KITCHENER PUBLIC LIBRARY

3 9098 02339587 3

W9-DGW-466

THE DARKEST LEGACY

ALEXANDRA BRACKEN

HYPERION

Los Angeles   New York

Copyright © 2018 by Alexandra Bracken

All rights reserved. Published by Hyperion, an imprint of Disney Book Group.
No part of this book may be reproduced or transmitted in any form or by
any means, electronic or mechanical, including photocopying, recording,
or by any information storage and retrieval system, without written
permission from the publisher. For information address Hyperion,
125 West End Avenue, New York, New York 10023.

First Hardcover Edition, July 2018
First Paperback Edition, September 2019
10 9 8 7 6 5 4 3 2 1
FAC-025438-19200

Printed in the United States of America

This book is set in 11.5-pt. Edlund
Designed by Marci Senders

Library of Congress Control Number for Hardcover: 2018030730
ISBN 978-1-368-05752-3

SUSTAINABLE
FORESTRY
INITIATIVE
Certified Chain of Custody
Promoting Sustainable Forestry
www.sfiprogram.org
SFI-01054
The SFI label applies to the text stock

Visit www.hyperionteens.com

For Anna Jarzab, who loved these characters and their dark world first.
Thank you for everything.

The blood wouldn't wash out.

It ran red, red, red, down over my hands, curling over the bruises on my wrists and the scabs on my knuckles. The water pouring from the faucet, hot enough to steam the mirror, should have diluted it to pale pink and then clear nothing. But it just . . . wouldn't stop. The dried stains on my skin became fresh again, blooming from a rusted brown to sickening crimson. Snaking lines of it ran down the basin while the drain struggled to drink it all up.

The darkness of the tight room crept up on me, feathering the edges of my vision. I fixed my eyes on the flakes of dried blood stuck to the porcelain like loose tea leaves.

Hurry up, I ordered myself. *You have to make the call. You have to get the phone.*

My knees bobbed and the world tilted sharply down. I half leaned, half fell into the edge of the sink, catching its smooth edge with my hands. The caulking that held it to the wall crumbled with my added weight, groaning out a warning.

Hurry up, hurry up, hurry—

One by one, I pulled at the spots where blood had dried my blouse against my skin, trying not to choke on the vomit that threatened to come up.

The pipes shuddered inside the walls, the clanging coming faster and louder, until one final *bang* sent a hard vibration up through the sink.

Shit! I felt around the countertop, searching for something to catch the remaining hot water in.

"No, no, no—come *on*—"

Those timers—those stupid timers measuring out the room's supply of clean water, not leaving a single drop to waste. I needed this. Just this *once*, I needed them to bend the rules for me. The blood, it was on my tongue and teeth and coating my throat. Every swallow brought the metallic tang deeper into me. I needed to get myself clean—

With one last dull beat from the pipes, the water trickled to a thin stream. I picked up the motel hand towel, stiff from being bleached too many times, and shoved it under the faucet to let it absorb whatever water was left.

I clenched my aching jaw and leaned forward unsteadily, bracing my hip against the sink. After wiping a stroke of condensation off the mirror, I used the damp towel to dab at the scab on my lower lip, where it was split and swollen.

The crusts of dirt and blood packed beneath my broken nails hurt with the slightest pressure. My gaze fixed on those dark red crescents that showed through the chipped nail polish. I couldn't look away.

Not until the clump of hair landed with a wet slap against the sink.

The cheap fluorescent light fixture buzzed, flaring dangerously bright. It fed the snarling static trapped inside my skull. I couldn't understand what I was seeing. The small, jagged piece of flesh. The shape of the strands curling against the wet porcelain.

Not long black hair.

Blond. Short.

Not mine.

I opened my mouth, but the sob, the scream, locked inside me. My whole body heaved as I frantically twisted the faucets on and off, trying to wash away the evidence, the violence.

"Oh my God, oh my God . . ."

I threw the wet towel down into the empty sink, whirling toward the toilet and dropping onto my knees. As much as my stomach churned, nothing came up. I hadn't eaten in days.

I tucked my legs under me on the cool tile, reaching up to work my shaking hands through my hair, yanking at each sticky knot.

This wasn't working— I needed— I clawed my way up off the ground, reaching for the towel I'd abandoned in the sink. I scrubbed at my hair as the bathroom spun around me.

I closed my eyes, but all I saw was another place, another burning wave of light and heat. I threw out my hand, catching the empty towel rod and using it as one last anchor.

As I touched the thin metal, a sharp snap of static passed up my arm, prickling each individual hair. By the time it raced up the back of my neck, a frisson of power had already gathered at the base of my skull. Behind my closed eyelids, the bathroom's light flickered again, and I knew I should let go.

3

But I didn't.

I pulled on this silver thread in my mind, coaxing it across my nerves and through the thousands of bright, sparkling pathways in my body. The blue-white heat, like the heart of a flame, burned away the dark thoughts in my mind. I clung to the feeling of familiarity racing through me like unstoppable lightning. Inside the walls, the wires hummed in acknowledgment.

I can control this, I thought. Whatever had happened, it wasn't my doing.

The smell of smoldering drywall finally forced me to release my grip on the bar. I pressed my hand to the scorch marks on the dingy floral wallpaper, directing the power out of the wires and cooling the insulation before it could ignite. The insensible murmuring of the television cut off, only to snap back on a second later.

I can control this. In that moment, I hadn't been frightened, or even angry. I hadn't lost control.

It hadn't been my fault.

"Suzume?"

In the few days I'd known Roman, his quiet, calm voice had only broken a few times—in anger, in concern, in warning. But there was an edge to it now that I didn't recognize. Almost as if, for once, he'd let fear shape my name.

"You need to come see this," he called. "Right now."

I stripped off my ruined blouse and threw it into the trash can, then wiped my face one last time with the soiled towel before tossing that in, too.

My tank top wasn't as tattered or stained, but it did nothing to protect me from the damp chill of the motel room's window

AC unit. I limped forward on my broken heels, well aware that the split up the back seam of my skirt was growing with each step. There hadn't been time to ditch our clothes and find something more suitable for traveling. In a way, it seemed right to look as wrecked as I felt.

"What is it?" I croaked out.

Roman stood directly in front of the TV, his dark hair falling across his forehead. He was in his usual pose: his hand clenched into a fist, his knuckles resting against his mouth, his brows drawn together in thought. The sight of him there, carefully working through some plan, was actually reassuring. One steady thing in this mess, at least.

He didn't answer. Neither did Priyanka from where she sat on the bed, staring at the television screen. She had stripped a pillow and bunched up its pillowcase to stanch the flow of blood from a cut over her left eye. The sleeves of her yellow silk dress had been shredded, the fabric drenched with sweat, blood, and what had to be gasoline. The tattoo of a star on her wrist was dark against her brown skin. As she stared straight ahead at the flickering television screen, her free hand struggled to reload the pistol she'd stolen.

"Just . . . watch," Roman said tightly, nodding toward the screen.

The newscaster was a middle-aged white woman. She wore a bright pink dress that clashed with her look of severe concern. "Investigators are combing the scene of the incident, and the search is still on for the Psi responsible for the deaths of seven people. The victims are slowly being identified—"

The victims.

5

The static was back, buzzing in my ears. Out of the corner of my eye, I saw Roman turn to watch my reaction, his ice-blue gaze never wavering, even as the screen began to click on and off, matching my quickening pulse.

My own face stared back at me.

No . . . no. This wasn't right. The words drifting along the bottom of the screen, the angle of the footage they kept playing over and over again—this wasn't right.

The deaths of seven people.

"I need the burner," I choked out.

I did this.

"What burner are you talking about?" Priyanka asked. "The one you took is dead—"

I didn't have time for this. "The one you found in the manager's office and *conveniently* forgot to tell us about."

She opened her mouth to argue.

I cut her off before she could begin. "I can feel the battery's charge in the pocket of your jacket."

The dead. All those people . . .

Roman turned, stalking over to where the other teen had dumped her ruined jean jacket on the room's desk.

No. I can control it. It wasn't me. It wasn't me.

My hands curled into fists. Outside the motel, the power lines whispered back to me, as if hissing in agreement.

I didn't kill those people. I needed to talk to someone who would believe me—who could fight for me. If I had to take the phone from Priyanka by force, I'd do it.

"Come *on*," Priyanka grumbled to him. "This is ridiculous. You *know* I could just shut—"

"You *won't*," Roman said sharply to her before passing over the old flip phone and fixing me with a long look. "Tell me this is someone you trust with your life."

I nodded. There wasn't a doubt in my mind.

I only knew three numbers off the top of my head without the crutch of my cell phone's contacts list, and only one of those was likely to answer on the first ring. My hands shook so badly, I had to enter it twice, squinting at the small black-and-white display, before I hit CALL.

Roman cast a cold glare at Priyanka and she returned it with fire. I had to turn my back to them; I couldn't take their uncertainty, and I didn't want them to see mine.

The phone only rang once before it was picked up and a breathless voice said, "Hello, this is Charles—"

The words burst out of me. "It's not true—what they're saying. It didn't happen like that! The video makes it seem like—"

"Suzume?" Chubs interrupted. "Where are you? Are you okay?"

"I knew it!" Priyanka made a *cut* motion with her hands. "You called one of your government buddies? Are you really this brainwashed? They're tracing your call!"

"I *know*," I snapped back at her. The risks were real, but Chubs would have a plan. Would know who I should talk to. He knew everything, and now everyone. I could picture him in his office in DC so clearly, flanked by that enormous window and a view of the newly finished Capitol Building.

I could see other things, too. The cameras installed in the ceiling monitoring his every move. The tracking device he wore as a watch. The security detail outside his door.

The years of saying *yes, okay, all right* sped forward, slamming into me now. I almost couldn't breathe from the pressure of the realization—the knowledge of how quickly every small agreement had added up to this moment.

"I need you to calm down and pay attention to what I'm saying," he said sharply. "Where are you? A safe place? Somewhere hidden?"

An ugly feeling planted itself at the back of my mind, taking root there and sending a shiver down the ridges of my spine. The words poured out of me, and as much as I tried to stop them, slow them, shape them, they came out nonsensical. "Tell everyone that I didn't do it. He tried to— These men grabbed me before I could get away—I don't know how. It was an accident—self-defense."

But I remembered Roman's voice, the way he'd spoken so softly in the uncertain darkness of the truck: *For us, there is no such thing as self-defense.*

The truth of it suddenly crystallized around me.

Legally, I couldn't claim it. I knew that. Some part of me had recognized the danger in the new order when the government had issued it the year before, but it had felt so abstract—so reasonable.

The Psi could harness their abilities like weapons, drawing out their deadly sides. The balance of power between a Psi and non-Psi in any given situation would always be unequal. The government had enacted laws to prevent us from being targeted or hunted by anyone. We had special protections. It was only right the others had certain legal protections, too. After all, I'd seen it for myself countless times. Not every Psi had good intentions, and fury at the way we'd been treated in the past was never in short supply.

Every day, we lived at that crumbling edge of civility and

cooperation with the interim government. The only recourse was to work together, because the other option was no option at all. We couldn't let things spiral back into chaos. That would finally force the government's hand, and the cure would no longer be a choice, but the only way to claim our futures. And that was the marker that things had gone too far—that was the line we had all agreed upon, years ago.

My pulse was thrumming again, sweat breaking out along the back of my neck.

Chubs was so calm, the order so crisp: "You need to drive to the nearest police station or zone checkpoint and turn yourself in. Let them put you in restraints so they know you won't hurt them. All I want is for you to be *safe*. Do you understand?"

I could barely get the word out: "What?"

My whole body, everything I was, recoiled at the thought of turning myself over to be handcuffed and led away. This didn't make sense. He knew what it felt like to be trapped behind barbed wire, at the mercy of guards and soldiers who hated and feared us. He promised—they *all* promised—that we would never have to go back to that, no matter what.

The plastic cracked in protest under the force of my grip. I tried to keep my eyes focused on the faded art print on the wall, but it kept blurring.

They're not going to take me.

"This is a serious situation," he said, carefully crafting each word. "It's *very* important that you listen to exactly what I'm telling you—"

"No!" My throat ached as it scratched out the words, "What the hell is wrong with you? I want to talk to Vi—where is she? Put her on the phone—call her in, I don't care!"

9

"She's on assignment," Chubs said. "Either stay where you are, Suzume, and tell me where that is, or find the road to a safe place where you can turn yourself in."

My hand was icy as I pressed it against my eyes, taking in a shaky breath.

"Did you hear me?" Chubs said, in the same measured tone he'd adopted for every council session he was asked to speak at.

That was our lives now, wasn't it? Even. Steady. Accepting. Never allowed to get mad, never allowed to threaten, or even be perceived as a threat.

For the first time in my life, in all the years I'd known and loved him, I hated Charles Meriwether.

But in the next heartbeat, through the anger buzzing in my head, I heard him.

Somewhere hidden.

Find the road.

Safe place.

Did you hear me?

A small static shock traveled from Roman's fingertips to my shoulder as he brushed it. I glanced back, taking in his apologetic look as he pointed to the phone. Behind him, Priyanka didn't bother trying to stifle her groan of frustration.

"Okay," I said. "All right. I got it."

He was right. I don't know why I hadn't thought of it before now. I wasn't so far away from the place he was hinting at; if I could get past the cameras and drones monitoring the highways, it would only take half a day to get there. Maybe less.

Will you meet me? The words slipped through my mind, each quieter and smaller than the next. *Do you even care?*

Before either of us could say anything else, I hit END on the call.

Priyanka unfolded her long legs and practically leaped off the bed to take the phone out of my hand. She broke it into little pieces, taking out the battery and SIM card, all the while muttering, "Using my last phone to call the damn government. You don't just need help, you need full-on reprogramming. *Deprogramming*."

"Who was that?" Roman asked, his gaze piercing. "What's 'okay'?"

The last few days had threatened to kill me in a thousand different ways, with a thousand different cuts. But if there was one thing I knew how to do, it was smother the fear just long enough to keep surviving.

In darkness, you only needed to see just as far as your headlights extended. As long as you kept going, it was enough.

"I need a car," I told them calmly. I moved toward the motel's windows, pulling back the curtain to survey our options. I couldn't use the one we'd stolen before. The truck's engine was on its last legs, in any case, and it was almost out of gas. No way could it get me as far as I needed to go.

But stealing one out of the parking lot, or one nearby . . . I hated feeling this desperate again. They might have already labeled me a criminal, but that wasn't any justification to commit an actual crime.

"*You* need a car," Priyanka began, arching a brow, "or *we* need a car?"

I turned toward them again, pressing a hand against my collarbone. My fingers traced the jagged edge of a new scab there. Maybe this was the reason I hadn't let myself consider my options

11

fully, and why I hadn't gone straight there—from the moment everything had exploded, there hadn't been a second I'd been without the two of them. This place was secret for a reason, even from most Psi.

"You aren't involved," I said. "They don't have your faces or your names."

"Yeah, but for how long?" Priyanka towered over me in height, and part of me envied how forceful and confident it made her seem, even when her boisterous voice gentled to something like a whisper. Even when she looked like she'd been dragged beneath a truck.

Which . . .

I grimaced. She basically had.

"These people—whoever did this—clearly know what they're doing. You need our help." Priyanka gestured toward the television, and, with a look, I overloaded its circuits, flooding the device with power. The bloodied images flashed off with a biting *snap*.

"Okay, yes, that was very dramatic and a waste of a perfectly good TV that we could have sold for gas money, but you do you," Priyanka said. "The problem is, I didn't hear any kind of counterargument."

The fact that she thought I had to argue anything with her was the problem.

"I'll be fine," I insisted. "You're free to get the hell out of here."

Roman frowned. He raised one hand toward me. It fell away before it could touch my shoulder. "Think it through. Just from a reasoning standpoint. You don't know us well, and you might not trust us, and that's fine—"

"That's *not* fine," Priyanka said. "We're awesome and we haven't tried to kill you once. What more do you want from us?"

The truth, I thought angrily. I couldn't keep up this charade of believing them much longer.

"—but I know you've realized it, too. Priya and I escaped with you. They're going to assume we're together no matter what, at least initially, because there's safety in numbers."

I'm not getting away from them, I thought, pushing back against the nausea that realization brought with it. *Unless I fight them and escape.* They wanted to help me, but only because they wanted something else from me. Whatever their endgame was, they'd snapped a leash on me. Every time I tried to escape it, the lead only shortened.

"Isn't that all the more reason to scatter?" I pushed back. "To throw them off and force *them* to split up as well?"

"You may have a point," Roman said. "But there are benefits to staying together, at least until we figure out what actually happened. Two more sets of eyes to keep watch. Two more sets of hands to find food."

"Two more mouths to feed," I continued. "Two more opportunities to be spotted."

"As if you know the first thing about roughing it." Priyanka rolled her eyes. "Did you read about it once in your special reports? Have a kid come up onstage during one of your fancy little speeches and tell their sob story? Did you cry a few crocodile tears in front of the cameras to sell it?"

Every muscle in my body tensed to the point of pain. I could barely get the words out. "I don't need anyone to tell me a damn thing about it. I know what it feels like to be—"

"I wasn't aware government robots could be programmed to have feelings," she cut in.

I sucked in a sharp breath, a pure, unflinching anger

gathering at the center of my chest. It was a fire that fed itself. It rose through me, until I was sure I could breathe it out and incinerate the motel room faster than any Red.

"Priya." Roman's voice was soft, but like the edge of the sharpest sort of blade, it didn't need power or anger behind it for the words to cut deep. "Enough."

The mocking twist of her mouth fell away. Her eyes slid to the side.

I turned to look the other way, letting that same anger and pain turn to steam. Letting it drift out of me with my next long breath.

"You don't know the first thing about me," I told her, fighting to keep the words even.

The girl took a deep breath of her own, pushing her long hair back over her shoulders. She struggled a bit to say, "Sorry. You're right."

Roman looked back and forth between us. "We need to wrap this up and head out. Preferably in the next thirty seconds."

I blew out a loud breath through my nose, trying to quickly piece together an argument. The trouble was, they weren't wrong. When you were being hunted, it was better to stay within the protection of a group, have extra eyes to keep watch, than to try to navigate through danger alone. I'd learned that the hard way.

Just like I'd learned that sometimes the real danger came from the people inside your car, not the world outside it.

I can't take them there, I thought. *I can't risk it.*

If I kept pushing back, they'd know I was onto them and they'd do everything in their power to prevent me from slipping away. Priyanka had the evidence I needed to prove my innocence, and she knew it. As long as she kept it out of my reach, I'd have to stay with them, or risk pitting my word against video and eyewitness evidence.

I wanted to know who was responsible for this. The need burned like a snarling charge, blistering me as it collected more and more energy to it. It was a risk taking them with me to that safe place. It meant putting more than just my life at stake. But something was happening here, something bigger than I could have ever imagined. I would have to accept the risk and control it, if I wanted answers.

Here was another thing I'd been made to learn all those years ago: the world was never as simple as it wanted you to believe it was. Hard exteriors could hide soft hearts, a chosen family could be more important than a blood one . . . and even the safest of places could be made into a trap.

"All right," I told them. "*We* need a car. But I'm driving."

Besides, where we were headed there was someone who could take care of any unwanted memories they might make—and guarantee they'd never remember the way back.

ONE

Three Days Ago

THE WHEELS DIDN'T STOP TURNING ON THE ROAD. NOT for gas, not at signs or signals.

A glare of sunlight burst through the window beside me, washing out the words I was pretending to read on my cell phone's screen. A deep grumble from the engine and the renewed stench of gasoline signaled we were slowly picking up speed. The grind of the highway beneath us still wasn't loud enough to drown out the police escorts' sirens or the chanting from the sign-wavers lined up along the highway.

I refused to turn and look at them. The tinted windows cast them all in shadow, one dark blur of hatred in my peripheral vision: the older men with their guns, the women clutching hateful messages between their hands, the clusters of families with bullhorns, and their cleverly awful slogans.

The police cars' lights flashed in time with their chants.

"God!"

Red.

"Hates!"

Blue.

"Freaks!"

"Well," Mel said. "No one could ever accuse them of being original."

"Sorry, ladies," Agent Cooper called back from the driver's seat. "It'll just be another ten minutes. I can turn up the music if you want?"

"That's okay," I said, setting my phone down on my lap and folding my hands on top of it. "Really. It's fine."

The machine-gun-fire typing coming from the seat beside me suddenly stopped. Mel looked up from the laptop balanced on her knees, a deep frown on her face. "Don't these people have anything better to do with their lives? Actually, on second thought, maybe I should send a job recruiter down here and see if we can't get them on our side—that would be quite the narrative, wouldn't it? From hater to . . . humbled. No, that's not right. It'll come to me eventually." She reached for where she had left her phone on the seat between us and spoke into it. "Make a note: protestor reform program."

As I'd learned—and apparently Agents Cooper and Martinez had, too—it was best just to let Mel talk herself through to a solution rather than try to offer suggestions.

The car snarled and shuddered as it hit a bad patch of highway. The chanting grew louder, and I fought its tug at my attention.

Don't be a coward, I told myself. There was nothing any of them could do to me now, not while I was surrounded on all sides by bulletproof glass, FBI agents, and police. If we kept looking away, they would never think we were strong enough to meet them head-on.

18

With a hard swallow, I turned to gaze out my window again. The day's breeze tugged at the construction flags across the divide between the northbound and southbound lanes. They were the same shade of orange as the barriers protecting the workers as they went about the business of pouring new asphalt.

A few of the men and women stopped mid-task and leaned against the concrete median to watch our motorcade pass; some gave big, cheerful waves. Instinctively, my hand rose to return the gesture, a small smile on my lips. A heartbeat later, just long enough to be embarrassed by it, I remembered they couldn't see me.

Behind the thin barrier of dark glass, I was invisible.

The window was warm as I pressed the tips of my fingers to it, hoping the workers could see them through the tint like five small stars. Eventually, though, just like everyone else, the workers disappeared with distance.

Setting America Back on the Right Route! had been one of Mel's first publicity projects for the interim government established and monitored by the United Nations, back when she was still fairly junior in the White House communications office. It was a way to advertise new infrastructure jobs while also promising that roads would stop buckling under people's wheels, that the gas ration would, eventually, be coming to an end, and that deadly bridge collapses like the one in Wisconsin wouldn't happen anymore—not with reinforcements from new American steel. The proof of its success ran on newscasts every night: the unemployment rate was falling as steadily as the birth rate was beginning to rise.

Numbers were simple, real symbols that people could latch onto, holding them up like trophies. But there was no way they could capture the *feeling* of the last few years, that all-encompassing sensation that life was rolling out in front of us again, swelling to fill those empty spaces the lost children had left behind.

The same populations that had shifted to the big cities in desperate search of work were now slowly making their way back to the small towns and suburbs they had abandoned. Restaurants opened. Cars pulled in and out of gas stations on their assigned days. Trucks cruised down the highways that had been patched and knitted together again. People walked through newly landscaped parks. Movie theaters began to shift away from showing old films to showing new ones.

They arrived tentatively, slowly—like the first few people on an otherwise empty dance floor, waiting to see if anyone else would rejoin them in search of fun.

Almost five years ago, when we'd driven these same highways, the towns and cities we'd slipped in and out of had practically ached with their emptiness. Parks, homes, businesses, schools: everything had been hollowed out and recast in miserable, dirt-stained gray. Neglected or abandoned like memories left to fade into nothing.

Somehow, the government had managed to shock a pulse back into the country. It fluttered and raced in moments of darkness and frustration, but mostly held steady. Mostly.

The truth was, it had less to do with me than it did the others working day in and day out. I hadn't been allowed to do much of anything until I finished the new mandatory school requirements. President Cruz had said it was important for other Psi to see me do it, to demonstrate there were no exceptions. But it had been agonizing to wait and wait and wait, doing the homework of simple math problems Chubs had taught me years ago in the back of a beat-up minivan, studying history that felt like it had happened to a completely different country, and memorizing the new Psi laws.

And the whole time, Chubs and Vida had been allowed to do real, meaningful work. They'd moved from one closed door to the next, disappearing into meetings and missions, until I was sure I'd lose track of them completely, or be locked out forever.

But it was only a matter of time before I caught up to them. As long as I kept pulling my weight and proving myself useful, going wherever the government sent me, saying the words they wanted me to say, I'd keep moving forward, too. And someone had clearly seen my potential, because Mel had been reassigned to me, and we'd been traveling together ever since.

"How did I know they'd be back out in full force now that the reparations package has been announced?" Agent Martinez said. "I swear, people are never happy."

After four years of trying, Chubs and the Psi Council finally got a plan for reparations and Psi memorials through the interim Congress. All families affected by IAAN could apply to reclaim their homes and receive debt forgiveness. Banks had foreclosed upon most of them during the financial crisis sparked by a bombing at the old Capitol in DC, which had only worsened with the deaths of millions of children and the loss of jobs as businesses closed.

Watching the final deal go up for vote, seeing it *pass*, had filled me with a renewed sense of purpose and hope. I'd cried at the final *yea* vote. There'd been this pressure locked around my chest for years, so long that I'd gotten used to its ache. In that moment, though, it had finally released. It felt like taking my first deep breath in years.

Justice demanded time, and, in some cases, sacrifice, but with hard work and persistence, it *was* achievable. The kids who'd died, those of us who'd been made to live in the cruel camp system, none of us would be forgotten or brushed aside. Even the old camp controllers were finally being brought to court, with the hope of criminal prosecutions later.

They'd finally know what it meant to be imprisoned. It was what they deserved.

We still had so much work to do, but this was a start. A springboard to asking for—and getting—more. With this victory under his belt, Chubs was already at work trying to shift government research funding away from Leda Corp, which Psi and their families all agreed hadn't deserved to survive the purge of the Gray administration, given their starring role in developing the chemical agent that had caused the mutation.

"The real problem is that we have to announce road closures days ahead of time," Agent Cooper said. "They want us to alert the cities to secure the routes, but it's like a signal fire to these folks. It doesn't matter if it's you or someone else from the government."

There was a gap in the unbroken line of protestors as we moved along the highway. Farther from the rowdier ones, clustered in a small, tight group, were a few men and women, all holding signs of their own. They were silent, their faces grim. The SUV flew past them, forcing me to turn back in my seat to read them.

WHO HAS OUR CHILDREN? A chill curled down my spine as another one of the men angled his sign more fully toward me. It read, GONE—AND FORGOTTEN BY UN. Beneath the angry words were old school photos of children.

I sat forward again. "What was that about?"

The government had worked hard to identify unclaimed Psi and find new homes for them—as far as the reports I saw were concerned, all of them were now accounted for. I knew that after the camps had been closed a handful of Psi had run away, choosing that life over returning to the families who had abandoned them. But it seemed a little hard to believe that the kind of parents who were abusive or fearful of their children would stand out on a highway with homemade signs begging for answers.

"It's those damn conspiracy theorists," Agent Martinez said, shaking his head.

Of course. I should have put that together. A number of recent news clips had centered on the latest fearmongering line the Liberty Watch people were testing out—that vast numbers of Psi had been taken by our enemies to use against America.

Unfortunately, the rumors didn't seem likely to die off anytime soon. Joseph Moore, the businessman running against Interim President Cruz in the election, had recklessly parroted one of Liberty Watch's well-loved demands for mandatory military service for Psi and had watched his popularity numbers spike overnight. Now he repeated whatever script Liberty Watch gave him. If I had to guess, his people were floating the stories as a kind of trial balloon, to test future messaging for his next speech.

"But those pictures . . ." I began.

Mel shook her head in disgust. "This is a new thing that Liberty Watch is doing. They're taking photos like that off the internet and hiring people to stir up doubt and fear that the government isn't doing their job. But we, at least, know that they are."

Frowning, I nodded. "Sorry. They just caught me off guard."

I leaned my temple back against the window just as we approached another huddle of protestors.

"Oh God," Agent Cooper said, leaning forward to look up through the windshield. "What now?"

The banner dropped over the pedestrian bridge ahead of us, unfurling like an old flag. The two grown men holding it, both wearing an all-too-familiar stripe of white stars on a blue bandana tied to their upper arms, sent a chill curling down my spine.

LIFE, LIBERTY, AND THE PURSUIT OF FREAKS FOREVER
IT'S ONLY MURDER IF THEY'RE HUMAN

"Charming," Mel said, rolling her dark eyes as we passed under the bridge.

I rubbed a finger over my top lip, then picked up my phone, tapping through to the most recent text thread. ARE YOU STILL COMING TODAY? I typed.

I didn't take my gaze away from my phone's screen, waiting for the chat bubble to appear with a response. Out of the corner of my eye, I caught the reflection of Agent Cooper's mirrored sunglasses as he looked up into the rearview mirror, watching me. His already white skin looked a little bloodless as the sign's message sank in.

Agent Cooper didn't have to worry. There would be no crying. No emotional mess to mop up. Half the poison these people churned out with their signs, their radio shows, on their news programs was lies, and the rest of it was nonsensical. *Freak* was an old insult—sometimes you heard a nasty word so often it lost its fangs. That, or I guess your skin eventually could grow too strong, too thick to cut. My heart didn't bruise the way it used to—they were way too late to get in that particular blow.

24

I swallowed the thickness in my throat, squeezing the phone's case in my hand.

If they're human . . .

I cleared my throat again, looking out my window. The group of protestors was thinner on the ground, but growing in number again as we left the construction zone. "Everyone's entitled to stupidity, but they really abuse the privilege, don't they?"

Mel gave a weak laugh at that, reaching over to smooth back a strand of my hair that had come loose from its twist.

"Still, better call it in," Agent Cooper said, taking his hand off the wheel to nudge Agent Martinez. "It's not a direct threat, but they need to know they're one step away from taking it too far."

"Agreed," Agent Martinez said. "We need to start documenting everything, no matter how small. Build a case."

"Actually," Mel cut in, now reaching back to adjust the pins she'd used to help secure her locs into a bun, "it's probably best not to give that fire any air. It's what they want—we shut them down and they'll jump on a narrative about us violating their right to free speech. *Our* job is to tell the truth about the Psi, and the polls show that we've been hitting that ball out of the park. The people are on *our* side."

That was a small comfort, but it did help. Sometimes it felt like I was talking to everyone and no one at the same time. I never saw the words leaving my mouth reflected on the audience's faces, good or bad. They just absorbed them. Whether or not they internalized them was another question.

I glanced down at my phone again.

No response.

"I should tell you before we get to the venue," Mel said, turning more fully toward me. A bead of sweat rolled down her cheek, glinting on her dark skin. She reached down to adjust the air-conditioning vent toward her. "I received an e-mail from Interim President Cruz's chief of staff this morning saying that they're going to be sending along some new language for your speech. I'm not sure when it's going to come in, so I might need to add it directly to the teleprompter."

I didn't care if my sigh sounded petulant. They had to realize how annoying it was.

"Aren't they done tweaking it yet?" I hated not having time to practice new material and straighten out my delivery. "What kind of new language is it anyway?"

Mel slid her laptop back into her satchel. The battered leather case tried to spit up a few of the overstuffed folders inside it to make room. "Just some finessed points, from the sound of it. I know you could recite the speech backward and half-asleep at this point, but just keep an eye on the teleprompter."

I'd repeated different versions of the same speech a hundred times, in a hundred places, about the nature of fear, and how the Psi had reentered society with only a few ripples. But the added responsibility was a good sign that they trusted me more and more. Maybe they'd even add dates and use me again in the fall, for the big election.

"All right," I said. "But—"

It was the suddenness of the movement that caught my eye, more than the woman herself. She pulled away from the cluster of sign-wavers and bullhorn-shouters lined up along the shoulder to our left. Long, stringy gray hair, a faded floral shirt, a blue scrap of fabric decorated with white stars tied to her bone-white arm. She could have been anyone's grandmother—if it hadn't been for the flaming bottle she clutched in her hand.

I knew we were speeding, that there was no way it could be happening, but time has a way of bending around you when it wants you to see something.

The seconds slowed, ticking in time to each of her running steps. Her lips pulled back, deepening the stark lines of her face as she held the bottle high over her head and flung it toward the SUV, shouting something I couldn't hear.

The small firebomb hit the cement and billowed up with a loud, sucking gasp. It flared as it devoured the traces of oil and chemicals on the highway, blasting my window with enough heat and pressure for it to crack with a high, suffering whine.

My seat belt locked against my chest as our car swerved sharply to the right. I craned my neck, watching the road blaze with a wall of red and gold.

"You guys okay?" Agent Cooper bit out, slamming his foot onto the gas. Mel and I were both thrown back against our seats again. I reached out with one hand, gripping the door to steady myself.

Up ahead, one of the cop cars swerved and blared its sirens. The crowd of protestors scattered into the nearby woods and fields like the cowards they were.

"Holy shit" was Mel's response.

Fury stormed through me, twisting my insides, clawing at them. I shook with useless adrenaline. That woman—she could have hurt another protestor, Mel, the agents, or one of the police officers. *Killed* them.

Heat writhed inside me, giving form to my fury. A sharp chemical smell burned the inside of my nose.

It would be so easy to get out of the car and find that woman. Grab her by the hair, throw her to the ground, pin her there until one of the officers caught up with us. So easy.

The charge from the car's battery seethed nearby, waiting. *You think that's enough to scare me? You think I haven't had people try to kill me before?*

Plenty had tried. A few had come close. I wasn't prey anymore, and I wouldn't let anyone turn me into it again, least of all an elderly woman dabbling in a bit of bomb-making with her unpleasant friends.

A single cooling word got through my scorching thoughts. *Don't.*

I forced myself to release my hold on the door. I clenched and unclenched that hand, trying to work out the tension still there. That would be exactly what they wanted. Get a reaction, prove that we're all monsters only waiting for the right moment to break out of our cages.

She's not worth it. None of them are.

She wouldn't be the last one to try to hurt me. I accepted that, and was grateful for the protection we all had now. There was no room for ghosts in my life, whether they were living or dead. Ruby used to say that we'd earned our memories, but we didn't owe them anything beyond their keeping. I guess she'd know better than most.

We were moving forward, and the past was best left to its darkness. Its ashes.

"It's all right," I said, when I trusted my voice to be calm. "It's okay."

"That was the definition of *not okay*," Mel said, her tone brittle.

"I think you have your direct threat," Agent Cooper said to his partner, never taking his eyes off the road.

I flipped my phone over from where I had pressed it against my leg, ignoring the pulse pounding at my temples. Even with its rubber case, the screen flickered as a single lance of electricity crawled out of my finger and danced over it. I dropped it back onto my lap, silently praying for the phone to turn itself back on.

Damn. I hadn't done that in such a long time.

Finally, after another agonizing second, the screen flashed back up again. I swallowed against the dryness in my throat, opening the same text thread as before. My message was still there, still waiting for a response.

"About ten minutes now," Agent Cooper said. "We're almost there."

The phone buzzed in my hand, making me jump. Finally—

I glanced down, fingers flying over the screen to input my password. The thread opened.

COULDN'T GET AWAY. SORRY. NEXT TIME?

"Hey, everything okay?" Mel asked, resting a hand on my arm. Her eyes were soft, searching. I had the stupidest urge to lean my head against her shoulder and shut my eyes, shut out the world, until we got to where we were going.

She must have seen it in my face, because she quickly added, "Should we move the event? Even delaying it a few hours might help. I almost went into cardiac arrest, so I can only imagine what that just did to you."

The smile I plastered onto my face was so wide, it actually ached. "No, I'm all right. Really. No delay necessary. Besides, if we push back this one, we might hit traffic and miss the Japanese embassy event."

The embassy was reopening their Japan Information and Culture Center and had asked me to do the honor of introducing a documentary film by a fellow Japanese American Psi, Kenji Ota. To say I was excited was an understatement; I'd only met Kenji once in passing, but for weeks now I'd been looking forward to having the chance to connect with someone who'd come from a similar background and experienced the same things I had.

"Can we go through today's schedule?" I asked. "Make sure I have it down?"

Mel squeezed my wrist reassuringly. "You're amazing. I don't know how you stay so strong in the face of all this. I meant what I said, though. I can ask about moving the event."

I shook my head, my heart skipping at the thought. The second President Cruz's director of communications suspected I couldn't handle the stress of this job, I'd be taken off it. "There's no need. I promise."

"All right," Mel said, looking just a little relieved. This would have been a nightmare for her to reschedule. She reached into her bag and pulled out a folder with the day's date and began to run through our itinerary, matching hours to actions.

I dropped the phone back into my own bag, trying to find something to ward off the pressure building in my chest. It pushed at my ribs like it could split me open and reveal the raw mess inside.

Maybe I should have responded? Or would I have just bothered him more?

"Nine thirty a.m., the dean will introduce you. . . ."

Next time? I was tempted to take the phone back out and reread Chubs's message, just to make sure I hadn't imagined it. My mind couldn't stop whispering those two words, wouldn't let go of that question mark—that one small symbol that had never existed between any of us before.

TWO

Once upon a time, I went months without saying a word. More than a year, in fact.

It happened by accident at first—or not by accident, exactly. I still struggled to explain it, to justify why I silenced myself. It was as if the barbed wire that surrounded the rehabilitation camp had cut me so deeply the night we escaped, all the words in me had just bled out. I'd been so empty under my skin. So cold. Weak enough for shock to spill in and take over.

The truth is, some things go beyond words: The sound of gunshots thundering through the night. Blood staining the backs of thin uniforms. Kids facedown, slowly buried by the snow falling from the dark sky. The feeling of being strangled by your own hope in that second *it* escaped the fencing and left you behind to die.

The next few days I was just . . . tired. Unsure. Questions would come at me, and I would nod. Shake my head. It took so much energy. I was afraid of picking the wrong words out of the messy darkness inside my head. Scared to say something the others, the boys who had saved me, wouldn't like.

Every second we spent driving in the van, I could see it: I

would tell them I was hungry or cold or hurt, and they would decide I was a problem, just like my parents once had. The boys would leave me behind somewhere just as quickly as they had decided to take me with them that night we'd escaped.

But they didn't. And, pretty soon after, I realized that they wouldn't. But by then, it felt more comfortable to pick up that ratty notebook we shared and carefully choose my words. I could spell out the exact response I wanted, no mistakes. I could choose when I wanted to say something. I could have that much control over my life.

The problem was that I *kept* choosing silence. Over and over again, I let myself fall into the safety of its depths. Painful things could stay buried, never needing to be understood or talked through. The past wouldn't come back to hurt me if I never spoke of it. The memory of snow and blood and screams couldn't rise up and bury me in its freezing pressure, its dark. I wouldn't need to admit to being scared or hungry or exhausted and worry the others. My silence became a kind of shield.

Something I could use to protect myself.

Something I could hide behind.

That was years ago now. I became known to the world for what I had said, not as the silent little girl with the shaved head and oversize gloves. I appeared on television screens and in front of crowds. She became a ghost, abandoned in the memories I no longer wanted to remember.

Words still seemed to sit a little heavier in my mouth than they did for other people. It was all too easy to slip back into those comfortable depths inside me, where there was quiet. Especially on days like that one, with the last lick of adrenaline making me antsy to move on to the next event.

I couldn't focus on any one thing, no matter how hard I tried. The two dozen rows of people in front of us became an indistinct haze of color and small, shifting movements. I lost the thread of whatever Penn State's steely-haired dean of admissions was saying, the same way I struggled to keep up with the campus tour he'd given us earlier. Now even his dark skin and blue seersucker suit were smearing at the edge of my vision.

I tapped one high heel down, brought the other up, tapped that down, brought the other up, working off the lingering buzz of nerves from the car ride in. I closed my eyes against the warm sunlight, but opened them again just as quickly when I only found the image of the old woman's snarling face there.

The air wept with moisture, so thick with late-summer heat it gave the sky a silky coating. My thick hair rebelled, swelling against the hold of the bobby pins, just at the edge of slipping out of its careful style. A drop of sweat rolled down the ridges of my spine, gluing my blouse to my skin.

Mel gripped my arm, her nails digging into me. I came back to myself all at once, pushing up onto my feet and letting the world open around me again.

The scattered applause wasn't even loud enough to echo back off the columns of the large building behind us, the one the dean had called Old Main. Not a good sign when it came to their interest level, but I could win them over. Being a *freak* meant that people were more than willing to stare at you for a while.

I stepped through the shadow cast by Old Main's clock tower. Setting my shoulders back, I licked my teeth to make sure there was no lipstick on them and lifted my hand in a wave.

The dean stepped away from the podium, which rested on top of a temporary platform that had been built out over the steps that led down to the grassy seating area. He swept his hands toward it as I approached, inviting me forward with an encouraging smile I forced myself to return.

I didn't need encouragement. This was my job.

The meager applause was lost again, this time to the music that poured through the speakers on either side of the bottom step down on the grass—some kind of fight song, I guessed. While I waited for the words to load on the teleprompter, I cast a quick glance around the audience, making sure to avoid looking directly into the fleet of news cameras positioned off to the right of the stairs.

"Good afternoon," I said, my hands grasping the lip of the podium. I hated the way my voice sounded as it blasted out of speakers—like a little girl's. "It's an honor to be here with you today. Thank you, Dean Harrison, for giving me the opportunity to address your incredible new class and inviting me to celebrate the reopening of your illustrious university."

I sincerely doubted there had been any invitations involved—Mel pitched all of these events based on population models and where she thought we would get the most media play. She always seemed to know just the right way to threaten someone to get a *No* magically transformed into an enthusiastic *Yes*.

Every speech was carefully altered at its beginning and end to fit the venue. These slight adjustments were the only variations in the usual routine. My grip on the podium relaxed as I settled into it. I swept my gaze back and forth, trying to take the crowd's temperature. Beyond the row of reporters, all scribbling on notepads or half-hidden by the phones they were using to snap photos, there was an array of people, spanning almost the full range of ages.

Parents and other family members filled the very back rows.

Farther in were the men and women a decade past what you might expect from typical college freshmen. All of them were trying to recover the educations they'd been forced to abandon when the majority of universities had gone bankrupt at the height of the Psi panic.

Then there were those my age, even a little younger. They sat behind the reporters, their thumb-size buttons visible on their shirts, as they were meant to be at all times. Many green buttons, fewer blues, and even fewer yellow ones like my own. And, scattered between them all, white.

I glanced down at the podium, pausing in my speech for a quick breath. *Blank.* The word slipped through my mind, as unwelcome as it was ugly. These were the ones who had elected—or had parents who had elected for them—to get the "cure" procedure. Specifically, the ones who had received surgical implants to halt and effectively neuter their brain's access to the abilities they acquired when they survived IAAN.

"We truly are the lucky ones," I continued. "We have survived the trials that the last decade has brought to our country, and they have united us in ways that no one could have predicted. Of course, we have all made sacrifices. We have struggled. And from that, we have learned much—including how to trust one another again, and how to believe in the future of this nation."

There was a loud, sharp cough from the far left end of the front row. It was just pointed enough to draw my gaze as I took a quick sip from the sweating water glass that had been left for me.

Two teenagers sat just behind the police officer standing watch over the left side of the audience. One, a girl with brown skin, glowing in her yellow silk sundress, had stretched her long legs out in front of her. They were crossed at the ankles, just above her strappy sandals. Her head had lolled to the side, her long ponytail of curly black hair spilling over her shoulder. The metallic-rimmed cat's-eye glasses had dipped down the bridge of her nose, revealing more of her features: full brows and high, slanted cheekbones. She also had what I assumed were beautiful, wide eyes, but there was no way to really confirm it, given that I'd apparently talked her right into a nice nap.

Irritation curled through me as I watched her mouth fall slightly open, and her breathing even out.

Oh, am I wasting your time?

Beside her was a boy, also about my age, more or less. He was such a study in contrasts that my gaze naturally held on him a second longer. His chestnut-colored hair had a hint of wild curl and was barely tamed, glowing with a faint red sheen in the harsh sunlight. His face was lean, but his features were so strong, the lines so distinct, that I would have believed anyone who told me they had carefully designed his face on the pages of a sketchbook. Even the tan on his white skin only seemed to make his pale eyes burn brighter in comparison. He met my gaze directly, his unreadable expression never wavering, not until the corners of his mouth tipped down.

I straightened, glancing away. "I realize that much has been asked of my fellow Psi, but we must establish limits on those perceived to be limitless. Society can only function with boundaries and rules, and we must continue to work to find a way back into it—to not press so hard against those markers as to disturb the peace."

The girl could get right up and leave if she was so bored with a talk about her future—but I let myself glance back toward them for a moment. She wore a green button, and he wore a yellow one.

I shifted my full attention back to the speech as I entered the homestretch. It was my least-favorite part: I'd plead with the Psi for patience with those who feared us, and plead with those who feared us to acknowledge the terror that we had lived in every day since IAAN was first recognized. It didn't feel like a fair comparison, but this had come directly from professionals. What did I know, when it really came down to it?

I stumbled, just a tiny bit, as unfamiliar words loaded on the screen. "And as we enter this new beginning, I think it has become all the more important to acknowledge the past. We must honor the traditional American way."

It was the new language that Mel had mentioned in the car. The teleprompter slowed, accommodating my unfamiliarity.

"That includes," I read, "honoring our original Constitution, the core foundation of faith, and the requirements of citizenship in our democracy. . . ."

The words rolled forward on the screen, even as they halted in my throat.

TODAY, THE INTERIM GOVERNMENT HAS VOTED ON AND APPROVED A BILL THAT TEMPORARILY REMOVES PSI-BORN, INCLUDING THOSE OF LEGAL AGE, FROM CURRENT VOTER ROLLS. THIS IS TO ALLOW THEM MORE TIME TO HEAL FROM THEIR TRAUMATIC EXPERIENCES BEFORE MAKING POTENTIALLY LIFE-ALTERING DECISIONS ON THEIR BALLOTS, AND SO THAT THEY MAY BETTER UNDERSTAND THE FULL WEIGHT AND IMPACT OF THIS SACRED CIVIC RESPONSIBILITY.

THIS IS ONLY A PROVISIONAL MEASURE, AND THE MATTER WILL BE REVISITED FOLLOWING THE ELECTION THIS NOVEMBER, AFTER THE NEW FULL CONGRESS IS SWORN IN.

A tremor worked its way up through my arms, even as my hands clenched the podium's glossy wood. The silence stretched on, punctuated only by the muffled sigh of the breeze catching the microphone. The audience began to shift in their seats. A woman in the second row finally stopped using her program as a fan, leaning forward to give me a curious look.

That couldn't be right. I wanted to look back at Mel, to signal that the wrong text had been loaded in. Whoever thought this was a funny joke deserved a fist to the throat.

The words scrolled back up, repeating. Insistent.

No—this was . . . The Psi already had stricter ID requirements. We had to wait until we were twenty-one before we could get legal driver's licenses. I'd given a whole speech about how it would be worth the delay, and how exciting it would be to finally be able to turn in a voter registration form with it. I filled mine out years ago, when Chubs and Vida were doing theirs. I hadn't wanted to be left out.

This must have . . . This had to have slipped by him and the other Psi on Interim President Cruz's council. They were probably already pushing back against it.

Except hadn't Mel said the language had come directly from President Cruz's chief of staff? Why spring it on me like this without any explanation or warning?

Because they know you'll say it no matter what, a small voice whispered in my mind, *like you've said everything else they've given you.*

Or . . . because the Psi Council had already refused to announce it themselves.

This time I did glance back over my shoulder. The crowd began to quietly murmur, clearly wondering what was going on. Mel didn't rise out of her chair, didn't take off her sunglasses. She motioned with her hands, pushing them forward, urging me to turn back to the audience. To keep going.

The boy in the front row, the one I'd noticed before, narrowed his eyes, cocking his head to the side slightly. The way his whole body tensed made me wonder if he'd somehow managed to read the words on the teleprompter, or if he could hear my heart hammering inside my chest.

Just say it, I thought, watching as the words rewound again, then paused. I'd promised them my voice, for whatever they'd need me to do. This was what I had agreed to, the whole point of coming here.

Just say it.

It would only be temporary. They promised. One election. We could sit out *one* election. Justice took time and sacrifice, but like the reparations had proven, it was best won through cooperation. We were working toward a better *forever* for the Psi, not just one year.

My throat burned. The podium trembled under my hands, and I couldn't understand why. Why now—why this announcement, and not any of the others?

Just say it.

The girl, the ghost from the past, was back, her gloved hands wrapping around my neck.

I can't. Not this time. Not this.

"Thank you for your time," I choked out, "it was an honor to speak to you today, and I wish you the best as you begin a new chapter of your lives—"

The teleprompter's screen blanked out. A second later, a single line of text appeared.

SOMEONE IS HERE TO KILL YOU.

THREE

I LAUGHED.

It was a jarring end to an unfinished thought, momentarily drowning out the persistent hum of the speakers and electronics surrounding me. The shocked sound somehow seemed to multiply as it ricocheted off the pillars of Old Main—like a single bullet summoning a hail of them.

Confusion spread through the crowd; I saw it in their faces, heard it in their murmurs. Bands of anger and resentment locked me in place, and the longer I stood there, useless and silent, the deeper I sank into the humiliation.

Someone with an ax to grind had clearly loaded fake text into the teleprompter instead of the new material Mel had given them.

Say something. Do something.

I should have realized it the second the language about the provisional voting measure had appeared on the screen and wrapped things up as naturally as I could. Instead, I'd frozen like a total novice and left myself open to the worst kind of speculation from the nightly newscasts. I could practically hear them now, dissecting the pause, replaying the moment over and over again, asking, *Is the girl well?*

I leaned forward and managed to squeeze out, "Thank you again, Enjoy your day."

Rather than settle the crowd, the words only seemed to stir them. Even the sleeping girl suddenly sat up, curling her legs back under her, glancing at the dark-haired boy beside her.

The dean stepped up to the microphone again, casting a nervous look my way. "Well . . . thank you, everyone. Please enjoy the refreshments and sunshine."

The last thirty seconds had felt like thirty minutes. Fake threat or real threat, it didn't matter: the wheels of the emergency protocol were now turning. Agent Cooper walked straight to me, his tie fluttering with each quick, clipped step. The words on the teleprompter were reflected in the silver lenses of his sunglasses before someone cut the power and blacked out the screen.

He wrapped an arm around my shoulders. To anyone looking on, it probably seemed like he was just escorting me off the stage. They might not have noticed that Agent Cooper was pressing me hard into his side, that his other hand was just a few centimeters away from the gun in his holster. The sun had baked heat into the sleeve of his dark suit and it burned everywhere it touched me.

"It's all right. It's all right." He repeated the words over and over again as the police officers turned to the university staff and began to wave them off the steps of Old Main. Most of the students and their families had risen to their feet and were milling around, talking to one another or moving toward the nearby table of food and drinks.

"I know," I said pointedly. My heel caught on a crack in the old stone, sinking into it. Instead of giving me a moment to ease it free, Agent Cooper yanked me forward, shredding the leather off it and leaving me stumbling toward Mel.

"Wait here," he said. "Martinez will come get you. I'll get the car."

That was the extent of our security protocol: shelter in place until safe transport could be secured. I nodded and Agent Cooper was off, heading toward where the car was under joint custody of the newly reinstated Pennsylvania State Police and the United Nations' new federal police force, the Defenders.

I spotted Martinez a short distance away, not heading in my direction, but interrogating the shrugging woman in the tech booth.

Mel's voice rang out behind me, cutting into my thoughts.

"—unacceptable! I asked you to guarantee a level of security, and you didn't deliver!"

My heels clicked against the stone as I pivoted and cut a straight path toward her. Mel turned away from the pale-faced university staffer, who'd been nodding, nodding, nodding, simply absorbing the publicist's lecture. Her face was strained with barely muted anger.

Because of her job, Mel had been trained to be changeable, to shift between many roles depending on who she was with or what she was doing. To me, she'd been a coach, a defender, a guide, and a protector. Incompetence, especially when it came to safety, never sat well with her. This security breach, combined with the car incident, had clearly rattled her.

"It's fine," I assured her. "Just someone looking for a reaction—"

"It's *not* fine," Mel said, her hand closing over my shoulder. She drew me behind the nearest pillar, out of the lingering news cameras' line of sight. "You were supposed to launch the voting order. That's why I pitched this event to the press!"

I took a step back, lips parting as I searched for the right words.

"I told them you were ready for bigger announcements, but if that's not the case—" she began.

"No!" Somehow I managed to throw off the shock that had blanketed my mind. "No, I *am* ready. It's just, it didn't seem like— It wasn't—"

Right.

I couldn't get the word out, not under the full force of Mel's disappointment. The day's heat was unbearable, but her words were coated with ice.

"It came directly from the interim president's office. They *chose* you for this announcement," Mel said.

"Why?"

Mel stared back at me like I'd asked it in another language.

I didn't look away as I clarified, "Why did they want *me*?"

Someone touched my elbow, silencing any reply I might have gotten from Mel. "Ma'am? This way."

The Defenders' uniforms were as crisp and new as the fighting force itself. The gray jacket was cut close to the body, allowing for a black utility belt stocked with nonlethal weapons and tools, including the signature batons with their motto stamped lengthwise in silver lettering: FOR THE COMMON DEFENSE. A red leather sash ran from the left shoulder to the hip, pinned in place with a silver badge over the heart.

I'd been in the focus group that helped to choose the uniforms. One minute, I was sitting next to Cruz's chief of staff and the man modeling the sample—the third of five final options— had come into the conference room. The next, I found myself standing at the door, heading out. I still didn't understand why the sight of that particular one had put my heart in a vise. It was a nice uniform. A fantastic one. There was nothing wrong with it, even if the colors were . . .

I drew in a deep breath as I looked to the Defender and nodded. I'd been so embarrassed when the chief of staff asked me what was wrong that day, and even more embarrassed when the designer explained the concept. The boldness of the crimson against the gray represented the hope for a stronger, more peaceful future in the face of a dismal past.

There was nothing wrong with the uniform, or me, and I proved as much when I voted for it.

The Defender, with her neat braid beneath her helmet, her sunburned white skin, and rigid posture had likely come out of one of the country's fighting forces and had gone through psychological evaluations and tactical retraining with the United Nations peacekeepers. She walked us forward with the controlled assurance of someone who was used to giving orders, or at least following them.

"Wait," I said, trying to pull my arm free. The Defender tightened her grip as she walked me back down the steps of Old Main, toward the speakers and the podium. I only knew Mel was still behind me by the sound of her heels. "Agent Cooper said to—"

"Not now," Mel said sharply, coming to stand beside me. She waved toward where a group of Defenders had lined up along the edge of the makeshift stage, keeping back the tide of curious attendees trying to snap photos and the few reporters shouting questions at her.

"What are the interim president's thoughts about the approaching elections? Has she seen the latest polling?"

"Mel, what can you tell us about the rumors of the UN General Assembly coming back to Manhattan?"

"Mel! *Mel!*"

Realizing how it must have looked to everyone, I stepped in close to the Defender's side, ignoring the pressing buzz in the back of my mind. The speakers were still humming as power moved through them, whispering something I couldn't quite hear.

But I heard Mel all too clearly when she hissed from her own plastered-on grin, *"Smile."*

I couldn't.

Across the impatient, jostling bodies, through the shouted questions, I accidentally caught the eye of the boy I'd seen before. He hadn't moved from where he stood in front of his chair, and now it felt like I had frozen in place, too. His brow creased as his gaze finally broke away from mine and locked onto the sight of a tall male Defender wading through the crowd.

The Defender who had my arm tugged me forward, down the steps. Not away from the crowd, but into it.

"Why are we going this way?" I asked. It would have been quicker to go the opposite direction, following the path Agent Cooper had taken to the other side of Old Main.

"Security protocol has changed," the Defender muttered. Her dark braid shone in the damp heat.

There's something deep inside you that shifts—awakens, I guess—when, at one point in your life, you come face-to-face with death and narrowly escape it. From that moment on, it's like an unacknowledged insight is plugged into your mind. It doesn't ring like an alarm when it picks up on something that's off. It doesn't always make your heart pound. Sometimes, there isn't the time for that.

Call it instinct or intuition or whatever word you have for self-preservation, but once it's there, it never goes away. And when it stirs, you feel it like a layer of static on your skin.

I should know. I'd felt it from the moment I'd accidentally stalled my family's car in the middle of the I-495. From that heartbeat before the truck rammed into the passenger side of the car. It's saved me too many times to ever risk ignoring it. As Vida always said, there are times you have to listen to your gut and tell common courtesy to fuck right off.

It was just a little bit harder to do that with cameras rolling. I didn't want to give anyone the satisfaction of seeing me afraid. I wasn't about to flinch again.

But . . . it wasn't just a feeling of unease. A faint new vibration coated the air, tickling along the edge of my ear, whining and burning.

In the blur of the crowd moving around me, I caught sight of the girl with the marigold-colored dress. She reached out and grabbed the boy's arm, pointing at something behind me.

I glanced back over my shoulder, searching for whatever they were looking at. The whining grew in intensity, melting into the hum of the speakers.

"We should go a different way," Mel said to the Defender in a low voice. "Avoid the crowd."

Yes. Yes we should. The attendees had bottlenecked at the only entrance, and therefore exit, in the security fencing. The day's heat boiled the stench of sweat and the mowed lawn, leaving a burning aftertaste in my mouth.

I turned again, looking for a clear path back up toward Old Main, for Agent Martinez, who seemed to have disappeared. But as the crowds parted, only one figure was still heading our way.

It was the male Defender, his uniform too tight across his broad shoulders, sweat gleaming on his white face. He lowered his head but not his gaze. It fixed on me a second too long. Before I could point him out, he was an arm's length away.

Close enough for me to see my face reflected in his gleaming badge.

Close enough to see that there were no silvered words along the length of his baton.

Close enough to see his free hand slip into his uniform jacket pocket. The deadly shape of the weapon there as he reached for its trigger.

I didn't think. I didn't scream. The old woman from the highway, her face, flashed through my mind as my arm shot up. My fingers strained forward, close enough to nearly brush the end of the baton. The man gritted his teeth, eyes narrowed with naked hatred. He raised the gun inside his pocket to level with my heart.

I fired first.

I pulled the charge from the humming currents in the air, distilling it into a single thread of electricity that jumped from my skin. I aimed for his chest, to give him just enough of a nudge to knock him off his feet, but—

"No!" someone shouted. The voice rang out through the air just as the Defender—whoever he was—raised his baton to catch the charge. It was wood, it should have only been wood, but the thread of light exploded into a crackling halo that surrounded the baton, flashing up to capture the man in a cage of furious power.

"What did you do?" Mel screamed. "Oh God, what did you—?"

But even her voice was lost to the roar of the speakers blowing out in a wave of fire and thunder.

FOUR

At first, there was nothing but silence. Smoke.

It sank deep into my lungs, driving out every last ounce of air. The heat was trapped inside me, bubbling up until I was sure it would separate my skin from my muscles and my muscles from my bones.

The pain came next.

Panic trilled inside my skull. The white-hot air and pressure had lifted me up off my feet just as the Defender disappeared into the torrent of scorched plastic and metal. The fire had caught his uniform and hair, coating him like a second skin before devouring him entirely. And I'd flown— My head hurt, and it was so dark, it was so dark—

My chest wouldn't expand to take in the breath it desperately wanted. I couldn't move. My nerves sang and screamed and stung, but the pressure, the pressure that ground me harder against the sharp, uneven stone—it was going to crush me.

Smoke rose everywhere. Ribbons of it spilled over me, stroking the open gashes on my arms and chest. My right arm was caught under a sheet of metal that had fallen over me. I tried to draw it back to my side, but my wrist caught on something jagged. I bit back a low sob of pain.

Think—think—

Mel. Where was Mel?

I twisted as much as I could, feeling the metal edge bite into my skin. *Can't stay down here— Can't stay—*

Someone is here to kill you.

Someone is here to kill you.

Bomb.

"Stop it," I choked out. *"Stop."*

It ran against every instinct, every single voice in my head screaming at me to get out, to move, to breathe, but I forced myself to stop struggling against the metal sheet. I forced myself to take in the burning air, every acrid gasp of it I could manage. *Calm down.*

It didn't work. The Defenders, Mel, the boy, the teleprompter, the green, green grass, it all spun together in my mind. I tried to use my broken nails to claw through the sheet that was pinning me in place. I was breathing, I was alive—all those times the darkness had tried to catch me, I'd slipped through it. I'd escaped. This wasn't it for me. I was alive.

I have to help them.

With a heaving groan, I arched my back, wedging my knees up under whatever had fallen on me to try to shove it off.

It wasn't until I felt the rough carpeting rub against my cheek that I realized what it was: part of the temporary stage they'd built for my speech.

I shoved at it again, and this time it skidded against the nearby steps, giving me just enough room to slip both of my arms in toward my chest before the metal collapsed back onto me.

Then, all at once, the pressure, the weight, the darkness—it was gone.

The metal sheeting trembled as a silhouetted figure struggled to lift it. But when the sunlight momentarily dimmed, I could make out his face clearly.

It was the dark-haired boy.

The second the weight was off me, I crawled as far away from it as I could. With a look of intense relief, the boy dropped the piece of the stage back onto the steps, sending another cloud of dust into the air.

Blood suddenly rushed through me, pounding in my ears, sending knives through my numbed legs. I swiped a hand over my stinging eyes. The ash swirled in the air like a fierce snowstorm, and, for a second, I wasn't there at all—I was somewhere else, my skin freezing, my body small.

A scream lodged itself in my throat.

The boy, his eyes bright, wrapped his hands around my upper arms and pulled me onto my feet before they'd even had a chance to feel again. He held firm, even as my ankles buckled and I dipped forward. The boy gave me a faint shake, trying, I thought, to draw my attention back to his face.

But I was looking past him.

Mel.

They looked like doll parts scattered across the ground in the wake of a child's temper tantrum. One of her heels stood upright on the step below me, as if she'd simply slipped it off the instant before the explosion's heat overtook her. The Defenders—the woman who had led us along, the man who'd had the gun—were dead, the gray fabric of their uniforms still smoldering.

The blast had scalped the grass, leaving a halo of overturned

soil and brick. A few members of the university staff and reporters were gravely injured nearby and were trying to crawl away
from the burning ground. Their skin and clothes were charred
almost beyond recognition.

I jumped as the first figure tore through the heavy veil of
smoke, smashing through the mangled security fencing. A woman
stumbled after him, her sundress torn and stained by the blood
running down her shins. Her expression was blank, as if the blast
had incinerated every thought in her mind. It didn't waver, not even
as she looked down at the severed arm she held in her other hand.

People fled in a thrashing mass of chaos, trampling the shattered
cameras, narrowly avoiding the injured and the dead and those who
were trying to tend to them. The ones on their knees on the ground
screamed silently into the chaos. Kids. Parents. Grandparents. Police.
Defenders. Blood, everywhere. Smoke—so much smoke.

It was just one spark.

It was just one jolt of power. It couldn't have expanded like
that, or jumped to the speakers. I had too much control. I turned
again, this time toward the place where the tech booth should
have been. Where Agent Martinez should have been.

The pressure on my arms increased again. My eyes were raw,
streaming with tears, as the boy adjusted his stance to block the
destruction. His mouth was moving, but I couldn't make out
more than a few of the words—they were pops of muted sound,
like he was shouting at me underwater.

"—go—*back*—hear—?"

He realized I couldn't hear him at the same moment I did. I
flinched, trying to shove myself away. My heartbeat kicked so high,
so fast, my vision went black. He held on tighter, this time clasping
my face in one hand, forcing my gaze back toward him again.

The storm of panic and fear swirling in my mind abated, just for a moment. He kept talking. One word. I couldn't tell if I was actually hearing him, or if I had imagined his voice, deep and gravelly: "Okay? Okay?"

My hearing wasn't totally gone, but nearly everything was being drowned out by a keening whine that came from everywhere and nowhere.

"Okay?" he shouted, inches from my ear. "Okay?"

I nodded, because I was alive. I nodded, because it was the only movement my body seemed capable of making in that moment. It wasn't okay—none of this was okay—

I couldn't even cry: My eyes were already streaming hot tears to clear out the dust and smoke. My brain couldn't sink into the grief.

He reached for my arm again, pulling me forward down the remaining steps. Toward the bodies.

I tried to pull back, to head into the safety of Old Main. None of this made sense. The explosion. The Defenders. This *stranger*—I hadn't made a habit out of following strangers since I was a child, so why was I doing it now? He could be involved. He could have . . . he could have rigged the explosion.

You did it, a voice whispered. *You lost control.*

I shook my head, trying to wrench myself free. I didn't. I knew my power.

The thought steadied me, echoing through my mind. *I know my power.*

It wasn't me. Dissolving into panic, getting caught in the snare of that horrifying possibility, wasn't going to do me any good. I clenched my jaw, willing my hands to stop shaking.

Plan: Get to the car. Find Cooper. Drive myself, and anyone else who needed help, away.

Focus.

The boy released me when he felt me tug against his hold. I straightened, looking up to meet his gaze.

"Not safe!" he shouted.

"No shit!" I shouted back. I pointed in the direction of where we'd left the SUV. *"Car!"*

His face changed beneath the streaks of grit, the intense gaze slipping into a look of surprise. Recovering quickly, the steely look of determination returned. He nodded and gestured for me to take the lead.

I turned. The girl I'd seen with him before appeared without warning, her yellow dress bright in the haze of smoke. There was a burn on her right forearm, as if she'd thrown it up to shield herself from the heat of the blast. She shouted something to the boy, who swung back around to see what was happening.

A rush of uniformed police and clusters of horrified spectators came toward the wreckage. Some of the survivors fell to their knees, putting their hands behind their heads; others ran blindly forward, toward the rifles in the police officers' hands. The Defenders among them had taken out their batons, but most broke away to tend to the wounded.

The first bullet hit the smoldering remains of the speaker seconds before the crack of the shot's discharge split the air.

The girl in yellow dove to the right. The boy reached for the back of his jeans, only to realize whatever he was looking for there was gone. Without a word, he turned sideways and gestured for me to do the same.

For a second I thought he was trying to direct my gaze toward something, but no—I knew this trick. Vida had taught it to me years ago, before the new government had taken root.

Turn to the side to give your attacker less body mass to shoot at.

Another flash appeared in the smoke-clogged distance. This time the bullet struck at my feet, splintering the stone. A shard sliced across my shin, nearly taking me down.

The boy surveyed the steps around us, his eyes landing on a different, smaller panel of the temporary stage that had been blown out in the explosion.

He bounded down toward it, and, in one smooth motion, kicked the sheet up in time for the next bullet to glance off it.

It was the smoke. They didn't know—they couldn't see who they were firing at.

"Stop!" I shouted. The word was ragged as it left my raw throat. "Don't shoot! *Don't shoot!*"

The shots flashed in the burning smoke. The last bit of speaker exploded into black shards that cut at me, fast and deep.

"It's me!" I screamed back. "It's Suzume!"

The boy threw us both down, grunting as the sheet of metal absorbed the force of the bullets' impact. It bent in, further and further, until it was a hairbreadth from his face.

"They don't know," I said, struggling against him. They thought it was the attacker. They thought someone was taking me hostage. He didn't get that. We needed to find Cooper or Martinez.

The boy made sure I heard every single word as he shouted, *"They know it's you!"*

I shook my head, blood exploding in my mouth as I bit my tongue. He was breathing hard, inches from my own face; I answered each gasp with one of my own. His weight wasn't braced on me, but the heat of him was. Droplets of sweat, his or mine, ran down my chest.

He's wrong, I thought. *He has no idea—*

"Are you with me?" the boy shouted. "Can you run?"

What was the protocol? What would Mel do?

"We should wait!" I said. "We need to let them see we aren't a threat!"

"Like hell we should," he shouted next to my ear. "I don't want to die here! Do you?"

No.

I don't know where the voice came from, the same one whispering the words on the teleprompter inside my mind: *Someone is here to kill you.* As those few agonizing seconds ticked by, the words slowly shifted, slithering and crackling like a serpent shedding its skin. *They are going to kill you.*

Someone almost had. But I wasn't about to lie down and let them do it now, or take a bullet by mistake.

Do you want to die here?

I looked at the boy.

He squeezed my arm, understanding. Then we were running toward the car.

The gunfire roared behind us like an ocean wave trying to catch our heels. The girl in the yellow dress appeared in the smoke, her eyes widening as she spotted us. She motioned for us to follow, yelling something I couldn't hear but the boy could. He looked toward me, then nodded in her direction.

I nodded back, following the path she cleared for us by shoving through the horrified witnesses and university staff on the upper steps. It was only then that the firing stopped. The boy ditched the sheet of metal he'd used to cover us.

What is happening?

A hand reached out to grab me, but slid right off the coat of dust and soot on my arm.

What is happening?

"—op! Stop right—! —ume!"

Cop cars and fire trucks tore up onto the lawn in front of Old Main, their lights blazing as they surrounded the edge of the ruined security perimeter.

They're here to help. They're here to take control of the situation. Finally, some kind of protocol was clicking into place. They'd search the area, make sure it was safe. They'd help the injured. They'd find whoever was responsible for . . . *this.*

It had to have been a bomb. It took out the speakers on either side of the stage and decimated the tech booth. I remembered that now—that it hadn't been just one explosion. It had been three separate explosions, within the space of that last breath I'd drawn.

Three detonations, that same dark voice whispered in my aching ears, *or a single powerful electrical current traveling through their shared conductor?*

My stomach churned, the bile there roiling. Now that the authorities were here, it would only be a matter of time before they figured out who or what was responsible—and whether or not it was connected to the warning on the teleprompter.

We followed the flood of running attendees and staff until the point where they met with a line of Defenders, who caught and corralled them, ushering them to safety in groups. I let out a heavy breath at the sight, at the small touch of relief it brought.

Instead of following them headlong into the human safety net of gray uniforms, the boy and girl swung a hard right at the edge of Old Main, toward the street on the other side of the massive building.

My feet slowed, even as people jostled me from all sides. The girl noticed I had fallen behind first, and motioned for the boy to keep going as she made her way back to me. An expression of disbelief overtook her soot-smeared face.

"Really?" she shouted. "Don't make me carry you!"

The Defenders were there to help. I looked between her and the swarm of them, including the few who had noticed us—who were pointing and shouting in our direction.

The Defenders were there to help.

The silver, shining words. The promise, the oath they all took. *For the common defense.*

But it had been a Defender who had guided Mel and me toward the speakers. It had been a Defender who'd had that gun in his pocket, even though they were banned from carrying lethal weapons.

I didn't let myself think it through. I just followed the girl. Her long legs easily outstripped mine as she caught up to her friend. I tucked my chin against my chest and limped after them as quickly as I could.

The fountain at the back of Old Main, repurposed and rededicated as a memorial to the community's Lost Generation, gurgled up water as if nothing had happened. This side of the building looked otherwise abandoned. The cars that clogged the small parking lot had been deserted, a few doors left open with the engines running. All except one.

It should have struck me as strange, but I was too relieved to care. I ran toward our SUV, noticing for the first time that the front headlights had been cracked and the hubcap melted by the earlier attack.

The boy tried to catch my shoulder, but I dodged away. My heart galloped as I all but slammed into the passenger side of the

SUV. I could just make out Agent Cooper's form through the tinted windows.

I pounded on the glass to get his attention.

"Cooper!" I shouted. This wasn't like him—I'd never seen him so still in all the years I'd known him. *"Agent Cooper!"*

The piercing drone in my ears grew louder and louder, pitching up and down with my pulse as I ran to the SUV's driver's side.

I saw the distorted shapes of the boy and girl through the shattered driver's side window and the hole in the front windshield before I saw Agent Cooper. He was slumped forward against his locked seat belt, blood still dripping from his forehead and pooling where his sunglasses had fallen into his lap. One of the lenses was blown out.

I reached inside, slicing my arms on the jagged edge of the window. I gripped his shoulder, his tie, then recoiled at the feeling of warm blood. The left side of his skull was broken in, exposing white bone. The speckled pink of soft tissue.

That last fading spark of composure I'd been clinging to was stamped out, and I was left in the clawing dark.

It poured over my mind, my eyes. I knew I was screaming by the burn in my throat. Heat gathered in the center of my palms, and the car's engine revved to life. The remaining headlight flashed, exploding out onto the asphalt. The flat, dull blare of the horn finally broke through the high-frequency wail stabbing into my ears.

What the hell is going on?

The air shifted behind me. I turned, throwing out my elbow, intending to catch the boy in the chest. I couldn't stand the idea of being touched, not with the charge from the car's battery flowing through my senses, giving me power, giving me control when seconds ago I'd had none.

A hand latched onto my head, yanking me back away from the car. My heels caught in the uneven paved surface and knocked me off balance. The rubber of the glove caught in my hair's twist and dragged painfully across my scalp.

I screamed again, punching back at whoever was behind me. The charge curled just above my knuckles and between my fingers, searing the air. It caught the attacker, but right in the thick chest plate he was wearing over his black jumpsuit. Everything, from the helmet he wore down to the soles of his boots, had been coated with a thick tire-like cover of rubber.

The pulse of power flared white as it met the resistance of his body armor and traveled out through the air, looking for another conductor.

Shit. There wasn't anything electrical on him that I could sense, not even a comm in his ear. *Shit!*

My body knew what to do a full second before my mind did. I went limp, making myself deadweight. The asphalt dragged against the back of my legs, tearing at my calves, but the shock of that one movement was enough for him to relax his grip in my hair.

I swung my leg so that my foot caught his ankle. At the edge of my vision, the boy came tearing around the side of the car, a small gun in his hands. He wheeled back in surprise as I shoved myself up off the ground and launched my fist one, two, three times into the attacker's throat.

"Down!"

I threw myself to the left as his first shot rang out. The attacker staggered back, pressing a hand to where his rubber vest had caught the bullet. The boy's face was utterly expressionless as he adjusted his aim by less than an inch and fired again.

What the hell? It was an impossible shot, catching the man between the low-slung helmet and the rise of the vest that covered the lower half of his face. Even Vida would have struggled to make it.

The man dropped to the ground, bleeding out onto the cement between us.

The boy took a step toward me. I took a step back, heart jumping into my throat. This wasn't just another Psi—this wasn't just another kid. The training that took . . .

"Who the hell are you?" I snarled.

He's part of this, that voice whispered. *Him and the girl.*

That unreadable mask faltered as he lowered his gun, only to draw it back up again, spinning toward the fountain.

The girl in the yellow dress was knocked back by another man dressed in solid black, but she went down kicking, beating her foot against his kneecap. Her impressive height and strong, athletic figure made them evenly matched—until the attacker trained his gun on her.

I took a running step toward them on instinct, but he wasn't alone—*we* weren't alone. Three more men, all in the same dark uniform, came running up from behind the police cars, guns trained on us.

"Go!" the boy shouted.

I swung my gaze to him as he squeezed off a shot at the other girl's attacker. He spared only a single look at me, then pivoted toward the girl. The soldier dropped both knees onto the girl's stomach, pinning her there.

The girl screamed in pain as she reached up to knock his helmet back, then clawed at its strap hard enough to choke him. With her kicking up to flip them, and the soldier trying to pin her, the boy couldn't get a clear shot.

"Priya!" the boy shouted. "Stop!"

The man—the soldier—whoever it was—reached into a pocket on his vest and pulled out a yellow handheld device.

It had been so long since I'd seen one, and an old model at that. Years and years and years, hundreds of miles from this place, on the road in the middle of nowhere. The memory invaded my mind, filled my mouth with static until I was sure I could feel sparks traveling over my teeth.

But when the White Noise sounded, I couldn't hear it. Didn't feel it.

It tore through the others, and I knew exactly what they were feeling, how it must have shredded their thoughts and set fire to their nerve endings. The boy fought to stay on his feet as blood began to drip from his nose. The girl went terrifyingly still. The man laughed as he punched her again and got no response.

The other men were on the boy in an instant, kicking and beating him until, finally, he collapsed onto the sidewalk. He strained to lift up his head, finding my gaze.

I read the word on his lips: *"Run!"*

I could. I could take one of the deserted cars left in the lot and be in the wind, be gone. The realization made my knees lock, my hands shake.

But I hadn't been able to leave that stranger at the gas station in West Virginia when she needed help. I couldn't leave these strangers now, not after they'd tried to help me. Even if it came to nothing, I had to try. I'd cheated death once today. I could do it again. I wasn't weak or small or frightened—I wasn't that little girl anymore.

He'd trusted me. I'd brought them here, right into this. I had to be the one to get us out.

The words blazed through my mind as I threw myself onto the man holding the device, raking my broken nails down the exposed skin of his cheek. I knocked him sideways off the girl, clawing until I could get the device in my hand. My fingers brushed against it, making it spark and crackle as the plastic casing melted down into its wires.

The others stopped writhing, but before I could try to wake them, a pair of arms locked across my chest. They hauled me up until my feet dangled over the ground. I bucked, trying to smash my head back into his face, but I only hit the helmet. Black stars burst in my vision.

"*Stupid bitch!*" the man yelled, throwing me back down. I slammed into the cement, gasping. "I'll fucking kill you, I don't care—"

"Easy!" someone else bellowed. "Come on, there's no time—"

A cloth reeking of damp, sickly sweetness was shoved up against my face. I crawled forward, toward the unconscious boy, only to have the cloth pressed in tighter. Chloroform.

Let me help—let me help—let me— I bucked against the weight that fell over me, hating the hot sting of tears in my eyes, and the way the growing darkness took the sight of him, the words, the pain from me, until all I had left was the deepest black of sleep.

FIVE

I FADED—IN AND OUT OF CONSCIOUSNESS, IN BETWEEN reality and dream, and through light and darkness.

My mind spun inside my skull, light as a passing breeze. The bite of the leather straps holding me down—across my shoulders, my stomach, my legs—was disorienting. Half of me was there. The other half was rising toward the cracks in the metal roof, pulling myself up on those narrow ropes of light. The shadows on the walls were like long-forgotten nightmares, circling their prey.

Each time I closed my eyes, a new scene played out. Campfires. Dark roads. Electric fences. Closer and closer, faces edged forward out of the darkness. They watched me, blurred and unreal. They were all here, everyone I had known. My friends. Caledonia's controller. Gabe. Mel. The old woman. My head was crowned with sparks and crackling threads of power.

They watched, but didn't come closer. Didn't help. They spoke in broken thoughts and uneven voices.

"—everywhere, looking for her—"

"Stay here, wait for orders—"

"The truck—"

My eyelids burned. They drooped shut under their own weight; the tears and crusts caught in the lashes were as heavy as lead. This time, there was only darkness.

There was nothing at all.

At first, I thought it was blood.

The metallic stench seeped into my nose, my hair, my skin until I couldn't escape it. I forced my eyes open, cringing at the intensity of the light from above. As the black spots floating in my retinas faded, I could finally make out the stains on the ceiling. On the walls around me.

It was only rust. But seeing it smeared everywhere, the red-tinged droplets falling steadily into a small pool near my head, made the bile rise in my throat again, until I was sure I would choke on my own vomit.

Breathe. I sucked one breath in through my nose, then released it slowly. Just the way Doctor Poiner had taught me in our very first session, three years ago, when the past suddenly grew teeth and started following me everywhere.

Breathe through the panic, she'd coached. *Find five things you can see, four things you can touch, three things you can hear, two things you can smell, one thing you can taste.*

Three walls, the ceiling, my shirt, I counted. *The ridges on the metal, the damp strokes of condensation, the clumps of rust both old and new, the rough wood of the floor beneath me. My heartbeat, drips of water, my breath. Gasoline and something rotting. My sweat.*

Breaking down all those senses one at a time made me realize something else: I could hear again. The static whine had subsided enough that it no longer blocked out every other sound. It was still there, though, buzzing like a fly trapped in my ear.

I took in another breath, trying to sit up. The straps keeping me in place creaked but didn't stretch. I was flat on my back and wet where my body touched the ground. Judging by the shape of the small space, it had to be some kind of shed—or a shipping container?

I craned my neck back, catching sight of two long, still shapes in the shadows. It all came back in a jolt that sent awareness shooting through me. Wherever I was now, they hadn't brought me here alone.

Someone was taking shallow breaths, pulling hard against their restraints. There was an edge of panic to it, and I had to fight to keep it from infecting me, too.

"Hello?" My throat felt blistered.

"Try to keep your voice down." The boy. He spoke so softly, I barely made him out. He was still tugging at his restraints when he added, "There are guards posted outside."

Some of the tension in my shoulders eased, making it easier to breath.

"Oh good," I whispered back, forcing a brightness into my voice. The patented Liam Stewart method of trying to defuse someone else's fears while swallowing your own. "I was worried escaping would be too easy."

"Too easy?" he repeated, momentarily forgetting the restraints. I was just about to explain the art of inappropriately timed sarcasm when he said, almost as if testing a joking tone for the first time, "Then . . . you'll be excited to know that it looked like they were armed with everything but flamethrowers."

I twisted to look at him again—the dirt-caked bottom of his sneakers, at least. His breathing had evened out somewhat, and even with the lack of light I could see him twisting his body to try to catch a glimpse of me. "No flamethrowers?" I said. "What kind of evil organization is this?"

"A particularly stupid kind," he whispered back, "one that was reckless enough to try taking you *and* foolish enough to under-estimate your ability to fight back. I think you gave them the shock of their lives."

It was what I wanted to believe more than anything in that moment: that I was capable of both getting us out of here, and making whoever had taken us regret it. That strand of confidence wove through me. "And that's too bad. About the flamethrower, I mean. I do know how to use one, you know."

"You say that like it's meant to surprise me," the boy said qui-etly. "Like I didn't watch you punch a man twice your size with a fistful of lightning."

That's right—I had, hadn't I? That memory was enough to send the aftermath of the explosion crashing back through my mind. Him and the girl being beaten and slammed against the ground. The armor the soldiers wore that blocked my power. The boy shouting at me to run.

Would he have told me to go if they were involved? Would they be locked in here—wherever *here* was—with me? He'd held himself together after the bomb in a calm, composed way. Even as the men attacked us, he'd seemed to sink deeper into that con-trol, as if he'd merely clicked into a different, more lethal mode.

But a minute ago, I'd heard his strained breathing. I'd felt his rising panic as if it had been my own pulse fluttering beneath my skin.

"I'm sorry," I whispered. "There's nothing funny about this."

"Don't be sorry," he said. "Humor is good for the alleviation of stress."

Now that I could hear him clearly, my ears picked up the faint trace of an accent. Polish, maybe? Russian?

I gave a faint laugh. "That sounds like something a friend of mine would say."

God. Chubs would be so worried. He and the others were probably losing their minds. He'd be my first call once I got us all out of here.

Get out, find a phone, make the call. It wasn't even enough to really be considered a plan, but I clung to it. Even if there were a hundred steps that I still had to sort out, it gave me something real to start planning for. Just the possibility of hearing his voice after everything was enough to make me test the strength of the restraints again.

"I've been informed that I have the sense of humor of a rock," he whispered, "which I'm interpreting as *nonexistent* and not *surprisingly colorful.*"

"I don't know, you seem to be doing okay," I told him, pulling at my restraints again. "We can work on it after we get out of here. You didn't happen to notice where that is, did you?"

It was a long moment before he responded. I heard him swallow hard, the creak of leather as he tried to move. When he did speak, his voice had gone hollow. Remote. "Storage container— some kind of rail yard."

The waves of fear rolled out, releasing the unbearable tightness in my chest, carving out pockets of paralyzing anxiety. In those places, something new bloomed.

Fury.

For the threat during the speech. For Mel. For the wounded. For Cooper. For shattering that small measure of peace we'd managed to scrape together after almost five years of struggling. For the boy and the girl caught in this dark web with me.

It had to be connected—the bombing, being taken. From the moment the Defender had walked me down the steps of Old Main, toward the second Defender with the wrong baton and the gun, to when we'd reached the lot and had been confronted by a man with protective tactical gear that had nullified my specific power.

They had targeted me.

"I'm getting us out of here," I told him, not bothering to keep my voice down. "Do you see anything around you we could use to pry up the bolts on our restraints?"

"Guards," the boy reminded me quietly.

Right then, I couldn't hear anything other than the wind blowing outside the storage container. My job required me to be so reserved, so careful with every small word choice, it felt like a relief to finally be able to say exactly what I wanted to.

"Let them listen, I don't care." I raised my voice, loud enough for it to echo off the metal walls. "I want them to know *exactly* how fucked they are the second we get out of here."

Silence. The boy shifted, craning his neck to watch what I assumed was the entrance.

"Is she—the girl—is she okay?" I asked. "It looked like she took a big hit. . . ."

"Priyanka? She's taken bigger ones," he said unhappily. "A word of warning: she's going to wake up in a few minutes and will absolutely fight you to be the first one out of here. Please do not forget to unchain me when the two of you escape." Somehow, he didn't need to raise his voice the way I had for it to carry through our prison. His words were pure ice. "And when you're done with them, I'll make sure no one will recognize they were ever human."

No response. Not even a bang on the door to tell us to shut up. No taunts, either.

I breathed in and out, cringing as a fat droplet of rust-stained water dripped onto my forehead.

"Maybe they're gone," I ventured. "Taking a break to do something else horrific. I should have asked before, but are you all right?"

"I just . . . want to get out of here," he said haltingly. He shifted again, and I wondered what he was trying to see. "Can you think of any reason why they'd want to grab you?"

So he was also operating under the assumption that they had targeted me, and he and his friend had just been collateral damage.

Collateral damage who happened to be able to fight with an efficiency I'd only ever seen in trained soldiers.

"To make a statement? For ransom?" I decided to feel him out, see what he'd tell me about himself before clamming up. "Why do you assume they weren't targeting *you*? Or Priyanka?"

"Because I'm no one," he said quietly. "And I can't imagine what they'd gain by taking Priyanka, unless they're just planning on selling us to the highest bidder. But even that doesn't seem likely, considering your high profile. It's too big of a risk."

"I doubt they'd risk selling *any* Psi. The government has shut down every attempt to illegally move Psi both inside and out of the country," I said. "That's why they keep such close tabs on all of us, to protect against that possibility."

"All right," he said slowly. "So what do you want to do?"

"What do you mean?"

"How do you want us to handle the escape?" he clarified. "I can't tell how long we've been here, but if the guards are really gone they might be prepping to move us."

As his words sank in, I felt something bright, something steady and calm break open inside me. He was looking to me again for what to do.

Relying on me.

"Normally, I love a good road trip, but we can't let them move us," I said. "If they come in to remove the restraints to bring us to another transport, wait until we're all freed. Then we fight."

"Agreed."

I closed my eyes briefly, exhaling through my nose.

"Don't be afraid," he said softly.

"I was about to say the same thing to you," I said. My bottom lip must have split open at some point after I lost consciousness, because the cut reopened as I spoke, and I tasted blood. "People will be looking for me, and once we break out of here, these assholes will have to face the full measure of the law for the lives they took. I'll make sure of it."

Silenced pooled between us once more. Finally, he asked, "What about me?"

"Well, you're welcome to help," I told him.

"No," he cut in. "I mean, will you do the same for me? Make sure I don't escape the law?"

"What are you talking about?" I said.

"The men," he continued. "The ones I killed."

The ones he'd dispatched with cool efficiency, and that expressionless mask on his face.

"That was self-defense," I said, wondering who I was trying to reassure. "Anyone with eyes could have seen that."

"For us," he said, "there is no such thing as self-defense."

"What do you mean?" When he didn't respond, I pressed: "Who are you that you could even do that? You're not just a student, are you? Why were you *really* at the speech?"

"It's not like that," he said quickly. "Suzume, listen—"

There was a labored groan of metal somewhere behind me. Daylight washed in, blanketing us in late-afternoon gold. My eyes watered the longer I stared at the opening, at the silhouetted figures there.

"I don't know who the hell you are—" I called out to them.

I was cut off by the clang of metal striking metal, and a sinister hiss. Gas billowed around us, choking the small space. The door slammed shut again, a heavy lock rammed into place. The air turned sour, chemical.

"Shit," the boy said, his words slurring. "Don't breathe. Try not to—"

My thoughts slowed as the sensation of spinning returned. The darkness was a whirlpool that came on too quickly for me to feel afraid, or wonder if I'd ever wake up again.

"Your name," I gasped out. "What's your name?"

I fought against the pull of unconsciousness, bucking up against the restraints. It wasn't right, none of this was right—I couldn't go without knowing—

A single word reached me before the world dissolved into darkness: "Roman."

SIX

THE NEXT TIME I SURFACED, IT WAS TO THE SOUND OF wheels against highway, muffled voices, and the loud, wet breathing of a man hovering above me.

I was flat on my back again, the thick heat baking me from all sides. The stench of hot rubber was everywhere. I was being steamed alive in my own sweat.

"Shit," came a grumbling voice. "Fucking light . . ."

A joint cracked as the man rose, stepping on my shin as he moved away.

I fought to stay awake. To take in what was around me before unconsciousness crept up and pulled me back under.

The space was pitch-black, save for the narrow light attached to the top of the man's helmet. He wore the same black uniform as the ones who had grabbed us, but his skin was as white as a ghost's in the dark. His form took on an unnatural sheen—it was like searching the shadows of a lucid dream. The haziness of my vision made me uncertain if he was really hanging a bag of yellow liquid up beside me, or if it was a hallucination.

It wasn't.

The light on his helmet sputtered. He knocked a fist hard against it, letting its full glow sweep down over Roman's sleeping form. He used his boot to roll him off his back and onto his right side, facing away from me. Save for his shallow breathing, Roman didn't move, not even as the man knelt behind him, fussing with the bag . . . the . . .

My mind struggled for the word.

Roman's hands were bound together behind his back with a black zip tie. I couldn't see them, but I assumed his feet were secured with a few more. My own ankles rubbed together uncomfortably, and there was a bite from something hard digging into my skin there.

As the man looked up and shone the light on it, I could see liquid drip down from the bag and glide through the thin tube that connected it to Roman. The needle in his forearm was secured with a heavy bandage of tape.

But . . . I squinted, waiting for the splotches of black to clear from my vision again. His and Priyanka's IV bags were hung awkwardly from the straps on the ceiling, ones probably meant to secure shipments.

My own arm began to hurt in the same spot. There was a new, unrelenting pressure where a needle had been slipped beneath the thin layer of skin. A clear tube connected it to an IV bag on a metal stand. The first few drips of the same yellow liquid slid down the line toward my arm.

Spots of every color floated in front of my eyes, but the fresh surge of dread pushed back against the coaxing of whatever drug this was. My hands filled with hot sand as I tried to move them.

I couldn't. My wrists were locked together. Not with zip ties, but actual handcuffs, lined with rubber. Sweat poured down over my forehead, my throat, my chest.

The drug left a rancid taste in my mouth as it seeped into my body. Within the space of two heartbeats, it became harder to focus on the sight of the man hovering over Roman. But when his back was finally to me, I turned my head toward the IV line, taking it between my teeth and yanking—*hard*.

The long needle pulled partway out of the vein. The tape hissed as the edge lifted off my skin.

I tensed, my hands curling into claws. Watching the man's back. Waiting.

He didn't turn around. He coughed without covering his mouth, smearing sweat and snot against the sleeve of his black shirt. My ears filled with static as I took the plastic tube between my teeth again. I didn't look away from him, even as my heart began to bang in warning.

The tape gave way, lifting enough for the needle to slip out. The drug spilled over my wrist and the back of my hand, dripping onto the rubber mat beneath me.

The man rose again, pulling a cell phone from his pocket. He tapped out a message. Its screen cast a faint blue light on his face. That, combined with the glow from his helmet, was enough to confirm what I already suspected.

It was a semitruck of some kind. Every inch of it, from the inside of the door, to the ground, to the walls, was covered in old tires, cut open and melted together again in a tarry black quilt.

Thoughts were sharpening in my mind again, fragments piecing themselves together. I looked to the IV stand over me, then toward the haphazard way the others had been strung up.

Our suspicions had been right. *They were only after me.*

The boy was a Yellow, too, wasn't he? I'd seen his button, and I assumed the kidnappers had as well. But I was the only one in proper handcuffs, lined with rubber. The girl was a Green, considered relatively harmless by most of the population, but her hands had been bound in front of her, and her ankles were locked together with zip ties of her own. If they were only ever after me, why hadn't they just killed the others—witnesses—outright?

One possible answer was leverage. What was better than one hostage? Three of them. They could kill one or both of the others as a sign to show how serious they were about doing the same to me.

But there was this instinctive feeling I had about Roman and Priyanka that I just couldn't shake. It had seared through me like an electric current from the second I saw Roman fire that first shot, and it hadn't disappeared since.

I hated feeling suspicious of Psi who needed help; it made me more nauseous than the sedatives. If I questioned the motives of every stranger in a terrifying situation, I would never have opened the van door for Ruby all those years ago.

But the attackers, these two Psi, the men who had us now . . . Everyone in this situation was too well trained. No one shot like Roman did without hours of practice and instruction. No one fought with the confidence of Priyanka without having done it before.

Maybe they were part of this after all. I wanted to believe that all Psi were on each other's sides, but I wasn't stupid. There was the rumored nihilistic Psion Ring group, for one thing, constantly floating threats that undermined the work the Psi Council was doing. Or, the kidnappers could have hired these two to act as bait, knowing I'd be more likely to accept another kid's help. If that was the case, they'd done their job well.

But . . . they were tied up and drugged, too.

As Vida always said, the best way through bullshit was to wade in, hold your nose with one hand and a grenade in the other, and cut straight through it. Right now, I needed to eliminate the immediate threat and then wake up the others for answers. As the only one of us currently conscious, it fell on me to figure out exactly how to do that.

"Changing the Op—" The man stuffed his phone back into a leather pouch on his belt and took two swaying steps toward the wall that aligned with the truck's cab. He pounded on it. "You see that shit? Why the fuck should we take them there? The zone crossing is going to be a goddamn nightmare as it is."

I couldn't make out the muffled reply, only that there were two distinct male voices.

"Yeah, yeah," he muttered. His helmet light flickered as he swept it over us again, this time pivoting toward Priyanka, to my left. The IV bag above her was empty, sucking into itself as if wanting more.

The truck vibrated beneath me. I closed my eyes as he passed by. Priyanka's right leg shifted against my left as the man reached down and took her chin between his gloved hand, squeezing the soft skin of her cheeks. He stared into her face, bringing it close to his masked lips. He *tsk*ed at her, giving a mocking little coo.

Every inch of me went cold with fury. My fingers curled against the cuffs as I tried to slide my right hand free without making a big enough movement for him to notice. There was a gun at his hip and a knife in a holster at the other—but there was also the White Noise device on his utility belt and a smartphone in his pocket. And, if my senses were correct, a comm in his ear.

With a hiss, he shoved Priyanka's face away, letting her head slam back against the rubber mat on the ground. My top lip pulled back in a sneer as his gaze lingered a second too long at the spot where her dress had ridden up to her thighs.

Oh, so it was like that, was it? He was *that* brand of bastard.

I felt wild with the thoughts careening through my head. They urged me forward, cutting through to a part of me I didn't recognize. Here in the dark, I could be someone else. Someone who didn't stand in front of audiences, perfectly coifed, smiling, smiling, smiling no matter what the world threw in her face. There were no cameras. There were no protocols.

There was only escape. Survival.

The man turned, kicking Priyanka's leg aside to go for a small cooler near the door.

"You're lucky he didn't tell us to break your legs to keep you from running," he told her casually, the way someone would report the weather. *Cloudy, with a chance of agony.* "I argued for it, of course." He flipped the lid open, letting the flickering light on his helmet illuminate the bag of yellow liquid he pulled from the cooler. The light shifted, exposing her again to his gaze. "I would have taken special pleasure in smashing one bone at a time, starting with your hips."

I knew the drug was fading from my system by how fast the words jumped to my tongue. How clear they were, despite the dry ache in my throat. "You like leering at unconscious girls, do you?"

The bag of fluid jumped from his hand, slapping against the rubber mat. The truck's engine roared as it picked up speed. I felt the flare of its electric current as it flowed through the body of the truck, but I couldn't tap into it. Not with the layers of rubber insulation between it and me.

The man's light landed on the wet spot the drug had left on my side.

"You sneaky little bitch," he said in disbelief.

"Call me a bitch again and I'll show you how hard I bite," I said.

"That's some mouth you got on you," he said. "I've a mind to put it to good use, freak or not. Maybe I'll keep you awake, just to hear you scream."

He laughed, and that shadow that lived in me, that small, dark corner of my heart that made me feel so ashamed when it demanded *more*, began to shift inside me. To rise.

How many people have to die because of you, before you'll do something?

I stopped thinking. I shut down the carefully conditioned serenity. I let Mel and all of her lessons be carried out of my mind on a wave of anger.

Then I started to laugh, too.

The sound was haunted, ragged. The man sucked in a sharp breath as it reached him.

"Stop it," he barked, lurching over to me. His light washed out my vision, but I refused to shut my eyes to escape it. He stepped onto my ankle, and I had to bite back a cry of pain as he leaned his full weight on it. A dare, a threat.

"I think it's funny, too," I told him. "Really, truly funny how much your friends up there must hate you."

He was close enough for me to see his eyes shift, to confirm what I'd suspected: they thought the drugs would be enough. That the handcuffs would take care of the rest.

"What the hell are you talking about?" he demanded.

"They trapped you in here with me, didn't they?" I said. The cut opened on my lip as I smiled.

"Shut the fuck up," he growled, storming over to the back of the truck to retrieve the drugs. At the force of his words, Priyanka began to stir again, her bag still empty, waiting to be changed. "I can't kill you, but I can use these last hours to create your perfect hell. So try me, you freak bitch."

"What did I say about that word?" I asked.

I felt for the charge of his ear comm and seized it. Even with a throbbing head, it took only a second of focus to pulse it, to fry the small circuitry inside its plastic shell.

"Fuck!" he screamed, clawing at his ear. A thread of smoke wove between his fingers as he tried to yank it out.

"They lined everything with rubber to protect themselves and the truck. But they didn't even tell you to leave your electronics with them." I lifted my cuffed wrists. "They made you think I had to actually touch you in order to hurt you, didn't they?"

His free hand went for his belt, to the White Noise device.

It was nearly impossible to explain what I could do to anyone who hadn't experienced it themselves. Most of the time, it was important to pretend that I didn't have the power at all; that I couldn't hear the song of electronics buzzing and vibrating against my senses, or feel the buried electrical lines growling beneath my feet.

It was frightening—it had always been, from the time I was a child. The vastness of that power. The innate charge inside my mind only ever wanted to connect, to join and complete those nearby circuits.

I reached out for the batteries. They reached out to me.

The device exploded in his hand. A hot shard of plastic landed on my shin as he fell back, stunned by the sound, the pain. But I wasn't finished, not until I had the battery of his phone in my mind's grasp.

"Say you're sorry," I rasped out.

"You . . . *bitch*!"

The battery exploded inside his uniform pocket. The fire caught on his black pants, traveled up his side, to his neck, to his face, to his helmet. He screamed so violently, falling to the ground to try to roll the flames away, I was shocked the others didn't stop the truck. The heat spread out through the rubber and melted it beneath him.

I sucked in a breath and sat up. The darkness pushed toward me from all sides, coated in smoke. I forced myself to stay upright, to watch.

The man writhed and groaned, trying to drag himself to the door. He was within arm's reach of it when his body gave one final tremor and collapsed. The fire burned until it couldn't, trailing out in thin, glowing veins across the rubber mat. As the last flame went out, the only thing left to me was darkness—darkness, and the sound of the wheels against the road, keeping time with my own driving heartbeat.

SEVEN

"HOLY . . . SHIT . . ."

I jumped at the sound of Priyanka's voice.

The girl turned slightly to the side, jolting as the dry IV line tugged back at her. She jerked her bound hands forward, ripping the empty bag from its strap.

"Here, let me do it," I said. Easier said than done. My ankles were locked together by loops of zip ties. I had just enough range of movement to get my knees under me and inch over to her.

The chain linking my handcuffs clicked and strained as I pulled off her tape in one go, ignoring her sharp "Shit, ow!"

"That's what hurts?" I said in disbelief. The man's helmet light was still glowing against the wall beside her. I'd made sure not to fry the device, thinking we might need to use it. Now it only illuminated her collection of cuts and bruises. Seeing them seemed to wake up my body to the reality of my own injuries. For a second, the pain took my breath away.

I shook my head, trying to clear the throbbing as I removed the IV line from Roman's arm.

"I'm adding it to my list of complaints," she muttered.

Roman let out a soft sigh as the needle slipped free, but he didn't immediately rouse like I'd hoped.

I tugged down the bag of yellow fluid, turning it toward the helmet's light to try to find some kind of label. About a quarter of it was gone. It looked like he'd gotten a higher dose than both Priyanka and I had, and I didn't know how long he'd be out, or if we'd have to try to break out of the truck without him.

It would be easier. I couldn't stop the thought from welling up in my mind. One less person to potentially have to run from. One less reason to question my gut.

But also one less person to fight off the people who had taken us.

I released a hard breath. Who was I kidding—I was never going to leave either of them behind to the mercy of these people. For one thing, I wouldn't be able to look myself in the eye again. If there was even the slightest chance they were innocent bystanders, then I was going to give them the exact same chance I had to get out of here.

"Where the hell are we?" Priyanka asked, the words slightly slurred.

The thick curtain of her wavy black hair fell over her shoulder as she propped herself up on her elbow and, finally, pushed herself fully upright. The drug was clearly still working its way through her system; she had that slightly glassy look of someone whose brain was caught up in a fog. Which meant that I had an opportunity.

In another time, and in a very different world, I would have felt guilty for trying it, but this was life or death. And I was going to make it out of this truck alive no matter what.

"I'm a little more concerned about who took us," I said evenly. "Did you recognize any of them?"

"Why are you asking me that?" she said, reaching her bound hands up to touch a spot on her cheek where a new bruise was forming. It was the size of a fingerprint. "Shouldn't you have some sort of catalog of bad guys we can work through? Who are the idiots who are always out screaming on highways and at speeches with signs?"

"You mean Liberty Watch?" I said.

"If they're the ones who think that you Psi should make up some sacrificial army, then yeah, Liberty Watch."

Ice prickled down the length of my spine.

"*You* Psi?" I don't know how I managed to get the words out. I don't know how I managed to smile when panic's numbing fingers were stroking my face. "How hard was that hit you took?"

A heartbeat of silence passed between us before Priyanka reached up and pressed a hand to her face. "Yeah. Wow. My mind is a mess right now . . . I'm—" She sucked in a breath through her nose, glancing down at Roman. "I'm . . . I'm one of those . . . a prodigy."

"Excuse me?"

"Oh . . . a Green? Whatever the government has decided the 'correct' label is," she said.

None of this felt right. None of this. Were they not even Psi? I hadn't seen them use their abilities—they looked young, but so did plenty of adults who weren't affected by IAAN.

Do something, I thought, feeling my handcuffs' lock again. *Don't let them get free before you do.*

I leaned forward, bracing the bottoms of my palms against

the ground, crawling forward, toward the dead man. Priyanka's gaze was almost suffocating as she watched me. My breath caught with the effort it took not to turn and meet it head-on.

Keys—I needed the keys to the handcuffs. I felt across the man's charred chest for anything that might have once been a pocket. The smell of burned hair and skin made me gag until I finally had to hold my breath. The utility belt around his waist was in better shape, but the few pouches attached to it either had cigarettes stashed inside, or were empty.

What I was doing was horrifying, but my mind had switched back into survival mode. The only thing I could really focus on right now was getting out of this truck and staying alive.

If the handcuff keys had been on him, they'd either melted or had been thrown off him as the man had tried to save himself. The better bet was that they were with one of the soldiers up front.

"It's bad enough that we have to announce our abilities with those hideous buttons, but why do we have to use the labels they gave us?" Priyanka asked. "Why did you government-Psi types keep *that*?"

My fingers trembled as they brushed the hilt of the small knife attached to the man's utility belt. This could work. I just needed to wedge the blade between the small links and use enough force to break one of them.

My eyes fell upon the gun at his side, and when I finally glanced back at Priyanka, she was looking at it, too.

Then her dark eyes shifted, meeting mine.

Shit, I thought, my fingers tightening around the hilt of the knife as I pulled it from his belt. *Say something, say anything . . .*

But it was Priyanka who broke the silence. She clucked her tongue, her smile too easy to be completely natural. "What a shock, no response. Did your speechwriter not give you any canned one-liners to use?"

I knew a lot of Psi didn't necessarily see the point of the work we were doing with Cruz and the interim Congress—but they also didn't see half of what we were up against. It was always easier to be cynical than actually roll up your sleeves to help.

"Well, you're clearly not a fan of my work," I said, keeping my voice neutral. "But I guess that makes sense. Roman already told me you weren't really there for the speech."

That was a lie, but her lips parted in surprise all the same.

Dread braided with disappointment, until I could no longer tell one feeling apart from the other.

I wanted to be wrong.

I wanted to believe them.

It was like I could see the flurry of thoughts and excuses moving behind her dark eyes as she flicked away each option, searching for a best one. She finally settled on the one I expected: outright denial. "Clearly his brain was fogged by whatever drug they pumped into his system. We were there because we had to be, as members of the new class."

It was tempting to keep digging, especially as the lies began stacking up like a house of cards. But one wrong move on my part, however slight, could send everything crashing down on me, escalating an already dangerous situation. A little suspicion would read as normal, but if Roman and Priyanka did have something else planned for me, pushing them too hard for answers would only make them close ranks and shut down.

I had exactly one guaranteed way of making it out of here and contacting DC: alone.

"Good point. He could have just misheard me, too," I said.

"Your families must be worried sick about you. Did you see if they were hurt? As soon as we're out of here, we'll find a phone for you to call them."

Or we'd see if they made an excuse not to. Or pretended to put a call through.

"Ouch with that assumption," Priyanka said. "Roman is my only family, and vice versa."

Shit. The forced lightness of those words pinged against my mind as truth. Shame burned in my throat. I shouldn't have brought families into this. God knew I didn't ever want to talk about mine.

"Sorry," I said with weak smile. "I'm a bit on edge. To answer your earlier question, though, I have no idea what group they could be. Antigovernment, anti-Psi, the Psion Ring . . ."

Priyanka held out her hands for me to cut the zip ties there, the rigid lines of her posture finally relaxing. I cut the ties binding my ankles together before taking care of hers. By the time her hands fell back into her lap, her expression was no longer shuttered; she lost that defensive glint in her eye, and, for a fraction of a second, her lips traced out a faint smile. There and gone.

But I saw it.

Who are you? I fought to keep my face blank, even as the hair stood up on the back of my neck. *Who the hell are you?*

"Well, you can cross the Psion Ring off that list," Priyanka said. "It wasn't them."

"How can you be sure?" I asked.

The group was like a ghost; they had countless agencies trying to track them and reports of violence done in their name, but they'd never stepped out of the shadows. Many people assumed that they were some remnant from the Children's League, but everyone affiliated with the League was accounted for, and most had moved directly into government work.

"Because," Priyanka said, "we used to work with them."

The truck swayed as it hit a bad patch of road. I stared at her.

"Oh, come on. I saw the expression on your face when you watched Roman take those guys out," she said, looking down at him. "You're not stupid, and you have a working set of eyes. It's obvious we've had some kind of tactical training. I'm surprised you didn't put it together yourself."

Her tone was so baiting, I felt my temper rise and had to take a breath.

"I didn't think the Psion Ring actually existed," I told her. *And where's your proof?*

"Well, that would be because the *whole point* is to operate under the radar and covertly push for the things no one in the government is willing to give us," Priyanka said, swaying with the movement of the truck. "More importantly, it's Psi-only."

Clever. I pushed back the strands of hair glued to my face, considering it. She'd picked the one group the government, myself included, knew next to nothing about. I'd hated the idea of the Psion Ring from the moment I'd heard about it. The last thing the Psi needed was a rogue element causing chaos.

"So you were there to do . . . what? Report back on what I said?"

"We were there for a fresh start," she said, her voice taking on an edge. "To try to get our lives straight again after leaving an organization that got to be too much. Too violent. They were broadcasting your speech, remember? What information would I be gathering that I couldn't get by sitting in my dorm room and turning on the TV?"

I could think of any number of things, actually. Security protocols, identifying the car we'd used, studying Mel or the agents and analyzing potential threats.

"At least then I could have been lying on my bed, eating Pop-Tarts," she said. "Do you think we wanted to be there listening to you tell us what the government was going to take away from us next? It was a mandatory event. They all but dragged us out of the dorms."

If there was one thing I'd learned about liars, it was this: they gave you way too many details. The Pop-Tarts were a nice touch, but she wasn't the only one who could spin a detailed cover story out of nothing.

"Well, sorry to disturb your busy day," I said. "Those dorm rooms were nice. Southgate, right? I got a tour from the dean right before my speech. That's where they finally found the missing mascot head, right?"

Lie, lie, lie. Southgate wasn't the one dorm they'd reopened—it wasn't even a dorm at all. As far as I knew, the mascot's head had never gone missing, either.

There was a silence that stretched a second too long before Priyanka looked me in the eye and said, smoothly, "Yeah. They found it in the oven of the third-floor kitchen."

Liar.

It should have filled me with some small feeling of victory, but it only set my nerves ablaze. My skin felt like it was slowly being cut away the longer she stared back at me, as if daring me to call her out. To see what would happen when I did.

My grip on the knife was slick with sweat. I tightened my grip on it again, drawing it closer to my body.

"I'm glad you got out. Of the Psion Ring, I mean," I said. "I'm a little surprised that a group that basically sounds like a terrorist organization simply let you go, considering the secrecy surrounding it."

"We had to fake our own deaths to get out," she said sharply. "And go ahead, call them what you want. At least they're trying to do work on behalf of the Psi."

"No, they're ruining *our* work," I said. "You can't burn a house down when we're all still inside it. You have to come in and sit down at the table if you're going to create lasting change. The Psion Ring has only succeeded in scaring people, which makes the job of the good guys that much harder."

"You really believe that, don't you?" Priyanka said.

I didn't want to fight with her about this, and I didn't have to justify myself, either. I worked with the government because even with its flaws, it was still our best bet for protection and security.

I held up my cuffed hands, feeling strangely hollow as I forced myself to shrug.

Finally, Priyanka's gaze fell back on Roman. She blew out a long sigh, then started again, her voice softer. "Look. While I will confess I am not unfamiliar with certain criminal elements in this country, these guys honestly just seemed like your run-of-the-mill, stereotypical bad guys. They were clearly trained, so maybe ex-military? Former PSFs hiring out their services to third parties? I mean, would it kill you to just . . . ?"

"What?" I prompted.

"My stupid, heroic Boy Scout of a best friend survived a bomb blast and still ran *toward* you, not because of who you were, but because he thought you needed help. And yet, it feels like you think we're the bad guys," Priyanka said. "Can we please just focus on getting out of here?"

An unwelcome flicker of guilt moved through me. The rawness of her voice had been . . .

I looked away. If it turned out this was all true, I could feel guilty and apologize later. For right now, I needed to smooth things over. "You're right. I'm sorry. I'm just trying to make sense of what happened."

"What's . . . happening . . . ?" a soft voice interrupted. Then, stronger, "Priya?"

Both of us startled as Roman rolled onto his back. He blinked fiercely in the dim light.

"I'm here," she said as she leaned over him. "You okay, bud?"

Moving slow, dragging himself out of the pull of the drug, Roman tried to get his feet flat on the ground. The zip tie restraints around his ankles locked up where they were looped through the ones binding his wrists behind his back.

That one small tug of resistance was enough to send a shock through his whole body. Roman jerked, turning back onto his side with a thin sound of panic.

"It's okay, it's okay." Priyanka's voice rose as he continued to struggle against the restraints. "Roman, just wait. Don't do it—don't you dare—"

Roman's body contorted into an agonized pose, his shoulders hunching forward, the muscles of his back and arms straining—

"I'm not popping it back in again!" Priyanka said. "Don't—"

There was a sickening, wet *pop* as the zip tie that had locked his hands behind his back snapped, and his left shoulder dislocated.

I reared back at the horrifying sound. *What the hell?*

Priyanka gagged. "Jesus! Will you stop hulking out on me?"

Roman struggled to sit up, keeping one hand pressed against his shoulder.

"Oh, no you don't," Priyanka said. "You're not going to do it right—let me—"

She braced one hand against his shoulder and set her jaw. I had a half second to look away before she realigned it. The only noise from Roman was a grunt of pain, and then a long sigh.

"What? You're not going to chew through the ankle restraints?" Priyanka groused, watching him examine them. The truck swerved right, rocking all three of us. "Or are you done showing off?"

He looked down at the zip ties, cocking his head to the side. Considering.

"I . . ." I began, awkwardly holding up the blade. "Knife?"

"The man didn't say anything about who they are or where we're going?"

Roman's dark head was bent over my handcuffs as he turned my wrists this way and that. His touch was soft, and it confused me, just for a second, into forgetting that his palms and fingers were covered in calluses, the kind that come from handling many weapons over many years.

I hadn't noticed before, but the back of his right hand was covered in a web of dark scars. It looked beyond painful; I turned his hand slightly to get a better look, but Roman immediately tugged it back.

"Sorry," I murmured. What could have caused something like that? Fire?

Roman kept his face turned down, even as he returned his hand to the cuffs.

"It was a stupid thing I did," he explained quietly. "My fault."

When I didn't respond, he looked up at me through the strands of his tousled hair, bright eyes rimmed with full lashes. Even if his face betrayed no hints to his thoughts, those eyes had currents of emotion in their depths. The danger was that they kept drawing me in, even as my head was telling me to look away.

Eyes of a poet, hands of a killer.

Who the hell are you?

"We really owe you," he said, nodding toward the dead man. "He must have had no idea what hit him."

In the moment, it had felt like I had no other option but to attack the man, but now I wondered if I'd made a mistake in revealing what I could do. "He deserved it."

My skin heated under the scrutiny of Roman's gaze, but my head was a mess. He looked at me the way he did when he helped me out of the wreckage from the bombing. It was a potent combination of relief and gratitude, and I didn't understand it.

Distance, I reminded myself.

I pulled my hands back, straightening the best I could. "Anyway, the only thing I got from him is that they changed the Op in some way. He did mention we still have hours ahead on the drive."

I tried not to think about the context in which that little piece of information had come up.

"Op." Priyanka snickered, repeating the word. *"Op."*

"What's your problem?" I snapped.

"I need you to stay very still for just a second," Roman interrupted, his voice as quiet and steady as the stretch of road beneath us. "I can't get the cuffs off without a key, but this should give you a better range of motion."

He brought up the tip of the knife, wedging it between two of the narrow links connecting the cuffs. If he could keep his hands steady in this situation, even with the swaying of the truck, I sure as hell wasn't going to let mine shake.

"It's just funny to hear you say that," Priyanka said, pitching her voice up higher. *"Op."*

The metal links split and my wrists fell away from each other.

"You find yourself in handcuffs often?" I asked Roman, rubbing at the metal rings still circling my wrists.

He looked down at the knife's blade, clearly trying to decide how to answer. "Are we still trying to relieve stress?"

My nerves were sparking, flaring hot and fast with no sign of burning out. So, yes.

Priyanka held up her hands. "Could we now turn our attention back to the situation at hand? How many people do we think are in the cab of the truck?"

"I heard two voices respond to the guy back here," I said, crossing my arms over my stomach.

Priyanka rose to her full, impressive height, knocking into one of the empty racks that lined the roof of the truck. *"Ow, dammit.* All right, then, spark plug," she said, her hand rubbing her head. "You're up. Can you stall the truck?"

"What did you just call me?" I asked.

Roman sighed, giving Priyanka a look. "She means that you're classified Yellow. A surge of power could stop the truck's engine, right?"

I nodded. "But if they've insulated the cab, too, it's going to be a problem for us."

Roman's mouth flattened for a moment, his brows drawing down in thought.

"You're a Yellow too, right?" I pressed. "I didn't imagine your button?"

In spite of everything, including my fears about them, it would almost be reassuring to have another Psi like me here. It would help explain why I felt a small instinctive tug toward him, even now. Yellow-classified Psi could connect to each other as they felt out the same electrical currents—one flicker of power brushing up against another.

Some days, that passing sensation felt like the only reassurance that I wasn't alone.

"You didn't imagine it," he said. "But you have the better control by far, and I don't know how useful I'll be. How do you want to play this?"

I rubbed at my face, thinking. Control would be key here. It meant the difference between stopping the engine and exploding it, which could kill all of us. "I can take care of the engine. It's going to come down to using the element of surprise. One of you can get the door open; the other is going to need to be ready to fire at any of the soldiers who come back to investigate."

Roman nodded, his gaze sharpening with focus. "I'll take care of them before they can get out of the cab. Priya will get the door open. Does that work for everyone?"

I was surprised when Roman flipped the knife in his hand, catching it by the tip and passing the handle over to me. I took it, swaying with the movement of the truck, and realized a second too late he'd only done it so he'd have both hands free to take the utility belt off the dead man.

Including the gun.

Shit. Why hadn't I grabbed it the second he'd freed my hands?

"Could I *possibly* do more than get a door open?" Priyanka

said. "Just so I don't, you know, fall asleep waiting for you guys to save us?"

Roman cast an anxious look in her direction. "It'll be enough for now. Don't rush the horses."

Priyanka gave him a look. He let out a sound of exasperation. "What is it in English?" he asked.

"Don't be in such a rush," she said. "Or hold your horses. I like that one, though. A point to Mother Russia."

I'd been right. English wasn't his first language.

He nodded. "I just mean that it's better to be careful and not overdo it if we don't have to."

"Okay, but counterpoint: Is it even possible to 'overdo it' with assholes like these?" Priyanka asked. "Can't we also use the opportunity to send a message straight up to the top? To whoever might be running this show?"

"We just need to get out of here alive." His tone had a note of pleading.

"And find out who's responsible for grabbing us," I added, watching them both for their reactions. Their expressions betrayed nothing.

"I hate it when you use that earnest look." Priyanka blew out a frustrated sound. "It always makes me feel like I'm about to tell you that your puppy got hit by a car."

"Priya."

"All right," she relented. "I'll get the door open—but I want the knife when she's done with it."

My heart gave another hard kick. I tightened my grip on the hilt. "Wait—"

"God, what's the problem now?" Priyanka demanded.

Everything, I thought. It would leave me without a weapon, but I was never defenseless. I had my power. "Nothing. Never mind."

Out of the corner of my eye, I saw Roman shift toward the front of the truck. I turned to find him staring down at the gun in his hand, a pensive look on his face.

As if feeling my gaze, Roman looked up, and I quickly knelt on the rubber mat. Pressing the blade of the knife to it, I sawed at the heavy material until it broke through and clinked against the metal truck bed below.

The engine's power surged across my senses, the voltage registering like lightning in my blood.

Roman checked the cartridge of the gun, his frown deepening.

"How many shots do you have?" Priyanka asked.

"Three." He moved past me to press his ear up against the wall dividing us from the cab. "You're sure you heard two voices?"

It was my turn to give a bad answer. "He asked a question and two voices responded. That's all I've got."

Roman nodded.

"Ready?" I asked.

He took the knife from me and cut a section of rubber away from the wall.

Get out, find some kind of ID on these people, get away. With that last thought, I let my mind connect with the engine. Its knot of electricity was so powerful, it burned away the rest of the world.

I grounded myself on the rubber mat. "All set here. Can we get this show on the road?"

"All right," he said. "Once we're out, head west. Don't stop running for anything."

"And if we get separated?" Priyanka prompted.

96

"Like hell we will" was his only reply.

"Stay on the mats," I told her. "Just in case."

Priyanka gave me a bland look as she stepped over the man's body to take the knife from Roman.

The image of the Defender, his whole body seizing as I sent the charge toward him, flashed behind my closed eyelids.

"Just in case," I repeated, when I realized the others were waiting. My fingertips pressed into the ridged floor, searching for that powerful connection again. "Tell me when. . . ."

Priyanka positioned herself at the door, the soldier's knife in one hand, the other on the latch to the truck's gate. At the edge of my vision, I saw her nod.

Roman waited a beat longer before shouting, *"Now!"*

I fell into the blinding-white power that flooded through my mind. I called it out, pulled up and up and up, feeding it back tenfold until the engine stalled out with a metallic bellow. The truck swung left, the wheels on the right side lifting off the road as the driver tried to regain control.

Roman braced his back against the side of the trailer and fired two shots into the wall that separated us from the cab.

The wheels locked, skidding in the opposite direction.

"Holy sh—!" Priyanka's voice cut off as she was thrown against the door.

The world rocked up and down, around, around, around. I released my hold on the current, breaking it. The last of its power caressed my spine, purring against my senses.

With a bone-jarring finality, the truck slammed down on all four wheels and rolled forward slowly, coming to a stop. Roman raised his brows at me. I raised mine.

"Well, that was some demon's idea of fun." Priyanka shook

out her whole body, recovering enough to shove the truck's gate open. Dusky light poured in from behind her, revealing a landscape of flat green fields and little else. "Come on, before—"

I felt it a split second before the others did—the spark as the engine reignited. The truck suddenly shot forward, and Priyanka fell.

"No!"

Roman's shout was drowned out by the hail of bullets that tore through the wall separating the trailer from the cab. They pinged against the exposed metal, roaring as they shredded the rubber. The air filled with black and metal ribbons, the stench of hot rubber clogging the already thick air.

Priyanka had grabbed the metal edge of the trailer, her legs pumping under her, as if trying to run at the accelerating speed of the truck. With a gasp, she hauled her elbows onto the trailer's lip, one hand reaching for the door's strap. There was a scream of gears as the truck swerved hard to the left, knocking her back down.

Bullets whistled and banged around my head as I saw her pulled farther beneath the truck, until only her white-knuckled fingers were still visible.

Priyanka wasn't being dragged, I realized. She was using whatever strength she had left to hold her tall frame between the scalding hot metal of the axles and undercarriage and the bite of the road.

"Kill it!" Roman shouted, throwing himself flat on his stomach as the spray of bullets poured through the wall. He flipped over, trying to use the holes left behind to aim at the figure moving there, climbing over the two bodies between him and the wheel.

Three. There had been *three* of them, not two.

One more bullet.

"I can't," I called. "I'll electrocute her, too!"

I crawled over to the edge of the truck. Priyanka had tucked her long legs up under the lip of it, bracing her feet against something I couldn't see. Her hands and the top of her head were the only thing visible. The road streaked beneath her, ready to tear her apart.

Priyanka set her eyes on something past me, her face going blank. I was close enough to see her pupils flare as she took in her next gasp of exhaust and air. Her adrenaline must have been off the charts.

Sound exploded out from the cab of the truck and the relentless grind of the wheels slowed with a few sputters.

"Grab my hand!" I called, reaching out to her. "Priyanka!"

I wasn't sure she even heard me. I barely heard myself over the road, the screaming radio from the cab, the thrum of blood in my ears.

"Priyanka!"

I reached for her hands just as she released her grip and the dark, tattered road snatched her.

EIGHT

I WAS THE ONE WHO SCREAMED.

At the edge of the truck's trailer, I watched as she slammed into the road, curling in on herself just enough to miss the monstrous wheels as they sped forward. She rolled, over and over, her body limp as it took the beating. When she finally came to a stop, I couldn't even tell if she was breathing.

Get up, my mind screamed. *Get up!*

She didn't. She wasn't moving—she—

"Suzume!" Roman shouted. He crawled toward me, keeping his head down. Whoever was up front had stopped firing, giving him just enough time to reach out and take my arm. "We have to do it again!"

The sound of my name, combined with his touch, shocked me back into action. I nodded, following him back over to the opening I'd cut in the mats. His hand returned to my shoulder, steadying me as the truck swayed.

Roman looked to me, and when I nodded, we both reached down. My awareness of him exploded as his power brushed mine the instant before our hands touched the metal of the trailer.

This time we didn't just stall the engine—we melted it into liquid steel.

The truck stopped so violently, its joints folded into themselves. The back wheels of the trailer lifted off the ground, tossing Roman against one wall and me against the other. The burning power of the connection between us went out with one last shock to my system.

Finally, the truck jerked to a full stop. Roman pushed himself upright. I blinked rapidly, trying to clear my vision, before taking off on shaky legs. I jumped down onto the road.

I stumbled toward the dot of color that was Priyanka, only to realize it was growing bigger, brighter, as she half ran, half limped toward me. Scrapes and road rash covered her arms, shoulders, and legs.

"Are you o—?" I began to shout.

"You left him?" she yelled back. As soon as I was within reach, she grabbed my elbow and turned us back toward the truck.

The only sight that greeted us was a man in the black tactical gear climbing out of the driver's side of the cab, his handgun trained on us. The white of his skin had turned bloodred with fury.

Priyanka charged forward a step, her fist raised, apparently unbothered by the fact that the knife was a silver glint on the road a mile back. One cut on her head was bleeding profusely, leaving a trail of crimson down her front. Her palms and knuckles were raw from the road; I was in agony just looking at her.

"Don't you fucking dare," the man said. He tossed a glance up toward the truck's trailer. "Anders? Anders, *report!*"

Anders's body rolled out, falling bonelessly into the road. Roman stepped out of the shadows, gun drawn.

One bullet.

"You want to risk it? Really, kid?" the man snarled, looking at him. "I don't need all of you. Which death do you want to live with? Hers?" He swung his gun from Priyanka to me. "This one will make more of a statement."

"Shoot him!" Priyanka snarled as the man came closer, shifting from foot to foot, like she might burst out of her own skin. As he passed behind me, one hand came up to clasp the back of my neck. Heat rose off his body armor, and spittle flew out of his mouth each time he breathed.

Roman's aim didn't waver, even as I saw him shift his weight to his back foot. His eyes darted from the man behind me, to my face, then back again. A muscle in his jaw rippled; I couldn't tear my own gaze away from the line of sweat that trickled down his temple, over the high planes of his cheek, off his chin.

The barrel of the gun kissed my spine.

Drop, I thought, trying to remember the move Vida had shown me years ago. *Startle him.*

And potentially get myself shot in the process. The soldier was vibrating with fury behind me—fury, or fear.

"Let them both go," Roman said, his voice calm. "One chance. You don't have to die."

I narrowed in on his face, the world blurring behind him. The strained lines around his mouth. The naked pleading in his eyes. *Don't do this. Don't make me do this. . . .*

"Just kidding," the man said, aiming the gun back at Priyanka. "Boss told me I could shoot—"

The bullet caught him just beneath the rim of his helmet, passing through his right eye. The blood spatter whipped across the side of my head, momentarily stunning me.

There was a single beat in which Roman stared at me in horror. Then he pitched forward, falling off the trailer into the road.

"Oh my God!" I said, running toward him. "What happened?"

"Roman!" Priyanka gripped him by the shoulders, lifting his upper body off the ground. "Roman, can you hear me?"

"Was he shot?" I forced myself to stop just short of them.

"He's okay," she said quickly, her own voice strained. "Just fainted. He gets . . . he gets these stress migraines. They knock him out."

Sunlight glinted off the truck's passenger-side mirror. I spun on my heel, cutting a straight path toward the cab before my mind had even made the decision to try.

"What the hell are you doing?" Priyanka called.

I climbed up onto the running board, yanking the heavy door open. The body of one of the soldiers slumped against my chest, knocking the air out of me. My arms shook with the effort it took to shove the soldier back inside the cab. Roman's bullet had caught him from behind, exploding through his neck.

Finally, with his hot blood painting my palms, I managed to push the man's immense weight off me. The body slid toward the one in the middle seat; the soldier there had simply slumped forward against the dash, as if he'd fallen asleep.

The hot stink of death overwhelmed my senses. My breath came in shorter, harder bursts as I searched the floor and dashboard for some kind of paperwork or identification.

Phone, I thought. The man in the back had had one, before I'd fried it. Even a burner could provide some kind of information about who they'd been in contact with. The pressure building at the back of my mind finally released when I found a slim smartphone tucked inside the closest soldier's bulletproof vest.

Password locked. Of course. No service, either. My fingers fumbled with it, smearing the man's blood on the screen. But I didn't need a password to use it to take a picture. I slid my finger left across its cracked surface and brought up the camera.

As quickly as I could, I snapped a photo of each soldier. The UN had facial recognition databases they could search for any match to these people. The pictures would be more than enough to ID them. The real question was if I could break away from the others long enough to send the evidence back to the government.

"Again, I ask: What the *hell* are you doing?"

I spun toward the voice, pulse throbbing in my veins.

Priyanka watched me from below, a gun in her hand. She must have taken it off the soldier Roman had shot. Its barrel was pointed somewhere between the ground and me.

"I . . . evidence," I said, showing her the phone. "Listen, I think we should split up. Scatter, so they can't easily track us—"

"I *need* your help," Priyanka cut me off, her voice tight. "I can't carry him alone, at least not far enough to matter. I can't. I'm not— I'm not enough. I need help."

I fought to keep my eyes off the gun in her hand.

I can't say no, I realized. If I stopped pretending everything was fine, so would they. And without knowing what their end-game was, I couldn't predict how she would respond or how she'd try to keep me here.

I just had to make it back to DC with the phone. If she got desperate to keep me here . . .

"Do you know what it takes for me to ask for help?" Priyanka said, her voice ragged. Whatever adrenaline surge she'd experienced, it had played itself out. Her legs, covered in darkening bruises and gashes, were trembling with the effort of staying vertical. "Do you think I would ask if I didn't absolutely have to?"

I swallowed and made the decision. I just had to stay alive for now. There would be another chance to get away from them. I'd make sure of it.

"Here," Priyanka said, holding out a hand covered in road rash and blood. "I'll hang on to that phone for you."

My grip on it tightened. "I'm good."

"I have pockets," she said, her voice as direct as her gaze. "I would hate for you to lose it."

The gun was still in her other hand. Every instinct I had was screaming at me as I slowly placed the phone in her palm and watched as it was tucked into her ripped jean jacket.

Feeling trickled out of my limbs as I climbed down out of the cab. We hurried back toward where she'd left Roman stretched out and prone in the shadow of the semitruck.

"Let's get out of here before the cavalry comes galloping over the horizon," Priyanka said, kneeling to get one of Roman's arms over her shoulder. I did the same.

"And go *where*?" I asked, scanning the open fields on either side of the road.

In response, the long grass waved back at us, combed through by the faint breeze. Miles to the west, to the east, to the north, to the south, there was nothing but prairie and open sky.

Nothing but us.

NINE

NIGHT HAD TURNED THE EMPTY HIGHWAY INTO A DARK ribbon of asphalt, one that stretched on endlessly to the distant horizon. It felt like I was chasing the moon, only to have it remain just beyond the reach of the headlights.

The thought was jostled out of my head as the wheels hit a pothole. The worn-out shocks on the truck launched the three of us off the bench seat. Priyanka's forehead smacked into the window she'd been resting it against. I glanced over at her quiet grumbling, but, within seconds, she'd once again given in to the exhaustion tugging at her mind.

My eyes slid down to the small lump in her jacket pocket, back to the road, then back to that same pocket. Biting my bottom lip, I reached across Roman's body, careful not to brush the slight rise and fall of his chest, fingers straining toward her jacket.

Get the phone, stop the car without waking them up, run like hell away from them.

Except Priyanka shifted, turning so her back was fully to me.

Even without the seat belt strapped across my chest, there was no way of reaching the phone without climbing over Roman.

"Shit," I breathed out, turning my full attention back to the road. My hands gripped the wheel so tightly, I felt the old leather crack beneath my palms.

Priyanka and I had walked for hours, carrying Roman's unconscious form between us. Wild grass turned to cornfields, which had led us to an abandoned farm and a junker truck left to be buried by a collapsing barn. All I'd had to do was use the last bit of power in the house's generator to jump the engine.

The truck was an old model, with its best years in the rear-view mirror and a broken fuel gauge, the latter of which added some unwelcome mystery about how much gas we actually had. Liam would have loved it, though. He'd call it a "classic beauty," and name it after some old rock song.

Maybe . . . he could be my second call, after I let Chubs know where I was and that I was okay. If I still had the right number.

I rolled down the window's hand crank, hoping some fresh summer night air might keep the fog of fatigue from creeping too deeply into my thoughts. We had to hit some kind of home or motel or even gas station eventually. The trick was just staying awake.

I hadn't had anything to eat or drink in what felt like days. No rest outside of the drug-induced stupor they'd put us in. Maybe that's why Priyanka hadn't fought me to drive—she really thought it would only be minutes before I pulled off the road and tucked into sleep, too.

I glanced over at her again. The gun was in her lap, her hand resting on it. The phone I'd stolen from the soldier hadn't had a signal at all—either there were no cell towers out here, or someone had figured out what had happened and immediately discontinued service to it. In the end, it didn't matter. I'd probed what was left of its battery with my power as we'd climbed into the truck, but it had already died.

Awake, I thought. *Just stay awake.*

What my mind wanted was coffee. What I had was a radio.

The signal had started out dodgy, sputtering between songs and silence. It got stronger with each mile we gained, which made me hopeful that we were on the verge of finding civilization again. And even if we only got that one throwback station, it at least gave me something to do—Liam's favorite trick to stay awake: singing.

I whispered the words to the REO Speedwagon song, but my head felt like it was a thousand pounds, and I couldn't seem to grasp the melody.

"I've never heard this song before."

The truck swerved into the other lane. My heart just about rocketed out of my chest, shredding itself against my rib cage. "Jesus!"

"Sorry!" he rasped out. "I should have—"

"No," I interrupted, pressing a hand against my chest as I steered us back to the right lane. "It's all right." Adrenaline had dialed my nerves up to a hundred, and the way he was looking at me now, so *concerned,* filled me with this angry confusion. "You're awake."

Don't be nice to me, I thought, forcing my gaze back onto the road. *Don't pretend.*

"Where are we?" he asked, rubbing his forehead. He leaned

forward, turning to get a better look at Priyanka, assessing her with those bright, worried eyes of his. She didn't stir.

"No clue," I said curtly, sitting up a little straighter. "I'm just driving until we find someplace that'll let me make a phone call."

"How long have I been out?" he asked, sounding like he might not want to know the answer.

"A few hours," I said. "Long enough that I was starting to seriously doubt you'd ever wake up."

He swore quietly. "Hours?"

"Hours. Priyanka explained about your migraines," I told him. "How they're triggered by stress. Is that true?"

"They hit me like a hammer and take me out, but it's usually only for an hour at most." Roman ran his scarred hand over his face again. "What else did Priyanka tell you?"

It sounded like he didn't want to hear the answer. Of course. Maybe he'd be the easier one to drill for answers in the end.

"About your past with the Psion Ring," I said, watching his face for his reaction. "How you were at the school for a 'fresh start.'"

"The Psion Ring?" He leaned his head back against the seat, his mouth stretched into a tight grimace. I didn't miss the glance he slid her way. "Then she told you too much."

"Why?" I began, trying for playful. "Is it an I'd-tell-you-more-but-I'd-have-to-kill-you kind of operation?"

"Yes," he said flatly. "The more you know, the more dangerous they become to you. There are . . . added risks to you since you work in the government."

I ignored the cold prickle on the back of my neck, keeping that same joking tone. "Because they have spies in our ranks?"

"No, because you can report our involvement, and then we'd be taken in for questioning."

I glanced at him, stunned. "I won't do that."

"Why wouldn't you?" he asked, staring through the windshield. "It doesn't matter what you'd want to do personally—it would be your duty. Your responsibility."

I don't know why that rankled me. "I'm capable of working for the government and doing a little bit of off-the-books help if I have to. If it's true you want a fresh start and you left that life behind, then I have no reason to say anything."

But that wasn't exactly true, was it? The government had been searching for any leads on the Psion Ring for years. Knowing I had something potentially helpful would gnaw at me. Maybe I *would* feel like I had to say something.

That only mattered, though, if there was an ounce of truth to this story. And every interaction I'd had with the two of them pointed to it being a convenient cover, including Roman's reluctance to say more now.

"I'm sorry," he said in that quiet voice of his, the one that didn't disturb the silence so much as give it depth. "God, I'm so sorry. I don't know what else to say, other than thank you."

"Don't thank me," I said, ignoring the pull of those eyes. Pain had its own gravity, and his words were heavy with it, threatening to pull me in. "I really didn't do much."

"You stayed with Priyanka," he insisted. "You helped her."

Helped would have implied I had a choice. But even if nothing else he said was true, those words, at least, felt genuine to me.

"I'm going to make it up to you," he said, his low voice rumbling. "I won't forget this, and I won't ever let you down like that again."

At that, the words blistering with sincerity, I finally looked. Roman was watching me intently, his face a kaleidoscope of barely restrained emotions.

"You couldn't help it," I said, feeling my skin heat up again. The way he looked at me was like . . .

Like nothing.

Like a liar.

I turned back to the road. "It's fine. Really. Don't make a big deal out of it."

"It *is* a big deal," he said quietly. "It's my only deal. At least the only one that matters to me."

I didn't know what to say to that. I didn't understand why I *wanted* to say something to that. In that moment I felt as soft as a petal, when all I'd ever wanted was to grow a few thorns.

"Priyanka and I . . . We . . ." Roman struggled to put the thought together.

"You only have each other," I finished. "She told me that, too."

He shook his head, running a rough hand back through his dark, thick hair.

"What? Is that not true?" I pressed.

"It's true enough," Roman said, rubbing at the back of his scarred hand. "I had . . . I lost my sister. I lost her, just like we'd lost our mother years before. As hard as I tried to take care of her, it all fell apart in the end. The man raising us had the heart of a snake, and I couldn't save my sister from him. I couldn't keep my family together."

I tried to swallow whatever was lodged in my throat. "I'm sorry."

"Even if it doesn't make sense to you . . . when I say that what you did in helping Priyanka means everything to me, it's the truth. It's my absolute truth."

"I understand," I said before I could stop myself. "Probably better than you think."

I hadn't been able to keep my family together, either.

Maybe this was all a play, part of whatever their bigger plan was—get me on their side by working some quality emotional manipulation. Even as the thought crossed my mind, I wanted to brush it away. The only times I felt like they were being real were the ones where their control over the situation slipped and they spoke or acted from a place of deep feeling. These little glimpses of who they were beneath the deception, two kids who fought like hell for each other, made me think the endgame wasn't to hurt or kill me. Or at least I hoped.

It was a good ten minutes before I realized Roman and I had been sitting in silence. I stole a look at him out of the corner of my eye, but he seemed as unbothered by quiet as I was.

For the first time in a long while, I didn't feel like I had to say anything. There was no one to comfort or convince. There was no one to charm or encourage. I disappeared into myself as I drove on, trying to find my center. I could breathe. Be still.

What I hadn't expected was how much Roman seemed to need it, too.

Some people feared silence. They did anything to fill it, talking about things that didn't matter, asking questions just to hear some kind of response. It seemed to me that a lot of people saw it as a kind of failure. Evidence that they weren't interesting enough, or that a bond wasn't strong enough. Or maybe they were just nervous about what it would reveal about themselves.

"Do you want a break?" he asked quietly, catching me looking.

"No, I'm fine," I said. I wasn't turning this wheel over to either of them. As long as I had it, I had some control over our destination.

I was so sure he'd fight me, make all the right arguments about how he'd rested and I was exhausted, but he simply nodded. Believing me.

"Why did you stop singing?" he asked.

"I was only doing it to keep myself . . . to keep my mind off other things," I said. "And I haven't recognized any of these last few songs."

Roman looked almost relieved. "Me neither."

All right. I'd bite. This was at least keeping me awake and alert. "What do you normally listen to? Or do you just not really listen to music?"

He pressed a fist to his mouth, considering. "It's . . . Priyanka tells me I have the taste of an old man. I like the classics. Older music. There's a word for it I can't think of?"

"Classics like orchestra music, or standards?"

"Standards!" he said, his expression brightening. "Sinatra, Billie Holiday, Nina Simone . . . Listening to them helped me learn English. They were the only records in the house where we grew up. I like them, too, because they're simple."

My brow creased. "In what way?"

"The voices, they're deep and complex, right?" he said slowly. "But the songs are usually uncomplicated in what they're saying— that they love someone, that they miss someone, that they don't want to have to say good-bye. It makes me wish all of life could be that way."

Roman suddenly sat up straighter, taking in a sharp breath. I turned back toward the road, searching for whatever he'd seen move in the darkness beyond the headlights.

"What?" I asked. "What is it?"

"I know this one!" he said, turning up the volume on the radio.

It took me a moment.

"You do *not*," I said in disbelief.

He held up his finger, waiting for the chorus, wholly focused on the dashboard. Then he opened his mouth to sing.

Even with the rasp of his dry throat, it was a beautiful, rich voice—the sound was as pure and bold as a bell, and completely at odds with his usual quiet way of speaking. For a moment I was so stunned by it, I missed what he was actually singing.

"*Come on, Eileen, I swear what it means,*" he sang, trying to keep his voice down so as not to wake Priyanka. "*In this moment you need everything / You are the best / Oh, I swear you're the best / Stop your hurting / Come on, Eileen—see?*"

I let out a shocked laugh. He was so pleased with himself, I almost couldn't say it. "Those are *not* the lyrics. What do you think the song is about?"

Roman's expression turned serious. "She's discouraged and he's trying to cheer her up. Bolster her courage."

"He's trying to convince her to hook up with him," I explained. "He's basically badgering her."

"No." He looked almost scandalized. "Really?"

"Really," I confirmed.

Roman angled his head toward the radio, listening to the next verse. Then he leaned forward and turned the radio off.

After a minute, he explained, "I like my version better."

"You know," I said, "I think I like your version better, too."

Roman shrugged and turned back to the road, and I did the same. Silence settled between us again, but as the miles faded in the rearview mirror, so did the easiness of that moment. A cold, creeping realization spread over me.

Dammit.

I'd just . . . slipped. The conversation had felt genuine, and I was so tired I'd lowered my defenses. I wanted to believe that I'd opened up as a way to convince him that I'd fallen for their game, but that would have been lying to myself.

There was only one thing I needed to remember.

All of this was impossible, and none of it would ever be real.

TEN

A FEW HOURS SHY OF MORNING, WE SPOTTED A MOTEL sign in the distance, its VACANCY light on. For dozens of miles it had been nothing more than a faraway spark, and now the sign turned the sky violet with its glow. The sight of it tangled my thoughts, knotting them with unwelcome memories of other motels, in other empty places.

"Phone lines," I said, pointing them out. A feeling of triumph bloomed in me as I added, "At least I'll finally be able to make my call."

The only questions were what they'd try to do to stop me, and what they'd do when they realized they couldn't.

As if on cue, Roman asked, "Can you pull over here a second?"

I slowed the truck, but didn't pull off onto the rough shoulder.

Roman stared out at the motel, brows lowering in thought. "I was just thinking . . . maybe we should approach on foot. And not check in with the employees."

I translated that into the crime it was. "You mean break into a room and use it?"

"The hotel manager or staff would be able to identify us to

116

anyone who came looking," he explained. "The kidnappers could have beaten us here and bribed the workers to call in a sighting of us."

"That terrifying thought aside," Priyanka said, "we also look like we escaped a murder scene, so maybe it is best to approach with some caution, especially since a hotel manager out here is likely to have some kind of gun."

I glanced down at my shirt, my stomach turning at the sight of the blood on it.

"That too," Roman agreed.

"Let me go ahead, then," Priyanka said. "I'll scope the place out, see which rooms are open, avoid rushing any horses."

"Why don't you both go?" I suggested innocently. "Or I can go, and the two of you can stay here."

"Or Roman could go," Priyanka said. "Or you *and* Roman could go. Thank you for helpfully laying out all the possible solutions."

"That's not all of them," Roman said absently. "None of us could go, or all three of us could go together." Seeing the look Priyanka sent his way, he said, "What? That wasn't all of them."

"I should go," I said, fighting my frustration. I needed to get into one of those rooms myself, not give them time to find an excuse for why we should move on. "I could go in, make the call, and get out before anyone notices."

"You're the most recognizable one of us," Priyanka said. "Someone is going to notice."

"No one is going to notice," I shot back, and that was the truth. I was used to moving unseen, even if I was slightly out of practice. "I have more experience with this kind of thing than you do."

"Somehow," Priyanka said, "I really doubt that."

I slammed my foot down on the brake in anger, and it was the only opening she needed. Before I could get the truck moving again, she unbuckled her seat belt and jumped out, calling, "You two can enjoy coming up with all the possibilities of what could happen to me together."

Priyanka took off at a limping run, her legs losing their stiffness as she wove through the tall grass and stray clusters of trees, making a wide arc across the field to approach the hotel from behind. Gritting my teeth, I guided the truck onto the shoulder and threw it into park.

I was shaking with frustration, and no matter how hard I gripped the wheel, I couldn't stop.

"Tell me what that look means," Roman said. "Are you all right?"

"No," I said, and left it there for him to figure out.

Priyanka's distant form reappeared at the edge of the motel's lot twenty minutes later. As she neared, it quickly became apparent that the blood on the shoulder of her jean jacket and dress was bright, meaning fresh, and that she was holding a palm against the skin above her left eyebrow for a reason.

Roman let out a sigh and reached over to turn the engine off, taking the keys from the ignition. He slid across the seat to open the door for her. Priyanka didn't bother climbing back in.

"Good news, bad news," she said, way too brightly for someone with a gushing head wound. As she leaned in, I saw that her pupils were dilated again, and she had that look of almost feverish excitement. Her words seemed to chase one another out of her mouth.

Roman's whole body tensed as he took in the sight of her. "Start with the bad."

"*Welllll*, you see," she began, "I happened to be trying to look into a room's window to make sure it wasn't occupied, and the manager—this little white dude—he just pops out of nowhere at me like a damn weasel. I didn't really want to wake anyone sleeping nearby, so I followed him back to his office, playing the innocent, desperate ingenue. And, well, it turns out he's got a little side business, this one of the narcotics variety. I basically *had* to knock him out, use his belt to chain him to the office's toilet, and blockade the bathroom door."

Theft and assault. Perfect. This was going to be so much fun to explain to Chubs.

"You call that being careful?" Roman said.

"I actually call that a citizen's arrest," Priyanka said. "I was just doing my civic duty in God's country."

"Did you at least kill the security cameras?"

She gave him a look. "You think this is the kind of joint that has working security cameras? A better question is if I stole the illicit bundle of drug proceeds out of his pocket, because, yes, I did."

She tugged out a large roll of UN-printed dollar bills with their signature pale-blue paper and holographic security foil and tossed it to Roman, who caught it with an unhappy look.

"This isn't going to get us much," he said. "Maybe a tank of gas or two."

"You're joking," I said, reaching for it. The weight of the bills alone told me it was at least a thousand dollars. "And anyway, you can't keep that. . . . It's . . . evidence."

"When was the last time you had to buy anything?" Priyanka asked. "Everything costs a hundred dollars, an arm, *and* a leg these days."

"I buy . . ." I began to say. What had I bought recently? A scarf—a present for Cate's birthday. But of course I wasn't paying for food, or clothes, or gas. I was an employee of the government living in government housing. That made me *lucky* and *grateful*, not out of touch, like she was implying.

I met people almost every day and heard their stories. Things were tight with everyone while people reentered the workforce and new companies opened their doors. If a dollar didn't buy much now, it would again soon.

"Things," I finished lamely.

"Is this dirty money?" Roman asked, turning back to her. "Traceable?"

"Let me put it this way: either the guy is an employee of Leda Corp moonlighting as a crappy motel manager in the middle of nowhere, or he's in deep with whatever network is set up in this zone."

"Network? Like a crime network?" I asked. "You really do have a vivid imagination."

"Okay," Priyanka said. "Keep believing that. I, on the other hand, am going to believe what I actually saw: he was better stocked than most pharmacies. In either case, you should be thanking me. Now it can all be returned to the bosom of democracy and justice along with everyone's favorite Psi sweetheart, Suzume. You're welcome, America."

"Hilarious," I told her.

"I know, right?" she said. "But you won't be laughing when I tell you that their phone lines are down."

The words trickled through me, slowing the blood in my veins as they sank in. Roman cast an anxious look my way.

"You're sure?" Roman asked.

Priyanka shrugged. "Must have been a storm or something."

Of course. Anger shot through me, blistering hot. She had to have shut it off somehow. They were never going to let me call for help, not before they got whatever it was that they wanted from me.

"You're welcome to test it yourself," Priyanka said, all innocence.

"I think I'll do just that," I said as I climbed down from the truck.

"How did you reopen the cut on your head?" Roman asked, reaching over to inspect it. Priyanka shooed his hand away with her free one.

"Calm down, I'm fine. It's a flesh wound, et cetera."

"Did he hit you?"

She looked insulted.

"No. I mean, he put up a fight . . ." Priyanka began. "Well, a li'l fight. A cute struggle. It made me giggle."

"You hit your head on a door frame again, didn't you?"

Priyanka's full-wattage smile dimmed, but her words didn't slow. I could see her pulse fluttering in her throat again, too fast to be normal. "I'll have you know I hit my forehead on the window when he jumped out of the bushes squealing at me like a little troll."

"Wasn't there also supposed to be good news?" I asked.

Priyanka reached into the partially torn pockets of her dress. Hooked on her index finger was the loop of an obnoxiously large wooden keychain, and a silver key. "I got us one of the bigger, and

I'm assuming less shitty, rooms. I'm guessing we have about an hour before the manager wakes up and gets enough of the duct tape off his mouth to start screaming."

Oh God.

Roman looked to me, as if waiting for my approval. I gave a reluctant nod.

Just this once . . . I thought, feeling smaller and smaller as I trailed after them. I remembered what this felt like, too: breaking the law, turning yourself invisible to avoid getting caught. My hands shook so hard that I had to press them flat against my sides.

I could do this again. Just this once.

Just one more time.

As Priyanka passed by me, an expected spark of electricity brushed up against my mind.

I angled toward her again, spreading that silver thread of my power out, letting it feel for a connection.

It found one.

There was something electrical in Priyanka's pocket besides the cell phone I'd taken from the kidnapper. Something with power in its battery.

She turned toward the motel, leading the way. Roman subtly slowed and drifted back so that he was a step or two behind me. He marched me forward like the prisoner they believed I was.

But in the soft, milky light of early morning, I let a small smile touch my lips. I knew what that power signature was.

Another, different cell phone.

A chance.

ELEVEN

Present Day

THE CAR SMELLED LIKE DAYS-OLD FRENCH FRIES AND drove like it was slouching toward its millionth mile. The engine clogged and churned pitifully each time I sped up, and the brakes screeched as I slowed. It *did* have a full tank of gas, but that was only because I'd shown Roman how to use the motel's garden hose to siphon from the other car in the parking lot.

This was a routine I knew. Find a car. Siphon gas. Change the plates. I latched onto the familiar steps, because I didn't want to think. Anything was better than mentally replaying what I had seen on the television.

Me, killing that Defender. Me, sending out a bolt of bright electricity that ripped through the speakers and tech booth, making all of them explode in turn.

I'd been hoping one of the reporters on hand had captured the attack on camera. At least two of them had, but both videos were set from behind the Defender who had approached me with the gun. Only someone recording from my right would have captured what actually happened.

I couldn't shake it, even as I stalked down the interstate to retrieve the truck's license plate and swap it with the one on the gray sedan we were taking. Of all the cameras there rolling . . . there had only been that one angle?

By the time I had the license plate in place, Priyanka and Roman were already in the car, the supplies in the trunk along with the water bottles and snacks Roman had selected from the vending machine.

No one said a word as we drove east using the car's dashboard compass. It was at least an hour before we knew where we were: Nebraska. Over a thousand miles from the attack in Pennsylvania, which had occurred three days ago.

The men had held us for *three days* while the rest of the country, the UN, its peacekeepers, the Defenders, and local police searched for me. While they sent out drones to scan blocks of cities and highways for any sign of me. While my face was plastered on newscasts and, I assumed, on the few social media sites that the interim government had approved access to.

The search is still on for the Psi responsible for the deaths of seven people. . . .

It was another hour before cars started appearing, cities began sprouting up, and the highway widened around us. I felt like an ant caught under glass; unable to move and slowly being burned alive by the sunlight.

I swallowed hard, reaching for the water bottle in the cup holder. Roman opened the cap and passed it over. I drank it down, crushing the plastic as I finished, but it did nothing to ease the ache in my throat.

"Are we going to talk about this, or are we just going to ignore the fact you're a wanted fugitive?" Priyanka asked from where she'd sprawled across the backseat. "I'm fine with either, I just want to make sure that we're all on the same page. Also, I'm bored."

I gritted my teeth. "I'm glad you have the luxury of being bored by this situation."

"We do need to discuss a plan," Roman said, almost apologetically, "if only to get through the zone crossing. Did your friend give you any sort of way to get . . . wherever we're going?"

"Yeah, and by the way, what friend was that?" Priyanka asked. "The one who is on the Psi Council, or . . . who were the others? Stewart and . . . Ruby? Was that her name?"

I shut that down quickly. "It was Charles."

Priyanka knew Ruby's name. After the media storm following the camp closures and, later, her disappearance, *everyone* knew Ruby's name and that she was wanted by the government. This wasn't an innocent question.

I bit the inside of my mouth to keep from saying anything else. After everything, the lies stacking on lies, it couldn't be that simple. That obvious. My personal history was out there, along with the knowledge I'd been close to Ruby and Liam. It wasn't totally unreasonable for them to assume that I was secretly in contact with my friends and might turn to them in a time of need.

Still, the thought was like cold fingers closing over the back of my neck. That would mean, what? That they'd set everything up to get the wheels moving in this direction? That they were just taking advantage of the situation we were in now?

Shit. *And here I am taking them right where they want to go.*

There were two options in front of me. The first one was to

get the cell phone with the evidence on the kidnappers back from Priyanka, and then, once we were in Virginia, make a run for it. It would avoid exposing the existence of the safe place, along with everyone in it, to harm.

As for the second . . . There was a way I could use Haven to trap Roman and Priyanka without ever bringing them to the house's secure location.

When I'd pieced together my plan in the motel, the second option had seemed like a fallback—the thought of even bringing them near Haven made my skin crawl—but now I wasn't so sure. If Roman and Priyanka were interested in finding Ruby and Liam, my friends wouldn't just want to know about it, they'd *need* to.

Playing the situation out like that was tricky, but I could control and limit those risks as long as I was careful.

I could do this. I *could*. They'd backed me into a corner, but they didn't realize I'd already walked them into another one.

A mile up the road, the electronic billboard flashed on. Static swept over it as it received its transmission. When the image finally snapped into place, it wasn't an ad or traffic alert.

It was my face. Fourteen feet high and glowing. The headshot slid across the screen, allowing red flashing text to appear alongside it.

IF YOU SEE THIS PSI, DIAL 9-1-1

HIGHLY DANGEROUS

DO NOT ENGAGE

My foot slipped onto the brake, jerking us forward in our seats. A car speeding up behind me honked, swerving to pass.

"Um," Priyanka said mildly. "I can't say that's your best photo. You look like you want to punch someone."

They'd used my Psi ID photo. The one they'd specifically told me not to smile for. The result was a mean mug shot that Vida had found so funny she'd printed and framed it.

Not so funny now.

One mile down the road, the next billboard flickered on. IF YOU SEE THIS PSI . . .

With the flashing distraction of the billboards, the new power sources registered in my mind slowly, quickly growing like a swarm of bees. The vibration of their electricity was muted compared to the nearby car engines, but harmonized with them in a way that set my hair on end.

"Suzume—" Roman began.

"I see it," I choked out.

The cars a few miles up were slowing, bottlenecking as the highway narrowed down to one lane. Just beyond them, red and blue lights flashed. Several uniformed police officers and Defenders walked from car to car, opening trunks. Overhead, making slow passes with their cameras and scanners, were drones. All state-of-the-art technology commissioned by the United Nations, as one of their parting gifts.

I sucked in a hard breath, holding it as I cut off the car in the next lane and blindly took the nearest exit.

"Definitely not going to raise any red flags with that move," Priyanka said, hanging on to one of the car's grab handles.

I accelerated onto the surface street, making a hard right on red without looking. Someone honked, but the sound faded under the sensation of something electronic tailing us in the sky.

Shit, I thought, picking up speed with another turn, narrowly missing a cyclist about to enter the crosswalk. I cringed, but the drone was still in the rearview mirror.

"Priyanka, can you just—?" Roman began.

"Already on it," she said. I'd thought she'd tossed the burner she'd broken apart, but she'd only stuffed the pieces into her jacket. She quickly reassembled it, leaving out the SIM card, then reached into her pocket, to retrieve the other phone. The one with the photos.

"What are you doing with that?" I asked sharply.

"Relax," she said. "I'm taking a small part from this one to modify the other one. The phone's storage and your pictures won't be impacted."

I wanted to lunge back between the seats and pry the phone out of her hand, but she'd already flicked out one piece and inserted it into the other.

"I swear to God, if you mess up that phone . . ." I began, gripping the wheel.

"I'm not messing anything up except that drone," Priyanka said, her voice calm. "The phone is going to emit a low-grade signal that'll scramble the drone's feed before it can transmit its footage. We're now a permanent blind spot, as long as I can keep this phone charged. Same with any highway cameras—it'll make them blink as we drive underneath." She turned in her seat, giving the hovering black device a wave. "See? Farewell, drone."

I swung the car into the first deserted strip mall I found, watching in no small amazement as the drone peeled off, turning back in the direction of the highway. We jerked to a hard stop behind a shuttered dry cleaner. I yanked on the parking brake and turned off the engine.

I hadn't even thought of the newly installed highway cameras we'd find along the way to Virginia. They were a new security measure, meant to help prevent smuggling and crime. They were *also* programmed to flag any car where the passengers seemed to be intentionally altering or masking their faces. A very useful thing . . . when you were not the one being tracked.

"You're sure we're okay?" I'd seen other Greens pull miracle tech results from a few wires and an empty tuna can, but this was wild, even to me.

Priyanka pretended to look offended, pressing a hand to her chest.

I don't know why I looked at Roman for confirmation when he had been just as dishonest as her. Maybe because if there was one single thing I believed about them, it was that they would never risk each other's lives or safety if they didn't have to. They had every reason to want to escape the camera's eyes, too.

"It works," he assured me. "The drones will just signal that they're experiencing a routine error, and the highway cameras won't know to switch on to take the photo or video to begin with."

Breath fired in and out of me, cranking up my pulse. I leaned forward to rest my forehead against the wheel. I shut my eyes, trying to bury the memory of the billboard in that darkness. When I opened them again, Priyanka was holding a plastic grocery bag in front of me. "Please don't throw up on the upholstery. We have to share this space."

"Priyanka!" Roman said.

"Don't pretend like you weren't thinking it, too," she said.

I pushed her hand away.

"I'm—" *Angry. Confused. Scared.* So many different terrible things at once. But I didn't want to give any of those feelings power by acknowledging them, so I changed the subject. "I'm fine. How did they know to look for me out here?"

"It is an enormous search field . . ." Roman said, smoothing a hand back over his mussed hair. "They've likely been expanding it out from Pennsylvania each day."

I forced myself to sit up, even as feeling was slow to return to my body.

"Can you tell us where we're going?" he asked. "If they're checking the highways, we can just make it a point to avoid them."

No we couldn't. Not the whole way. "Virginia. I'm taking us to a safe place there. Somewhere off the grid."

A place where I'd be able to send the photos of the kidnappers to Vida and Chubs, and start piecing together the connection between them and the bomb.

Priyanka leaned forward between the seats. "I like the sound of that."

I hated to give them even that much information up front, but sharing some small bit of information might make them think I was starting to trust them. Besides, even if I did get the chance to run from them, Virginia was a big state. They could spend years driving around, searching aimlessly.

"So we are going to have to pass through a zone crossing," Roman said. "How do you want to do this?"

It didn't matter how we approached, we'd have to cross at least one zone checkpoint. We were currently in Zone 3. The boundary for Zone 1 ran along the western edge of Pennsylvania, West Virginia, and Virginia, with Virginia also serving as the southern boundary for Zone 2, which began at North Carolina and stretched down to Texas.

The zones had been important in the early days after the United Nations' intervention, mostly for administrative purposes. They dictated how supplies were divided and organized, and allowed for smaller, more manageable areas for the peacekeepers to monitor. Now we were only months off from our first real election in more than five years, and the dismantling of the zones would probably be one of the first items the newly elected Congress voted on.

It was impossible to cross zone lines off-the-books, so to speak. All the access roads were blockaded. Everyone crossed using one of many checkpoints along the major highways and interstates. License plates were photographed and cars were scanned and put into the system to keep track of who was coming and going.

The thought made me turn toward the others.

"How did the kidnappers do it?" I asked, drumming my fingers on the steering wheel. "How did the truck get from Zone One to Zone Three without raising any red flags? Even if it didn't go through a scanner, there should have been a visual cargo search."

"I wish I could tell you that everyone loves rules as much as you do," Priyanka said. "Except more people seem to love bribes."

Bribing wasn't an option for us. Even with the cash, I couldn't risk being ID'd. They'd just installed facial-recognition cameras at all the checkpoints, and I had no doubt that the UN peacekeepers who monitored the flow of traffic were stopping people for more thorough checks as they looked for me. The fugitive.

Roman glanced at me. "We could try going on foot?"

"No," I said, bracing my elbow against the door. "I know another way."

I didn't want to do this—it was selfish, not to mention criminal, to reveal this to people without a security clearance—but we didn't have the time to wander and look for a gap in their fencing or security monitoring. I'd only found out about this loophole by accident, when we'd been forced to change our travel plans from Zone 1 to 3 because a group of Liberty Watch supporters had barricaded the main checkpoint. Agent Cooper had let it slip.

"There's an unmonitored side route," I admitted. "The government sometimes uses it to bypass traffic or backups at the checkpoints."

A state route that ran along Lake Erie in New York and Pennsylvania. The government's transportation team had planned to reopen it to the public for lake access and to ease some of the traffic from the main checkpoint. They set up smart visual-ID cameras and everything to monitor the flow of traffic during phase one of Setting America Back on the Right Route! But, at the last minute, the Canadian government had lodged a formal complaint—they'd said the cameras, which faced the lake, could be used to monitor Canadian ships in Canadian waters, and violated their citizens' right to privacy. They claimed that it could be considered domestic espionage, given their role in the United Nations.

The government had left the cameras up for later use, but they weren't turned on. The interstate wasn't monitored.

"*Quelle surprise,*" Priyanka said.

"How frequently is it used?" Roman asked. "Would anyone think you'd try to use it?"

Those were all good questions that I had no real answers to. "I don't know. I think we should try it and see."

It wasn't a good option, no. But it was the only halfway-decent one I could come up with, and if it was a choice between that and nothing it would have to be enough.

TWELVE

IT TOOK ABOUT A HUNDRED MILES FOR ME TO TRUST that Priyanka's device was working, and a hundred more to feel confident I could keep us away from the major cities and towns that would have aerial-drone crime-monitoring support. The drug weasel's cash dwindled down as fast as Priyanka had predicted, just buying enough gas ration cards to keep the tank half-full.

Priyanka napped on and off during the twelve hours it took to get to Ohio, snoring faintly in the backseat, her long legs bent up toward the roof of the car, but Roman never let himself drift off. Not even for a second.

Neither did I.

At midnight, we finally stopped for a break. I parked the car across the street from a little diner, far enough from it to remain unnoticed but close enough to keep watch of everyone on the other side of its glowing windows. A man in a little white hat was wiping down the counter, chatting with two tipsy-looking patrons who were happily sharing a plate of pancakes. Behind them, a TV flashed a news report about Europe.

"She's really taking her time . . ." Roman said, looking slightly on edge. His eyes darted between the diner and its bathroom, which was situated on the right side of the building, outside like a gas station's would be. That setup was the only reason we'd deemed it safe enough to stop and use.

"It's all right," I said. "She should take her time. She didn't get a chance to wash up at the motel."

Thanks to me.

Roman reached forward, nudging the POWER button on the radio.

I really did not have the emotional bandwidth to listen to news reports about the incident and my supposed involvement. I reached to turn it right back off, but Roman's quiet words stopped me.

"I know it might be painful to hear what they're saying, but we should stay on top of the news and monitor their investigation."

I pulled my hand back onto the wheel.

He was right, but the memory of the explosion, of what had happened to Mel and the others, was still so close to the surface. I was already replaying it in my head on a near-constant loop, trying to figure out what I could have done differently to save them; the thought of hearing someone else discuss those last, horrible seconds made me want to bolt from the car.

"All right," I managed to get out.

Roman hit the scanner and let the stations fly by, counting up and down as they searched for this zone's primary radio channel.

The static poured in and out of my ears, broken up by weak channels and fragments of half-forgotten songs. When Roman finally found the right station, it was so strong that the broadcaster all but screamed at us. He flinched, fumbling with the knob to turn the volume down.

"*—don't disagree with Mr. Moore, and, in fact, we've tentatively agreed to work with him in a more meaningful way on his Personalized Independent Training Facility program. The reports that his company has sent on the results at the pilot facility have been very encouraging. It's no secret that I'm not entirely sold on PPS, but I remain open to it so long as his pilot facility passes government inspection next month. As you know, we have not had access to it—Yes, next question—*"

I had recognized President Cruz's voice at her first word, but I'd also recognized her tone. It was an exhausted reluctance, the kind that came with finally being trapped in a corner after years of narrow escapes.

"What's PPS?" he asked.

"Privatized Psi Schooling," I said, trying to focus on what President Cruz was saying. She must have gone in front of the press pool that morning. Brave, considering the news. "Sort of like a boarding school for Psi, with the focus on getting them better reintegrated into society by giving them skill sets they can use in the workforce."

"I thought there was supposed to be . . . independent living communities? Didn't you do a presentation on them?"

Irritation buzzed through me—not at Roman, but at what had happened to squash those plans. "That was voted down because they were deemed too expensive for the recovering economy. A few companies, including Moore's, put in bids to finance different school and living projects, and his got picked."

If kids were being taught valuable skills in a safe, clean environment, then I couldn't really complain. Especially when the original idea—one still startlingly popular with a number of Americans—had been setting aside remote stretches of land, building a few structures, and trapping the Psi inside its electrified borders.

"No, George, I agree, both with you and him," Cruz continued. *"These programs could be a great option, especially for the unclaimed Psi. Twelve volunteered to make up the pilot facility's first class, and we're hoping to be able to move another fifty out of foster situations and group homes into the school. But, again, it's only after Mr. Moore finishes his initial testing and submits the program to more thorough inspection."*

"How many kids are . . . unclaimed?" Roman asked, hesitating on the ugly word.

"One thousand, one hundred and twelve," I said. "Most are in foster homes, but a lot of the older Psi live together in group homes. The government monitors all of them, and they have special caseworkers checking in constantly."

He turned back to the road, his expression troubled.

"What is it?" I asked.

"Nothing," he said. "Just . . . I'm surprised you aren't more against them. You were in a camp."

I glanced over, startled. "What does that have to do with anything?"

After the interview I'd given years ago that went out to the world, and the talks I'd participated in since then, it had seemed like there wasn't a person on earth who hadn't heard the story. So many people knew the details, it had stopped feeling wholly mine.

"I thought you'd hate him because what he's proposed could be seen as similar to them," he clarified. "Sorry, I didn't mean to bring up—"

"It's fine." I was fine. "The kids in Moore's program

volunteered to go, and they're guaranteed to get out. The images of the facility I saw make it look like the height of luxury compared to what we had." I hadn't thought to ask before now, but I was curious. "I take it you weren't in a camp, then?"

He shook his head. "No. We survived on the outside. We weren't ever in the camp system."

"How?" I asked. I'd lived rough with the others for a time, and it had been nearly impossible to stay ahead of skip tracers and PSFs. Even civilians looking to make a rare quick buck by reporting a sighting were a threat to us. I wondered if the government had *any* official record of Roman and Priyanka at all.

"We found a vacant house and stayed there," he said, rubbing the back of his scarred hand with his other thumb. The words were remote. Practiced. "A neighbor brought us food."

It was an appropriate lie, somehow. That kind of thing only happened in dreams.

"What was it like," he asked, "being in the camp?"

"What's there to know that's not already out there?" I asked. "It was a prison in every sense of the word. They controlled everything about our lives, including when we slept, and when and what we ate. They had us work to keep busy. It was like walking through hell soaked with gasoline and trying to avoid being set on fire."

The churlishness left a bitter taste in my mouth, and an uncomfortable silence between us. After a moment, I said, "It was like living with your heart in a cage. Nothing escaped. Nothing got in."

At home, before Caledonia, before the Collection, before I'd ever manifested my power, I'd grown up hearing stories passed down from older relatives about their time in internment camps here in America during the Second World War. I'd known the government had forcibly imprisoned Japanese Americans and seized their property, subjecting its own citizens to a harsh existence simply because of the belief that anyone of Japanese descent was dangerous by default. And still, when the bus that took me and a number of other kids to Ohio had rolled through Caledonia's gates, I'd been naïve enough—young enough—to hope that this "rehabilitation center" would be everything they promised on the news: a medical program to keep us alive, an isolated school, and a place where we could live without fear.

The experiences weren't the same, and there was no real comparison to be made between them. I only wished I had listened to the stories more carefully, that I could have somehow made that history feel more immediate to me, because I think knowing not to hope for the best, recognizing that the government and the president weren't always paternal figures that wanted to care for us, would have saved me some small bit of pain.

"I'm sorry you were made to go through that," he said in that quiet voice of his. "I understand why you work so hard for the Psi."

I didn't know what to say to that, because I didn't want to agree. I didn't want there to be anything shared between us.

Priyanka appeared at the door to the bathroom, carefully shutting it behind her. She glanced toward the diner, checking to make sure the people inside had their backs turned, before crossing the street.

The pressure in my chest had built to the point of exploding. "Actually," I said, opening the door, "I think I'm ready for a little break."

I shut it behind me, not making eye contact as I passed Priyanka. She turned, tracking my path to the bathroom. As I neared the building, the server walked out from behind the counter and moved toward the windows to start cleaning the tables.

I ducked down and crawled forward until I was just under them, waiting. Warm, damp air filled my lungs and smoothed against my skin.

"Suzume Kimura, the Psi responsible for the horrific attack at Penn State, worked in her office!"

Every muscle in my body tightened at the sound of my name in Joseph Moore's silky voice coming from the television inside.

"Interim President Cruz was never elected to her position, but was instead appointed by her UN puppet masters. Every bad deal she accepts from them attacks the interests of everyday, hardworking Americans. She has lined the pockets of our foreign overlords and, instead of shaping the generation of Psi, she's only managed to nurture their radical elements. How can her judgment be trusted? How can she be impartial on the subject of Psi, when her very daughter, Rosa—who, by the way, has yet to make a single public appearance since her mother's campaign began—is one of them?"

I wanted him to take my name and Rosa's name out of his filthy mouth. The girl was living in Canada, attending school there after someone had tried to kidnap her on her way home.

"We don't need a new American dream—we need to reclaim the one that was stolen from us the day we agreed to allow the rest of the world to solve our problems. The first step is the loyalty oath—" The cheer that followed made me shudder. *"Yes! Exactly! And—let me finish, let me finish—the second is to ensure an attack like the*

one Kimura and her fellow degenerates pulled off can never happen again."

Degenerates.

Fury ate at me. All that work . . . all the speeches . . . every emotional lashing I'd taken and responded to by simply turning the other cheek . . . it was one step forward and a thousand steps back.

The broadcaster returned, noting, *"Though the Cruz administration has repeatedly dismissed the Liberty Watch Party's demands for a loyalty oath as being unnecessary, the attack at Penn State seems to have prompted a change in that policy."*

I crawled forward, rising only when I reached the bathroom door. From this angle, I could see the images on the television reflected in the front window.

The press secretary stepped up to the briefing room podium. Her words were tight with suppressed emotion. She and Mel had been close friends. She had known many of the reporters covering the event. *"To ensure the safety of the public and the continued cooperation of the Psi, we will be implementing two new policies beginning Monday. First, all Psi, even those in the custody of their families, will be assigned a local government counselor who will process any requests to travel across zone lines as well as other legal paperwork. Second, at their first meeting with these counselors, all Psi will be asked to sign a document agreeing to not commit acts of violence or treason in any form against the United States."*

So, a loyalty oath. I took a step forward in disbelief, needing to see the screen itself, just to prove that I wasn't trapped in a nightmare.

This was going to be nearly impossible to walk back, even after I proved my innocence.

The broadcaster returned with, *"That may not satisfy Liberty Watch and other organizations who have voiced fears that not enough is being done to control the Psi population in America, as well as their desire to see them in mandatory military service—"*

Across the street, the car's headlights flashed. Startled, I turned toward them, only to see Priyanka slam her fist down on the steering wheel, letting the horn blare out through the night.

"—yes! She's here! I'm telling you!"

I spun back toward the inside of the diner. The white woman at the counter was shouting into her cell phone, and the man who'd been sitting next to her was already on his feet, coming toward the side door—toward me. The server reached beneath the counter, pulling out a shotgun and aiming at me through the glass.

There was no time to think it through. I seized the white-hot current of power flowing through the ceiling lights and fluorescent signs and *pulled*. They blew out in a roar of glass, leaving the people inside screaming.

The car's brakes squealed as it skidded to a stop along the road. I ran for it, ignoring the pounding footsteps behind me, keeping my eyes on where Roman had rolled down the window. He aimed the handgun just over my shoulder.

I pulled the back door open and dove inside, letting the force of Priyanka's acceleration slam it shut at my feet.

No one said anything. I curled onto my side, breathing hard as shudders of adrenaline and delayed fear rocked me.

Finally, Priyanka said, her voice light, "Everyone awake now?"

I pushed myself up, too embarrassed to meet Roman's worried gaze. *Stupid . . . So stupid . . .*

It was a minute, maybe more, before Priyanka's phone blared out a familiar tone. The Emergency Alert System.

Roman didn't read the message aloud, but I could see it clearly over his shoulder.

FUGITIVE PSI SUZUME KIMURA SEEN
IN AREA.

SILVER TOYOTA LICENSE PLATE ENDING
WITH D531

STAY ALERT. DO NOT APPROACH IF SEEN.
CALL 9-1-1

A drone appeared in the dark sky, rocketing over us with a scream as it headed in the direction of the diner. And a minute after that, sirens. They were distant, but their wailing stayed trapped in my head, even as miles and hours passed. Even after we were far enough away for me to release what had happened to memory.

But I couldn't. Inside me, the past was colliding with the present, and the only thing I could do was just stay awake long enough to survive the nightmare it created.

THIRTEEN

My FACE WAS EVERYWHERE.

Countless billboards. On the TV screens of homes we passed, in automated news alerts delivered to Priyanka's burner phone, and on thousands of flyers posted on streetlamps, in the windows of stores, and in gas stations.

Roman had brought one back for us to look at during our last gas stop hours before. It was identical to the message and photo on the billboards, with one key difference: there was a second phone number to contact, and a small line of text at the bottom: *This notice is brought to you by Moore Enterprises, in conjunction with the Moore for America campaign.*

Later, we'd heard Moore issue the threat himself on the radio. *"If Cruz can't find Kimura, even with her vast resources, then I will."*

I'd looked up at the others and said, as calmly as I could, "I think I'm going to need a disguise."

"Now we're talking," Priyanka had said. "I don't know about you, but I'm dying to look like I didn't just crawl out of my own grave."

We entered the edge of the small town so quickly, I didn't

catch the name as we blew past the sign. Roman eased up on the gas, slowing down to get a better look at its potential as a stop. The station wagon let out a pitiful whine as he shifted its gears. It had been too risky to keep the sedan, and pure luck we'd found the new ride abandoned next to a rail yard.

After a series of neighborhood streets cradled in the shade of overgrown trees, signs of renewed life had appeared. Work crews were out fixing downed power lines or clearing dumpsters full of junk and shrubs away from newly painted homes. Cars were parked in driveways, not abandoned in ditches along roads. People stood out in their lawns, talking to neighbors or walking dogs.

It's working, I thought, feeling some small bit of hope for the first time in days. The government, for all the criticism leveled at it every single day, was improving lives. As soon as I had cleared my name, I'd work even harder. Help even more people.

But that small touch of life clearly had passed over the old strip mall up ahead. It looked like a snake's skin, frail and silvery in the disappearing light. Most of the glass storefronts were still boarded up, and the others had been halfheartedly blocked off with police tape and NO TRESPASSING signs.

I caught sight of a large bin and pointed to it. "There. That'll work."

Roman cracked a faint smile. I hadn't gotten control of the wheel back since the diner incident, and I didn't think I was likely to. Not when we were within reach of Virginia. In the end, it wasn't worth fighting. They were welcome to drive themselves right into my trap, just like I was welcome to use them as two extra sets of eyes to keep watch.

"Seems okay . . . ?" Roman said, guiding the car behind the massive bin.

Garbage bags of clothing had piled up so high, its lid was one strong gust of wind away from blowing off. Children's toys and bicycles were piled up alongside it, collecting rain and dirt. Unwelcome memories. There was no way to tell how long this stuff had been sitting out here, ten years or ten days.

"We'll wait here for you," I told him, unbuckling my seat belt. As the only one of us not drenched in blood, Roman was in charge of getting gas—by bribing someone to give up one of their ration cards, or by bribing the station attendant to run the pump off the books.

Roman rolled down his window. "Just . . . be careful, okay? I won't be long."

"Don't worry, Ro," Priyanka said. "I'll find you the fluorescent tie-dyed shirt of your dreams."

It was his long-suffering look as he drove away that almost made me laugh. Almost.

Priyanka was already busy sorting through the nearest bags of clothes that had been piled up outside the donation bin. "Oooh . . . Now *this* is what I'm talking about."

She used a box of books as a step stool, pulling down a tied-off garbage bag. The arm of a purple silk blouse dangled out of a tear in the plastic. She hummed happily, digging through it.

With my hands on my hips, I turned to assess everything else that had been dumped here. There were whole tubs of appliances, bedding, and decorations left out like ruined junk. The wasteful-ness was almost offensive. Then again, people always seemed to unburden themselves of belongings when they were trying to get out from under the weight of memories.

I went through the nearest bag of clothing, my hands still-ing for a moment on a pink floral blouse. With a deep breath, I pushed it aside, reaching for the oversize Cleveland Cavaliers shirt beneath it. Digging past the dresses underneath that, I found a pair of jean shorts that seemed like they could work, as long as I used a belt or length of rope. I kicked off my battered heels, shoving them in the bag and taking out the white tennis shoes at the bottom of it. Only a size too big. Not bad.

That done, a second list began to sketch itself from memory. Food, water, containers, blankets . . .

I set three piles aside, starting with the blankets, then took what pillowcases I could find. They always made useful bags for carrying things when backpacks weren't available. One small pot for boiling, one small pan for cooking or additional self-defense. Knives, always good. One fork and spoon for each of us. More than that, and they'd clatter inside our bags, keeping us from moving silently. No batteries. One flashlight that seemed to be working for now, even if the beam wasn't strong. The real coup would have been canned food or toilet paper, but those were truly one-in-a-million finds.

"Did you forget to tell us that you're taking us camping?" Priyanka stared down at me, brows raised. "I'm all for roughing it as long as that entails air-conditioning and a nice view."

Blood heated my face. I looked away, back at my orderly piles of supplies.

I had only wanted to stop to find new, clean clothes. I didn't need to grab any of this stuff, especially since we were heading toward Haven. I knew I was tired, but this . . . this was something else. It was like I'd slipped back into a pair of shoes I'd thought I'd outgrown. The donation bins, the empty street . . . The familiarity of it had overwhelmed me.

"Sorry," I muttered, forcing myself onto my feet. "Old habits."

I felt . . . *Embarrassed* wasn't the right word. The months we had all spent on the run, surviving on stolen vending-machine food and siphoned gasoline, weren't ones I really cherished.

Every day had been shot through with desperation and hunger. The only small slivers of light I'd been able to cling to were those flashlight-illuminated memories of my friends: Liam telling stories or singing off-key to his endless stream of favorite classic rock songs. Working out the clever little math problems Chubs wrote for me in the notebook we had to share. Wandering through the dark husk of a Walmart with Ruby, finding something I actually wanted to wear. Feeling safe. Feeling hopeful. Feeling loved.

When I thought of them now, it was like seeing sunlight come through a stained-glass window. Each memory had its own color, its own feeling, and together they created something beautiful held together by a dark frame.

Priyanka looked at me again, her gaze different from before. There was no longer any suspicion there, or even that impatient edge she got whenever I talked about my work. For once, she wasn't taking the measure of me.

If things had been different, I might have called it understanding.

"No, I mean . . . this is good," Priyanka said. I resented the kindness in her voice as she crouched down to gather one of the piles into a waiting pillowcase, how it made me feel almost feral for having done this. "You never know, right?"

"Right," I muttered, abandoning the piles of supplies for the bags of clothing I'd bypassed before. "Whatever."

Priyanka lingered behind me for a moment, watching. Why did it have to feel like this—like I was some wounded animal being released back into the wild? My head ached with the need to rest it against something, with the pressure building behind my eyes.

This is ridiculous, I thought. *You're fine.*

To prove it to myself, I let my mind reach out, searching for the faint voltage of the working phone's battery. It was like turning out an empty pocket. She must have left it in the car. The only electricity nearby was the streetlamp.

"Here," Priyanka said, passing me a bundle of cloth. "Hang on to this."

After a long beat of silence, I took it.

The shirt was made of soft denim. I shook it out, revealing bright embroidered flowers with looping vines at the shoulders.

"This is cute," I said, trying to smooth the wrinkles against my leg.

"The embroidery on it is gorgeous," Priyanka agreed. "Check it to see if there are any holes or stains I missed. . . ."

I ran my fingers softly across the seams and turned the shirt inside out, giving it a thorough inspection. In that moment, I wished more than anything that I'd found it first.

The boys had tried so hard to find clothes for me when we were traveling in Betty, and they hadn't understood what a difference it had made to me to be able to pick out something I liked for myself. As unhelpful as it was to wear bright pink on the run, it had let me feel some small bit of power to present myself the way I wanted to, in a world that was trying to render me powerless. It had made me feel like one of the magic girls in the manga I grew up reading, with their bright colors and beautiful costumes. Back then, that's what strength had looked like to me.

"You still with me, Sparky?"

I blinked. "Yeah. Sorry."

"That top would look cute on you with a bright skirt, but it seems sadly impractical for running and beatdowns."

"Wait," I said. "You pulled this for me?"

"Oh no, I'm doing the overwhelming thing again," Priyanka said. "Sorry. I just thought the colors would look great with your skin tone. It won't hurt my feelings or anything if you want to toss it back. I'm so used to having to look after Roman, I sometimes forget other people are actually capable of taking care of themselves."

"No, I love it," I said. I was just . . . surprised she had somehow perfectly nailed my taste. "I already grabbed clothes."

I tried to pass the blouse back to her, but she only looked at the Cavaliers shirt like it was crawling with lice.

"It's supposed to be a disguise," I said, wondering why I felt like I had to defend the choice.

"That thing is at least three sizes too big for you. Can't we just find you a big hat or something?" Priyanka said. "I mean, if you're going to be a fugitive on the run for your life, shouldn't you at least be wearing something you feel good in?"

I pushed it at her again, hating the way my throat tightened. The humor drained from her face as she finally took it back. Instead of returning it to one of the bags, she folded it and added it to her own pile.

"In case you change your mind," she explained.

"I won't."

Priyanka shrugged. "Anyway, bless you for thinking that wouldn't be a crop top on me. What about this for me, though?"

The blouse she held up was a dark floral pattern, slightly sheer, with long sleeves. There was just enough color to bring out the amber in her eyes. But after seeing her in the bright yellow dress, it seemed almost too subdued for her.

"Find high-waisted jeans and tie them off. If it wasn't a thousand degrees out, I'd say layer it with this—" I tugged out a soft violet sweater.

Her face lit up as she took it. "Maison de Dumpster is a treasure trove. This is vintage Dior!"

"Très Trash has a surprisingly good variety," I said, watching as she happily tried on a long vest, before adding that to her pile, too. She returned to the bag, digging something out from the bottom. "Usually it's just NASCAR shirts and baby clothes. Who is that for, though?"

Priyanka looked down at the faded floral T-shirt in her hands. It wouldn't have fit either her or Roman, but she didn't hand it over to me. Instead, it went into her pile, too.

A pile with enough clothes for three people, not two. Priyanka must have seen the moment I put it together, because her expression didn't just shutter, it shut down.

And I snapped back to reality.

Those last traces of warmth were stomped out by the silence that followed. It was a relief when she turned her back on me. I didn't have to hide the growing, bitter anger that was twisting me inside out.

You did it again, I thought vehemently. I'd gotten too comfortable. I wanted to blame her, cling to the idea that it had all been a careful manipulation to get me on their side.

But I was ashamed. I was ashamed that, at least for a few minutes, I'd welcomed it. I'd let that easy exchange soothe a deep, quiet hurt in me I'd been struggling to ignore. The one that, in all of its ugly truth, I couldn't bring myself to admit might be loneliness.

"Who are those for?" I asked again.

The station wagon swept into the parking lot, its brakes whining as Roman pulled up beside us.

"If I wanted you to know, I would have told you," she said, each word harder than the next. "Are you finished?"

"Yeah," I said, gathering up what supplies I could carry. "We're done."

In the backseat, I dreamed.

Distant roads roared at me like thunder, wrapped in ropes of snarling electricity. Familiar faces circled around me, choking off my view of what was coming in the distance. Each time I reached out to touch them, they blew apart like ash.

I heard Mel's voice, the words echoing on a crushing loop: *Should we move the event? Should we move the event?*

None of the people would move. None of them would let me search for Mel. . . .

Even when I opened my eyes, it was like peering through fogged-over glass. Light sliced through the darkness inside the car. My head rested against the seat belt strap, hair plastered to my forehead with sweat.

"All I'm saying is that if the Psi who supposedly was the poster girl for how reformed and 'human' they are does this, then we should be a hell of a lot more frightened of what the others are capable of. The Psion Ring is about to step out of the shadows and into the light now that their obvious leader has been revealed."

"You're so right, Carol. Think about how much government

information she's been feeding them. We're lucky that the Ring hasn't perpetrated anything worse than the Penn State attack, and that it's only been vandalism and theft of public property until now. But, clearly, their behavior is escalating. The precautions in place aren't enough. Cruz's assurances about their good behavior aren't enough. It's all very sad what happened to them, but deviants are prone to deviant behavior. I'm not saying President Gray was a perfect person, but even imperfect folks can be right some of the time—"

Someone let out a noise of disgust and turned the radio off. The numbing drag of sleep caught me again, and I shut my eyes, but the voices didn't stop. Their words fell like embers, burning out before they fully reached me.

"—so close, can't trust—"

"—we should just tell," the boy insisted. "We have to—"

"So close—" was the response. "It's not safe for her—"

For who?

"Lana would—"

"Lana's not—"

I needed to remember this.

Lana.

I needed to ask. . . . But the heavy darkness was claiming me again.

Lana.

Who wasn't it safe for—me, or Lana?

FOURTEEN

MAIN STREET IN BLACKSTONE, VIRGINIA, LOOKED AS IF it had been lovingly painted from someone's dream of what America had once been. It looked so perfect, in fact, that if I'd seen it in a film, I probably would have called it clichéd: striped awnings, brightly painted brick buildings, and old-fashioned streetlamps. Flags and patriotic bunting from the Fourth of July still crowned the street six weeks after the holiday, and a sign announcing the return of the local movie theater was strung between the two sets of stoplights.

The worst thing you could say about Blackstone was that it was a bit out of the way of Petersburg and Richmond. Its small size meant it hadn't merited the high-tech security cameras that had been installed in the bigger cities, and there weren't the telltale UN symbols on the dumpsters and fire hydrants. But those were hardly faults when it came to finding a place to hide a secret halfway house for Psi.

"Are we just driving in circles?" Priyanka asked. "Or are we waiting for something—or someone?"

I'd woken up in a bad mood, and nothing about the day had

done anything to take the edge off it, least of all the extra six hours it had taken us to reach the town with all the roadblocks and police checkpoints in place across the state.

Just as I'd expected, the closer we got to what they wanted, the tighter the leash became. Priyanka came with me if I needed to use a restroom. Roman stayed in the passenger seat, marking our progress on a stolen map. I'd finally been able to regain control of the wheel earlier in that morning, but only after lying that my friends would need to see me driving to know it was safe to let us in.

I was never going to be able to get away from them; once I'd gotten in the car at the motel, I'd sealed my fate, the same way they'd sealed theirs now. Everything else had been hope and delusion.

The day-old gas-station hot dog I'd eaten for breakfast sat like a brick in my stomach. "I'm just making sure that we haven't been followed. They prefer night arrivals."

It was easy to lie now. Just a simple matter of shutting down every stray feeling and keeping my focus sharp. Of course Ruby and Liam didn't prefer night arrivals. They also had a step-by-step process for kids in need to make contact with them. I still remembered it from my last and only visit.

But we weren't going to use it. We were going to make our arrival as suspicious as possible.

Priyanka's fingers danced along the backs of the two seats. Roman took the last sip of his coffee, his eyes on the street. The wind tore one of my WANTED flyers off a nearby streetlamp and skimmed it across our windshield. I would have laughed, if I were any less anxious about this. Instead, I reached up to pull my baseball cap lower and push my sunglasses up.

Roman's jaw tightened, a single ripple in that calm exterior. I wondered if there was something he wanted to say, or something he didn't trust himself not to.

"Fine," Priyanka said, bouncing a little in her seat.

I remembered almost nothing about the drive here, or even the dreams I'd had that left my throat feeling like it had been clawed at from the inside. But I did remember one thing. One word.

Lana.

It didn't matter if they were looking for Ruby, or if they were looking for whoever Lana was—they weren't ever stepping foot inside Haven.

Hours passed, carrying the sun in its wide arc through the sky. I moved the car several times to avoid the parking enforcement officer checking the time left on the parking meters. Eventually, I settled us at the edge of a cul-de-sac, in front of the construction fence on a house that had been torn down to its foundation.

Finally, at sunset, I put the keys back in the ignition and turned, letting my heart roar along with the engine. If I could keep it together, this weight would be off me soon. I'd be able to breathe again once all the lies and secrets were unraveled.

"Headlights," Roman reminded me, his voice thick with sleep.

"Not this time," I said.

It was a short drive outside the town, weaving through back roads and side streets, then looping back through them again one last time to make sure I wasn't being followed. The car's tank was dangerously low as I drove us away from the signs of suburbia into the sprawling dark forest.

When I was sure there was no one nearby, I briefly switched the headlights back on.

"What are we looking for?" Priyanka asked.

The length of blue tape flashed as the headlights skimmed over it, marking a hidden gate.

I slammed on the brakes. Priyanka gasped as her seat belt snapped over her chest. "That."

I pulled the car over and left it running as I got out. "I'm going to need help."

Roman joined me, shutting the door quietly behind him. We made our way over to what looked like a tall, overgrown blackberry bush and I carefully reached into it. The metal gate beneath it had absorbed all of the day's heat. The latch gave way with a loud *click*.

Roman had a small smile on his face as we pushed the barrier out of the car's way. I was standing close enough to feel the excitement vibrating off him. "Is this really it?"

The cleared lot started narrow at the gate, then funneled out to allow for parking. It was like an optical illusion. From the road, you wouldn't even notice that the trees were missing in an otherwise dense forest.

"This is it." I stepped out of the way as Priyanka climbed into the driver's seat and navigated the car through the gate. Roman and I made quick work of shutting and re-latching it behind us.

The few cars belonging to the residents of Haven were lined up neatly on one side of the clearing, most covered in camouflaged sheets. The sight of a familiar truck made my heart jump.

They're here.

Priyanka climbed out of the car with a low whistle. "Quite the setup," she noted mildly.

I smiled. "Oh, just wait."

"What should we bring with us?" Roman asked.

"Nothing," I said. "Actually . . . maybe the flashlight."

He nodded, dutifully going to retrieve it from the trunk. "Priya, where did you put it?"

She pivoted back toward the car, her long legs eating up the distance. "It should just be in one of the pillowcases—"

It wasn't. I had moved it when we stopped earlier, shoving it under the backseat. I had maybe a minute before they spotted it and my makeshift distraction was over.

From what I remembered, the cameras Liam and his father had installed were motion-sensing. They had to have switched themselves on as soon as the car pulled in, but they were disguised and insulated well enough in the trees that I only found the one nearest to us by tracing the length of the hidden cable feeding power to it.

I turned my face up toward the lens, giving it a clear look at me. Then I did the only subtle thing I could think of to indicate things were not okay. I brought up my arms, resting each hand on the opposite shoulder, creating an X.

Please still be using them, I thought, as I mouthed a single word: *Help.*

Liam had told me he was teaching the Haven kids about the old road signs the Psi used to use, including the X surrounded by a circle that had indicated a place wasn't safe. If the people watching, whether that was Liam, Ruby, or someone else, couldn't tell what I was signaling, maybe it would still be enough to signal that things weren't what they seemed—that something was very wrong.

"Found it," Roman said, shutting the back door. He switched the flashlight on, scanning it over the ground.

"What's wrong?" Priyanka asked, coming to stand beside me.

I let my hands drift down my arms, pretending to hug them tighter to my chest. "I just got cold for some reason. Must be the lake or something."

It had to be seventy degrees at least, never mind the humidity. Priyanka just shrugged.

"Let's go," I said. "We have to walk a little ways."

We had to buy Haven some time to figure out what was happening and what to do.

Roman kept pace with me, his head up, eyes sharp as he scanned the trees. He had the gun on him, but kept it tucked into the waistband of his jeans. I could see its outline through the close fit of his gray T-shirt. I'd debated telling him to leave it behind, but I hadn't been able to think of a way to do it that wouldn't have set off an alarm in his already cautious mind.

"While traipsing through the woods at night is one of my all-time favorite nightmares," Priyanka whispered from behind us, "I would dearly love to know what I should be looking for. A house? Some kind of tunnel?"

"It's not far," I whispered back. "Listen for the water."

The lake was a speck on most maps, looking especially insignificant next to the nearby Lake Lee—a fact that had not gone unnoticed or un–joked about by one Liam Stewart. But it was big and deep enough to require a boat to cross to the other side, where the trees were thicker on the ground and there was no road access to the structures hidden behind them.

I kept them going forward, meaning to swing them in a wide arc before looping back to this spot, but Roman suddenly straightened.

"I think it's this way," he said, nodding his head in the exact direction of the lake.

I turned before Roman could say anything else, reaching back to take the flashlight from him. The path wasn't as clear here; there were large rocks and a slope to contend with. I didn't need an excuse to make my way down slowly. By the time we reached the muddy bank of the lake, my heart was beating like we'd run all the way here from Nebraska.

I knelt down, motioning for the others to do the same. I angled the flashlight toward the opposite shore and switched it on, off, on, off, on, off. . . .

"What are you doing?" Roman asked.

"It's a signal," I lied, "to let them know we're friendly. They have a security protocol."

And this was absolutely not part of it.

Here we are, I thought. *Come and get us.*

"Ooh," Priyanka whispered, shifting her weight from foot to foot. "This feels very sneaky."

"Yup," I agreed.

"I think I see someone," Roman said, squinting at the other side of the lake. Sure enough, a moment later, there was a faint splash as something entered the dark water.

A boat, and the single person rowing it, took shape out of the night. The oars pulled through the water with ease. I rose to my feet, gripping the flashlight hard enough to feel a spark from the batteries snap back at me. Flannel . . . light hair . . .

It wasn't Liam.

As the boat neared us, the rower turned to judge the remaining distance. I actually recognized her. It was Lisa—one of the first teens that they'd gone to retrieve three years ago. She was eighteen like me, and, at this point, was probably one of the older Psi at Haven.

Not Liam. Not Ruby.

Lisa looked at me, her face brightening with recognition. With my plan in pieces, I managed to salvage one last useful bit of it.

"Who the hell are you?" I called.

She stiffened, freezing halfway out of the boat. Roman reached behind him, his hand hovering over the gun.

"I don't know you," I said, keeping my voice hard. *And you don't know me either. Come on, Lisa. . . .* "Where are the Psi in charge?"

Lisa's mouth opened. Shut. Fear flickered across her face.

Liam or Ruby should have come. Things couldn't have changed *that* much, especially when it came to security.

Something's wrong. Something else was happening here.

Priyanka stepped up behind me, her shoulders back. "Do we have a problem?"

Roman moved in close to my other side. If it were almost anyone else, I would have thought they were trying to back me up, not make sure I couldn't slip away.

No one said a word, and it was only because of that silence that we heard the branch snap. In the next instant, a voice barked out, *"Drop it!"*

Six figures, their faces obscured by black ski masks, poured out of the trees behind us, an array of rifles and pistols in their hands. They were camouflaged in dark shirts and slacks, and while none of it was military grade, it was good enough for an evening ambush. They'd used the distraction of Lisa's slow approach across the lake to surround us while our backs were turned.

One of them, a tall teen, stepped out in front, moving his finger to the trigger of his rifle as he said, calmer this time, "Drop it."

Roman had the gun in his hand before I'd managed to look behind me. That horrible, emotionless mask was back over his face as he shifted his gaze from threat to threat, assessing.

He could take them. The realization was like a knife to the gut. Roman wasn't the type to take chances. If he was ignoring the order, it was because he knew he'd win.

I reached out, putting a hand on the barrel of the gun. He glanced toward me, and there was nothing there, just ice. I pushed it down slowly, watching him swallow hard.

Finally, he switched the safety back on and tossed it toward the young man out front. I didn't like the look he shot Priyanka, or the message buried in it. I put my hands behind my head, kneeling on the ground.

"Just so there's no misunderstanding," I said, "I'm armed."

Check them for more weapons.

Lisa nodded at a different masked teen, and the girl stepped forward, briskly patting me down. Finished, she kicked me square in the back, forcing me to catch myself before I ate dirt.

"Don't touch her again," Roman warned. To my surprise, the gun was all he'd had on him. The only thing they pulled from Priyanka was the two phones. Lisa caught me watching them and shoved them in the pocket of her flannel hoodie.

Separate us, I begged silently. *Get me away from them long enough to find out what's happening. Separate us. Don't bring them to the house.*

"I can explain," I began.

The boy gripped my arm, hauling me back onto my feet. "You're damn right you will."

Priyanka took a menacing step forward, ignoring the guns pointed her direction. "Now, that's no way to talk to a lady, is it?"

I held up a hand, trying to mask my own surprise. "It's fine—it's okay."

The masked teen squeezed my arm. Reassuring, not threatening. "Take the others to the hole. We'll question this one."

"No!" Roman surged forward, forcing two of the teens to grab him and a third to point their gun directly in his face. "Don't—*please*—"

That one word took the air out of my lungs. *Please.* I forced myself to look back at Lisa, who watched the scene unfold, her expression pained. The game I'd been playing was starting to splinter around me.

The anger burning in his expression was real. The fear in his voice was *real*.

The others turned to Priyanka. She held up her hands. "I'm not going to be *dramatic* about it." Then, with one last nod toward me, she added, "But if you so much as scratch her, I'll redefine that word for you."

The boy drew me over to Lisa, to the boat, steadily guiding me into it. He made enough of a show of flashing his gun that I felt like I couldn't see what was happening to the others, not without exposing the whole charade.

He dragged the small boat back into the water, and, somehow, the three of us fit comfortably on it. As we drifted away, I took in a deep breath of the cool, moist air rising from the moon-bright water. The more the distance grew, the less I understood what had just happened. I'd expected them to try to fight being separated, knowing they wouldn't want their tool out of sight before they could use me, but . . .

Not like that.

The opposite shore was a few dozen feet away before the boy

pulled off his mask and took in a steadying breath of his own. Jacob.

"That was something else," he said.

"Seriously," Lisa said, a bit shakily.

"You all right?" Jacob was a good foot and a half taller than I'd remembered. Even sitting in the boat, he still had to duck slightly to look me in the eye. He'd been the quietest of the original three, almost painfully shy. At the time, I'd thought he resembled Chubs, both in appearance and in his energy. Now he looked like he could bench-press him.

"Zu?" he said, a bit more urgently. "You did want us to pull you away from them, right?"

"Yeah," I said. I had to fight the urge to keep from looking back.

"You didn't use the normal procedure, but we weren't sure if you just . . . didn't remember it," Lisa said, hesitating over the last part. "It's been a while."

"That was smart, using the X symbol," Jacob said. "Miguel figured it out right away. We rowed out behind the house and circled around the long way to meet you. Good call with the stalling."

I wanted to feel proud of that, or even just acknowledge that this insane plan had worked. Somehow, it was just . . .

Please.

"I'm all right, and yeah, that was what I was after," I said as we bumped into shallow water. "Safe to assume my new reputation has preceded me?"

I barely knew these kids; we'd only met once, and that had been minutes, not even a full hour of interaction. We all just happened to fall inside Ruby and Liam's bright constellation.

In that moment, though, with their sympathetic eyes on me,

that automatic assumption of my innocence, I could have hugged them both and never let go.

"Listen," Lisa began uneasily, "before we go in . . ."

The boat rocked against the water, but neither Jacob nor Lisa moved to get out. Then I remembered.

"Where are they?" I asked.

"Didn't Charlie tell you? Ruby and Liam left two weeks ago to do a pickup," Jacob said, "and neither of them came back."

Three Years Ago

I REALLY HATED TUESDAYS.

It was like the world had decided that Mondays were for easing into the week, but Tuesdays—Tuesdays were fair game. It was the start to the apartment being empty and quiet, when my phone went silent as a sudden rash of meetings swallowed my friends whole. Worse, it was the day Mrs. Fletcher had decided should be our math day.

I had no problem with math. I liked it, actually. It was straightforward in a way nothing else seemed to be in life. There was only one right answer, and usually only one right way to reach it. It had none of those uncertainties of writing and reading, where a single word could change the meaning of a sentence. Math was fine.

The problem was, this was math Chubs had taught me a year and a half ago, and Mrs. Fletcher refused to skip ahead because *true understanding can only be reached by adding one building block after another.*

Somewhere in the nearby living room, the text alert on my phone went off with a cheerful *ding*.

I sat up straighter, leaning back in my chair to peer around the edge of the breakfast bar.

Where did I leave it . . . ?

From that angle, all I could see was Nico's back. He sat on the couch, noise-canceling headphones plugged into the computer as he typed away on whatever program he'd spent the last week coding. There was no way to get his attention, to have him check to see who it was from—to see if it was finally *them*, after months having nightmares about the worst.

"No." Mrs. Fletcher didn't look up from the work sheet she was grading. Her red pen moved down the algebra problems, checking off the correct answers, crossing out the few that were incorrect. "Finish your equations."

I set down my pencil, giving her my sweetest smile. The one Vida told me should be illegal.

"What if—?" I began.

"No."

"It's almost lunch anyway—"

"*No.*"

I clenched my jaw. My bare feet bounced against the tile until I could feel the static snapping against my toes with each small movement. What if they only had a second to send a message, and they needed a response right away? What if this was the only time I was going to get to talk to them before they disappeared again for months?

What if . . . this was Chubs calling to tell me that it *was* the worst?

I didn't mean to let so much frustration into my voice, but it bled through anyway. "You do know this isn't real school, right? I don't need a hall pass."

Mrs. Fletcher finally looked up, setting her own pen down. The phone let out another *ding* from the living room, somehow sounding more urgent the second time.

Sorry, Mrs. Fletcher, I just need to see if that's one of my friends—yeah, the ones who went missing six months ago? You know, the wanted fugitives?

"Do you think I'm wasting your time?" she asked, finally.

That was an easy answer: *No.* But I couldn't force the word out of me.

She looked across the room, her watery gaze moving from the pots hanging on the wall of Cate's kitchen—still unused after months of takeout—to the living room, where Nico was ignoring us.

I couldn't tell what she was staring at, exactly. Everything in the apartment had this strange quality to it; it was too new, too perfect. It reminded me of the dollhouse I had when I was younger, where all the decorations and furniture came prepackaged, perfectly toned and sized to fit the miniature rooms.

As it was, most of the furniture *had* come included with the apartment lease. The couch and chairs in the living room had a weirdly overstuffed design, like they'd sprouted from the carpeted floors like fungi.

Cate must have come home in the early hours of the morning, because there were new stacks of case folders balanced at the edge of the coffee table. She'd likely only stayed long enough to shower and change before heading back out to work on whatever project she and Vida were currently assigned to.

Out doing *real* work, not basic algebra.

Mrs. Fletcher was only in her early forties, but the last few years had carried twice the stress, twice the fear, twice the anger, and it showed on all of us in different ways. There were two deep frown lines on either side of her mouth. One, I decided, for her students, and one for her own son, who should have been sitting at the kitchen table with her, if life were even remotely fair.

"It must be hard to adapt to a routine after everything," she said softly. "I'm sure this is unbearably boring after what you've seen."

I whispered back the same words Chubs had told me after helping me set up my room at Cate's new apartment. "Boring is good."

After he'd left, I'd sat alone on my bed, listening to the last comings and goings of the movers bringing the new bed for Nico. Unlike the other rooms in the apartment, our two small bedrooms hadn't come furnished. The movers kept referring to them as the guest rooms, and Cate corrected them each and every time. But there was truth in that. I was only staying until I got approved for my own apartment in the building where they'd set up Chubs, Vida, and the others working on the Psi Council.

I liked Cate—I liked her *a lot*. But it wasn't like either of us had any real choice in this arrangement. The law said any Psi under eighteen years old had to live with a non-Psi guardian, and she was the only adult my friends fully trusted. And Cate was too damn nice to say no.

The bedroom, for now, was my space. Cate offered to let me paint and decorate it however I liked, but that didn't feel right to me. All I had really wanted was the door. The one I could open and shut as I pleased. The one that locked from the inside, not the outside. The one that divided my own space from the rest of the world.

Boring *was* good. Every night, when I lay down on that same bed, I didn't have to be afraid of what might happen when I fell asleep.

"If not boring, then . . . foolish. For what it's worth, I do think I understand somewhat," Mrs. Fletcher said. "When you go through something so earth-shattering, everything else will feel trivial. Unnecessary. But, please . . . all I'm asking is for you to be patient with this. Learn everything you can before you go out into the world. It's something no one will ever be able to take away from you."

I looked up at her from beneath my bangs. "What do I even have left for them to take?"

"I hope you never learn the answer to that." Mrs. Fletcher let out a soft sigh, leaning back. "All right. Let's have a quick break—but after you check your message, turn the phone off, all right?"

I slid off my seat and forced myself to walk, not run, into the living room. Nico actually looked up as I passed him, searching the couch cushions for any sign of the cell phone. He pointed to the table beside one of the chairs.

"Thanks—" I began.

But he only gave me a small smile and returned to his work.

The phone's face was turned down, but the pink case Vida had bought me was bright enough to spot under the stray sheet of newspaper. My heart seemed to climb higher into my throat with each step I took.

Only to sink the second I turned the cell phone over.

It was Chubs. CAN YOU DO FAMILY DINNER TONIGHT INSTEAD OF FRIDAY?

What other plans do you think I have? I wanted to write. Instead I typed, SURE. YOUR PLACE OR VI'S?

MINE. WHY DON'T YOU MEET ME IN THE PARK
AT 6:30?

I glanced out of the window. The weather had been alternating between sleet and freezing rain that week. Both his and Vida's apartments had been bugged from the start. If we were meeting outside, he had something he wanted to share with me alone.

I'd felt the little pinpricks of the microphones' batteries the first time I'd visited his place. Later, when he was walking me out to meet Cate, Chubs told me not to worry about them—that the bugs would reinforce they could be trusted.

"All right, Suzume, ready?" Mrs. Fletcher called.

I quickly responded to Chubs's last message and turned the phone off, as promised. I had no idea how I was going to concentrate for the next two hours. "Ready."

Chubs was waiting for me at his favorite spot in Meridian Hill Park. It was a few blocks away from the small apartment building Cruz and the others had set aside for members of the Psi Council, which included at least one representative from each of the rehabilitation camps. Though the park's overgrown landscape had been tamed when it reopened along with the city's other green spaces and monuments, its most impressive feature, a grand fountain, was still turned off, and the only water that filled the nearby reflection pool was from the steady drizzle of rain.

Chubs didn't seem to mind, though. He sat on the ledge, staring up the fountain.

My feet slowed as I approached. Something about seeing him there sent a pang through me. It left me rubbing at my upper arms, trying to erase the prickling beneath my skin. He was drenched; he'd dressed for winter, but not the rain. No umbrella. No knit cap like mine. I cocked my head to the side. Not even gloves?

Something's not right.

He tucked his chin deeper into his scarf, rubbing his bare hands together. The wet briefcase at his side was almost identical to the one all the other business and government types were carrying as they hurried along the park's intersecting paths to get home. One young woman did a double take as she saw him, nearly tripping.

He instinctively reached out to try to steady her, but the woman yanked her arm in close to her side, paling. She put her head down and hurried away without a single word.

My heart clenched into a fist at his confused expression. That woman had no idea the kind of person Chubs was. I shook my head, forcing out a hard breath through my nose. That was the point of this. That's why he and the others were working with the Council. We had to prove to people they had no reason to be afraid.

She wasn't afraid, a little voice whispered in my mind. I knew what fear looked like, and that wasn't it. *She was repulsed.*

A few feet away, Chubs's security agent Frank frowned while he pretended to read a newspaper. But Chubs only sat back down, bracing his hands on the freezing stone. His shoulders were bunched up at his ears, as if he were trying to protect them from the cold. I couldn't tell if his expression had tightened because of the woman or because he had something on his mind—I didn't like either option.

The rain pattered loudly against my pink umbrella as I closed the distance between us. Finally, Chubs turned toward the sound of my quick steps splashing through the puddles.

"Nice night you picked for a walk," I said, holding my umbrella over the both of us.

One of the things I really loved about Chubs's smile was how rare it was; when you got it, you knew it was honest.

"Hey—" All of a sudden his eyes seemed to focus on me from behind his glasses. "Wait, where's your security agent?"

He meant Aurelia. She was even nicer than Frank and had taught me how to French-braid my hair. "She got recalled. The office said I wasn't a public figure anymore, and I could rely on Cate for anything I needed."

Frank glanced over at us, then went back to casually scanning the park. He stood, stretched, and moved to sit across from us on the path, giving us a little more space. His khakis seemed out of season, but Frank didn't strike me as the kind of guy who put a ton of thought into seasonally appropriate fabrics.

"We'll see about that!" Chubs huffed. "Not a public figure? As if you didn't have your name and face splashed out on the news for months. I just saw one of the channels replay your interview the other night! Unbelievable. I know exactly who's going to hear—"

"Do you think Frank only owns that one pair of pants?" I interrupted. "Should we buy him some kind of wool blend if you're going to make a habit of sitting outside in the middle of winter to think your deep thoughts?"

"Don't even think about stealing his clothes from his closet and ordering him new ones," Chubs warned.

"You look so nice in them, though, and I got all the sizes right, didn't I?" I said.

Chubs had always cared about his appearance, even when we were traveling in Betty. Liam used to poke fun at him for ironing his shirts, but that was just who he was. Chubs was a reliable, put-together person; during his first few press conferences he'd had to borrow one of his father's old suits, and it hadn't fit him right. He wouldn't take money from his parents to buy a new one, either— not when they needed it more to cover medical costs when his dad had open-heart surgery.

I asked Cate if Chubs could have a small clothing allowance so he didn't have to riffle through donation bins to find proper business suits. We petitioned Cruz, and she wrote me a personal check for the cost of three new suits Chubs could rotate through until he earned enough of a salary to add to his collection. A regular paycheck, however, was likely still years away. Chubs and Vida both currently worked for housing and a grocery stipend now that we were through the horrifying, mismanaged rationing of the months that had followed the United Nations ousting Gray.

Chubs worked so hard, only for people to cringe away in parks or shout obscenities at him while he took the Metro to his office. He deserved to feel good about this one thing.

"You made me think I'd gone into someone else's apartment, I almost had a heart attack—" Chubs's eyes narrowed on me. "Okay, distraction over. If an agent didn't drive you, how did you get here? If you took the Metro alone, please just lie to me."

"The Metro is totally safe now."

"Says who?" he said.

"Says *you* in a speech you gave last week, the one about why we don't need special fare cards to ride it," I said. "Also, *hi*."

Chubs was dressed in a sharp suit and dark overcoat, with a blue tie I'd picked out for him for his first day of work. It was almost the same exact shade as the blue pin he wore on his lapel. I pushed my hair off my shoulder, untangling it from the yellow one I'd stuck on my coat before heading out.

"Hi," he said, carefully avoiding the umbrella to hug me. "But, seriously, how did you get here?"

"Mrs. Fletcher drove me. She waited until I saw you before driving off," I explained into his shoulder. "Are you okay? This is a really long hug for you. . . ." The horrible thought crashed into me a second later. "Is it Vi? Is she okay?"

He pulled back. "She's fine. Do you want to sit for a minute?"

The rain was freezing into clumps of ice on my hat and shoulders. I couldn't feel my lips to know if I was smiling or drooling. "Um . . . sure?"

Chubs was only this cagey when he was trying and failing to keep something big secret. He kept shifting uncomfortably, sliding his feet across the ground as if to look for more solid ground. Liam called it his antsy dancey. The rest of America had yet to figure out that they could trust what he was saying simply because he'd wear any lie like an anchor around his neck.

"I have something I want to talk to you about," he began.

My pulse jumped. I nodded, drawing in a deep breath. Chubs reached over, unbuckling his briefcase. He glanced over at Frank once before sliding out a few damp sheets of paper.

"I want to talk to you about the importance of reading," he finished.

I stared, taking the papers when he handed them over.

"Because I don't already have enough schoolwork?" I asked.

"I found a few books that I thought you might enjoy and printed off reviews for you to help decide which ones you actually wanted. Reading can change your life," he said. "And open your mind—"

"I already got one lecture on the importance of education today," I cut in, tempted to hit him in the face with the paper. Why the cloak-and-dagger routine if he was just going to tell me I might like—I looked down at the paper—*Watership Down*. "Seriously?"

He leaned over, running a finger down the side of the review. "I thought we could compare notes, the way my parents and I used to."

It took me a moment, but when the realization came together, I almost jumped off the bench.

"Do you—" I swallowed hard, clearing my throat. "Do you trust these reviewers?"

"Yes," he said. "I've relied on them for years."

It *was* them. Only Ruby and Liam knew how Chubs and his parents used to pass messages back and forth to one another while he was on the run. I looked at the review closer this time—it was an e-mail from the online store they used, with the subject line "A Recommendation from user EleanorRigbyyy."

Little bursts of relief quaked through me as I finally released that dread I'd been carrying with me for almost six months. *They're okay. They're alive.*

But with that fear gone, there was room for something else in my heart. Something that was too hot and stinging to touch. In the second before he looked away, I saw that same feeling there on Chubs's face. Neither of us put it into words, but I felt it taking shape between us like a double-edged blade.

They left.

"Why don't you take them home and think about which one you want to read first?" Chubs took the pages from my hand and folded them small enough to fit into my purse. "Should we go in? I'm famished. I hope you don't mind I ordered Italian again."

There was only one restaurant that had been able to reopen in a twenty-block radius and that was Italia North.

"I aspire to one day have your passion for garlic bread," I joked, looping my arm through his when he offered it. The two of us, with Frank trailing a little ways behind, headed toward Chubs's apartment building.

This was our new normal, as much as the new government and their new laws were. Parks reopened. Meetings were held. School began. We stayed.

They left.

I couldn't keep the words from circling back again and again, even as Chubs told me about work and asked me about school. Even as we lived lives that were mostly good and mostly normal and the best kind of boring.

They left.

I understood why. I understood the choice. But some part of me would never fully understand how four had become two.

It was a testament to Cate's exhaustion that she didn't hear me sneaking out of the apartment at three o'clock in the morning.

I bundled up with my knit hat, a striped fleece sweater, a coat, and pair of boots with fuzzy lining. The combination still wasn't enough to stave off the blast of blisteringly cold air and rain that hit me when I pushed open the building's back door and stepped out into the alleyway. I ran past the building's dumpsters and a few parked cars, searching for the right one.

"Hey!"

My feet skidded across the wet pavement as I spun. The interior light of a nondescript dark blue sedan flashed on, revealing Chubs in the driver's seat. He was wearing a black turtleneck pulled up over his mouth and a black beanie that came down so low it almost covered his eyes.

I started toward the back door, only to remember again. *It's just the two of us.* I moved to the front passenger seat, quietly shutting the door behind me. The heat from the vent warmed my face as I buckled up and Chubs reversed back out onto the street. He searched the street once more before finally pulling his turtleneck down enough to speak.

"Vi wanted to come," he explained, "but we thought it would be too suspicious if the three of us suddenly disappeared."

"I think it's still going to be pretty suspicious that we're gone," I said.

His fingers drummed against the steering wheel as he leaned forward, squinting ahead at the dark street. The windshield wipers began to work harder, faster, as he finally picked up speed.

"Vi let Cate know today that you and I were going to take a trip together," he explained. "Between the two of them, they'll come up with a good reason for why we ditched Frank. In theory, I am supposed to have weekends off. . . ."

"It's Wednesday," I reminded him.

"Wednesday can be my weekend when I haven't taken a weekend in . . ." He trailed off.

"Never." I shook my head. "You have never taken a weekend off. I probably should have asked this first, but whose car is this?"

"Vida got it for us from . . . well, I didn't ask, because I know better," he said. "She checked it herself. It's totally clean of any sort of GPS or tracking system."

Did she even have to really search it? The car looked like it was older than the three of us combined. It probably didn't have hubcaps, let alone a GPS system.

"So . . ." he began after a while. "What did you think of the messages?"

There had been three altogether. Two from Liam and Ruby, and one from Chubs with instructions on meeting him later that morning. *We are alive and safe will explain everything if you come to us,* was the first message. The second, *Blackstone mural write name on wall leave rock buy tea shop across from it,* was slightly less comprehensible.

"I guess we should be grateful we're allowed to know that they're still alive. Still, this is so typical of Liam," Chubs muttered. "It can't just be a simple *Go to this random location and I will come pick you up.*"

"It's not like they're making us do a scavenger hunt," I said. The instructions weren't totally clear, but they were enough to get us started. Blackstone was a city a few hours south in Virginia. All we had to do was look for a mural and a coffee shop. "They're just being careful."

"You always side with Lee," he said.

"No I don't," I insisted. "Sometimes I side with Vida."

He didn't laugh like I'd hoped. He didn't switch on the radio, either, which bugged me less than I thought it would. Liam always had to have a song or news on in the background, like he couldn't stand empty air.

Chubs leaned an elbow against the door, resting his head against his palm.

"It'll never not be weird to see you behind the wheel," I told him.

"If I'd been able to hang on to my real glasses I could have taken over for Liam in Betty at least part of the time," Chubs said. "Though I doubt he would have let me. You know how he gets about driving."

"You're probably right," I said. "See? That was me siding with you."

Finally, a faint smile.

"I wish I could drive," I told him. "It's so stupid I have to wait."

"Such impatience," he said, reaching over to briefly drop a hand on my head. He hadn't done it in years. "Do you know how many things can go wrong when you're behind the wheel? And that's not even factoring in *other* drivers—actually, let's talk about something else that doesn't involve vehicular manslaughter."

His grip on the wheel tightened as we left the limits of DC and reached the beltway. Through the blur of rain pelting the windows, we could just make out the shapes of the new highway lights and cameras that would be installed over the next few months. Right now, though, our only real sources of light were the car itself and the glow of the capital's light pollution.

"Did I really always side with him?" I wondered aloud. "I swear I didn't mean to. . . ."

Chubs risked a quick glance at me, then fixed his eyes back on the road. "It's not about choosing sides. I shouldn't have ever said that. I'm sorry. You know how I get when my blood sugar is low. He's *Lee*—he's funny and nice and he dresses like a walking hug."

"He *does* wear a lot of flannel," I said. "But you're those things, too. Don't make that face just to try to prove me wrong. You are."

"I don't feel that way," he admitted. "But I always got that you guys had something different. I respect that. I've never been . . . It's harder for me to open up to people."

The headlights caught the raindrops sliding off the windshield and made them glow like shooting stars.

He was making it sound like one friendship was better or more important than the other. That wasn't true. They were just different. The love was exactly the same. The only difference was that Liam had lost a little sister; a part of me had always felt like he wanted to prove to himself that he could save at least one of us.

"I always understood you," I told him. "Just like you always understood me."

Chubs glanced over, swallowing. By his nature, he ran at a slightly higher frequency than the rest of us, but looking at him now made my whole chest hurt. The suits he wore seemed to hide how thin he'd gotten, and the shadows of the dark sky seemed to drag his face down.

I hated the selfish part of me that had been so excited to see our friends I hadn't even stopped to realize how much planning Chubs and Vida put into this. How careful they'd had to be, to make sure that no one else picked up on the hidden messages, or their arrangements.

Chubs had the most at stake if we were caught or followed. Vida would lose her active-agent status, but Chubs would be raked over the coals. He'd be made out to be a self-serving liar. Congress could claim he had knowingly misled them, and he could go to prison for lying under oath. The Psi Council was still in its infancy. It wouldn't survive the loss of its visionary.

"Are you okay?" I asked him.

"Of course," he said, too quickly.

"We're not in DC anymore," I reminded him. "No one's listening."

"Really, it's—"

"You never used to lie to me," I said, holding my hands over the hot air blowing through the vents, "so please don't start now."

Chubs sighed, rubbing a hand back over his hair. He usually kept it short, but it was clear to me that he'd gone several weeks longer than usual without getting it cut. "It's . . . hard. All of it. I'm sorry you haven't seen me much, and if I've been out of sorts lately. It just never stops. We make some people happy, we enrage another group. We try to change people's minds about us, and they only get set deeper in their ways because they don't like to be made to feel wrong. I'm trying to make sure everyone on the Council is organized and that we read absolutely everything, but we keep having to bend our original goals to fit with the rest of the government's. It's maddening, and those awful people who are on the news with their disgusting protest signs, those people who killed that Psi boy in California and claimed self-defense . . . it's . . . it just never stops. If we could just get *some* movement on reparations . . ."

The court system had already dismissed any number of civil suits brought against the government by families who had lost children to IAAN, or who had children who'd survived it only to end up in camps. Each and every time, the judges would cite the same reasons. The administration and Leda Corp *had* conducted reasonable testing to make sure Agent Ambrosia was safe. The intention on the part of the government *had* been to introduce the chemical to prevent biological attacks on our water supply.

The government *had* reasons to believe that we were an imminent threat, given our powerful abilities and the fear that IAAN could be spread by contact.

Interim President Cruz was working behind the scenes to cut a deal, but it would be years before anything definitive came out of it. Almost every single family in the United States had been affected, and the country was still drowning in debt and depression—there simply was no money to pay any kind of settlement.

They had issued an official apology on behalf of the Gray administration for not intervening. That had been a start, at least. But when Chubs had gotten a bill on the floor of the House that would have funded a memorial, the Speaker had axed it, explaining that the nation "needed time to reflect on the tragedy before they could properly mourn it."

"Chubs . . ." I began, reaching over to squeeze his arm. In all the time we'd spent traveling together, I'd never seen him like this. "Why didn't you say anything?"

"Because this is what I signed up for." He shook his head. "Wow, listen to me. I'm sorry, Zu. It's not as bad as all that. I'm just frustrated. I keep having to remind myself that the work is good, even if it's hard. A year from now, I'll look back on this meltdown and laugh at myself."

Things *would* and *could* get better. I believed that with my whole heart. But he needed help. He needed more of us to take some of the weight of the load off his shoulders.

"I think that optimism is going to get you kicked off Ruby's Team Reality," I said lightly.

"I'm tired of Team Reality," Chubs said, his voice tight. The car picked up speed, flying past the workmen repaving the other side of the highway. "I'm done with it. I'd rather be the fool who hopes and works toward change than the cynic who does nothing and laughs when his doubts are proven right."

I nodded. "I agree with you on that, too."

He smiled. "Thanks for listening. Sometimes I feel like I'm talking just to myself."

"We can all hear you," I told him. "You speak for all of us."

That same smile faded. "Not everyone."

With no one listening in, I could finally ask the question that had been festering in me for months.

"Did they ever hurt you?"

"They didn't bother to hurt me before they left," Chubs said, struggling to keep the bitterness from his voice. "They didn't even tell me they were leaving."

"I meant the people who questioned you about their disappearance," I said quietly.

Chubs had been questioned by the FBI in a way that I hadn't. Those same men who harassed him for weeks, following his every move, never turned to look at me. Two FBI agents had stopped by Cate's apartment to ask me a few questions about the last time I saw Ruby and Liam, but Cate had been present the whole time. And, after an hour, she'd made them leave. That was it.

At first I'd been almost angry about it. Like, of course, what would a little girl know about anything, right? But I'd seen what the investigations had done to Chubs.

I'd watched him sit in front of Congress, testifying under oath he had no idea where his "so-called friends" were, and answering all of their questions with "I don't know. I hadn't spoken to either of them for months." I was there when agents showed up during family dinner to ransack his apartment for evidence, seizing whatever they wanted, including his books, just to intimidate him. I witnessed the harassment his amazing parents had received from reporters, investigators, and people who just despised Psi until they were forced to move out of Virginia entirely.

The reality was, for once, my youth had protected me.

"No," he said after a while. "They just asked questions I still don't know the answers to."

I plucked the folded map from one of the cup holders. He'd marked our route to Blackstone, a small town I'd never heard of in the southern, central part of the state.

"It should be about a three-hour drive," he said, sounding more like himself. "Let me know if you get hungry. I packed some water bottles and protein bars. Is the temperature okay?"

"Everything's great," I told him. "Do you want me to turn on the radio or anything?"

"Actually, if you don't mind," he said, "I kind of like the quiet."

I smiled, sitting back to watch the rain. "Me too."

FIFTEEN

Present Day

NO ONE TOLD ME.

I took the worn path up to Haven at a brisk, hard pace, my arms crossed over my chest. The otherwise smooth, packed dirt was interrupted by a few scattered leaves and footprints that had been stamped in during the most recent storm. Each time I passed one heading the opposite way, back toward the lake, I wondered if it had belonged to Liam or Ruby.

But the thought only filled me with rage.

I felt the heat of it clawing under my skin like a charge desperate to find a circuit to complete, to renew itself.

They didn't tell me.

Two weeks. Two goddamn weeks they'd been gone, and Chubs couldn't find a second to mention it to me? Lisa told me they'd made contact with him immediately to let him know. He could have gotten word to me somehow, in person or through Vida. He didn't think it would matter to me that two people we love were just—just *gone*, and that they'd left Haven, the most important thing in their world, behind?

I knew I was shaking. Crossing my arms over my chest did nothing but trap the furious heat in, wrapping me in it.

"—see that it's grown quite a bit since you were last here. We have about twenty kids now. The youngest is nine. Suzume?"

Finally, I looked up from the trail.

At one point in its life, Haven might have been someone's summer home. A secluded house on a lake, with all the privacy anyone could ask for.

Liam and his stepfather had done considerable work expanding out what had been a simple two-story wood house. The dark, woodsy colors, all deep greens and browns, were meant to help the property blend into its surroundings. Despite the sharp angles of its roof, the first—and last—time I'd seen Haven, I'd had the wild thought that maybe the house had grown up out of the forest, rising up from dirt the same as any of the surrounding trees.

As we approached, the familiar rope lines peeked out through the trees, but . . . wait. We were still far away from the house, and the last time I'd been here, the ropes hadn't extended this far into the woods.

I tilted my head back, following the line that passed over our heads to where it was knotted to a tree on our right.

It was a live oak, massive in stature. A silver ladder leaned against its side, a bucket of hammers and nails hooked on it. Nestled between the sturdiest of the branches was the beginning of a wooden platform.

"It'll be Tree House Ten whenever Liam . . . well, when one of us gets to finishing it," Lisa said. "There are nine completed ones on the grounds. After some of the kids took to the first one Lee built, he and Ruby decided to create more to give others their own private spaces. Then it just sort of got out of hand, because Liam doesn't like the word *no*, and here we are with more tree houses than actual houses."

"They're great," I somehow managed to choke out.

"The kids usually sleep up there, too, unless the weather gets too hot or too cold and forces them to come into the house," Jacob added.

The sudden guilt that flooded through me was so overwhelming, I couldn't speak. The missing years had never felt more pronounced than they did standing there. Each tree house was like a cut that carved down to the bone. My body tensed with the urge to turn and run, but I couldn't tear my eyes away from them.

This is what you missed.

Why didn't I come back?

Look at what they did without you.

Why didn't I just find a way to call?

You don't belong here.

It was the last thought that made me reach up to my throat, trying to rub away the thickness.

"I know you don't agree with Haven . . ." Jacob began, misreading my look.

I held up my hands, cutting him off. "It's not that. It was never that."

"Then what was it?" Lisa asked.

"Lisa—" Jacob interrupted.

"No, I want to know," she said, turning to more fully face me. "You never came back, but they never stopped hoping that you would."

The accusation in her words, a realization of the truth I'd managed to sweep away for a time, brought me up short.

I'd hurt them. I'd hurt the two people who Lisa and Jacob and all the kids here loved. Even old wounds could reopen with the right amount of pressure.

I wanted to scream. I wanted to slam my fist into the nearest tree and let the years of silence between us pour out of me like blood.

Instead, I took a breath. I clasped my hands behind my back. I spoke in that careful, cool voice Mel had coached me on adopting. And that numbing self-control became my armor.

"I wanted to work to make sure we didn't need places like Haven," I told her. "This was their way of helping. I have mine."

Or, at least, I did.

Haven wasn't sanctioned by the government. It, and other places like it, would never be, because they brought kids outside the protection and monitoring the government provided. These places returned the Psi to the dangerous way we'd been forced to live before.

I'd never doubted that the kids at Haven had escaped from truly terrible situations. Abuse and neglect that came after being returned to their families, runaways who'd refused to go back at all, who'd been made to use their Psi abilities against their will . . .

I *understood*. I'd only struggled to understand why they hadn't been brought to us to find better living situations. Existing in the shadow of society was an invisible, fragile existence.

Lisa and Jacob exchanged a look. He gave a shake of his head, and the girl's shoulders slumped.

"Sorry," she started. "I just—"

"I get it," I told her. "I do. Let's just . . . figure out what's going on. I need to find a charger for that phone, and I need to hear everything you know about what's happening with—"

Lisa put a finger to her lips, looking up at the curious faces peering down at us from the houses.

They don't know, I realized.

"They're on a long pickup trip," Jacob said meaningfully. "They'll be back soon."

They were lying to the others—lying by omission, but still lying. It had to be to protect the younger kids, but I would have thought, given the circumstances that brought them here, they would have been given the respect of being kept informed.

"Come on," Jacob said. "Miguel is waiting for us in the Batcave. I'm sure he's already got some theories about your new friends."

As we made our way to the house's wraparound porch, the kid in Tree House Four sent a message can—an old coffee tin that had been weighted at the bottom—across a rope line to Tree House One. It zipped over our heads with a whispering sound. All the houses seemed to be connected to one another, and to the window that marked the attic of Haven. Where Liam and Ruby slept.

"Everything good?" Another teen, also dressed in black, jogged up from the back of the house. Her long braid swung out behind her, and she seemed winded.

"Yeah, it's under control," Jacob said, handing his gun over to the girl. "Jen, this is Zu; Zu, this is Jen."

"Hi," the girl said. "You made tonight pretty damn interesting. Should I go help the others?"

"They have it handled," Jacob said. Then he added sheepishly, "Could you do me one favor and put this away in the lockers upstairs? We have to go debrief Miguel."

"Sure," she said, taking his weapon. "If you don't need me, I'll put mine away, too."

Jacob ran up the steps of the porch, opening the door with a dramatic sweep of the arm he'd clearly picked up from Liam at some point. Jen went ahead of us, disappearing as she headed down the entry hall. I steeled my nerves and stepped through the doorway into the cool, cedar-scented air, almost forgetting to wipe my feet on the worn welcome mat.

That awkwardness I'd felt outside was nothing compared to what swept through me now; it was almost physically painful. What little familiarity I'd had with the place evaporated in an instant. I was vaguely aware of Lisa explaining the setup of the house as she walked in behind me, but most of my attention was on the hallway itself.

While the outside of the house had been designed to camouflage itself in nature, the inside threw colors and patterns at you from every direction. The rugs were a trail of dizzying yellow and blue; wildflowers burst from a crooked vase. A strand of colored lights wound up the banister of the front stairs.

But my eyes kept drifting to the walls. On our brief tour, years before, Ruby had explained that it was too dangerous to keep photos of the Psi who stayed with them, whether the kids were there for a few months or years. They had been thinking about encouraging them to leave a piece of artwork—so that the house, and all of its inhabitants, would never forget them.

Clearly, they'd made their decision.

The result was a mishmash of frames scattered over the

main hall and up the staircase. Most of the Psi had done drawings or paintings of Haven itself, but others had decided to do self-portraits. Some wove bracelets or potholders, others sewed messages, and some even melted beads together to make flat plastic flowers and smiley faces. Liam and Ruby had diligently framed them all.

The last one on the wall, a picture of a short, dark-haired woman and a taller blond guy, their arms linked, their faces smiling, was drawn in careful strokes of crayon. My face was reflected in the glass, and, just like that, I could see Liam's there instead of mine, smiling that dumb, proud grin of his.

"If you wouldn't mind . . ." Lisa gestured to the row of neatly lined-up shoes—sneakers, sandals, boots, all in different sizes— along the wall. I kicked off my tennis shoes next to a pair of dirty red rain boots.

The TV was on in the living room, a sweet, upbeat song chirping from the speakers. I glanced in and saw twelve or so kids riveted by an animated movie I didn't recognize. As we passed, a girl emerged from the room. She rubbed tiredly at her eyes, making a beeline for the bathroom.

Her crown of dark curls bounced as she came to a sudden stop in front of me, and her eyes went wide. "Zu?"

I stilled.

Oh God, I thought. *She saw the explosion, she thinks—*

But instead of running away, she let her face bloom into an enormous grin.

I actually could have cried, the relief was that strong. "Hi. Yeah."

She latched onto my hand, pumping it up and down. It wasn't a handshake, but a gesture of pure, mystifying excitement. As she looked up at me, her expression turned urgent. Serious. "Do you still like horses?"

"Do I—what?" I blinked.

"You said in your interview that you liked horses," she insisted. "Do you like Arabians, Percherons, Clydesdales, Lipizzans, or a different kind best?"

Lisa laughed. "Sorry, Sasha, she doesn't have time to talk right now. We have to steal her for a little bit."

"Okay!" the girl said, giving my hand one last shake. "You can come to our room—it's the blue one—and we can talk some more then!"

"Okay," I said, still mildly startled. She continued past us down the hall, giving Jacob a high five along the way.

I gave them both a questioning look.

"It's easier just to show you," he said. "Plus, it's on the way."

Lisa led us down the hall. We swung a left at the dining room, and just before we reached the kitchen, she stopped beside a bulletin board on the wall that was overflowing with newspaper and magazine clippings. One face smiled out from every single photograph.

Mine.

"Wow . . . this is . . ." I didn't have the words for it. I stared at the photographs from my speeches and publicity shoots, the articles about every event I'd attended.

"Sorry," Lisa said. "I hope you're not embarrassed. You know how Liam gets. I think he just . . . wanted everyone to know you."

Because you never came back.

"There's one for Charlie upstairs," Lisa said. "It's smaller, though. He doesn't get out as much as you do . . . did."

An old, battered hubcap hung over the massive kitchen table, taken from a van hidden deep in the woods near a different lake. I turned away, unable to bear looking at it a second longer. "Can we just go wherever we're going to talk now?"

"This way," Jacob said, nodding his head toward the back door.

The small room—which had clearly been added on to the original structure—was about ten degrees cooler than the rest of the house. It was no small feat, considering the back wall was lined with server towers. A built-in desk wrapped around half of the space, and every inch of surface area was covered in either screens or computer units.

Miguel sat at the center of it all, his fingers pounding the keyboard in front of him like a piano. He swiveled back and forth in his chair to the beat of a muffled song coming out of his massive headphones.

As we came in, he tore his gaze away from his task. The computer screens illuminated his naturally tan skin, making his face glow.

"Hiya, Zu. Long time no see," he shouted over the music in his ears, continuing to type. It was always amazing to see how many different things a Green's brain could process at once. Three different computer screens flashed with code as Miguel smiled at me—the confident smile of a heartbreaker who knew the exact level of charm he possessed.

Jacob let out a noise of exasperation, affectionately pulling the earphones off Miguel's head. The other boy caught Jacob's hand before he could pull it away, planting a kiss on the back of it, with a wink. Jacob pulled back his hand, flustered, but pleased.

If that wasn't confirmation enough that they were together, Miguel set his headphones down next to a photo of the two of them on the desk. A symphony of electronic beats and violins poured from the earpieces until Lisa leaned over and hit the MUTE button on the keyboard.

"Hey, Miguel," I said. "Thanks for getting my message."

Miguel ran a hand back over his dark hair, scratching just above where he'd tied it into a bun, and shrugged. "No problem. Glad everything worked out."

"Before I forget," I said, turning to the others. "Can I get those phones? Miguel, I'm wondering if you have a charger—"

He pulled open a nearby drawer. Dozens of charging-cable bundles were lovingly arranged inside. Lisa passed me the phones, and I handed them to him, pointing at the cell phone I'd used to take the photos of the kidnappers.

"Priyanka did something to that," I told him. "She took out a part and put it in the other—"

Miguel opened the back of both phones, and somehow did the exact reverse of what Priyanka had done in the car. Jacob put his hands on the other teen's shoulders, leaning over Miguel's head to watch. "She just removed its SIM card. No big deal."

At the sight of its screen finally lighting with power, I released a shaky breath. At least there was that.

"What's the status at the hole?" Jacob asked, searching the screens for a feed.

With two keystrokes, Miguel changed the footage on the monitor directly in front of him. "So far, mostly fretting. And pacing. A bit like you, I've got to say."

Jacob gave him a look that Miguel only returned with a small smile.

Sure enough, Roman was prowling back and forth across the

ten-foot space. His posture was rigid, and he seemed incapable of taking his eyes off what I assumed was an out-of-sight door. There wasn't much to the shed except a small bench to sit on, but it wasn't a hole in the ground like the name implied. I shouldn't have felt as bad as I did looking at them.

"This is quite the setup," I said. "What are they fretting about—the fact that they got caught?"

Miguel typed in another command, and the footage jumped back ten minutes. He keyed up the volume. I braced my hands on the desk and leaned in.

"—doing to her," Roman said, anger ringing through the words. "I'm so stupid! I shouldn't have let them take her out of my sight. Now we have no way of knowing if they're going to hurt her or not."

Priyanka had been feeling along the edges of the walls, as if searching for weak joints. At that, she glanced over her shoulder at him. "She'll be all right. Don't act like she's some helpless damsel. She got us out of most of the trouble we got ourselves into. If they try anything, she'll fight like hell."

"Still . . ." Roman said, stopping in the middle of the shed. His head fell back and he clenched his fists at his side. "I know. *I know.* I'm not doubting her. I just don't . . . I don't like this. We shouldn't have let them separate us—"

"It's a lot of that," Miguel said, speeding forward through the other footage. "'Should we break out and find her? She's coming back, don't worry. Should we try to talk to the kids outside? Why would they separate us? Et cetera.'"

I felt both Jacob's and Lisa's eyes on me as I stood upright again. My mind was spinning. "Well . . . it's not like they're going to reveal their plans out in the open for the kids standing guard to hear."

The footage caught up to the present, snapping out of fast-forward. I watched as Priyanka reached out to catch Roman's hand. After a small battle of wills, Roman relented. He slumped down beside where she'd planted herself on the bench, and Priyanka rested her head against his shoulder. Instead of closing her eyes the way I thought she might, she glanced up.

Directly into the camera.

"Is she a Yellow? She immediately identified the location of the cameras and mics," Miguel said.

Huh. A lucky guess? I couldn't imagine Miguel putting them anywhere remotely obvious.

"No, Green . . . at least that's what she told me," I said. "You guys don't happen to have a copy of the old skip tracer and PSF database, do you? I was hoping you might be able to search it."

"Sure do, and I already tried it," Miguel said. "Ran captures of their faces through the system. No records, though that database is almost five years old at this point."

"Roman said they avoided being picked up, which I'm guessing also means they avoided being registered, too."

"Or someone wiped their records," Miguel said. "What's their deal? How did you even link up with them?"

I gave them the details as quickly and matter-of-factly as I could, along with my theory that they might have been targeting Haven or Ruby and Liam all along. Another thought occurred to me. "You don't have anyone here by the name of Lana, do you?"

The boys looked to Lisa.

"No," she said. "I've been monitoring the tip lines these past few weeks and I haven't seen that name come up at all. Do you know what she looks like? What ability she might have?"

I shook my head. "All I have is the name. They were talking about her in a way . . . their tone wasn't malicious. If anything, they were both emotional about it. It didn't seem like they were tracking her on behalf of someone else, either."

"The mystery deepens," Miguel said, glancing back at the screen. "Haven's not a total secret to Psi. Word has been spreading a bit more recently. Maybe they just wanted to find a safe place for themselves?"

A thread of frustration wove through me. "Then why not tell me that from the start?"

Jacob shifted uncomfortably, silently communicating something to Miguel with a look. The boy read it and nodded.

"What?" I pressed.

"Think about it . . ." he said, not unkindly. "You work for the government. They could have been worried that, instead of telling them how to get here, you'd turn them over to the FBI or the Defenders for trying to dodge their monitoring system."

I felt nauseous at the thought. "I wouldn't do that. If they wanted to come here . . ."

You'd help them break the law?

It wasn't . . . it wasn't as simple as that. Nothing about our situation had ever been black-and-white; our lives were painted in shades of gray. I believed in giving kids choices, and in trying to protect them in whatever ways I could.

"Or," Jacob added quickly, "it could be that they just didn't think you'd believe them. Or that you'd shut down and refuse to say anything if they straight-up asked you. So maybe they came to the speech to try to ask you about it, and then they just got caught up in everything and figured you'd find your way here eventually?"

Lisa shook her head. "I don't know. . . . They repeatedly blocked her from going on her own."

I took a deep breath. We needed to put this aside and move on. Not knowing what was going on with Ruby and Liam had created a pressure cooker inside my mind, and it was about to explode. "Are they okay to stay in there for a little while longer?"

"Yeah," Lisa said. "I'll send some food and water down for them."

"And blankets," I said. "In case . . . It gets cold at night, doesn't it?"

The girl gave me a faint smile, nodding. She disappeared through the door, returning a few moments later.

"All right," I said. "Now, who's going to tell me what happened to Liam and Ruby?"

SIXTEEN

LISA SAT ON THE EDGE OF THE DESK, CROSSING HER arms over her chest. "I'm not even sure where to start. There wasn't any indication something was wrong when they left. Liam seemed sort of upset, but I figured it must have something to do with the kid he was going to pick up—"

"Wait, they were both gone from Haven at the same time?" I interrupted. "When did they change that policy?" As far as I remembered, they'd decided early on that one of them would always stay at Haven so the kids would have at least one constant in their lives.

"Miguel, Jacob, and I can take care of things here," Lisa said. "We fill in when the situation calls for it."

Miguel leaned back in his chair, swiveling more fully toward the rest of us. "It's a recent thing, in any case. I don't think either of them liked it, but splitting up let them cover more ground and rescue more kids."

"They didn't leave together?"

The three of them exchanged looks that made the hair rise on the back of my neck.

"Tell her," Jacob said, finally. "Neither of them would feel like it's betraying their trust. It's Zu."

Lisa didn't look entirely convinced. That sharp pang hit me again.

I don't belong here. I'm not one of them.

Ruby and Liam were no longer mine, not the way they had been before. I'd hurt them, the way they'd hurt me, and while these three had been welcoming, it didn't mean my last visit wasn't on their minds, too.

"Listen," she said finally. "You know how they are. The main reason they started traveling separately is because their network has grown and they started getting more tips about kids. I didn't really think anything of it. It brought some new stress—"

"They've been fighting," Jacob said, finally getting to the point.

Miguel nodded, adding, "We have no idea what about."

"It's been in that Mom-and-Dad-are-whisper-fighting-because-they-think-we-can't-hear-them kind of way," Lisa said.

"You're joking," I managed to get out. Ruby and Liam didn't fight.

"Nope," Jacob said. "In the meantime, Ruby's been leaving on her own more and more. All of us worry when she goes, but it puts Lee in a real funk. He goes and mopes in the woodworking shed, and everyone ends up with some kind of deformed carved animal they have to pretend to love to make him feel better."

I blew a strand of hair out of my face. "That sounds about right."

"Here's the thing, though," Lisa said. "Her trips were becoming longer and longer, but she stopped bringing kids in. Ruby's always been quiet, but lately it's like . . . she's gone."

Ruby had this way about her; she could slip so deeply into her own mind that sometimes it felt like she was vanishing in front of your eyes. But she loved these kids and she loved this place. After everything she'd been through, Ruby must have relished the quiet of the land and the cozy madness of the house in equal measure. Whatever was bothering her had to be big to disturb the tranquillity she'd found here.

"What happened with this recent trip?" I asked. "I saw Liam's truck, and I was so sure he'd be the one rowing across the lake."

"Miguel was using Lee's truck to pick up supplies from the drop site," Lisa explained. "That's why he didn't take it. Ruby left, and then, maybe a day or two later, we got a tip through the network about a Blue kid living rough near Missouri, so Liam felt like he had to go check it out."

"And neither of them have made contact since then?" I asked.

"Liam has," Jacob said.

I straightened. "He did? Why did you make it sound like he'd gone missing?"

"Because we haven't heard from him in over a week," Miguel said. "He called in to say the tip was bogus and we told him that Ruby had gone off the grid. Her cell phone tracker had been switched off completely. He went to look for her himself. Then we lost his phone signal, too, and only got a text message via an unknown number saying his phone was busted and he was still looking for her. He hasn't responded to any of our messages since. As far as I'm concerned, he's missing, too."

"Our theory is that he might have thought he was being followed and didn't want his phone calls traced back here," Jacob said.

"He wouldn't want to worry you," I agreed. "The idiot. Do you have Ruby's last known location?"

"We do," Miguel said. "The estimated address is 1020–1024 Cypress Street in Jackson, Mississippi. It's basically in the middle of a field."

"Does that mean anything to you?" Lisa asked.

I shook my head. *Not at all.* "It's really nothing but a field?"

"There was no satellite footage of her there," Jacob said. "So either it's a mistake, or . . . she's not somewhere that we can see."

The edges of my vision went blurry as his words sank in.

"She's not dead," I told them, my voice sharp. Final. "She's not. If anything, she might have ditched her phone there to throw someone off."

Lisa's face crumpled. She pressed a hand to her forehead, looking exhausted. They'd been here for two weeks, obviously pretending with the other kids that everything was fine, when, privately, they'd clearly assumed the worst.

"I don't know what to think," Jacob said. "There's that bounty out on her. She could have been taken or turned over to the government. Some criminal group might have grabbed her. Any number of foreign actors could have been looking for someone with her ability. Or . . . she decided to leave. On her own."

All the muscles in my body seemed to tense at once. When she and Liam had left, I'd felt . . .

It didn't matter what I'd felt. I had always understood they'd acted for Ruby's protection. After her father had been shot shielding her from some hateful monster's bullet while they took a walk through the park, the threats against Ruby had gone from being something to scoff at to something to actively worry over.

Her father had survived, but Ruby's faith in the world hadn't. She had a power, and a control of that power, that set her apart from the rest of us. It put her at the very top of our food chain and ensured there would always be a bright red target on her back for everyone who feared her and what she could do.

"You can rule out the government," I said. "Don't forget how many former Children's League kids work in it. One of us would have heard about her capture or seen something come up in the various systems."

We had friends at every level of the government, in every department. Not to mention Nico had monitors set up in the system to flag anything like that. Plus, the government was the leakiest ship out there. You couldn't keep the capture of the most powerful Psi secret for long. Someone's ego would eventually demand credit.

"I think they would have made an announcement," Lisa said. "Ruby always said that the fact that she'd gotten away was more harmful to the government's reputation than anything she could actually do to them."

"What are you thinking?" Miguel asked me.

"I'm thinking . . ." I took a deep breath. "Is it a coincidence that Ruby goes missing and then someone targets me shortly after?"

"There might be something there," Jacob said. "The timing is suspicious, and the two of you are high-profile. It could be a message to the wider world—no Psi is untouchable."

It wasn't just that Ruby was powerful, it was her story that mattered. She had completed the circle and destroyed the place that had held her prisoner. She was a symbol. *Our* symbol.

I shook my head, frustrated by all the missing pieces. "She really didn't tell any of you what was going on, or give any clues about why she was pulling back? Was she working with any of the kids one-on-one before she left?"

"Owen," Lisa said softly. "She's been working with Owen. But he's . . . fragile."

"In what way?" I pressed.

"He's a Red," Jacob clarified. "Project Jamboree."

That brought me up short.

"I want to talk to him," I said, "if it wouldn't be too hard on him."

"You probably won't get much," Miguel warned. "Owen is not what we'd call a talker."

"Would you be if you'd been subjected to that?" I said. "Not much is still more than nothing—"

The sudden, sharp ring of a phone blasted through the room, launching all of us to our feet. Jacob let out an uneasy, awkward laugh, but still darted for it. "Betty Jean Pizza, can I take your order—? Oh, yeah. She's here. Hang on." He turned and held out the phone to me.

With a deep breath in through my nose, I pushed myself away from the desk. I took the phone and unwound the coiled cord, drawing it back out of the Batcave and into the kitchen for a modicum of privacy.

Even with another deep breath, my words still shook. "Did it even *occur* to you—"

But it wasn't Chubs.

"Shut the fuck up and listen to me. I only have a few minutes before they realize I'm gone."

"*No*," I shot back, "you listen to me for once, Vi. What the hell is going on? Ruby and Liam have been missing for two weeks and you didn't think I would want to know? Don't pretend like that's brand-new information. Chubs tells you everything."

"Of course I know," Vida said, her tone hushed. "What do you think I've been doing these last few weeks? I've been hauling ass all over this country looking for them."

. I gripped the phone, ignoring the current of static that brushed over my fingers. My anger deflated, just slightly. "Did you find them?"

"No," she said. "Not yet. But I'm not calling about them—I'm calling about *you*. Are you all right?"

"Not really," I told her. Mel, Agent Cooper, the reporters . . . the memories cut through me like a hot blade. Admitting it was enough to bring tears close to the surface again. "But I'm not hurt."

"Tell me, as fast as fucking possible, what happened."

"You saw the footage?" I asked. "The angle—"

"It was jacked as hell," Vida said. "I've seen meth labs less suspicious than that camera angle."

The story burst out of me, the words rolling over each other in a rush to get out. "I have a phone. I took photos of the people who grabbed us—how should I get them to you?"

"I need you—and those photos—to stay planted right where you are until I get there. Don't send the files anywhere. I don't care how secure their network is, we can't risk anyone tracing them back to Haven."

"I want to do something more than sit here and wait . . ." I began, frustrated.

Suddenly there were voices crackling in the background on the other end of the line.

"I didn't realize stupidity scorched retinas, Murphy," Vida snapped at someone. "It's a personal call. Give me a goddamn second. Yeah, to my dead mother. No, I don't give a shit—"

"Vida?" I said. "Vi?"

"You still there?" Vida's voice sounded thin, so unlike her. "I have to go, I'm sorry. Listen, I love you, okay? Don't do anything stupid. Just stay where you are, and one of us will be there soon. Okay?" She paused. *"Okay?"*

Nothing about that was *okay*.

"I'm not going to just hang out while the killers are out there and Ruby's—"

The line went dead. The shock of the dial tone wormed through me, hollowing out my core.

"I love you, too," I whispered. I leaned against the kitchen counter for a moment, pressing the receiver to my forehead. Just as I set it down, I noticed a stack of newspapers on the counter.

The top one was from a month ago, and featured a bold headline: *CEO in Chief?* I picked it up, reading the first lines: *As corporate fixer Joseph Moore purchases another shipping company to add to his empire of cable, cars, and containers, his supporters make the case for him to fix the highest office in the land.*

I threw the paper down in disgust and turned back to the Batcave, where the three of them weren't figuring anything out so much as arguing about it.

"It's not the craziest idea, if they're trying to frame her—"

"Frame who?" I interrupted.

Jacob swung around, the hands he'd been using to emphasize his words falling back to his side.

Miguel jerked his thumb toward him. "This adorable clown thinks we should bring in the two from the hole and see if they're willing to tell us anything about the Psion Ring."

"The only problem with that is that I don't think they were ever actually in the Psion Ring," I pointed out. "I really believe their story was made up on the fly."

"I could question them," Jacob offered. "See if they're willing to ask me to stay, or about whoever Lana is?"

"No," Miguel interrupted, looking unhappy about the risks associated with that. "If they lied to Zu, they'll lie to you. I can't keep a secret from you, but, unfortunately, that superpower only works on me."

"We can't keep them in there forever," Jacob argued. "And while they don't know exactly where the house is, I'm pretty sure they could figure it out now."

"I'm sorry," I told them. "I thought Ruby might be able to help with that."

"You didn't know." Miguel shrugged.

Lisa passed by his chair, bringing her face close to one of the monitors. She pointed to it—to the image of Roman waving his arms and Priyanka shouting something. "They wrote something on the ground. . . ."

Miguel swiveled back to the screens, sending the footage to the largest screen at the center. The film was grainy, but the words were still clear.

TURN OFF THE PHONE

"Shit," Miguel said, unmuting the feed.

"Turn off the phone!" Priyanka was shouting. *"Turn it off!"*

"What phone?" Lisa said. "What are they talking about?"

Miguel seemed to figure it out a full five seconds before the rest of us. He swept the cell phone I'd brought in off the charger. Its face glowed as it was turned over. He only needed one look at it to start breaking it apart. *"Shit!"*

"Wait!" I cried. "The photos—!"

The walkie-talkie on Jacob's belt suddenly flared to life with crackle of static. *"Jay? They've been going on for ten minutes—"*

I felt it then, the flare of sudden heat against my nerves, the electricity moving through the nearby wires as it intensified from a hum to a scream.

A second later, Haven's power shut off.

SEVENTEEN

IN THAT MOMENT, IN THAT DARKNESS, NO SOUND COULD possibly have been more terrifying than the clang of bells as the old-fashioned trip wires surrounding the house were set off.

But then I heard a little girl scream.

Miguel shot to his feet and started for the door that led outside. I caught him, holding him in place.

"The generators—" he began.

He was so much taller and heavier than me, I struggled to keep him in place until Jacob helped me. "We don't know what's out there."

"Yeah, and we won't if I don't get the cameras and emergency floodlights on!" he said, finally wrenching away.

Lisa blocked the door, holding out both arms. "We don't have time. You and I need to get the kids and get to the trapdoor."

"The power—" he protested.

"It's too late," she barked, hauling Miguel toward the kitchen door. "Let's *go*, while we still have time."

"Ben?" Jacob said into the walkie-talkie. "Ben! Anyone? Can anyone hear me?"

He looked to Miguel in the darkness.

"They must have something jamming the frequencies," Miguel explained. "Which means—"

"They're well-trained and well-armed," I choked out.

"We've drilled for this," Lisa said. "We need to wake up the kids in the tree houses."

"No," Jacob said quickly. "We need to get them quickly and quietly. If we make a lot of noise alerting the kids, the intruders might attack immediately."

The agitation on Miguel's face broke as he nodded, moving to pull pieces out of each server. He dumped them all into a bag that had been stowed beneath the desk. As soon as Lisa opened the door, I heard the confused voices of the kids upstairs. She cupped her hands around her mouth, calling softly, *"Free Bird! This isn't a drill! Leave everything!"*

In response, feet pounded down the stairs, heading our way.

"The escape hatch is in the laundry, under the dryer," Lisa explained to me, catching Miguel's arm again as he reached the doorway.

"I'll get the kids in the tree houses," Jacob said, looking to me. I nodded.

"Please be careful—*please*," Miguel said, returning only long enough to lock Jacob in an embrace.

"I'll see you soon," Jacob promised.

After one last long look between the two boys, Miguel followed Lisa out.

"I'm sorry, I didn't know . . . the phone . . ." I began.

Jacob gave a sharp shake of the head. "Even Miguel missed it." Seeing my face, he gripped my shoulders. "You should go with Lisa and the others."

The horror blanketing my mind was ripped away by his words.

I did this. I'd inadvertently brought the kidnappers here, and had been careless enough to think they wouldn't track the missing phone. I wasn't going to leave this place until every kid was safely away from whatever—and whoever—was coming for us.

"No," I said. "*No*, Jacob. We need weapons—"

"They're upstairs," he said, already heading that way.

The kids who had been sleeping in the bedrooms ran down the staircase as we ran up. Lisa was in the hallway, waving them forward toward the laundry, counting them off as she went.

She called the last number just loud enough for us to hear: "Eight!"

"Nine in the tree houses?" I confirmed with Jacob.

"Four at the hole," he said.

A string of white-hot cusses streamed through my mind. The hole—Priyanka and Roman were either sitting ducks, or the safest of us all.

We charged up into the attic. To Ruby and Liam's bedroom.

Their room hadn't changed at all since the last time I'd been there—it was almost disarming. There was the same tufted green rug, adopted from Ruby's grandmother; and along the windows of the far wall—the one where all the lines from the tree houses connected—were the striped curtains she had made for them. Aside from the desk, the two nightstands, the bed, and a bookshelf, there was no other furniture in the room.

Which wouldn't give anyone up here much cover, if it came to that.

The last two of the Haven kids were waiting for us up there. Jen and another girl with raven-black hair had already pulled heavy weapons cases out from under Ruby and Liam's bed and were assembling the guns.

"What's going on?" Jen demanded.

Jacob dropped to a crouch beside them. I did the same, only I moved to the edge of the room's enormous windows, the ones that overlooked the tree houses. I kept my back to the wall.

"Is it a raid?" the other girl asked, unable to keep the note of fear from her voice.

"No," Jacob said, sliding a pistol over to me. "Something else."

A scream rent the air—somewhere in the darkness wood snapped, splintering loudly as it crashed to the ground. I moved onto my knees, scanning the shadows between the trees. "I don't see anything—"

Thin red beams of light pierced through the underbrush. Gun sights, sweeping up over the ground to the front of the house.

"Take cover!" I shouted, throwing myself away from the wall. The two girls dove across the room and crouched defensively by the door. With a single sweep of his hands, Jacob upended the bed and bookshelves and sent them sliding our way, barricading us behind them.

"We need to check out the back and make sure they don't have the whole house surrounded," he said. "Jen, you're with me. Zu and Ana, I need you to stay here and cover us."

His voice disappeared beneath the battering hail of gunshots. They pierced the side of the house, spraying through the wood siding. Shards of glass and plaster whipped into a hurricane of sound and violence.

"Did they make it out?" I asked, smoke and debris filling my mouth. "The house kids?"

I didn't hear any noise downstairs. They must have made it to the hatch. They had to have escaped.

But the kids outside . . .

The gunfire had stopped, but their screams hadn't.

"Help! *Help me!*"

"Get out! Run!"

My next thought sent a chill deep into my core. If the intruders wanted the kids dead, they already would be.

"They aren't going to kill them," I told the others. "They're going to *take* them!"

Jacob crawled through the broken furniture, dragging a rifle after him. He braced it against the blown-out window's frame, looking through the gun's sight. A gash on the bridge of his nose sent blood streaming down over his face.

I followed, bumping up against the other side of the window, the pistol gripped tight in my hand.

"Can you get a shot off?" I whispered, craning my neck to see out of the corner of the window.

He couldn't. Not without hitting the kids being dragged out of the trees, kicking, scratching, hollering.

"Why aren't they using their powers?" I whispered.

The other kids had to know these people weren't friendly, and we could hear them trying to get away, even in the face of the intruders' guns. Something else had to be preventing them from using their abilities. Something we couldn't see from up here.

The men in all black—they looked like monsters. They'd painted their faces to blend in with the green of the forest, and their body armor was as heavy as any soldier's going into war.

Just like the men who had kidnapped us in Pennsylvania.

213

Horror gripped me. This place . . . it had been Liam and Ruby's dream, and I'd turned it into a nightmare. The evil had chased me here, and now it was going to infect the lives of these innocent kids.

I switched off the safety and checked the cartridge, then slammed it back into place. I hadn't felt the heavy, bitter kiss of a gun in my hand since I was a child myself, when Vida had given me the training no one else was willing to. After, I'd sworn I'd never hurt anyone, let alone kill them. There wouldn't be any need. Not with the world we were creating.

We wouldn't need to fear every stranger and their intentions.

We wouldn't have to protect ourselves, or claim self-defense.

We wouldn't feel the cold brush of death on the backs of our necks every time we stepped outside.

My hand tightened on the gun. *You are not going to take these kids.*

"Where are you going?" Jen whispered as I approached the doorway. "Zu! You can't be serious!"

I shouldered past her, ignoring the protests of the others.

It was almost like the soldiers had sensed it, like they somehow knew the exact moment to truly crush me.

I only made it one step before the White Noise switched on.

The same second I realized I was still on my feet, I saw that no one else was.

The sound blared from speakers outside, enveloping the house like hurricane winds. It hummed and intermittently squealed. But it was just . . . there. Too loud, too aggressive in the way it invaded my skull, but there was nothing blistering about it.

Not for me.

Jen moaned, her legs curling toward her core, her hands jammed against her ears. Across the room, Ana was struggling to push herself up off the ground, swaying like she'd been drugged. A few feet away from her, Jacob craned his neck around, his face red and sweat-slick from the effort it took to push back against the White Noise.

"G-*go!*" he managed to get out.

I ran.

The explosion at the university, I thought, pounding down the stairs. I'd been standing so close to the speakers as they'd blown . . . My ears hadn't been able to pick up much of anything after, and while my hearing had eventually returned, it was completely possible that I just couldn't hear the mind-clawing frequency layered into the White Noise anymore.

Where is it coming from?

I forced myself to slow as I came down the last few steps. The hallway was a mess of paper and glass; the art that still clung to the walls was crooked or upside down.

Taking a deep breath, trying to envision how Vida would approach this, I raised my gun.

The floorboards near the door creaked. I spun toward the sound. A dark form dressed in head-to-toe black stood in the doorway, the barrel of his rifle aimed at my head.

Instead of raising my pistol, I threw up my left hand. His earpiece was enough. I seized control of that small bit of power and amplified it until it burst like a firecracker against the side of his face. The other electronics on him—the flashlight looped onto his belt, the scope on his rifle, the Taser—crackled, rippling as I drew a white-blue charge out of them. Their plastic casings made a horrible *snap*, like a bone breaking clean, just before they exploded.

"Fuck!"

The man screamed as he went down, trying to yank off his belt to pat down the fire. I started toward him, my mind darkening with the thought of finishing him, punishing him, for coming to this safe place. One step forward, one more. The gun was steady in my hands.

Two shadows moved along the exterior of the front windows, just beyond where he'd fallen to the floor, groaning. They streaked toward the porch; I wasted a second watching them through the patchwork of holes they'd made in the front door before turning and bolting.

I ran down the hall, passing through the living room and into the kitchen. The door that led outside from the laundry room was still locked, but I didn't take any chances. I drew the short curtain draped over the door's window to the side, keeping my back to the wall. A glint of silver caught my eye. I pulled the erasable chore chart off the wall beside me, angling its silver frame to reflect the space just outside the door.

No one was coming. I ducked out into the fog that had rolled up from the lake. The smell of damp earth was everywhere, mingled with gun smoke. The White Noise continued to blare; it was next to impossible to hear anything over it, including my own steps as I made my way deeper into the woods, trying to track the pulse of power the speakers emitted.

I glanced left, along the path. The same figures in black were pulling the limp bodies of kids down from the tree houses. I pivoted toward them, my finger so tight on the trigger of the gun I was surprised I didn't fire by mistake.

One by one, in a horrible chain, they dragged the kids farther down the path, toward the lake. My mind was screaming at me to fire, but . . .

I can't. I could maybe take down one of the men before alerting them to my location. I bit my lip hard enough to taste blood. No—I needed to stop the White Noise. I needed the others to be able to use their abilities to help me stop this.

"Come on . . . where are you?" I whispered. The White Noise filtered through the forest, blanketing every square inch of it until it seemed to be pouring out from everywhere and nowhere. It hadn't knocked me out, but the intensity of its core sound meant I couldn't focus on any one thought for long. I was navigating through the forest on sheer instinct, feeling out the charge.

I was so distracted that I tripped over the first speaker.

My knees absorbed the dull shock of my landing. I felt across the rocks and piles of mulch for the speaker's case. I hadn't uncovered any wires, which wasn't good news—it meant it wasn't connected to the other speakers, and I was likely going to have to find them one at a time.

I shook my head, letting that silver thread uncoil in my mind. My heart jarred as my power connected to the device. I coaxed the charge hotter, stronger, until the battery began to blister inside. The casing melted with a squeal, finally cutting off the sound.

Jumping to my feet, I braced a hand against the nearest tree and cast my gaze like a net, searching the trees.

Someone was screaming, begging, "Don't, *don't!*"

My jaw clenched. *Move,* I thought, *move!*

The tree to my right exploded, bullets turning its bark and leaves into splinters. A jagged shard caught me across the cheek, the shock and sting enough to make my eyes water and my vision swim. I dropped, falling beneath the line of fog, clutching at the place where warm blood was now dripping down over my chin.

None of it mattered. An electric circuit sang out from behind an overgrown fern, dousing everything in the audible fire that was White Noise.

Close—I was so close. The speaker's power licked at the fine hairs of my ears, my face, my neck. Mud seeped through my jeans as I crouched, focusing my attention on connecting to the device's power signature, even if I couldn't see it. This one must have been larger than the first, because the charge pushed back twice as hard against my senses.

A sharp pain snapped against the base of my skull. Tingling warmth exploded there, the sensation crawling up and down the length of my spine as my hands flew back, searching for the wound, for the place the bullet had cut through bone and nerve and muscle.

But it wasn't there. No blood, no gash—

As suddenly as the knifing pain had come on, it disappeared, throwing off my sense of balance. I barely caught myself on my hands as I tipped forward. Crawling, I tore at the mud and under-brush, calling to the silver thread in my mind, trying to spark it in the direction of the speaker.

Nothing.

A trill of panic, higher even than the White Noise, wormed its way into my chest.

There was no prickle of awareness of the speaker's power. No pulse of its current. No static to curl against my mind as I entered its circuit.

Nothing.

I staggered forward through the foliage until I found the device. I slapped my hand against the speaker's hard shell. I felt nothing. I was alone in my own body with only that emptiness in my head opening its jaws, devouring me whole.

There wasn't a single spark left in me.

My power was gone.

EIGHTEEN

"WHAT . . . THE HELL?"

I clenched my hair in my hands, squeezing my eyes shut, concentrating on the silver thread, imagining it there, coiled in my mind. The longer I crouched, my heart kicking at my ribs, the deeper I fell into that spiral of horror.

Someone screamed—they screamed *my name*.

I snapped back into myself, registering the weight of the gun in my hand and the reality of that moment. The White Noise was shredding the silence, and it seemed to only scream louder the longer I stood there, doing nothing, feeling nothing.

But in the dark chaos of the moment, a single, clarifying thought managed to get through.

"Like you need psionic powers to destroy a speaker, you idiot," I breathed out.

Shutting out the sounds and movement on all sides, I took aim and fired directly into the face of the device. It leaped off the ground as the shot pierced it. A second bullet finally silenced it.

The other speaker was close enough to track by sound alone.

I braced my feet against the ground, swiveling until my ears pricked with pain, pinpointing the direction of the sound. My gaze narrowed, searching through the fog, the darkness, the trees—everything that stood between it and me.

It was an impossible shot—impossible because I couldn't see to aim, and I couldn't get any closer, not with the men and kids on the trail. Instead, I pointed up, aiming at the thick arms of the oak that supported the unfinished frame of Tree House Ten.

It felt like the gun was trying to rocket out of my hand as I fired, unloading the clip on that branch. Bullets swarmed the trees like wasps, coming in from every direction, but I didn't stop shooting, not until the massive branch cracked.

I threw myself down as it split off the trunk. I heard, rather than saw, the branch crash to the ground, taking with it the beginnings of the tree house Liam had built. The wood pounded the ground, and, in the end, I hadn't needed to find the exact location of the speaker. The limb and debris buried it, muffling the White Noise.

A branch snapped behind me. I spun, catching a glimpse of something moving in the corner of my vision. I trained my gun at it.

At a girl.

The teen was a shade of white too pale to be truly healthy— her skin had hollowed out beneath her wide eyes, and her cheekbones looked too thin, like you could strip away her clothes and see where all of her blue veins connected to her beating heart. Full, dark lashes framed her startlingly blue eyes.

I relaxed, just slightly. At least one kid had gotten away from the tree houses.

"Are you all right?" I asked.

She reached up, touching the small gold flower charm on her necklace as she stared at me. Clearly overwhelmed by what was happening.

"You need to run," I told her quickly. "Go in through the back of the house and take the hatch in the laundry room out—the others have already gone ahead."

The girl smiled, but it didn't reach her eyes. "Thanks for letting me know."

I hadn't heard the man come up behind me, but I sure as hell felt the butt of his rifle cracking against the back of my skull.

Lights burst in my vision, and I dissolved into agony, into darkness.

"—u! Owen—!"

That was . . .

My legs dragged against the damp ground, feeling like they were filled with sand.

"Zu!"

That was . . . The name . . . Owen was . . . The thought was there in my mind, just out of reach. It fluttered beneath the insistent tug of sleep, and each time the name was called out, only one color flashed in my mind.

Red.

My eyes snapped open, and the memory of the last few hours crashed into me, taking the air out of my lungs.

Haven. The girl. The man in the black. The rifle.

Captured.

My hands . . . I tried to lift them, to claw at the tight pressure I felt at the back of my neck. The man, his radio buzzing just above my head, hauled me over stone and root and thorny brush. Everything below my waist felt like it had been carved from stone, but my upper body was air, so insubstantial that I wasn't sure I was even fully there.

The dirt suddenly softened beneath me, evening out. Blood rushed into my limbs along with that painful, hot sand sensation as feeling returned to them. The man had me by the scruff of my neck with one hand, twisting my shirt's collar until it choked me.

"Owen! Owen, don't!"

The fog wound up through the night, swirling the shades of midnight. I squeezed my eyes shut again, trying to clear the dizziness. When I forced them open once more, I couldn't see the house.

But I *could* see a kid, no more than thirteen, as he stepped onto the trail, standing between us and the rest of Haven. With his skin and shirt, Owen was as white as a ghost. An easy target.

I kicked at the ground, trying to slow our progress. Ahead, a handful of other soldiers in black were struggling with their own bundles of squirming, writhing weight. The kids kicked and clawed, and the men laughed. They *laughed* at us.

Why is no one using their abilities?

I reached for that silver thread in my mind again, but there was nothing, nothing, nothing. I couldn't feel my attacker's electronics any more than I could his heartbeat.

They can't, I realized. They must have all had that same block put on their minds as I did.

It could have been a sound that none of us could detect, or some unknown toxin mixed into the fog that closed off that part of our minds. It could have been a million things causing it, but the result was the same for all of us. For the first time in a decade, there was nothing inside me to call on. I had no power.

They've taken this from us, too, that rebellious voice whispered.

No. Even without our abilities, none of us were helpless. I shifted my weight sharply, hoping to startle the man into loosening his grip on me. Reaching back, I drew my broken nails against the hand gripping the back of my neck. But instead of finding skin, I scratched against thick, rough fabric.

He shifted his hand down, driving his fingers deeper into my neck. I twisted and strained, gasping to try to fill my lungs. Black exploded into my vision again. The pressure eased as my body went slack, but not enough to pull away.

"There's another one." The man's voice was rough and deep with amusement, but I couldn't tell who he was referencing, me or Owen.

Smoke curled in my nose, sharp and distinct. My gaze shot to the house, sure that the men had decided to torch it, to truly destroy every good thing.

Then fire raged at my back. Heat baked through my damp clothing in waves, stroking at my skin without burning it.

The man screamed, dropping me into the dark. As my vision cleared, I saw the flame at the center of his chest grow, then climb up over his head in a burning, golden wave.

The numbness hadn't affected all of us. Owen—Owen still had his power.

It was all I needed to see. I rolled away, stomach heaving at the stench of roasting flesh. Soon, it wasn't just one scream tearing through the air. I flipped over and pushed myself up onto my knees.

The men caught fire one by one, howling like the pack of wolves they were as it overcame them. I had the wild, fleeting thought that, from a distance, scattered in an arc on the trail, they looked like birthday candles.

The flames burned so bright, with such devastating intensity, the men only had mere seconds to scream before their lungs were singed.

As soon as the kids pulled themselves free, they ran for the house. It looked like all of them were unharmed beyond the roughing up the men had given them.

The kids gave a wide berth to the boy who still stood at the center of the trail, his gaze dispassionate as the figures that once had been men twisted into monstrous charred shapes on the ground. Wind carried the fire from their remains to the house, fanning them out over the siding and porch.

"Owen!" I called, jumping to my feet.

The boy turned his gaze on me.

This is why, that same dark voice whispered. Why it had been so easy to accept those controls Cruz and the others had put in place for us. Why that doubting part of me had been able to nod, to repeat their reasons for putting legal constraints on us. Why people would always be afraid, and why it had felt like we had to accept whatever small shred of freedom we'd been given.

No one should have power like this.

No one should be punished for using that power to protect themselves and others.

This was terrifying.

This was *necessary.*

My stomach rioted as I took another step closer to him. *He's a kid. He's just a kid.*

He *had* control. He didn't need to *be* controlled.

"Owen," I said, softer. "That's enough. . . ."

The rising flames from the house illuminated his face in a warm glow.

Then a flicker of awareness. Sudden fear, like that of a young child, pooled in his eyes.

"It's okay," I told him, holding out a hand. "You're all right—"

Haven's screen door slammed open and shut.

We both spun, but Owen was faster. Two men jumped down from the porch, guns drawn, and got no more than a step toward us before the first one went up in a horrifying *whoosh* of flame.

Blinded by fire and smoke, the first man ran, stumbling, back toward the house, collapsing onto one of the porch's wooden posts.

I couldn't move. My vision went dark at the edges, and I wasn't seeing the soldier, I was seeing Mel. I was seeing the Defenders, the reporters, the bystanders torn apart by the explosion.

Stop it, stop it, stop it— I shook my head, feeling like I was about to vomit. Within seconds, the flames had snaked up in the dark wood and spilled across the porch. The second man shot Owen a terrified look, freezing in place.

The boy only stared back. His forehead wrinkled, first in obvious confusion, then in outright alarm. He clutched at his head, letting out a soft moan of pain.

No. It had him, too.

The girl stepped out from behind the trees again as if materializing from the night sky. Her hands were in her oversize jacket's pockets, her gaze focused on Owen's hunched form. Her lips twisted in a cruel mockery of a smile.

Her?

As quickly as she'd appeared, she was gone again, fading back into the fog and darkness. It couldn't be a coincidence—the band of pressure tightened on my mind. Somehow, she was . . . the girl was doing this to us. But if Owen hadn't been immediately affected, it meant she had to target each Psi individually for her numbing grip to work.

Seeing an opportunity, the second soldier on the porch raised his gun.

"No!" I dove forward, throwing my arms around Owen to try to shield his small body.

A shot rang out.

A heavy body slumped to the ground, all clattering equipment and rustling fabric. When I didn't feel the bite of a bullet, I pulled back, hands flying over Owen, inspecting him, feeling for the wound, for blood.

"Okay," he mumbled, the words shaking with the rest of him. "I'm okay."

A cry sounded. One of the soldiers, a woman, charged at us from where she'd been combing the woods, her equipment rattling. She got no more than a few steps before her body suddenly lurched up into the air with the impact of a bullet, slamming into a nearby tree.

Owen and I turned just as Roman burst through the swirl of smoke and ash, taking aim at one of the soldiers fleeing with a kid on his back. His eyes narrowed as he adjusted his arms, then fired—piercing the soldier in that slice of exposed skin on his neck, between the girl's torso and the man's bulletproof vest.

"See? It's not always the worst thing to arrive late to a party," Priyanka called over to him, covered by a different tree. There was a slight edge to the words as she added, "Never underestimate the power of a dramatic surprise entrance. You okay, Zu?"

They didn't run.

Snapping out of my shock, I dragged Owen behind the nearest tree, trying to cover him as much as I could with my body.

"Zu?" she called again.

"Okay!" I shouted back, my voice raw from the smoke and the staggering relief that arrived both unexpected and uncontained.

They're trying to help.

They should have run—but somehow, they'd known something was coming, and they'd tried to warn us. They'd rushed into the fray to help all these kids.

The two teens who had been guarding them burst out of the trees, rushing past me. Each had a sobbing kid clinging to their back.

"Owen," I said, leaning down to look him in the eye. His skin was feverish to the touch. "You need to go with them, all right?"

"I can help," he said quietly.

The heavy smoke fell over us like a curtain. Even when I breathed through my mouth, I could taste it coating my tongue.

And Owen . . . He flinched at every gasp or soft cry as the kids who'd been guarding the hole crossed paths with the charred remains of the soldiers.

"You already did," I promised. "The only way you can help now is to go with them to safety."

One of the guards held out her hand to Owen, urging him forward. He pulled away from me, but instead of taking the girl's hand, he raised his arms.

"What are you doing?" I asked him. "Owen!"

The flames narrowed and rose like mountains where they covered the house, invincible, gorging themselves on the pure air and wood frame. But then Owen smashed his hands together with a single loud clap, and, all at once, they were smothered.

With one last reluctant look at me, he ran after the others.

A second too late to warn them, I remembered the girl, how I'd told her where to go to find the Haven kids who had already evacuated.

Thanks for letting me know.

That had been before the fire. She, or one of the soldiers, would have had time to go after them. To hurt them.

I spotted Roman as he ducked behind a tree, taking a moment to reload his gun.

Stopping only long enough to pick up the pistol that had fallen from the female soldier's hand, I soared toward him like an arrow. Bullets thundered through the air as I ran.

Roman spun toward me, a wild look of relief on his face as I slammed into the trunk, dropping down beside him. One hand reached out, cupping the back of my head to draw me closer. He had to shout to be heard over the gunfire. "Are you all right? Tell me they didn't hurt you—"

No—no time for that—

"They know how to find the kids," I gasped out. "They're going to go after them!"

His body went rigid. "Like hell they are. Priya!"

Priyanka was all color and motion, backlit by the lingering patches of fire in the trees. She ran for us, dropping to slide on her hip and leg across the last few feet of mud. Wincing, she said, "Okay, don't let me do that again. Looks awesome, feels terrible—"

Roman cut her off. "There's some kind of crawl space or escape route out of the house." He glanced at me, confirming. I nodded. "They found out where it is. Can you take care of it while we finish here?"

Her expression turned grave. "Yeah. Where is it?"

"Under the dryer in the laundry room," I said. "There might still be a few kids trapped upstairs in the attic. Call out for Jacob when you get inside and let him know we've got everyone."

She nodded, tossing her long hair back over her shoulder. "I'm going to remind you that heroes frequently die, but the morally mediocre people almost always live to see another day. Don't do anything that's going to piss me off."

And with that, Priyanka bolted for the house, leaving us to cover her as one of the remaining soldiers opened fire from somewhere in the forest. The screen door snapped shut behind her, then fell completely off its frame. A section of the porch collapsed with a sigh of cracking wood, burying the bodies there.

I reached out, gripping Roman's arm to reclaim his attention. "You should have run. What are you even doing here?"

Streaks of soot covered Roman's face, and his dark hair had fallen into his eyes, but it was impossible to miss their startling shade of blue. It burned in the darkness, pulling me in a bit closer.

There was a quiet catch in his throat, as if he'd skipped a breath. Then his dark lashes lowered, and he allowed himself a ghost of a smile. "We would have come sooner, except that noise—you took care of it, didn't you? The second I pulled myself back up off the ground, I thought, *There's going to be nothing left for us to do but watch as you sweep up the rest of them.*"

I straightened at the words, only to realize there had been nothing mocking in them. His genuine tone and that slight, almost amazed curve of his lips made me brace a hand against the ground, unsteady.

"I'm the reason they're here," I whispered back as he turned back to the forest, adjusting his grip on the weapon. "This is *my* fault. That stupid phone—"

He reached over, gripping my shoulder. "It's not your fault. If anything, it's mine. I should have thought of it. I know better. I *know* how people like this work. You were the one who did everything right in this situation."

"I should have known, too," I said, shaking my head.

In the panic after the power went out, I hadn't even thought to wonder how they'd anticipated the attack. But now that Roman was here, in front of me, as calm and steady as always, I reclaimed some small bit of center. Of clarity. "How did you and Priyanka know we'd plugged it in?"

He risked a glance at me. "We heard the helicopters in the distance. We'd been so careful on the drive not to be followed or seen, so it was the only explanation either of us could come up with."

There was another faint scream in the distance—a girl's. We both whirled toward it.

"What do you want to do?" Roman asked.

"Split up," I said, starting to rise. "You go left, I go right, and we meet back up at the lake. Is that where the helicopters landed?"

He shook his head. "There wasn't room to land. They dropped them. That gives us some time while they wait for transport."

I nodded, breathing in the smoky air. My eyes held that image of him rising from the ground, so solid and unafraid.

"You should have left," I said again. *Thank you for not leaving.*

"Come together," he said, "leave together."

Before I could respond, Roman's expression shifted again. The searing look of determination became what could only be pain.

Not pain. *Agony.*

Roman's breath exploded out of him as it hit. One hand shot out, feeling through the air for something to grip—something to use for balance. It landed on my outstretched arm, and I had to fight to keep him from collapsing back onto the ground.

He shook his head, sweat beading on his face with the force of the cry he was holding in.

"Roman!" I said.

This wasn't like the migraine before; that had been as simple as something unplugging his consciousness. Now his body locked, jerking as if the pain had its hands on his throat and was slowly strangling him.

"What's wrong?" I demanded, checking his pulse, gripping his face in my hands to keep him from pounding his skull against the rocks. "What's happening? *Roman!*"

"Kids . . . get . . . kids . . ." he gasped out. *"Go!"*

I let him fall against me, sliding my hands beneath his shirt, feeling along the hard lines of his back and shoulders for a bullet wound or shrapnel or anything to explain why his gaze had gone so unfocused. His fingers tightened on my forearm, pressing hard enough to bruise. A warning.

"You know I don't like having to do this."

The girl. She tucked her hands into the pockets of her jacket, tossing her long hair over her shoulder. "You make this so hard. I don't know how else to get through to you."

I looked between her and Roman. His lips were moving, struggling to get the words out. She wasn't just locking his mind, it looked like she was *attacking* it.

Roman cried out, his legs thrashing on the ground as she took another step forward.

"I'm trying to help you. I should kill you myself for what you did. I'm supposed to, you know. Kill you. Some days, I even think I might want to." Her voice was low, seething. It was only then, with the clarity of the hate in those words, that I realized the gunfire had stopped. "I don't know what happened to you, Roman, but you need help. It's not too late. Come with me, and I'll make sure you're safe. I'll protect you."

I stood up, gun in hand. A cold fury gripped me, steadying my aim. "Whatever you're doing to him—to all of us—stop."

That dead-eyed smile was like a single fingernail running down my spine. "No."

I licked the sweat off my top lip. My finger tightened on the trigger. "Then give me one reason not to kill you."

"Because," Roman said weakly from behind me. "She's my sister."

NINETEEN

"LANA . . ."

The girl's gaze had been trained on me, unblinking. Now she turned toward Roman, her eyes narrowing with a look of outrage.

Lana.

Roman used the tree to pull himself up from the ground. He staggered forward, his knees bobbing dangerously. His eyes looked glassy, almost feverish with pain.

Fury stormed through me, and I didn't bother to stop it. She was going to kill him—she was going to kill him, and the only way to stop her was to kill her first.

Don't make me do this, I thought, watching her.

"We had to go," he said. "We had to. All of this time, we've been looking for *you.*"

The knowing, after all these days of guessing, slammed into me like a fist.

I was right.

She was shaking her head, backing away. "You're the one who needs help. I'm trying to save you! I'm going to save you!"

Someone called out for her.

"Here!" she yelled back, ignoring the gun I had trained on her. "Here! I found him!"

"Don't . . . don't . . ." Roman's voice was faint. "Solnyshko . . ."

Then I felt it. The twist.

It was like molten liquid pouring into my skull. A scream tore out of my throat. Every joint in my body strained, stretching and contorting. I hit the ground, banging my left side against the root of the massive tree. The gun slipped from my hand, spinning across the dirt and leaves.

Through the blur of tears and smoke, I saw one of the soldiers approach us, dragging a boy after him. Fear shot through me as I struggled to get my hands against the ground, to push myself up.

"Stop, Lana!" he begged. "I'll come with you, all right? Please—don't do this!"

"You'll come with us no matter what," Lana said. "*This*"—I screamed again as the boiling pressure increased—"is so you understand that there are *consequences* to your actions."

A shot cracked out. The soldier was there, and then he wasn't. A spray of blood burst from his neck, and he stumbled back, pressing a gloved hand to it. The shock of the hit made him release his grip on the boy, who bolted the instant he was free. Some of the heat in my mind eased enough for me to lift my head and look for Roman.

But the shot had come from the remaining section of the porch. The gun was still smoking in Priyanka's hands as she lowered it, her eyes going wide.

"Lana!" The word broke from her like a joyful sound, only to be fractured by disbelief.

"Stay back!" I managed to shout through the agony. "Don't come any closer—"

The girl turned, and I wished I could have seen her expression—if it was still that tight mask of rage, or if it mirrored Priyanka's exhilaration as it faded into horror.

Priyanka looked first to Roman, then to me, before turning back to Lana.

"What are you doing?" Priyanka jumped down off the porch, her long legs quickly closing the distance between them. Lana tried to back away, refusing to look at her.

The distraction Priyanka provided was enough for the painful heat and pressure in my skull to momentarily ease. I drew myself up enough to try crawling across the ground, straining to reach the gun I'd lost.

"What do you think?" Lana spat. She looked between the three of us with all the feral suspicion of an animal that knew it was about to be cornered.

Priyanka stopped, and, like there was some magnetic force between them, Lana froze in place as well.

"I really don't know," Priyanka said softly. "Explain it to me while we get the hell out of here."

Something switched off in her, and Lana's tone went flat again. "You're not going anywhere. You're mine."

"You're damn right I am, Sunshine," Priyanka said, trying for a pained smile as she knelt down beside Roman, checking his pulse.

Oh, I thought, putting that much together as well.

"That's not . . ." Lana began. Her nostrils flared as she took in a heavy, uneven breath. "Don't. You know what I meant."

"I know a lot of things," Priyanka said slowly, rising again. Roman tried to follow, but could only get himself onto his knees.

"I know the Lana I loved wouldn't hurt others, especially not her brother."

"Just like Pri would never leave me, right?" Lana seethed.

Priyanka struggled to control her expression, but her eyes gave her away. "What's happened to you?"

Lana clenched her fist, taking a step forward. "He made me stronger. No one, not even you, will hurt me again. He's the one who took care of me. And now he's the only one who deserves my loyalty."

One word rose through the pain ratcheting up in my mind. *Who?*

"Who . . . the hell . . . is *he*?" I got the words out through gritted teeth. Both of them ignored me, wholly focused on each other.

Priyanka held out her hand. "Just . . . come with me. We've been trying to find you—this whole time, we've been trying to reach you."

"Liar," Lana whispered, but she didn't back up again. She stared at Priyanka's outstretched hand. It trembled where it hung in the air, and I could see in her face, no matter how hard she was working to disguise it, that Priyanka was halfway to heartbreak.

Still, she took another step toward Lana. "We have so much work to do, remember?"

Whatever daze had taken over Lana's mind was ripped away. *"No."*

The gun's register sounded a split second after the bullet slammed into the tree inches from Lana's head. Jacob had taken position on the porch and was already lining up his next shot. The boy I'd seen before hung behind him, tears streaming down his cheeks as he spoke, clearly explaining what was happening.

In the distance, helicopter blades sliced through the night air, growing louder by the second. Priyanka lunged for Lana in that moment of interruption, but the girl was faster, both on her feet and in processing her odds. She crashed through the underbrush, jumping over a downed log before disappearing into the trees.

"No!" Priyanka called, running after her. "Lana!"

My vision split in two as the band of pressure around my mind released with a hard snap of pain. Roman shuddered and gasped beside me.

Static roared through my mind, my ears, filling my veins. The welcome caress of power fired through me, erasing the terrifying silence in my mind.

"You all right?" Jacob called, jogging over.

I waited for the dizziness to pass before accepting his help up.

Roman had shoved himself up onto his feet, turning to follow the path Lana and Priyanka had taken through the woods.

"They still have Sasha!" the boy shouted from the porch.

Shit. I gripped Roman's arm. "Go after Lana, I'll—"

At that, Roman gave his head a hard shake, pulling away. "No, I'll go. Can you find Priya?"

I was still just disoriented enough that it took me a second to comprehend his words, and by then, he was already running, stooping to pick up a different gun from the ground. Then he disappeared, too, wrapped in darkness and smoke.

Jacob put a hand on my shoulder, making me jump. "You okay?"

"Is it just Sasha?" I asked.

He nodded and the relief was so pure, it brought tears close to the surface again.

"Take him," I said, angling my head toward the boy. "We'll bring Sasha."

"I'm taking that as your definitive vote for trusting them," he said, wiping the sweat off his face.

I turned back toward the smoldering forest, scanning for any sign of movement. "I tend to find saving kids from being kidnapped and murdered pretty endearing."

He clucked his tongue. "Makes it unanimous, then. She saved both my and Jen's asses when she busted into the house. Consider her extra endearing."

More than that, though, I finally understood what was going on. The darkness I'd sensed at their edges, shaping their lies, hadn't been some horrible intention. It had been a person, and she was nothing I ever could have imagined.

Like us, but not.

I took off, calling out Priyanka's name as I moved off the trail and into the woods. My mind raced. What Lana could do . . . the fact that she could affect our minds the way she had, suppressing our powers and driving stakes of pain directly into our nerves, made me think she might be Orange-classified. The only two I'd known, Ruby and Clancy, hadn't had the exact same ability, after all. He could plant suggestions, manipulate feelings, and maneuver bodies, but only Ruby had been able to directly affect someone's memory.

I slid to a stop at the sight of Priyanka coming toward me, her arms crossed tight against her chest, her head down. Her whole body shook, and her face looked as if every emotion had been wrung out of her.

"Are you all right?" I jogged toward her.

She shook her head, momentarily unable to find the words. Priyanka looked . . . not helpless, but lost. "I couldn't . . . I wasn't enough. I couldn't make her stay."

I didn't know what to say other than "I don't think anyone could have."

"I could have. I *should* have. But I promised Roman not to take it too far." Even though she didn't repeat them, I saw the echo of the words on her face. *I wasn't enough.*

"I thought she'd head back toward the lake for the helicopter extraction," Priyanka explained, her voice betraying her exhaustion, "but it's like she became the darkness. She must have gone a different direction. I couldn't make her stay . . . I couldn't make her stay."

The words, how she kept repeating them, made Priyanka sound like she was drifting away. I gripped her arm, trying to steady her.

"Do you want to look for her?" I asked. "The ground's damp enough that we can probably track her with better light."

In truth, I didn't want to go after the girl who had just tried to hard-boil my brain. But I couldn't take the thought of her out there, doing what she did to another Psi. It hadn't just been the way she'd hurt us. It had been the way she'd *relished* it.

"No. If we keep chasing her, she'll run farther and faster," Priyanka said miserably, rubbing her forehead. "We have to find a way to get her to come to us."

When I didn't answer, Priyanka must have read my thoughts on my face. "Listen . . . Lana is . . . She's different."

"I missed that part," I said wryly.

She bit her lip. "She's not herself. That's not *her.* I don't know what they've done to her, but that's not the Lana I knew."

"Let me guess, she's usually a ray of sunshine." I remembered the nickname Priyanka had used a second too late to stop myself. "Sorry."

She lifted a hand, waving it off. When I started back toward the house, she followed.

"But clearly there's a connection between her and the kidnappers," I pressed. "So what's the story there?"

Priyanka looked like she might be physically ill. "I . . . think that the kidnappers might have actually been after me and Roman. I'm sorry—I'm *so* sorry. I wasn't sure until I saw Lana here. He . . . they must be trying to drag us back."

I wasn't sold on her theory. There were still too many pieces to this that didn't fit together. The warning on the teleprompter, for one. And if the kidnappers were just after Roman and Priyanka, why stage a whole explosion? But a larger question loomed.

"Who's 'they'?" I asked. "The Psion Ring? She mentioned a 'he' too. That 'he' made her stronger."

Her expression was so distant, I wasn't sure she'd heard me until, at last, she said, "I don't know. Someone could have . . . someone could have taken over the Psion Ring. Changed things. They didn't use to work with non-Psi, but things . . . they change. We weren't supposed to leave. Ever. Someone wants us back."

Priyanka seemed to be genuinely struggling to pull herself together enough to speak. "When we left, she didn't come with us. We never should have left her, but it was unavoidable. It was, I swear."

"I believe you," I said, startled by how badly she seemed to need me to understand. Her eyes were haunted.

"We tried to make contact with her, but we couldn't reach her. And in the meantime, they've done *this* to her. . . ." Her hand slid up, clenching in her hair.

"Are you talking about her power?" I asked. "It seemed like she could be some kind of Orange, but how could she do *that*?"

"I don't know, I don't know—they've— Lana was a gentle, sparkling person, not—not whatever *that* was." Priyanka looked near tears. "Somehow, they've trained her to hurt people. I shouldn't have left her."

I couldn't keep my family together, Roman had said. *I couldn't save my sister in the end.*

In a way, he'd tried to tell me the truth. As much as he'd been able to while still protecting her. At the time, I thought he meant that his sister had died, so I hadn't pressed him on it, knowing the exact degree of pain that came with blaming yourself for another person's death.

"She's still in there," Priyanka said. "I know she is. She hasn't taken off my mother's necklace—that little gold flower, did you see? I know she seems angry, but there's still love in her. We can reach her."

I hadn't sensed any of this supposed love, and was covered with enough cuts and bruises to make a strong counterargument. But Priyanka's feelings for Lana were unequivocal.

"Why did you want to come here?" I asked.

"Because we'd heard about Daly—about your friend, Ruby," Priyanka said. "We'd heard that Lana might have left the Psion Ring, and we were hoping she'd be here, or your friends might have heard something. I was so stupid to think she could have gotten away from them."

My thoughts were too tangled to put them into words.

"You were right to hope they would help," I said. "They would have, no questions asked. But they're not here. About two weeks ago, Ruby went missing on a run to pick up another kid."

The wind ruffled the trees overhead.

"Holy shit," Priyanka breathed out. "Seriously?"

Her voice was lost to the scream of a helicopter ripping through the air overhead—moving not toward the lake, but away from it. Priyanka and I exchanged a look.

We took off together, weaving through the forest back to the trail, only to find that Roman was already there. He ran up the dirt path at a steady clip, Sasha clinging to his back, her tear-streaked face pressed against his shoulder.

"It's done," he said quietly, then looked to Priyanka. She shook her head.

"We should go," I said. But Roman had turned again to the forest, that hard look of determination back on his face. We didn't have time to chase after someone who didn't want to be found, not right now. "Come together, leave together. Right?"

His eyes found mine, but the prickling heat I felt at the base of my skull had nothing to do with that look, and everything to do with a familiar power signature nearby.

Drone.

I was running again, leaving the others to follow as I moved up the path. My feet slowed until, finally, I saw it. The spiderlike device whirred as it floated over the bodies of the soldiers, passing over the scene in slow, intentional passes. It lit the ground beneath it, which only would have been necessary if it was taking photos or video.

Miguel had destroyed the phone with the original set of photos—but if this device had photos of our attackers, I wanted it. As Mel always said, people want to believe, they just needed a narrative plausible enough to justify it. Mine, at least, had the benefit of being true.

I heard Priyanka and Roman catch up behind me, but didn't turn. I began unraveling the silver thread of power in my mind, only to cut it off. It would be too easy to fry it and render it useless. So, instead, I raised the pistol. The drone was about as big as a cat, which was probably not a comparison I should have let my brain make as I tracked its movement and aimed.

"What are you doing?" Roman whispered.

The drone hovered low over the porch, scanning for something. I took a deep breath in, adjusted the angle of my arms, then fired.

The bullet tore through one of its wings. It bobbed, trying to adjust and forcing me to shoot out a second one. The drone crashed into the charred wood of the porch, skidding across it.

"Careful," Priyanka warned as I approached it. "The camera's probably feeding directly to someone."

"Good," I said, gripping the drone and turning it over. Glancing back over my shoulder, I found Roman watching me, his anxious expression fading. Priyanka knelt beside one of the soldiers, searching his pockets and belt, removing his flashlight and sliding something into the pocket of her jeans.

The drone's propellers stopped spinning, but there was still a small red light on beside the glossy camera lens.

I brushed the dirt off it, just so it would have as clear an image as possible.

"I don't know who the hell you are," I said. "But if you come at me or my loved ones again, you better pray to God you actually kill me, because I'm right behind you and I've got nothing else to lose."

The red light blinked off.

TWENTY

AT THE END OF THE LONG, CRUDE TUNNEL DUG BENEATH Haven was a storm drain that opened into a trash-strewn field. We found the others there, sitting together in a tight cluster, the kids leaning against each other's shoulders and backs, fighting to keep their eyes open.

Lisa and Miguel had gathered the late arrivals from the tree houses and were tending to cuts and bumps, plying them with water and tight hugs. The first-aid kits open in the wild grass already looked empty.

Roman climbed out of the sludge-filled pipe first. Ankle-deep in the sopping-wet mess, he took Sasha's arm and steadied her as she took the big step down. Priyanka used his shoulder for balance as she followed the girl toward where Jacob and some of the others were sorting through a pile of soot-stained belongings. Someone must have gone back into the house to gather up a few things to take with them.

Finally, Roman turned back toward me, raising his hands as if to help me down the way he had Sasha. Instead, he hesitated, ghosting a touch over my forearm before I took his hand and stepped down. Roman stared at his own hand the whole time, as if he had to focus all his attention on this simple task.

"Are you all right?" I asked him.

Roman startled, glancing up at me through his mussed dark hair. "I'm not hurt."

"I meant about Lana," I said. "Priyanka explained to me a little of what happened. I wish you had just been honest with me."

"I should have," he said. "I'm sorry, Suzume."

"Zu," I corrected.

He met my eyes again. "Zu. I know it doesn't matter, and I don't expect forgiveness, but I wanted to tell you the truth a thousand times."

"But you also wanted to protect your sister," I said. *From me.*

"She's been surrounded by danger from all sides since the day her powers manifested. There's almost nothing I wouldn't do to protect her. To reach her," Roman said. Then he added, somewhat ruefully, "Lying to someone who was supposed to stay a stranger didn't feel like that big of a sacrifice at the time."

"Funny," I said. "I was trying to keep you a stranger, too." If there was one thing I was always going to understand, it was doing whatever it took to protect the people you loved. "I set up you and Priyanka to be captured when we got to Haven. Can we call it even?"

His face went slack as my words sank in and he replayed that moment in his mind. To my surprise, he laughed softly, pressing his hand to his head and tilting it back. My eyes fixed on the strong line of his jaw, where there was a small scar just below his right cheek. "Priyanka was right. I'm an idiot. You, on the other hand, are amazing."

It was spoken as a simple, direct statement of fact. It made me want to believe him, to let that warmth permeate my whole self until it became reality. But all I needed to do was look around me to find the truth. "Yes, amazing at ruining lives."

The humor left his expression. "That's not true."

"Isn't it?" I said. "I shouldn't have turned on the phone. I'm not stupid. I really do know better, but I did it anyway, and I brought hell down on these kids. I destroyed the one place they felt safe."

I'd almost single-handedly killed this dream. The thought of facing Ruby and Liam now left my chest too tight to breathe.

"You did what any of us would have," he said. "For all we know, they could have been tracking it even when it was off."

"They would have caught up to us before we ever made it out of Nebraska," I pointed out.

He gave me a stern look. "You're interrupting my attempt to make you feel better."

"You know what would make me feel a lot better?" I told him. "Another rousing rendition of 'Cheer Up, Eileen.'"

"Well, all right." Roman sucked in a deep breath.

I held up my hands, stopping him. "Kidding."

Roman's face turned more sober the longer he watched me. "I meant what I said before. If you hadn't gotten the noise turned off, none of us would have made it out of there. Everyone pulls a bad card. What matters is how you ultimately play it. You didn't run. You stayed and fought."

"So did you."

Roman ducked his head slightly, absorbing the gratitude in my words. "You had it handled."

Behind him, Priyanka broke away from Jacob and the older

teens and strode toward one of the clusters of kids. She swung the powered-down drone out in front of her.

"Hello, tiny Psilings!" she said, forcing brightness into her voice. "I'm your new friend Priyanka, and I'm going to show you how to disassemble a drone and steal its useful parts!"

Roman turned, watching as she knelt beside them. "She's not hurt, either."

I knew what he meant. "They were together?"

He nodded, his composure slipping just enough for bone-deep exhaustion to slip into his voice. "We've all been close since we were kids, but the two of them became something more. They were serious for about two years. From the time we were sixteen until just before we left her."

"And when was that?"

"About six months ago."

What felt recent to me was probably a lifetime to them.

"Zu! Are you all right?" Lisa called, waving me over. Several of the kids nearby watched Roman and me with big eyes. I had to look away from their ashen faces.

"One second!" I shouted back, then looked to him. "I have to tell you something. Ruby has been missing for about two weeks, and Liam's in the wind. If you want to go after Lana, then this is where we're going to have to split up. I need to find them."

Roman looked deeply troubled by that information.

"What?" I asked.

"I don't think we should split up," he said. "Hear me out—I don't think it's a coincidence that your friend went missing just before someone tried to kidnap you."

"I had the same thought, but Priya believes the kidnappers were after you," I said. "That it might be the Psion Ring."

He gave his head a sharp shake. "No, Lana is working with someone else and she's trying to . . . force us into the fold, the way she was. Somehow, all of this is connected."

"You think someone forced her to do this?" I asked, trying to subdue my disbelief. But even as I doubted that, Priyanka's insistence that something was different about her kept rising back up in my mind.

"I think she's been . . . programmed. What's the word?"

"Brainwashed," I supplied. "You really think so? I've seen Reds who have gone through conditioning, and they can barely function beyond taking orders."

The thought made me look back across the field, searching for, and finding, Owen's small form sitting away from the others.

"You don't know her," Roman insisted. "Lana changed. Someone has planted a seed of rage in her. They've done something to her. There's no other explanation for why she's like this."

Lana did seem troubled, but not in the way the Reds who had undergone Project Jamboree were. That reconditioning had been like a disease of the mind, one that stomped out their spark of life. But Roman, obviously, would know how Lana had changed better than I would.

"If we found your friend Ruby together, could . . . could she help Lana?" he asked, the words shaking slightly, as if with barely restrained hope. "Get through to her?"

"Ruby's problem is that she can't *not* help, so yes, I think she would try," I said, wondering at how that little bit of heaviness eased away from me at the word *together*. "I agree with you that, somehow, all of this—the kidnapping, the frame job, the attack—is connected. Ruby's a piece of it I don't understand. You see things more clearly than I do."

"That's not true," he said, almost abashed. This was a thing with him, I realized. He'd always swat down my attempts to compliment him, but when it came to praising me or Priyanka, he refused to let us do the same. "You knew right away Priyanka and I were lying."

"No offense, but neither of you actually are good liars," I said. "And anyway, someone once reminded me that there are benefits to staying together."

"Two more sets of eyes to keep watch," he confirmed.

"Two more sets of hands to find food," I finished.

I could do this alone. I knew that, and I could see in his faint trace of a smile that he did, too. When he looked at me, he didn't see a little girl who needed to be carried and protected. He didn't see someone who needed to be saved.

I could find Ruby—and catch up to Liam in the process—and I could figure out who was behind all of this by myself. I just didn't want to if I didn't have to.

A sharp snap of static bit both of us as I brushed past his shoulder. Roman let out another surprised, breathless laugh.

"Sorry," I said. "Comes with the territory, as you know."

"Yes," he said, that small smile fading.

I accepted his offered arm for balance as we navigated through the mud and released it just as quickly. I was too conscious of everything. The warmth of his skin, the tight band of muscle over his bones, the bump of my hip against his as I straightened. I started toward Lisa, only to be caught again by his soft voice.

"I don't want to be your stranger."

I glanced back. "Then don't be."

Watercolors couldn't have begun to capture the sky in that moment, just as it prepared to brighten for dawn. The cruelest truth about life is that it just goes on—the sun rises, gravity keeps your feet on the ground, flowers open their faces to greet the sky. Your world could be dissolving with grief or pain or anger, but the sky would still give you the most breathtaking sunrise of violet warming to shell pink.

Miguel and Lisa sent me twin looks of relief as I came toward them. Jacob stepped back, allowing me to join their circle.

"I'm sorry," I said, my throat aching. "I should never have come back here."

"Don't say that," Lisa said. "Ruby and Liam would have wanted you to come. You were exhausted and under incredible stress. One of us should have thought to check the phone."

"But the house . . ." I closed my eyes, and all I could see were Ruby and Liam standing at the edge of the collapsed porch, their dream reduced to ash and cinders.

"I'm not going to pretend this doesn't completely suck," Jacob said. "They left us in charge, and while we got everyone out, it still hurts. But Haven is people, not a house. You could ask anyone here and they'd tell you that. As long as we can take care of each other, it doesn't matter what roof is over our heads."

I nodded, but the guilt didn't ease.

"—and this is the standard prop," Priyanka said, from somewhere behind me. "It pulls the quadcopter-style drone through the air, while the pusher prop at the back does what the name implies and pushes it forward. This is the memory card, which I will be taking with me. Ooh, and do you know what this is?" She paused for effect. "A *motor mount*. You should always check to make sure it isn't cracked and the screws aren't loose."

I looked back, just in time to see several small heads nod, riveted. My eyes found Roman, whether they meant to or not. Sasha had waved him over and sat him down in the center of a circle of younger kids. Judging by her big hand gestures and the way stoic Roman's cheeks were going pink, she was clearly regaling them with the story of her escape. Another one of the girls stood up and helpfully smoothed down his mussed hair for him.

"—emergency plan is already in play," Jacob was saying, pulling my attention back to him.

"Are those the supply bags?" I asked, nodding to the large camping backpacks interspersed among the kids. Liam had mentioned them to me in passing during my last trip; they were outfitted with just about everything you could need for living rough for a while. The black trash bags they'd been wrapped in were currently being used by the kids as blankets to cover the ground.

"They are," Lisa said. "There's food, water, first-aid kits, and just about anything else you could want. It'll tide us over until Liam's dad and his friends get here."

At my surprised look, Miguel held up a flip phone. "Sent the distress-code word as soon as I was through the tunnel. He's checking the backup shelter for squatters and any monitoring, but he should be here fairly soon."

A backup shelter. I took in a deep breath, eyes closing for a moment. That was a small relief, even though I'd never doubted that Liam and Ruby would have some kind of emergency plan in place if the house was exposed.

"And then what?" I asked.

"We'll find a new house, or build one," Lisa said. "And the littles will come to love that place, too."

I glanced over to where Owen was sitting, alone. A few of

the kids tentatively tried to approach him, to lay careful, hesitant hands on his shoulder, but he didn't react to any of their touches. He stared straight ahead, toward the sunrise. I knew, without seeing them, how empty those big dark eyes would be.

"What are your plans, Zu?" Miguel asked. "There's room for you here with us."

"I'm going to go find them," I said.

"I thought you would say that," Lisa admitted. "I'd rather have you safe here with us."

"People are looking for me," I reminded her. "As much as I want to stay, you guys will never be fully safe if I'm with you. Not until I fix this mess."

"With them?" Jacob clarified, tilting his head in their direction.

I glanced back at them—Priyanka, still showing the kids various parts of the drones, letting one of the Yellows zap what I assumed was a tracking device in it, and Roman, dropping a daisy chain he'd made onto Sasha's head like a crown. She beamed up at him, the white flowers like stars in her dark hair.

"Yeah," I said. "I think I can handle them."

"Figured as much," Miguel said. "You'd better take the getaway car."

"Getaway car?"

"Liam stashed a Toyota sedan in the woods, about a hundred yards past that line of trees," Lisa said, pointing across the field. "Bring one of the packs with you. It'll have everything you need, including a burner and a charger for it."

I shook my head. I'd already taken far too much from them. "I can't—"

"You can," Lisa assured me. "We won't need it."

That's what it came down to in the end. Need. If nothing else, we needed the burner, both to communicate and for Priyanka to create another device to make the cameras blink. Need made us do things, take things, we never would have otherwise.

"Please," Miguel said. "Just try to check in with us. If you get any information, to let us know you're okay . . ."

"I'll try," I promised.

"Wait," Lisa said suddenly, turning back toward the pile of items salvaged from the house. Digging under some of the drawings, she pulled out a singed photograph and handed it to me. "I thought you might want this. I grabbed it from their room."

It was a picture from five years ago, taken by Vida, of me, Chubs, Ruby, and Liam standing in front of Betty the van, out in the middle of the forest near Lake Prince in Virginia.

At the time, Liam had wanted to go looking for Betty so he could bring her in and fix her up. But by the time we found the old van, nature had done its worst to her engine and undercarriage. It would have been a nightmare to try to get a tow truck in there to haul her out. So we left Betty behind, as a kind of monument to what we had done together—who we had been together.

Liam had taken one of the hubcaps, though; he tucked it under one arm and Ruby under the other.

I looked so young in the photo, dressed in bright pink, face beaming. My hair was in a long pixie cut and the way I was smiling so wide made me seem almost impish. Chubs had glanced up at the sky, clearly exasperated by something that Vida had said the instant before she took the picture. Liam was looking over my head, smiling in Ruby's direction. She was still in a walking cast after what happened at Thurmond, and was leaning back against

Betty's passenger door for balance. Her smile was small, but . . . peaceful.

I thought Chubs had had the only copy of it. He'd shredded it an hour before he testified in front of Cruz, UN representatives, and interim members of Congress that he no longer considered them friends, and that he had no idea where on earth they'd gone.

I took the scrap of memory, tucking it into my back pocket for safekeeping.

"Are Lee and Ruby going to meet us there?" I heard a boy ask Lisa. He twisted his hands together, turning his fingers into anxious knots. "Are they going to be able to find us?"

They are, I thought, *because I'm going to bring them back to you.*

But before I went looking, there was one last person I needed to talk to.

Roman looked up as I walked by him and headed for the lone figure sitting a few dozen feet away.

Owen had scrubbed the soot from his face, but the attack had left its mark on him. His expression was vacant as he held a blanket to his chest despite the heat. It was obvious that even his small stature and quiet, almost doe-like nature wasn't enough to fully counteract the fear others felt at learning he was a Red.

"Hey, Owen," I said, kneeling down beside him. "We didn't really have a chance to meet before. I'm Zu."

Nothing. No movement. Not a word.

"Thank you again for what you did," I continued. "I can't say it enough. *Thank you.* None of us would be here now, safe and together, without you."

His only response was a slight nod as he tucked his chin against the blanket.

"Are you all right?" I asked him. Even at dawn, the humidity was setting in, and the blanket looked like it was made of wool. "Are you cold?"

He could be in shock, I thought. Owen, however, didn't make any move to wrap the blanket around himself. He didn't move at all.

"I have to ask you a question, if that's okay," I said, taking his silence in stride. "It's about Ruby."

Another nod. Progress.

The others had said Ruby was working with him one-on-one, trying to help him break Project Jamboree's hold on his mind. This might be a long shot, but if she had mentioned *anything* to him about her trips, even in passing, it could be useful.

"Do you remember what the two of you talked about when she last spent time with you?" I asked. "She's misplaced her phone, and we're trying to track down where she might have gone."

This wasn't my first encounter with a Red who had been part of the ill-fated Project Jamboree, but it didn't make it any easier. President Gray's brainwashing program had been designed to turn them into weapons of mass destruction, but ultimately had only broken their minds and wills.

Ruby had worked with a number of them, until the world had tried to break her, too.

The longer I sat there, the longer that silence went on, the tighter my throat became. "It's all right," I told Owen. "You don't have to say anything. But you should know that your voice is necessary, and you deserve to be heard."

He looked up again, brow creasing, and I realized I'd had it wrong. It wasn't that his gaze was empty; Owen's eyes were like the deepest part of the sea, the darkness disguising every feeling, every fear, forcing them all deep below the surface.

"Well, no problem," I said, tamping down the frustration I felt. "I'm really glad I got to meet you, Owen. If you think of anything, let Jacob or Lisa know. They can pass it on to me."

I had just started to stand when a small voice said, "It's for Ruby."

"What is?" I asked, freezing in place. I turned to see him let the blanket fall into his lap. "The blanket?"

Owen nodded, not meeting my gaze. His thumbs ran along the edge of the blanket. "She's so cold."

It was only when those words ran through my mind a second time that I understood what he'd said. "You mean she *was* cold the last time you saw her?"

"She's cold," Owen said. "She's so cold."

"I'm not sure I understand," I said. "Did she say something to you before she left?"

His dark gaze lifted from his blanket again. "Just good-bye."

My pulse was already thrumming hard in my veins before I turned—before I heard Miguel's *"Oh, shit!"* from across the field.

He, Lisa, and Jacob were huddled over one of the burner phones, each of their faces looking more horrified than the next. A short distance away, the burner phone they'd given us began to blare in Priyanka's hand. Roman was already there beside her, and even from my distance, I could see the color drain from his cheeks.

The static was growling loudly in my ears again as I made my way over to Priyanka and Roman. They both glanced up, not saying a word as they passed the phone over to me.

At first I didn't understand what I was seeing. There was a live-streaming video of an airplane burning, its broken pieces strewn across a runway. The camera shifted over to the sight of a motorcade roaring away from it, police lights flashing.

The words scrolled across the bottom of the video, their truth blistering.

JOSEPH MOORE'S CAMPAIGN PLANE EXPLODES ON RUNWAY

"What is happening to this world?" I heard Lisa say.

AN EXPLOSIVE DETONATED JUST BEFORE THE CANDIDATE WAS DUE TO BOARD. TWELVE CREW AND STAFF ARE DEAD. NO SURVIVORS.

"I don't understand," Jacob said. "Why would anyone do this?"

SUZUME KIMURA, LEADER OF THE PSION RING,
CLAIMS RESPONSIBILITY

TWENTY-ONE

THE SEDAN WAS AS OLD AS IT WAS PLAIN-LOOKING. IT was the kind of car Liam had always favored: safe and completely nondescript. The beigest of beige. His only other requirement, aside from a decent engine and standard safety features, was a working radio. I would have left it off, except we needed to hear the latest updates about the bombing and the fallout from it.

An hour into our drive, I had the shock of hearing a recording of my voice, one that had clearly been cobbled together from a number of other speeches. *"This is in retaliation for all the crimes against Psi."* An hour after that, I had serious thoughts about melting the radio altogether.

The only channel we were able to pick up for miles and miles and miles wasn't the official zone channel, but a new one clearly unsanctioned by the interim government called Truth Talk Radio with Jim Johnson. It featured an endless programming loop of subjects that became progressively viler with each passing hour.

My mind was buzzing with anxiety and impatience. Roman had insisted on resting in the car and waiting until we had the cover of nightfall before hitting the road. I hadn't been able to drop into sleep the way the others had; the impatience to go, to get to Mississippi, was itching beneath my skin. Even if Ruby wasn't there, I told myself, her last known location was the only lead we had.

"I mean, listen to this—it's unbelievable. Just listen," Jim Johnson said, his voice so smug it made my skin crawl.

Then it was a different voice coming to us over the airwaves. President Cruz's.

"As a result of the act of terror perpetrated at the airport," she said, her voice as steady and bold as it almost always was—it was a voice that was never allowed to be wrong—*"I am temporarily reassigning the Defenders to a new role in the protection of our country. They will use all the many resources available to them to track down these . . . rogue Psi elements, the so-called Psion Ring. To that end, they have been authorized to use force in situations that call for it. They will be offered new specialized training that focuses on the unique dangers of dealing with psionic abilities. Those who previously received training in such matters will be cleared for duty in the next twelve hours."*

There was only one group who had "previously received training" in dealing with us: former PSFs. The thought chilled my blood.

But President Cruz still wasn't finished.

"In exchange for their assistance in the identification of potential members of this domestic terrorist group, as well as any information they might have about the histories of these Psi, the interim attorney general will be dropping all charges against the remaining camp controllers who are still awaiting trial."

The splotches in my vision reappeared, and if the two-lane road hadn't been deserted, I would have pulled us over onto the shoulder to breathe through the panic. I wasn't just shaking—I was glowing with fury.

Liar.

I could still hear her voice, her promise. *You'll never have to suffer as you did in the past. This is a new world, and it belongs to you as much as any of us.*

There was going to be so much work to do when I got back to DC. For the first time in years, Cruz would hear me go off-script. She'd hear every thought storming through my mind.

"I've got none other than Joseph Moore, presidential candidate for the Liberty Watch Party, on the line. Mr. Moore, it's great to have you back on the program."

"Great to be here, as always."

"The circumstances are horrible—can you assure the listeners that you and your family are all right?"

Moore let out a deep sigh. *"My wife is rattled, and the campaign staff has been made to face an unimaginable reality. We lost so many good folks. The only thing we can do now is mourn them and pull out a win in honor of them."*

"Was that supposed to be him grieving?" Priyanka asked. "Because that *whoosh* in the background sure sounded like him seizing an opportunity."

"On today's welcome news: Were you surprised to see the interim president cave on these points?" the host continued.

"Of course Cruz finally gave in—she's seen both her dismal polling numbers and the writing on the wall. Look at her favorite pets: one turns out to be behind the Psion Ring, and the other has finally been forced to disband that ridiculous sham of a council. I expect we won't hear from him for quite some time, not until they're through interrogating him."

Chubs. The car lurched to the right with the force of my reaction. Roman reached over to steady the wheel.

"Sorry," I breathed out. "Sorry . . ."

"That's your friend?" Roman questioned. "The one you called before?"

I gave a weak nod.

"We've also received unconfirmed reports the Psi Council has been dissolved, but what makes you believe they're interrogating him?" the newscaster asked.

They had him. They had probably grabbed him for initial questioning after the explosion, and then, when I'd called him directly, I'd confirmed that we were still close. That he might know where I'd go, and who'd I'd seek out for help or shelter.

"Well, he's the link, isn't he? Between Kimura, and even Daly and Stewart, who still have yet to be found. Who's to say they aren't involved with the Psion Ring, too? That he isn't a mole for them? That's the question I'd be asking."

No. God, no—

I wished I wasn't driving. My body wanted to curl into itself, just for a moment, and let my bones and skin deflect the truth.

I hadn't just destroyed Ruby and Liam's dream. Someone was using me to destroy Chubs's as well, and I was powerless to stop it.

Not for long, I thought, gripping the wheel harder.

"It's only a matter of time before Cruz is forced to face the truth," Moore was saying. *"In her heart, I think she knows that her UN overlords are running this country into the ground with their un-American restrictions. She's got no shot at winning the election as long as she refuses to initiate some kind of program to reeducate the Psi on how to be members of our society. It's one generation, but it doesn't have to be a lost one. Rather than brush them aside, let's ask them to work for this country. Haven't we seen that across history? Training for service will get them off the streets—heck, it might even reestablish our dominance in global politics."*

"Her reluctance truly makes you wonder if the United Nations has any intention of releasing their death grip on us. Mark my words, they will cancel this election before they let you win."

"That is ridiculous," I snapped.

"Let's hope that's not true," Moore said. *"At this point, I think we can all agree on one thing: even Gray was a better president—"*

I slammed my clenched fist against the volume button. I only meant to shut it off, but the spark that jumped from my knuckles to the dash crawled over the display. Joseph Moore's rant ended with a satisfying *snap.*

Roman gave a tentative poke at the buttons, but the second the host's voice came back on he switched it off entirely.

I forced myself to take slow, deep breaths until the sound of my heartbeat faded from my ears.

"I know we need to keep monitoring the situation," I began.

"That wasn't monitoring the situation so much as listening to a man pet himself for being so smart and so pretty," Priyanka said. "But why didn't Cruz say *one word* in your defense? They're not even pretending to investigate what's happening."

It was as if Mel's voice jumped to my lips. I saw the strategy so clearly laid out in front of me, I couldn't believe it hadn't occurred to me before now. "I'm political poison at the moment. It's better that she doesn't go out of her way to remind people she's associated with me."

But . . . the first time I'd heard her voice coming through the radio, days ago, she hadn't tried to defend me or say there had to be another explanation, and that *had* cut me deep. Truthfully, I wasn't sure how to keep that small wound from festering.

"Like *hell* it's better," Roman said.

"Strong fighting words from Roman Volkov," Priyanka said. "If you won't be mad, then we'll be mad on your behalf. How's that?"

"Volkov," I said. "Is that Russian? Ukrainian?"

"Russian," he said. "That's where my family comes from."

I nodded. "But you grew up here? You and Lana?"

"Yep," Priyanka confirmed, but didn't elaborate. Fair. I didn't want to talk about my family, either, and I already knew they'd been in a bad foster situation.

"For the most part," Roman said. As if he felt my frustration, he added, "It's complicated. I wasn't born here."

There were a few international cases of IAAN, usually when the mother had recently traveled to the United States and drank the water for a time before returning home, but there were a number of other possibilities, too, including that his mother had been born here, or lived here, and simply had him in another country.

I would have asked, but Roman turned, gazing out the window, his knuckles pressed to his lips. Here, but far away.

"I still can't believe it," Priyanka said after a while. "That move of dismissing the cases against the camp controllers is the most cold-blooded thing I've heard of in a long time. That woman was never our friend."

No. Back then, in the beginning, we'd all known that, but it had been a kind of partnership. She had been someone who had been willing to work with us. She'd even been someone I'd respected.

"You know, the ironic thing about Cruz is—"

I stopped myself.

"Is what?" Priyanka prompted.

You don't have to watch your words, I reminded myself. But I'd spent so long trying my hardest to represent the interim president in the best light, talking about her this way felt deeply unnatural to me.

"The only reason Cruz is in power is because of us. The Children's League rescued her from Los Angeles after the bombing. They got her through Gray's heavy military patrols that would have arrested her for treason like all the other California politicians. Instead, she worked with us. She positioned herself with the UN when they were ready to intervene," I explained. "So, no, she's probably not our friend, but her daughter is one of us, so she has a major stake in our welfare."

"It makes sense," Priyanka said. "But if she truly wants to stay in power, won't she have to move with the tide?"

"Once the election's over, things will settle down," I said. "And once I clear my name, she'll pull back on these executive orders. Right now, we need her to do whatever it takes to get votes and beat the hell out of Moore."

"I sincerely hope you're right about her long game," Priyanka said, "but right now it feels like we're the chess piece on the board that's going to be sacrificed first."

"You don't even play chess," Roman cut in.

"True," Priyanka said, "but I'm fluent in grand analogies."

I shook my head. "It's just politics."

One of the checkpoints where Zone 1 met Zone 2 was in Bristol, Virginia—or, at least, it had been.

"You're sure about this?" Roman asked.

"The checkpoint got light enough traffic that they decommissioned it two months ago as a test run for winding down the other zone-crossing spots," I explained. "Unless they have people stationed there to look for me, we should be able to pass through it with only camera eyes on us." I met Priyanka's gaze in the rear-view mirror. "And you can handle that, right? Do we need to charge the phone's battery before we go?"

"No, we're good," Priyanka said, holding up her device. "Only one camera? We meet at last, Luck."

"Luck isn't anthropomorphic," Roman told her.

Priyanka shot him an indignant look. "Everyone knows luck is a lady."

As it turned out, luck might have been a lady, but she was also an absolute bastard.

Ten miles later, the glare of searchlights from the fully operational zone checkpoint in Bristol swept back and forth over the highway ahead of us. I stared at them in disbelief.

The checkpoint looked like all the others. It hadn't been hastily reassembled in the search for me—it had never been broken down to begin with. Massive electrified fences framed the stark concrete booths and adjacent administrative buildings. Armored vehicles of all sizes were parked along the highway, narrowing it to two lanes: one that ran in through the two booths, and one that ran out of them.

Most of the checkpoints had started with simple trailers, but over time those structures were cemented to the ground, planted like knives in the otherwise beautiful countryside.

These buildings were meant to be imposing. Even now, having passed through so many of them, my whole body felt weighted down by every wrong thing I'd done in my life.

"Maybe you had the date wrong?" Priyanka suggested softly.

"I gave a whole speech about it," I said, looking up toward the highway lights and the cameras built into their eyes. They were all so modern—slick and silver, without any hard angles. Completely at odds with the natural green landscape surrounding them.

"Someone either asked me to tell a lie, or they changed their mind and hoped no one would notice."

Both options were equally infuriating to me.

"Next idea?" Priyanka asked.

"Only idea: we go on foot," I said, waiting for an approaching drone to pass over us and head the opposite direction. "Find a car on the other side and continue on to the address we have. There's still at least one more can of gas in the back, right?"

We opened our doors as one, stepping out into the night. Roman dutifully collected the supplies out of the back, including the bolt cutters Liam had stashed there.

I was about to shut the driver's side door when Roman tossed me a small rag.

"Better wipe it down," he said.

I stared back, not understanding.

"Fingerprints." He said the word with such care, wrapping it in an apology, as if he could soften its implications.

Fugitive.

"Oh. Right." He'd wiped the last two cars we'd used himself.

"Don't worry," Priyanka said, leaning against the side of the car. "It gets easier."

I briskly rubbed the towel over the steering wheel and dash, then turned my attention to the prints on the doors and trunk. "What does?"

"Doing what feels like the wrong thing for the right reasons." Priyanka stared off toward the checkpoint's distant lights. "Eventually you realize the only way to live is by the rules you set for yourself."

"These are extenuating circumstances. Life can't always work that way," I said. "People have to be held accountable. There has to be some kind of system. We take care of it, and it takes care of us."

"Maybe," she said, without any bite in her voice. "I really don't know. Lately accountability feels like obediently putting a collar around our own necks and trusting people who hate us not to tighten it. If a system is broken, how do you fix it when you're trapped inside of it?"

"Isn't it better to try to fix something with potential than to smash it into a thousand pieces and hope whatever comes next is better?" I asked. "I'd rather work within a flawed system to carve out my place than shut myself out by not participating at all."

Roman came to stand beside me, glancing between us with a look of faint worry. It was less an argument than a discussion, though. Priyanka confirmed as much when she draped an arm over my shoulder.

"What do you think?" I asked him, genuinely curious. As always, he considered his words before saying them.

"Breaking a bad cycle can sometimes break a system," Roman said. "But breaking a system will always break the cycle. It's only a difference in the degree of certainty."

"On that poetic note," Priyanka said, taking the can of gasoline from him. "I think we should head out before someone starts patrolling the highway."

We followed Roman's near-silent steps off the paved road into the wooded area that lined the right side of the highway. I'd expected him to take us just out of view of the central checkpoint buildings, but we continued walking through the trees long enough for blisters to form and then open on my feet.

At one point, I realized my eyes had adjusted to what had

initially felt like a pitch-black night. The outlines of trees and Roman's tall form sharpened in relief, until I could see the veins of their leaves and the folds in his T-shirt as it clung to his strong frame.

"Wanna see Roman's magic trick?" Priyanka whispered, clearly bored.

I raised my brows.

"Hey, Ro, what time is it?" she asked, keeping her voice casual.

"No. I don't like this game," he told her.

"It's not a game," she swore solemnly. "I just want to know. For reasons."

Roman gave her a suspicious look over his shoulder, his hands gripping the backpack's straps. "Reasons."

"Really, really important reasons."

He gave her one last glance before turning his gaze up toward the sky. "One thirty-five."

As soon as he had his back turned, Priyanka held up the flip phone, showing me the time on the screen with a gleeful look on her face. 1:36 a.m.

I snorted, which made Roman look back again.

"Swallowed . . . a bug," I told him. "Haven't we gone far enough? Are you looking for a particular section of the fencing?"

He hitched the backpack of supplies higher, then unhooked the bolt cutters from where he'd slid them through one of the straps. "No. Just hoping for a section with no fencing."

"Why?" I asked. "We have bolt cutters."

"Because," he said quietly, "it's a felony to tamper with government property and pass through zones without permission."

Oh.

Priyanka suddenly found the phone very interesting.

I crossed my arms over my chest, cupping my elbows as I tried to think of what to say. Of course he'd registered how uncomfortable that would make me. Roman missed very little, if anything. I'd been in front of cameras and audiences for so long, I'd come to think of that as being known. But this was being *seen*.

"That's what you're worried about?" I said lightly. "What's trespassing to someone accused of murder, treason, and terrorism, right? Here, let me do it." I gestured to the bolt cutters.

I meant what I said into the drone's camera. Right now, with my friends missing and scattered, with my reputation shredded, I didn't have much to lose. I could still go back to the government, I could still make things right—but that was *eventually*, and this was *now*. I just had to do whatever it took to keep going.

"I could do it," he said. "I don't have the control you do, but I could try, and at least then you wouldn't have to live with this, too."

"It's all right," I told him. "I want to."

I couldn't say exactly what made me do it. It was his worried expression, the way he clenched his fists at his side, the small kindness of it. The power rattling the chain-link fence. It all registered like tiny quakes in my heart.

I rolled up onto my toes to press my lips to his cheek. It was such an unfamiliar texture, the rough scrape of his scruff growing in. His skin warmed where I touched it, and I lingered there a moment longer than I'd meant to, taking in the smell of the car's leather seats, of the sweet green woods surrounding us.

There was no resistance in his grip when I reached out and took the bolt cutter from him. I stepped back until the warmth faded and only that startling, gentle urge remained, still as confusing as the moment I'd first felt it. He didn't say a word as I turned south, toward the place I felt the electrified fence calling out to me.

It was a simpler version of what we'd seen near the checkpoint, only eight feet high instead of twenty. But the electricity prowling back and forth across it was no less lovely or lethal. It turned frenzied at my approach, like an excited pack of dogs. The silver thread in my mind slipped out, connecting with it, guiding it away from a section of links in front of me.

All that mattered was getting to the other side. I was allowed to be angry right now. I got to be furious about the lie about the checkpoint closing, and that it was yet another thing standing in my way.

I brought the bolt cutters up and cut the first strip of metal before I could stop myself.

When I'd finished, I kicked out the loose piece and stepped through. Keeping one hand on the fencing, I waved the others forward. Roman went first, stealing a glance at my face as he passed by. Priyanka only let out a long, impressed whistle.

When they'd both gone on ahead, I turned back once more to see what I'd done.

And saluted it with my middle finger.

"Can you see anything inside?" Roman's voice crackled over the walkie-talkie as Priyanka and I walked across the pavement toward the dark blue sedan. Lisa had forced us to take one of their sets, and while I hadn't wanted to, I owed her. Big-time.

"Not yet," Priyanka replied. "Nothing moving, at least."

The satellite view of the estimated address hadn't been deceptive, exactly, but it hadn't been accurate. Instead of an empty field, the vehicle was parked in the dead center of a large paved lot. The kind that might have been used for a supermarket or a mega shopping center. That *should* have been used for something. Instead, there was only the massive cement footprint of a building foundation, and a few scattered pieces of timber and cinder blocks in the nearby field.

"This is creepy, right?" Priyanka said. I had to jog to keep up with her stride. "A little creepy?"

The air was so thick with moisture, it seemed to hiss at us as we moved through it. My hair rose into waves, sticking to my cheeks and neck, and all I could taste was the leftover syrup from the Waffle House breakfast Priyanka had bought us. That, and my own sweat.

My body tensed more and more, even as the heat did its best to melt me down to my raw nerves. By the time we were close enough to make out the shape of the seats inside the car, I could barely breathe.

She's not in the car. She can't be in the car.

Roman had given me one of the guns from Haven, and it hadn't left my hand since we'd stepped onto the lot. I raised it slightly, aiming at the car as we approached it from behind.

I nodded to Priyanka, and she moved to the passenger side as I approached from the driver's. The car's battery was dead. I wasn't picking up any spark of electricity anywhere nearby, save the walkie-talkie in Priyanka's hand. The part of me that had secretly feared this was some kind of elaborate trap almost relaxed.

The sedan was unlocked. The smell of stale, hot air greeted me when I threw open the door. A bag of what had formerly been M&M's sat wilting in one of the cup holders. Less than a foot away, a key was sticking out of the ignition. An empty water bottle remained in the door.

I slid into the driver's seat, breathing in the heavy air. I closed my eyes, trying to picture Ruby there, in that same place. Green eyes staring straight ahead.

What were you doing here?

Why would she ever come to a place like this alone?

"Should I open the trunk?" Priyanka asked carefully.

"Oh God," I whispered. "I didn't even . . . I hadn't thought of that."

"I don't know if this is going to make you feel better, but based on my limited experience with dead bodies, I think we would have smelled it by now," Priyanka said. Sweat poured down over her face and neck, wrapping her thick, wavy hair into tighter curls.

I nodded, resting my hands on the steering wheel. The car rocked as she opened the trunk. It swung up in the rearview mirror.

Please, I thought. *Please . . .*

"Empty!" she called back. "Oh, wait—"

At her note of surprise, I shoved the driver's door open again and jumped out.

Priyanka took my arm, tugging me forward. It *was* empty. The exterior of the car was covered with a light sheen of dust that had been spotted by recent rain, but inside was almost pristine.

"No, look—" She pointed toward the cover on the spare-tire well, which hung slightly open. Priyanka pulled it off and inside, there was a gun. Fake ID papers. And Ruby's cell phone.

"I see dust, about five miles back," Roman said. *"Someone's coming."*

I grabbed all three, pressed the cover back into place, and stepped away so Priyanka could slam the trunk shut again. Our footsteps pounded against the heat-cracked surface of the asphalt until we found the dirt road out again.

Up ahead, about a mile away, Roman was using the remnants of a burned-out gas station to cover our own car. Seeing us, he lowered his binoculars—judging our actual distance, no doubt—then pulled them back up to his eyes to gaze at the road behind us.

I threw a quick glance over my shoulder. Just long enough to see the flares of red and blue lights flashing through the screen of dust.

Priyanka and I took a hard turn as we reached the car, sliding to a stop on the other side of it. We kept low to the ground beside Roman.

"We should go," Priyanka said. "Come on."

"No, they're turning into the parking lot," he said. "We need to stay until they leave."

I spun back just as the cars crossed onto the paved surface. They surrounded Ruby's car in a jagged circle.

"Let me see," I said, reaching for the binoculars.

I blinked, trying to adjust to their strength. Uniformed men and women surrounded the abandoned car, guns up. It was a strange mix of forces: UN peacekeepers, FBI, Defenders, and—

Vida.

Her brown skin shone in the afternoon sunlight, but it took me a moment to recognize her with her dark hair. She'd stopped dyeing it years ago, when she'd been named as a special assistant to the interim director of the FBI. It hadn't sat right with me the first time I'd seen her with it, and now, as she wove in and out of the uniformed officers wearing her trim, professional-looking suit, it felt like I was spying on a stranger.

I lowered the binoculars, my throat too tight to say anything.

"How could they have found the car?" Priyanka whispered. "They couldn't have followed us. . . ."

"Is it possible they found the Haven kids?" Roman asked. His brow creased as he raked a hand back through the waves of his hair.

I shook my head. Even in a situation that made no sense, there was one thing I was certain of: "Vida never would have let the government near them. If she showed up at Haven and found it the way we left it, she'd know to contact Liam's stepfather, Harry. It's possible he told her what he knew and she had to give something to the government to keep them from getting suspicious."

Or maybe she thinks you're guilty after all.

"I'm going to try to power this up again," Priyanka said, holding up Ruby's cell phone. "Let's hope the heat didn't get to it."

She disappeared into the backseat, rummaging through the seat pockets for the charger, hissing out a cuss when she accidentally bumped her head against one of the handle grips.

"Vida is the smartest person I know," I told Roman. "And probably the toughest. She can handle whatever this is."

That was the truth, on both fronts. Chubs might have been book smart, but Vida had an innate understanding of the world. She had a vault for a mind and an uncanny ability to figure out what was important about a detail and apply it to any given situation. I had watched her do it many times in envy.

Roman nodded. "She'd have to be, to keep up with you."

The idea of Vida keeping up with any of us was so absurd, I

almost laughed. No, Vida set the ruthless pace in these kinds of situations, and we were lucky if we could keep within sight of her.

"You'd like her," I said, trying to lighten the heavy thoughts raining through my mind. "Well, I take that back. You might be a little overwhelmed. But she'd like you once you showed her the appropriate amount of skill and deference."

"Noted."

I pulled the binoculars back up. All the doors to Ruby's car were open as they searched inside. Vida hung back, pacing with the impatience of a lion waiting for its next meal, phone pressed to her ear.

That was what I struggled with. Not the changes in my friends—we all had to change, in big and small ways—but those pieces of them I recognized, and missed.

"She'd been out looking for Ruby and Liam on her own." It still stung to remember that both she and Chubs hadn't told me about any of it until it was too late. "And when I spoke to her at Haven, she was with other agents in DC. Something must have happened for her to come here, searching with government agencies."

I handed Roman the binoculars, unable to watch anymore.

"Your friend Charles might have told the government Ruby and Liam were missing because he was worried what could happen to them in the meantime," he suggested. "They have the resources to conduct a far more thorough search. Or he or Vida might have told them in an attempt to clear Ruby and Liam's names of any involvement with the Psion Ring or the recent bombings. Or . . . I don't know. What do you think?"

That was just it. I used to know their hearts better than I knew my own. I should have been able to guess exactly why Chubs and Vida were acting the way they were. I should have known, with a thousand percent certainty, what they'd try to do and how.

But I didn't.

"Ruby and Liam *aren't* involved with the Psion Ring, right?" I asked suddenly. "Was there ever any sign of their involvement? Did their names ever come up? Any information on the secret organization I'm supposedly running right now would be useful."

I don't know why I hadn't thought of it before, but if Ruby wasn't already involved with the Psion Ring, then they might have wanted her to be—and if she hadn't gone voluntarily, they could have taken her. Ruby's power would have made it difficult, but it wasn't impossible, especially if they kept her subdued.

Or if Lana used her ability on her.

Instead of bringing the binoculars up to his eyes, Roman merely turned them over between his fingers, studying its shape. I knew his reluctance to talk about the Psion Ring was tied to wanting to protect me, but I needed to know. "I never heard either of their names tied to the organization."

"What kind of operations do they run?" I asked. "Everything they've been accused of? Who were some of the people involved?"

"Everyone senior . . . they used code names. And the usual— small acts of disruption. Nothing like what they're claiming on the news. I don't think they have the resources for that."

"Good," I said. "They must be loving the attention they're getting right now. Hopefully I can intervene with the truth before they take it to another level."

His skin was splattered with dust and sweat, and with all the humidity, his wavy chestnut hair seemed even thicker. Roman swiped a sunburned cheek against his shoulder. My eyes found that small scar on his jaw again.

A hard knock against the rear window made me jump back.

Priyanka stared at us through the tinted glass, one eyebrow arched. "Get in, kids, we have to combine our powerful minds into a brain trust to crack her password."

"It's zero-five-zero-one," I told her as I slid into the driver's seat.

"No it's not," Priyanka said, then actually tried the numbers. "Yes it is. Dammit. That wasn't fun at all. What's zero-five-zero-one?"

"Liam's birthday."

"*Aww.* But terrible for personal security."

After one last look through the binoculars, Roman joined us, taking his usual place in the front passenger seat. "They're towing her car away. The road should be clear in a few minutes."

"Okay, there's only one message: 'Come home. Don't leave it this way,'" Priyanka read. "But the actual number shows up as blocked."

"That's probably Liam, then," I said, a new, sick feeling writhing in the pit of my stomach.

Don't leave it this way? Leave what? Haven? Him?

All of us?

"Did she look up any addresses?" I asked.

Priyanka let out a soft hum. I felt Roman's eyes on me, but couldn't bear to see what was in them.

"Let's see . . . Raleigh, Tampa, Jacksonville, Nashville," Priyanka said, scrolling through the list of addresses. "Wait. This one keeps coming up—it's in here at least four or five times. It's in Charleston—Zu, do you recognize it?"

She held up the phone for me, using her thumb to point it out to me. The moment I saw the street name, my blood iced over.

Ruby, I thought. *Ruby, what are you doing?*

"Yeah. I recognize it," I said. "That's where they keep Clancy Gray."

TWENTY-TWO

ON A STREET SHADED BY HEAVY MAGNOLIA TREES THAT had lived to see too much history, in a little pink house with a wraparound porch and window boxes spilling with flowers, lived the sociopathic son of a murderous ex-president.

"I've got to say, the flag is a nice touch." I nodded toward the American flag posted at the edge of the porch, an exclamation mark of bold red, white, and blue in an otherwise pastel street. "You can almost believe he didn't try to destroy the country."

I'd parked the car on the street a few houses down, in front of a grand old home with a for-sale sign promising AUTHENTIC SOUTHERN LIVING. We were just close enough to downtown Charleston, or at least the historic part with all the tourists, for me to feel uneasy about idling too long.

"They never did find his dad, did they?" Priyanka asked, resting her arms on the front seats as she leaned forward.

"No. He's still a fugitive. They think he escaped the country in the chaos of the UN coalition taking control." I shook my head. "Never thought I'd have something in common with President Gray."

For all that the man had done to us, it was the strangest thing—I just couldn't remember what he looked like, not unless his photo was right in front of me in the paper or on the news.

It was the strangest mental block. For the longest time, he'd been nothing but an impression; a voice that haunted us, reminding each Psi how very wrong we were. On the bus radio as they drove us through our camp's barbed-wire gate. On the announcements they sometimes played over our many silent dinners. Pouring out of Betty's speakers in the middle of nowhere.

"The mailbox says 'Hathaway,'" Roman said.

"He and his mother are hiding in plain sight as John and Elizabeth Hathaway." Cruz had given us this information years ago because she knew we'd check for ourselves anyway, but nearly everything else I knew about him could be categorized as a rumor. "She remembers their past life. He doesn't."

"Head injury?" Roman asked, eyes narrowing in interest.

"Ruby." I didn't tear my gaze away from the front of the house. Its sweet, old face was like a kindly grandmother whose gentle demeanor and endless supply of warm cookies hid her ugly, racist past.

The general public had held up Lillian as a hero to her husband's villain, which left their son to be cast as the victim she'd fought so hard to save. In that narrative, Clancy Gray had of course received the cure procedure happily, to prove to others that it was safe, much like he'd supposedly volunteered to go to Thurmond, to prove to American families the camps' "rehabilitation" programs worked. Most people believed the Grays were still living in seclusion outside DC, but Lillian had refused any sort of government position, claiming she just wanted to take care of her son in peace and quiet.

Considering she'd done such a bang-up job the first time, I was shocked that they'd let her.

Then again, Lillian knew things most people didn't—and Mel used to say that if you could keep someone happy, you could usually keep them quiet. Of course, Clancy had known all those things once, too, before Ruby had taken those memories. Closed them off. Did whatever it was she actually did.

Why did you come here?

The front door opened. All three of us slumped down in our seats.

A man in sunglasses emerged, glancing up and down the street before stepping aside to let a woman pass.

Even with her pale hair dyed brunette, Lillian's alabaster skin and regal bearing were unmistakable. She worked in one of the labs at a nearby college, from what I remembered.

"So there is a security detail," Roman said.

"Cameras, too—above the front door and probably at the back," Priyanka said. "Detail would have to be small to avoid anyone noticing it . . . one, maybe two meatheads."

I looked between them, mildly alarmed at the comfortable pattern of their conversation.

Like you've never stolen anything, I thought. *Or broken in anywhere.*

Roman nodded. "Private security, most likely, if Ruby was able to visit without being nabbed by the government."

"I think so, too," I said. "They initially froze the Gray family assets, but they released them after she agreed to serve as a witness against her husband when he was tried by proxy. They can definitely afford full-time security."

Lillian and her bodyguards piled into a black Range Rover

parked on the street and took off in the opposite direction.

Priyanka cracked her knuckles for maximum effect. "Well. I can pick any lock and turn any camera blind. But there's an easier way. It just depends on what Zu wants to do."

"I need to try to talk to him," I said. "To see if she actually went to see him."

"I'm going with the two-guard theory—one for mama, one for baby boy," Priyanka said. I had to keep from rolling my eyes; Clancy was twenty-six now. "If he's still here, and not doing whatever it is amnesiac former First Sons do with their time, best bet is to go through a back door or window. The porch rail is tall enough that we could use it to climb up onto the roof. But we're going to have to draw the guard's attention away with some kind of distraction."

She stared at Roman until he looked at her, confused. "You want me to shoot him?"

"What? No! That's less distraction and more *murder*." Priyanka shook her head, throwing a hand against her forehead dramatically. "Alas, the life of the theater calls to me again. You can probably sneak in easily through the side gate into the backyard. Just wait for my signal."

"No idea what that means," I said. "But are we doing this?"

Roman leaned forward, sliding one of the guns into the waistband of his jeans.

"Okay," I said. "Guess we are."

I moved to the sidewalk, meeting Roman there. He reached up, adjusting the lip of my baseball hat so it shaded more of my face. Before I could ask how we were going to approach the house, he looped his arm over my shoulder, pulling me closer to his side.

"Sorry," he murmured, guiding us down off the curb. "See if you can stand it for a little while."

"Yes," I whispered back, glancing both ways as we crossed the street toward the house. "This is definitely the worst thing that's happened to me in recent days."

It was early enough in the morning that the Charleston weather hadn't reached unbearable levels of humidity. A faint breeze smoothed over my cheeks, bringing with it the heady smell of the magnolia blossoms and nearby jasmine.

From what I could see, there was a pathway to the back of the house, blocked only by the smallest of white gates. Still, I was surprised when Roman led us over toward the house next door, giving me a blinding smile and laughing at nothing.

I laughed back, grimacing at how loud and sharp he sounded on the otherwise quiet street.

"We are pretending to have a wonderful conversation," he told me, turning me so that my back was to the neighbor's carefully groomed hedge. He walked me back toward it, his wide shoulders blocking my view of the street.

And the street's view of me.

"And it is going wonderfully," I said.

Somehow, I hadn't realized how tall he was until he was standing close enough that I could feel his chest expand with every breath. I looked up at him, eyes tracing the sharp edge of his jaw as he turned his gaze toward the house. I wasn't sure what to do, so my hands decided for me. They slid across his hips, fingers weaving together again behind his back.

He startled, his hands landing on my shoulders, almost as if he'd needed to catch his balance. I glanced down at his right hand, taking in the raised scars that covered the back of it.

I'd thought I was doing a good job of keeping my anxious thoughts about confronting Clancy to myself, but Roman asked, "Are you sure you want to do this?"

"*Want* is not really the word I'd use in this situation," I said. A shudder passed through me, and I knew he was close enough to feel it. "The past just feels a little closer to me than it did in the car."

Somehow, he seemed to understand what I meant. "If it gets to be too much, or if it feels like something is off, signal me— what did you use at Haven to get their attention?"

I crossed my arms over my chest, each hand clutching the opposite shoulder.

"That works," he said. "How about one for okay"—Roman demonstrated, pressing his right hand to his left shoulder—"and two for not?"

I drew in a breath, nodding. "All right."

Priyanka's hard knock on the door finally tore my gaze away from him. She took a deep breath, then began to pace, letting her shoulders slump as she ran her hands back through her thick hair. I could see her muttering something, but we were too far away to hear what it was.

Finally, the door swung open. A bald man in a dark polo and khakis stuck his head out. At the sight of him, Roman's body tensed. Mine responded in kind.

"Oh, thank *God!*" I choked on a laugh at the sound of the rich southern accent Priyanka was suddenly putting on. "Sir, I'm in desperate need of your kind assistance—I've come to y'all in dire need, one southern lady to a southern gentleman—"

I winced. "We should probably hurry."

"Roger that," he said.

Roman took a small breath before stepping back and breaking

the circle of my arms. He moved in front of me, keeping an eye on the porch. Priyanka had angled herself away from us and the pathway, forcing the man to keep his back to us.

Unlike the house next door, this path wasn't paved with crushed oyster shells, but simple pavers. My heart jammed into my throat as Roman boosted me up over the small fence before jumping over it himself. I didn't understand how someone with such a big body could move so quietly.

The narrow pathway was lined with small lanterns and hedges spotted with flowers, but I didn't feel any cameras or other security devices hidden in them.

"Should we try to use the porch rail to find a window?" I whispered. "Is it—?"

I slammed into his back as he stopped dead at the end of the pathway. He reached behind him, for me or his gun, I wasn't sure.

I stepped to the side, edging past him.

The pathway opened to a side yard bordered by white fencing and the same tall hedges. There was a small garden bed of flowers and vegetables that curved along one side of a round patio table. A plate of food, half-devoured, along with a basket of what looked like toasted bread, had been set out on the table. My stomach ached at the warm smell of it, the way the butter melted on its prim dish.

The figure sitting there was hidden behind the sheets of the *New York Times*. A pot of tea or coffee sat waiting for the nearby cup. Finally, he folded the paper closed, then neatly in half, turning his attention to the pot in front of him.

Coffee. As he poured it, its aroma filled the small garden, bleeding into the sweet perfume of the roses blooming nearby.

That same icy touch crept over my skin until it froze me in place.

He looked the same—not as when I'd last seen him, but the first time, at East River. His dark hair had grown back, and his form had filled out either with care or age. He was no longer lean, half-starved like the rest of us had been at the end, but strong. Still, the tidy button-down shirt, the crisply ironed slacks, and the preppy sunglasses masking his eyes were pure Clancy Gray.

It wasn't right. This wasn't right. He didn't deserve to be here, looking so healthy—so *content*. After everything he'd done, after so many good people had died instead of him, *because* of him, he got this small, carefree slice of bliss.

As if my thoughts had reached out to him, he looked up and smiled.

"Hi," Clancy said, setting his cup back down onto its saucer. "Ruby told me to expect you."

When I first met Clancy Gray, it had been like stepping into a dream.

At the time, none of us had known the careful way he was orchestrating things at East River. How he played each of the kids there, including the four of us, like notes in the grand symphony of chaos he was secretly conducting in his mind. We had been so exhausted when we'd arrived, hungry and desperate for even a few minutes of safety. Clancy had all but literally opened his arms to us, shining that perfect smile, every tooth straight and white. Everything about him perfect.

The kids at East River had worshipped him. He'd made sure of it. That was his thing, of course—pinpointing exactly what each individual person needed and wanted more than anything, and giving it to them. A thought would appear in your mind, and you would just accept it as your own. If the hairs rose on your arms when you caught him watching you, your first instinct was to chastise yourself for being a bad friend to someone who had given you so much. After all, if so many other kids adored and respected him—what was wrong with *you* that you had a problem with him?

But there was something wrong with his eyes. They were like cold rain, and when the mask slipped, you felt that ice sink down to your soul.

Even now, without his abilities, or the memory of his years as a monster, there was still something in his gaze that just wasn't wholly there. Maybe it had been taken from him, the way we'd all had pieces of who we might have been stripped away. Maybe he'd never had it in the first place.

He lowered his sunglasses, staring at me over them. I took a step forward, embarrassed of every hard, quickening beat of my pulse. It wasn't fair to hate someone so much, to *despise* them for the pain they caused your friends, and to still feel frightened enough to want to crawl out of your own skin and run away.

You're here for Ruby, I reminded myself, clutching my hands behind my back. *Ask him and then go.*

Static ran through my fingers, only to release with a hard *snap* as Roman stepped up behind me and touched his hand to mine.

"Ah," Clancy said, turning back to his plate. His tone had lost some of the imperious quality it used to have, but it was still as carefree and confident as anyone born with too much money and too much privilege. "I can tell you used to know me. Huh. Ruby mentioned the two of you were friends, but she never brought up the fact that you and I had met. She told me that I should be patient with others so they know they don't have to be nervous about saying the wrong thing."

"Ruby's giving you advice now?" I asked.

He reached for his coffee again. "Yes. She's good at it. Even my mom listens to her. Wow, I'm being rude—do you want any of this? I can get a few more cups from inside."

As hungry as I'd been a few minutes ago, my stomach was too tight to get anything down. I shook my head.

"We're good," Roman told him.

"Well, at least have a seat," he said. "Or stand if you're in a hurry, I don't mind."

Another thing that hadn't changed about Clancy: he still talked way too much.

Roman looked to me, waiting to see what I wanted to do. After a deep breath in, I nodded, moving to the chair directly across from Clancy. Roman followed, standing behind me. One hand curled over the back of my chair. His knuckles brushed my shoulder, a grounding touch as nerves fired throughout my body.

I folded my arms over my chest, sitting back. "So you recognize me? You know who I am?"

"From the news, yes," he said, giving me another close look. "Both good and bad reports. I suppose none of the bad is actually true, then?"

"No, it's not," I said. "Your security might not be so quick to believe me, though."

"Security?" Clancy repeated, cocking his head to the side. "No, those men are my mother's assistant and driver. Why in the world would we need security?"

"Because you're . . ." Oh, damn.

"Famous," Roman finished.

Clancy laughed at that word. The sound crawled over my skin. "I guess? Having the first documented case of memory loss as the result of the cure surgery will do that. Mother always has coworkers coming in to run tests to see if anything's changed."

I bit my lip, clenching my hands together in my lap. I needed to be careful here. His mother had constructed this new identity for him. He didn't remember anything about his past life beyond that she was his mother. Nothing about his father being president, nothing about his ability, and nothing about the chaos he'd caused.

I'd been wondering how Lillian explained his memory loss to him. A side effect of the surgery, huh? It must have been exhausting trying to keep him from finding out the truth. Someone's full-time job, at least.

"Every once in a while, someone tries to snap a photo of me while we're out to eat, but I don't really get it. If people want to know how I'm doing, all they have to do is call us and ask. It'd be my pleasure to tell them that, no, I still don't remember my childhood or what it felt like to be a Green, but I'd be more than happy to read them the thesis I'm working on for school."

"Yeah," I said, humoring him. "And what's that?"

Another too-easy smile. *"The Intersection of Faith and Violence in the Early Years of the Plymouth Colony."*

There was a faint twinge of something in my mind. I brushed it aside. I'd have time to analyze his tone and perpetually condescending smile later, when we were way the hell away from here.

"You said Ruby mentioned that we would be coming," I said. Reaching into the back pocket of my jeans, I pulled out the photo of the four of us, bending it so only Ruby and part of Liam were visible. "Is this the girl you're talking about?"

"Well, yeah," Clancy said, resting his hand against the table. I glanced up at Roman, but he was watching the way Clancy was absently stroking the handle of the butter knife. "That's Ruby.

She's a friend of mine from childhood. The only one who cares enough to still visit. How do you know her?"

Hearing him call Ruby a *friend* made me want to lean across the table and punch him. As if sensing that, Roman nudged me again with his knuckles. It felt like a question.

I pressed my right hand to my shoulder, disguising the movement as I leaned against the table. "She took care of me for a while," I said. "When was she last here?"

"Ruby was here about a month ago, but she stops by regularly. About every three months or so, sometimes more frequently," Clancy said.

That often? My hand slid down my arm. I had no idea she'd ever gone to see the Grays one time, never mind what sounded like a dozen visits. Liam wasn't controlling, but he could be protective to a fault. Given the direct role Clancy had played in his brother's death, I'd wager Clancy was the person he hated most in the world. The idea that he'd be fine with Ruby coming down here, where she could be spotted, to spend time with this reformed cockroach . . .

Unless she didn't tell him, either.

"You're worried about her, too, aren't you?" Clancy leaned forward, resting his arms on his legs. "She just seems so . . . lonely, you know? Exhausted and sad, like the weight of the whole world is on her shoulders and everything has become unbearable. She opens up to me sometimes—about feeling trapped, or alone. It makes me wonder if I'm her only friend."

"No," I said, more coldly than I meant to, "you're not her only friend."

"I didn't mean to offend you. She so rarely talks about the people in her life, it was a natural conclusion to draw. But to get back to your original question, the last time she visited, she told me she was leaving and wouldn't be back for a long time. That people might stop here looking for her. Did she really leave in that big of a hurry?"

How stupid was my little heart—of course she hadn't meant me specifically. She'd been talking about any of us who might notice when she was gone.

"Yeah," I managed to get out. "She up and vanished. We're concerned."

"I don't blame you," he said, running a hand back through his hair. "It feels like it was inevitable, somehow. Like what she really wants, more than anything, is to just be alone."

The static was back, growling in my ears again. "She didn't tell you where she was going?" I asked, feeling that last bit of hope slip away.

He shook his head. "No—but she did leave me a number, in case of an emergency."

"You could have started with that," Roman said.

"I wanted to make sure you weren't here to hurt her in any way," Clancy said, giving him a sharp look.

No one has ever hurt her more than you.

But she came *here.* She turned to *him.*

"John?" A man's voice called from inside. "You're going to be late for class—"

Priyanka's distraction was over. I pushed up out of the chair, torn between running back for the pathway and gripping Clancy's shirt, shaking him until he gave me that number.

"Ah, sorry," Clancy said, rising quickly. "What's your number? I'll text you the one she left with me."

Shit. I didn't want to give him the number to our only burner, but it would be easy enough to replace. After I rattled it off, Clancy repeated it back to me. "Got it."

"John!" the man called again, his voice closer. Roman was already at the path, motioning me to follow. Clancy grabbed my arm before I could. It wasn't a rough touch, but the press of his fingers against my skin made me feel like I was being injected with poison. He stared at me, cocking his head to the side, as if picking up on the scream echoing inside of my head.

"I can't believe I got to meet you," he said, with a smile. "You're famous. It must be difficult, though, to speak on behalf of all Psi. To ask the world to believe things you might not totally believe yourself."

I stared at him, fighting the need to pull away. The silver thread in my mind coiled. A spark burned across my tongue.

"Do you enjoy the touring?" he asked. "I don't think I would, were I in your position."

In my . . . The words trailed off, replaced by stray memories. Years ago, sitting in the mess of Caledonia at my room's assigned table, just below the glossy portraits of Clancy and his father high up on the wall. His voice slithering out of the speakers as they played a message from him that served as our "orientation." *My name is Clancy Gray, and I used to be like you.* . . .

After he'd manipulated his way out of Thurmond, Clancy's father had used him as a roving mouthpiece, selling desperate parents on the dream of a future cure at the camps. He was living proof that we could change. That we could be *fixed*.

The nausea grew so acute, I lifted both hands and crossed my arms over my chest.

That's not me. That's not what I do.

"John!"

"Ah, my summons." Clancy turned back toward the house. "Good luck. It's always nice to meet another friend of Ruby's."

He left the plates, cups, and food on the table as he stood to go inside. Clancy had always had a habit of making everyone else do the dirty work for him.

I sprinted for the pathway, forcing Roman to match my pace. *That's not me.* I got three steps into the protective cover of the hedges before my legs turned to sand beneath me. *That's not what I do.*

Roman caught me by the arms, holding me upright. "What's wrong? Are you all right?"

I shook my head, letting him guide us forward, step by step, moving too quickly for my numb feet. There was a suffocating pressure in my chest as panic stole up on me. I shook hard enough that my teeth chattered. The street blurred in my vision, smearing like wet oil paint.

"Are you all right?" Roman asked, sounding frightened. "Did he do something to you?"

You're okay, you're okay, you're supposed to be okay—

"No," I whispered. "He didn't do anything. He didn't do anything."

We stepped into the street and out of the house's shadow. And as soft and easy as a sigh, the crush of feelings pulled back, and I broke free. Tears flooded my eyes. I couldn't have stopped them, even if I had wanted to.

"He didn't do anything," I said again.

That hadn't been Clancy. It hadn't been the monster that had hurt my friends. But he'd still managed to find my softest parts and sink his teeth into them all the same.

"He's a prick," Roman said, with as much anger as I'd heard from him. "He was doing everything he could to make you feel bad—"

"No," I whispered. "I think, for once, he was telling the truth. I think she left us."

TWENTY-THREE

WE DROVE IN SILENCE, ROMAN BEHIND THE WHEEL, Priyanka in the front passenger seat.

Me, once again, in the back.

I leaned my head against the glass, trying to will myself to sleep.

Clancy's voice had wormed deep into my thoughts, burrowing through every plan I tried to make about what we should do next. In the end, I gave up trying and let the others choose. I didn't trust myself to make any kind of decision.

It wasn't just that she had gone to see Clancy, knowing the risks, knowing who he was and what he had done. It was that she had chosen to confide in him. Anyone could lie about another person's exact words, but he had seen something that Ruby never let slip. When I'd first met her, she hadn't even wanted to be touched, she was so locked inside her own fear. And while she'd learned control and had become stronger, those darker storms moving beneath her skin hadn't left, they'd only morphed.

Trapped by people's expectations and needs, alone in what she'd seen and what she could do. *Lonely.*

I was here, I thought. *I was here the whole time.*

I couldn't keep from wondering if I had done this somehow. By working with the government, by not going to live with them at Haven—did that lock the door on our friendship? I'd only been trying to help her live a better life. I wanted that for *all* Psi. She could have used our contact procedure to get in touch with me. I would have come to her. Instead, I waited for a call that never came.

I should have made the call.

Still, there was a small part of me that clung to the belief that Ruby wouldn't just walk away. From Liam. From the kids at Haven. From her friends. From her family. From the world. The more I tried to picture it, the harder it became. The only times Ruby had willingly distanced herself, it had been to protect us.

But things were different now, and all of us were, too. So much could have happened between when I'd last seen her and the time she'd vanished. She could have been swallowed by her old, familiar darkness and left us for good.

I leaned between the seats and turned on the radio, just to see what terrifying crime I'd been accused of that day.

When the familiar voice came over the speakers, I thought my exhausted mind had spun it out of thin air.

"*—out there, if you're listening, turn yourself in. Please, Suzume. Turn yourself in.*"

"Who's this chump?" Priyanka asked as Roman pulled into an empty rest station parking lot. He turned the engine off, but none of us moved.

"*You're a delegate in the Virginia state House, are you not?*"

I closed my eyes. Of course. Of course he'd gone on Truth Talk Radio.

"*I am. I've had thoughts about resigning, but staying and fighting for the American way is the only thing I can think to do to counteract the evil Suzume has injected into our fragile world."*

"Okay, no, seriously, who is this asshole?"

I cracked an eye open. Priyanka looked ready to jump through the sound system and strangle someone. Roman had gone stiff, his hands still gripping the wheel. An orange glow from the rest station's lights filtered through the windshield.

"My father," I said dryly. "Can't you tell by the love and warmth in his voice?"

"Her mother, Akari, and I wanted her home—we wanted to work with her and to try to reform her ourselves—but she refused, and she has gone out of her way to hurt us and others ever since. And, of course, Interim President Cruz interfered and made an exception for her. I could not believe my eyes when I saw her speaking on the government's behalf. If that's not reason enough for people to vote for Joseph Moore, I don't know what is."

Priyanka looked at me. "I'm going to need a meat cleaver and your home address."

Even Jim Johnson was intrigued by this statement. *"Can we consider this your official endorsement of Joseph Moore, Delegate Kimura? Isn't that the same man who, citing the ineffectiveness of Cruz, has been using his own money to fund a search for your daughter to bring her to justice?"*

"Yes," he said. *"In fact, I would like to say this to Mr. Moore—"*

Roman was the one to switch the radio off. I didn't have it in me to move. Didn't have a thought in my head, not at first. There was just this feeling like a balloon at the center of my chest, and I thought if I did anything at all in that moment I might actually burst.

But, somehow, the others' twin looks of concern were worse.

"I'm going to use the bathroom," I mumbled, popping the door open. The air was drenched with the smell of grass and the days-old garbage spilling out of the trash bins. I started for the women's restrooms, only to double back. My body seemed to know what my mind wanted before it did. I opened the trunk and took out the small first-aid kit, bringing it inside with me.

The sensor lights switched on, filling the filthy restroom with harsh light. I stood in front of the cracked mirror, and the girl I saw through the fractures, through the scrawl of graffiti—I didn't recognize her.

The kit that Ruby or Liam had packed contained various over-the-counter medication, bandages, and a pair of small sharp scissors. I took out the scissors and set them on the edge of the sink, staring at them like they could tell me my own thoughts.

"Am I about to witness a makeover montage?" Priyanka asked from the doorway.

I looked over. "I should . . . disguise myself, right? My face is all over the news. . . ."

And I'm not her. I wasn't Suzume Kimura, spokesperson for the interim president. I wasn't Suzume Kimura, daughter of a state assemblyman. I wasn't Suzume Kimura, leader of the Psion Ring.

I was just Zu.

"Unless you're planning on mutilating your face with those blades, a haircut isn't really a disguise. . . ." Priyanka cocked her head to the side. "I would say bleach it, maybe, but that would fry your gorgeous hair and make your scalp feel like you've dunked it in a fiery hell pit. Not that I speak from personal experience, of course."

There wasn't a more elegant way of putting it. "I think . . . I just want to look different."

I felt hollowed out, like all the ornamentation and training had been shaken off me. I wasn't that little girl I'd seen in the photo from Haven, captured in a single carefree moment. But I wasn't the polished, pretty girl on the news, either. As hard as I'd tried to be.

"Is that ridiculous?" I asked her.

Priyanka came toward me, her expression contemplative. "No, it's not. The only way to live is by following whatever message your heart is beating out for you."

"Did you read that on a greeting card?" I asked.

"No, on some kind of blood pressure medication ad," she admitted, "*but* it doesn't make it any less true."

I turned back toward the mirror and picked up the scissors again. That first soft snip cut through the restless buzz that had been moving through me, momentarily stilling it.

"Dang, you aren't playing," Priyanka said, delighted. "How short are you going?"

I showed her, gathering a few inches in my hand and cutting just below my chin. The long strands fell into the sink, curling around the drain. I stared at them until I wasn't seeing my hair, but a chunk of someone else's scalp. My vision shook along with the rest of me.

"Why don't you let me finish?" Priyanka suggested quietly, taking the scissors from me. She turned on the water and wet her hands, running them through my hair again and again until the tangles were gone, along with any last trace of dirt and smoke-scent.

I noticed the tattooed outline of a dark blue star on her wrist again, but before I could ask her about it, Priyanka demonstrated where she was planning to cut. "You want it that length, right?"

It was about an inch beneath my chin. I nodded, murmuring, "Thank you."

Weaving my fingers through each other, I clasped my hands together in front of me, squeezing until I couldn't feel them shaking anymore.

"No problem, I live for this," she said, snipping away. "When I see people upset, I just start grooming them until they feel pretty again. Roman won't let me near him with scissors. I used to cut Lana's hair all the time but . . . now I only ever get to do my own."

"Roman doesn't let you cut his hair?"

She met my gaze in the mirror. "Do you think I'd let him wear it so scruffy if I had a choice? But, no, it's a thing with him. Always has been. I don't know. Friendship is weird. I think it only works when you finally figure out what buttons you have to push to help them and what buttons are triggers that'll only hurt them."

"Are you my friend?" I hadn't meant to say the words, and I could hear that unbearable loneliness rooted in them.

Priyanka's hands stilled. "Of course, Sparky. I liked you from the jump, pretty much against my will. You're a great lesson in not judging a book by its government-groomed cover."

She leaned down until her face was next to mine in the mirror, giving me a devious little grin. I returned it with a tremulous one of my own.

The quiet *snip, snip, snip* of the scissors was soothing, almost hypnotic. As each long strand fell away, I no longer felt that anxious tug that was trying to pull me apart from all directions.

When she finished, Priyanka put a comforting hand on my head, running her fingers down through my wet hair again.

"Are you all right?" she asked, serious this time.

All right had become relative.

"I don't know why it still gets me so upset," I said, my throat aching. "It shouldn't. I hate them—I've hated my parents for years. It wasn't even just what they did to me, it was what they didn't do. Even after the camps fell, I kept thinking . . . maybe? Maybe now? They'll have seen that I was a good girl, and that I wasn't a danger to them. But they never came. They never called. Not until they needed me."

"What happened?" Priyanka asked. "What did he mean when he said Cruz intervened on your behalf?"

It had been the one rule Cruz had been willing to bend for me, and I'd felt guilty about it for years now—I'd felt like I owed it to her to do whatever she asked in return.

"You know how there was a policy put in place for reclaiming kids after the camps fell?" I asked. "Many of us were teenagers, a good number older than sixteen, and most felt like they shouldn't necessarily have to go back to parents who had turned them over to the government in the first place. Who had made them feel unwanted."

"I can understand that."

I nodded. "The UN and Cruz's people felt strongly that parents still had legal claims on those of us under eighteen. The compromise was that, if the parents didn't come to claim their kids, and their kids didn't want to go back, they wouldn't force the issue. Parents would be allowed to file claims of guardianship at any point, but in the interim, the government would re-home them."

Something flickered in Priyanka's expression when I said that. "What is it?"

"Nothing." She shook her head.

I watched her for a moment, waiting to see that same hesitation again. It never came. "Well . . . for a number of years, I lived with a friend—Cate—and the other kids she'd been looking out for. Then one day, I got the call. My parents wanted me. They *wanted* me. They applied to restore their guardianship and sent a letter to me along with the paperwork, saying how sorry they were, how frightened and confused they had been. My cousin, Hina, and her parents had been pushing me for years to try to talk to them. But I didn't want to go. Not really. The last time I'd seen them, they'd been so angry with me—I'd caused a horrible car accident in the middle of a busy highway, and it almost killed my mother."

"Shit," she breathed out.

I nodded again. "But . . . I had to set a good example. I had to show other kids that this could be a fresh start for all of us, and old wounds could be healed—insert whatever clichéd phrase you like there. I went. I got in a car, and I was driven to Falls Church with all of my things. We were about two miles from the neighborhood when I saw the first sign."

"A *Stop, Don't Come Any Closer, These People Are Bullshit* sign?"

"Kimura for Delegate. *A Better Tomorrow with Kimura.*"

Priyanka caught on quickly, and I loved her for her look of complete outrage. At the time, I'd felt like maybe I was making too big a deal out of it, that it was just a coincidence. It had been Agent Cooper driving me that day. He'd realized what was happening and had offered me the choice that no one else had. He'd risked disciplinary action over it.

"We parked a ways back from the house because we had to. There were so many news vans parked up and down the street. A nice little crowd, too. Everyone was waiting. He even had a banner hanging over the house's garage door: *Reuniting our families, reclaiming our future!*"

"I can't decide if I want to punch something or scream," Priyanka said. "What did you do?"

"We backed up and returned to DC," I said. "I never had the guts to read the news coverage from that day, but it must have been everywhere. I got questions about it for years, even after Mel put a ban on them."

Chubs and Vida had been waiting for me the second I got back. Chubs had hugged me so tightly I thought I wouldn't feel anything anymore. That would have been a relief. Instead, I held it in and had dinner with them, then raged and sobbed in private, with the shower running.

That's one of the few things rehabilitation camps gave you: the ability to hold in tears on command, and the knowledge of how to cry so no one will hear you.

I hadn't spoken to Hina or my aunt and uncle in almost a year. They were good, kind people, and had fallen out with my parents for years over my parents' decision to send me to a camp. I knew they'd been frustrated when I didn't move back to California to live with them, and I knew that frustration had only deepened when the wedge between me and my parents turned into a canyon. I just didn't want to hear their explanations, I didn't want to be cajoled. I wanted to *work*.

I turned to look at her and accidentally knocked the first-aid kit off the sink with my elbow. Priyanka and I both knelt to pick it up. In the process, something slid up out of the back pocket of her jeans and clattered against the floor. At first glance, it looked like the burner phone, but the rectangular device was a matte black, with no screen. Inside its casing was a faint charge.

"Backup battery for the phone," Priyanka explained, sliding it into her pocket as we stood. "In case we have to ditch the car. I was going to charge it in here for a while."

It must have been run down to nothing. The power whimpered as my mind brushed against it.

I tucked the first-aid kit against my chest, shooting her a grateful look. "Roman's probably getting worried. . . ."

"I think that's a *definitely*, not a *probably*," she said, now looking at herself in the mirror. "I'll be out in a few. I might try to wash my hair in this hellacious little basin."

I nodded, making my way to the door. Just before I slipped out into the warm summer night, I looked back. Priyanka had braced her hands against the rim of the sink and was staring at herself in the mirror, searching for something I wasn't meant to see.

TWENTY-FOUR

SOME PART OF ME HAD EXPECTED TO FIND ROMAN outside the door standing guard, but it looked like he hadn't moved at all. He was still gripping the steering wheel, staring out the windshield. I opened the front passenger door and dropped into the seat, shutting the door as quietly as I could.

For a long time, we sat in silence, watching the door of the bathroom. I didn't understand the tension I felt radiating off him. It wasn't directed at me, and neither was his look of quiet frustration.

"The haircut's that bad, huh?" I said lightly.

He looked over, then looked again. "Oh. No—I mean—"

"I'm kidding," I told him. "Everything all right?"

"Yes. No." A thread of anger pulled through the words. "He's wrong. About everything. He doesn't know you at all."

"Who's wrong?" I asked. "My father?"

He nodded, his brows low and his jaw set.

"Some of what he said is true," I said. "I did refuse to go home. I did hurt them by causing an accident. I did fail to live up to their expectations of what my life would be. But I take some umbrage with that one, mostly because I didn't exactly choose to have my power. I just chose to keep it."

Neither of my parents really bought into the concept of shikata ga nai, the knowledge that some things in life were simply outside of your control thanks to circumstances. My dad in particular was the type to believe that, with enough careful planning, there was little in this world that couldn't be brought in line or contained. One of the reasons it had been so hard to hang on to my anger after they sent me to school on Collection day was because I understood. I really did. My power had been anomalous to their worldview, and they struggled to rationalize it as much as I struggled to control it.

Roman turned in his seat, his eyes blazing. "There is nothing disappointing about you."

I leaned back, resting my temple against my seat's headrest. I didn't want to say anything. I wanted to live inside those words a little longer, even if there was a voice in my head whispering that I was a fraud. "I wish that were true."

He shook his head. "I know what failure is. I have failed so many times in my life, I can't even begin to understand how I'm still here. But you survived that camp, you used your voice to try to help others, you fought like hell against those kidnappers, you *saved* us from them—you, alone. You've navigated us this far, and you haven't backed down from anything, even as you've taken hit after hit. That's not *disappointing*. That's incredible."

I ducked my head slightly, a riot of emotion moving through me. In the backseat, I could have hidden that from him. The backseat was safe that way. You didn't have to join the conversation. You didn't have to be seen.

But I wanted to be seen. Because when Roman looked at me,

he only saw the person I was now. Someone capable, strong, and in control. Not the little girl with her gloves who only had control over her voice.

"How have you failed?" I asked him. "I can't even imagine it. Every time I get to the edge of being afraid, I just have to look at you. You hold it together, and you never miss a shot. You think every possibility through." Then I added, teasing, "You sing like an angel. . . ."

He let out a soft laugh, his hands slipping from the wheel and into his lap. His left hand rubbed absently at the scars on the back of his right. "I want to be that person you see."

"You *are* that person," I told him. "We don't have to be what anyone else wants us to be."

Roman smoothed his hair off his face. That same distance had returned to his eyes.

"My father lived and died to the rhythms of violence," Roman began. "He did odd jobs, and was always at the mercy of whoever he had a debt to or agreed to work for. My mother kept us away from him, but he was like a bruise on the heart of the family. We couldn't escape the stain of what he was doing, not fully. He was a terrifying man."

I waited for him to continue.

"My mother made me promise I wouldn't be like him. She really put a notch in my nose about it." The phrase was a new one for me, but I took his meaning. "I promised. Again and again. I'd go to school, become a doctor, or a fisherman, a banker, a teacher . . . anything but that. And here I am, good at the one thing I hate more than anything."

"Roman . . ." I began.

He tried to lighten his tone, but it didn't quite take. "I also promised her that I would take care of my sister. Taking care of Lana has always been my responsibility, from the time we were little. I couldn't even do that much. I looked away for a second, I focused on something else, and she slipped away."

Roman scrubbed at his face with his hands, letting out a frustrated sound. I felt for him and Priyanka right then, even more than I had before. They both did their best to hide it, in whatever ways they could, but seeing Lana had rattled them. Being near them was enough to feel the deep pain burning beneath their skin like a live wire.

"Sorry. I'm feeling sorry for myself," he said slowly, bracing his head against his hand. "I didn't expect to see Lana there, and to have her be like that was . . . I don't have a word for it."

I did. *Devastating.*

"I can't imagine what you've been through, even though I'm trying," I told him. "Nothing about failure is final unless you accept it. We're going to find Lana, and we're going to help her. I have no doubt about that, unlike everything else in this situation."

"Proving your innocence, you mean?" he asked.

"And getting justice for the people who died," I said. That was the most important thing in all this. "But if Clancy was right and Ruby left on her own, it means my theory about her disappearance being connected to the kidnappers just got knocked out. I'm not sure how I'm going to collect evidence now if we're on a completely different trail."

"Once you have the evidence, though, what are you going to do with it?" Roman asked. "Is there anyone in the government you still trust enough to give it to?"

The way he said that last part gave me pause. "What do you mean by that? You think the government is involved?"

"No, no," he said quickly. "I meant someone who would take it seriously and get it into the right, unbiased hands."

"It's government," I said dryly. "Everyone's got a bias. Everyone's picked a side, I just have to find someone on mine. The only way to beat this narrative they've built about me is to create one that's even stronger. One that's unassailable."

"Similar to what you did for the camps," he said, putting it together. "Creating the media package of interviews and footage."

I nodded. "Stories are powerful. You can give people a list of facts and they'll be dismissed or ignored. People believe what they feel is true. So I have to make them feel something. I have to make them angry on my behalf, sympathetic to the victims, and try to restore some of that trust Moore is chipping away at."

"Sounds nearly impossible," he said. "So, all in a day's work for you."

For the first time in days, I smiled.

I want to be that person you see.

Priyanka barreled toward the car, her face glowing with excitement.

"Uh-oh," Roman said, turning the key in the ignition. But before she reached us, he turned to look at me one last time and said, "I more than like your hair. You look like yourself."

I knew what he meant.

"What's up?" I asked Priyanka as she slid into the backseat and slammed the door shut with flourish. She must have gotten a good charge on the extra battery. The power had jumped from a spark to a steady flame.

"Your genius friend has had a genius moment," she announced. "Remember how, after we tried calling the number creepy Clancy texted and got the invalid-number error message, you told me to leave it alone so you could have time to think about what you wanted to do, et cetera?"

"*Priya,*" Roman said. "The point?"

She gave him an exasperated look. "I did a quick search on the area code, except the area code isn't in use."

"Really?" I asked.

"It's close to three-three-four, which is an Alabama area code, so I tried that number, and that one had also been disconnected."

"You think it's a typo?" I had never known Clancy Gray to get facts incorrect. If this was the number she'd left with him, I had a hard time believing that he hadn't tried it at least once, if only out of curiosity. He would have known it wasn't connected before giving it to me. I told the others as much.

"I was thinking about that, too," Roman said. "If his aim is to protect Ruby, then he might want to see how quickly you'll follow up for the correct information. How eager you are to track her down. That, or he's giving everyone who comes looking the same bad information to throw us all off her trail."

"Or he just didn't check and was helping out a friend by passing along the information she asked him to," Priyanka said. "Which is what I'm leaning toward now that I know it's not a phone number at all, but something else entirely."

She held up a scrap of newspaper she'd picked up somewhere, pointing out where she'd tried out a few ways of breaking the number up into coordinates. The last one was circled.

"This is the only one that brought up an actual address when I searched it," she said. "It's just outside of Athens, Georgia. It looks like a little house."

"Do you want to go?" Roman asked me.

"It's a long drive, but if there's a chance that she's there, I think we have to try, right?" I said.

"We can do that," Roman said softly. "But we're going to have to find more gas. And get more supplies. Food, water, and the like."

"Except we don't exactly have money for all that," Priyanka pointed out.

They both turned to me, but there wasn't another choice. We all knew what that meant.

"I'll find us a drugstore that's closed for the night," Roman said. "In and out."

Thank God the economy had recovered enough to reopen drugstores we could steal from. I should have felt worse about it than I did, but the world had taken so much from me over the last week. Maybe it was okay to take this much back from it.

I hated the feeling of waking up without realizing I'd nodded off almost as much as I hated opening my eyes to an empty car.

I sat up, trying to swallow the sour taste of sleep. There was a little water left in one of the bottles in the cup holders. I drank it down greedily, wiping my mouth against my sleeve.

As promised, Roman had found us a drugstore. The store was dark from what I could see through the windows, and the parking lot was empty, but it didn't do much to soothe my spiky anxiety. I had no idea how long they'd been inside.

Roman had taken care to leave the car outside the halos of light from the streetlamps. I rolled down the windows, trying to wake myself up with some cooler, cleaner air. Small bursts of power indicated security cameras nearby. Even with Priyanka's device, I didn't want to risk getting out and having one capture my face. Instead, I climbed awkwardly over the console and into the driver's seat.

Roman's limbs were so much longer than mine that I had to shift the seat up a good foot. I caught sight of them in the rearview mirror as I adjusted it. Their voices carried farther in the quiet night than either of them seemed to realize.

"If something happens—" Roman was saying.

"I don't need it," Priyanka shot back. "What I need is for you to let me do whatever I have to do. I shouldn't have to hold back because *you're* scared."

Roman didn't say anything, but I caught a glimpse of his face as he walked up to the driver's side, the deep unhappiness and worry there. When he saw me, Roman jerked to a stop, and then climbed in the back; Priyanka took the front. Both slammed their doors shut.

"What was that all about?" I asked. "What do you have to do, and what are you scared of?"

"Nothing," Priyanka said even as Roman said, "Everything."

I blinked. "Okay."

"Roman wouldn't let me take money out of their safe," she said, handing me a packet of Goldfish from her plastic bag, "that's all. I don't like feeling useless when I know I could be doing more."

"You are not useless," I told her.

I couldn't see Roman's face in the rearview mirror.

"Are we good?" I asked.

This time, neither of them answered.

TWENTY-FIVE

I PARKED THE CAR ALONGSIDE A CRACKED DRIVEWAY, staring up at the small house at the end of it. My head was heavy and ached with the need to sleep, but my heart had been galloping since we crossed the Georgia state line.

"Here," Roman said, passing me a water bottle. I took it gratefully, chugging until it was gone.

Priyanka squinted at the structure through the darkness. "Wow, what a super-fun murder house. Can't wait to go in."

Roman slid the rest of the way across the backseat, rolling down the window. "No movement inside. No lights."

The white cottage-style house appeared bigger on second glance. The left half of it had been built into the hill's natural curve, adding a lower story to the home. Over the years, wildlife had crept up on the property. The trees in the backyard were overgrown and threatening to topple onto the roof.

It looked abandoned. But that didn't mean it was.

"I'm glad we came," I said. "Even if this is a dead end, at least we can rule it out."

I hadn't put enough hope into this to feel truly disappointed if that ended up being the case. The idea of Ruby living in a place like this only filled me with more dread.

"Let's go have a quick look and be on our way," Priyanka said. She reached into the backpack at her feet for one of the flashlights, prompting me to pull the other one out from the seat pocket.

The night was alive with a symphony of cicadas and moaning power lines. Heavy cables stretched over the front yard. As I passed beneath them, sound became sensation. Every nerve in my body lit up with awareness of the electricity around me. The streetlamp, another house's garage door, and something . . . *something* inside the house.

My footsteps stilled. Priyanka swept her flashlight's beam over the front of the house. Roman clicked off the safety on his gun.

An object moved at the edge of my vision. I switched on my flashlight, searching for the small wind chime I'd thought I'd seen hanging at the slumped edge of the porch.

I hadn't imagined it. The wind chime glinted as the beam's glow passed over it. A breeze swept up from behind us, making it shiver out light notes, but I couldn't tear my eyes away from that small piece of glass. The one shaped like a crescent moon.

I bolted ahead, jumping up over the stairs and onto the porch.

"Zu, wait!" Priyanka called. She lunged, catching the back of my shirt. "Slow down. You don't know what, let alone *who*, is inside."

"I think it's her," I said, breathless. "There's a power source inside, something electronic. . . ."

"This place could be rigged to explode," Roman said. "The door could be on some kind of trigger."

"Okay, I wasn't thinking *that*," Priyanka said. "Thanks for the mental image, though."

He reached over us, grabbing one of the boards nailed over the front windows. The rusted nail keeping it in place slid free with one strong pull. Roman peered through the window, angling his body just enough to keep from giving anyone inside a target to shoot at.

"It's clear," he said, moving in front of the window to pry another board loose.

"There's some kind of machine in there," I told them. "The feeling is faint, but . . . it's almost like it's not fully on or off?"

"That's not exactly reassuring." Priyanka turned toward the door, raising her booted foot. "One way to find out."

She kicked it open, splintering the door from where it had been locked into its frame.

Roman ducked inside first, doing a quick visual scan of the house.

"Zu? Priya?" he called. "I think you'd better come here. . . ."

"Every time someone says that, it's bad news," I said, taking in a steadying breath.

"Well, we didn't blow up just now," Priyanka said, dropping an arm over my shoulder as we stepped inside. "How bad can it be?"

I'd been prepared for bad. I hadn't been prepared for this.

"Huh," I said, putting my hands on my hips.

"Hello, gorgeous," Priyanka cooed.

The house was devoid of furniture. Even the cabinets in the kitchen had been stripped of their doors. As far as I could tell, the only thing inside the house was a freestanding server rack, complete with a monitor. It was the source of the low voltage I had felt outside.

Roman circled the server rack, kicking at its cord. It was still plugged into the wall, but the system had clearly idled. "Is it malfunctioning? It doesn't seem to be on."

"There was probably an outage and it just needs to be rebooted," Priyanka said. "Want me to do the honors?"

I wiped my finger along the monitor, slashing through the thick dust. No one had been here recently. Certainly not Ruby. But if she'd sent us here, I wanted to know why. "Yeah. Turn it on. Let's see what information she felt was too dangerous to keep at Haven."

Priyanka passed her flashlight to me, cracking her knuckles. "I've been dying to get my hands on an Arclight four hundred. This one is a few years old, but it's the sweet, sweet rose of secure servers. You've got to have careful hands to avoid its thorns."

Roman returned my perplexed look with one of his own.

Priyanka hummed as she went down the row of machines on the rack, pushing buttons. The change in the flow of electricity was immediate, stroking my senses as the machines warmed up and began to whir. There was a small keyboard drawer just beneath the monitor. She tested a few of the keys.

"Leaving it here where anyone could break in and steal it seems like a big risk," Roman said slowly. "You said they had a solid security and tech setup at Haven, including a server, right?"

"Yeah," I said. "Then again, big risks can have big rewards."

"It just seems . . . careless. She wouldn't be able to stop anyone from taking it," Roman continued. "It's not a close enough drive for her to intervene if someone tried."

My heart began to pound. "You think it belongs to someone else?"

"I think she was trying to make sure that someone would know about this place," Roman said simply. "In the event she couldn't get to it herself."

"Ah!" Priyanka let out a happy little noise. "I don't need to reboot at all—the plug for the second server came loose. Here we go."

Priyanka beamed as the screen switched on with an electronic *beep*. The difference in the flow of power to the devices was immediate; a sudden surge erupted from the nearby outlet, flowing through the veins of wiring like blood.

Giving Priyanka a worried glance, Roman moved back toward the window and took up post there, keeping watch of the street. "Something about this doesn't feel right. I'm going to check the perimeter of the house, make sure there's nothing going on."

By the time I looked back to acknowledge what he'd said, Roman was already outside.

The keys clacked like machine-gun fire. In the darkness of the house, the computer screen cast Priyanka in an eerie green glow.

"Anything?" I asked, coming to stand beside her. The endless scrolling code was meaningless to me.

She chewed on her lower lip. "I need another minute. The security on this system is—"

The screen blanked out.

"What just happened?" I asked.

Priyanka's fingers flew over the keyboard. "I don't know—"

The screen flickered. A word appeared.

UPLOADING . . .

Over and over, that same word.

```
UPLOADING . . .
UPLOADING . . .
```

"Uploading *what*?" I asked.

Priyanka typed in a command.

```
FILE TRANSFER UNKNOWN USER
UPLOAD COMPLETE
ARCHIVE 1 DELETED
UPLOAD COMPLETE
ARCHIVE 2 DELETED
```

"Shit," Priyanka said. "Someone is downloading and deleting the material off the server."

"Who?" I demanded. "Isn't there some way to tell?"

```
UPLOAD COMPLETE
ARCHIVE 3 DELETED
```

She looked between the door and the flickering screen.

```
UPLOAD COMPLETE
ARCHIVE 4 DELETED
```

"Let me unplug it—"

"No, don't unplug it, it could corrupt the data," Priyanka said. "Just— Oh, screw it. Let's go, you skiddie."

Her hands moved from the keyboard to the monitor. She gripped it tightly, closing her eyes.

"Priya?"

They flashed open again, just as the screen exploded with more lines of green code. Letters and numbers flew across the screen, flickering between the upload status and a list of encrypted files.

"Can't . . . get in . . ."

UPLOAD COMPLETE
ARCHIVE 5 DELETED

"Priya? *Priyanka!*" As I reached for her, a static bolt jumped between my finger and her shoulder. I bit my tongue at the snap of pain, but she didn't so much as flinch. Her eyes were wide open, her pupils the size of pins. They tracked back and forth frantically, as if she were caught in a REM cycle.

"Can't . . . need . . ."

UPLOAD COMPLETE
ARCHIVE 6 DELETED

When I connected with a circuit, I'd always imagined myself dissolving into a million particles of light and energy. I knew it was impossible, that I hadn't actually become the electricity, but reason could tell you one thing while instinct told you another. Watching Priyanka now, her body as stiff as the server's rack, all I could think of was a plug slipping into an outlet.

The screen pulsed with files, images, code, flittering across the screen too quickly for my mind to grasp what I was actually seeing. Priyanka's eyes rolled back into her skull, still sliding back and forth as if she were scanning lines of material faster than any human could.

```
UPLOAD PAUSED
UPLOADING . . .
UPLOAD PAUSED
UPLOADING . . .
```

The door shut behind me. I whirled around in time to see Roman's face fall as he took in the sight of her.

He shot across the room, coming just short of touching her as Priyanka's whole body began to vibrate. I couldn't tell where the power source to the servers began and Priyanka ended. Roman snapped his fingers in front of her face. "Damn you, Priya, let up!"

"She told me not to unplug it—"

"*No*, don't do that!" Roman barked. "It'll send her into shock. I need—I need you to go into the car. The trunk. There are two bottles, one's labeled *metoprolol* and the other *haloperidol*. I need one syringe."

"What is this?" I felt like I was begging. "How is she doing this?"

The flood of information on the screen matched the tremors working through her, the flickering of her eyes, the rattling of the devices on the rack. Distantly, I was aware of the sharp trill of the servers, the smell of smoke and melting plastic.

She's in the computer.

Her mind was . . .

Roman set his shoulders back, taking in a deep, steadying breath. His hand hovered over her arm, but didn't touch her. "Take the gun off me and hold on to it."

I did, sliding it into my own waistband. "What's happening?"

"You're going to be all right," he said—not to Priyanka, but to me. "*Please*. Get the metoprolol and haloperidol."

As Roman finally grabbed on to Priyanka, the lines of his body went painfully rigid.

"I can pull her out . . . don't . . . unplug . . ." he murmured.

He jerked, swaying slightly on his feet. His eyes snapped shut, but I could see them moving beneath the lids, that same trance-like state.

"I'm going to kill you both," I muttered. "Just as soon as I wake up from this hallucination."

That was the explanation I clung to. It could be that I was still in the car, still asleep, and this was . . . what had Chubs called it? Sleep paralysis, where your mind is awake enough to feel ter-rorized by your nightmares, but your body is locked in a prison of unconsciousness, unable to react or fend off the monsters.

Whatever this was, this connection to the machines, it wasn't psionic. But, no, that wasn't right, either—it *could* be psionic. That term encapsulated anything related to unnatural powers of the mind. It just wasn't like anything I'd ever seen.

One thing was for certain: they sure as hell weren't Green or Yellow.

The machines whined pitifully, power choking their internal circuit boards. Every sound in the room aside from our breathing was unnatural. Clicking, pulsing, whirring, beeping.

I shook myself out of the daze and ran for the door. Grass and mud splattered against my ankles as I crossed the lawn and fumbled with the trunk's latch. Roman had left the car unlocked, which struck me as a careless move for someone who otherwise thought of nearly everything when it came to our safety.

He thought this might happen, I realized. He must have.

I tore open the drugstore bags, picking through the boxes of medicine and food until I found the bottles I needed. One, the metoprolol, was in pill form and the other, haloperidol, was in liquid form.

The syringe—that's why I needed it. I found a box of them and dumped them out, clutching a handful. Neither of the boxes had instructions on how to administer them.

"Of course not, because it's supposed to be done by a fucking doctor," I muttered. "What the *hell*—?"

A sudden spark of power shot across my senses, burning through every other thought. My adrenaline kicked in as I straightened, searching for the source. Distant, but coming nearer. Three . . . four . . . five . . . six sparks. Low-grade power like . . .

Comms. Soldiers.

I pressed the medicine to my chest and bolted for the house, shoving the door open with my shoulder. My feet slid across the dusty floor, coming to a dead stop.

The bottles and syringes tumbled from my arms as I reached back and pulled out the gun I'd taken from Roman.

"Back. Up."

Lana hovered beside Roman and Priyanka, staring at them through the curtain of her wild hair. She hadn't touched them; she hadn't seemed to have done anything to them. Yet.

The girl didn't move. She only looked at me with that thousand-yard stare. "Where's her medicine?"

"Back up," I warned her again, switching the safety off.

The sparks were close now, just on the other side of the house. Another extraction team.

As soon as that thought registered, another came right on its heels: I still had my power.

"Blue star . . ."

My gaze shot back to Priyanka. She was trembling harder now, as if it were taking every last bit of strength she had to hold on.

"Blue star," she was muttering, "blue star, blue star, blue star . . ."

The words tugged at something in my mind, some memory.

"That's right, Pri. Figured it out, have you?" The girl was fixated on Roman's and Priyanka's stiff forms, watching through heavy-lidded eyes as they worked. Then, like puppets whose strings had been cut, they collapsed to the floor, still writhing. Lana ignored me, ignored the gun, and went for the medicine.

I fired a shot at the ground beside her, stopping her. Outside, the team of soldiers that had come to support her was gathering. I only had seconds before they stormed the house.

My gaze fixed on the other girl. Lana's presence alone wasn't what caused the suppression. She must have had to will it to happen, just like the rest of us. And right now, I was still free of it.

My silver thread of power wove through each of the sparks outside. I seized control of the batteries on their comm units and urged the electricity forward, tugging until I heard the soldiers begin to shout in agony.

All six power signatures went out. No new ones approached.

A few of the soldiers were still alive; I heard them groaning in pain. The first attack hadn't been enough to erase the threat they posed. Not completely. The thread found another, bigger power source. The AC unit idling outside.

Lana looked up slowly, her eyes narrowing, and I seized that one last opportunity.

The explosion from the unit knocked us both off our feet, sending the gun sailing out of my hand. My vision blacked out as my head cracked against the ground.

When I came to, Lana had pushed herself up off the floor. She staggered to her feet, pressing a hand against a cut on her forehead. The back wall of the house was on fire. Tendrils of it raced along the floors and ceiling, pouring more smoke into the room.

She dropped down onto her knees beside the liquid medicine, clutching one of the syringes in her fist. She jabbed the needle into the open bottle and filled it with surprising care, eyeing the measurement.

Roman groaned from the ground, his legs curling in pain. He didn't seem aware of his sister or the explosion. There was no world outside of whatever agony was scorching him from the inside out.

Lana crawled toward Priyanka, the syringe in her hand. I dove for her, tackling her back to the ground.

The lance of pain that skidded across my brain still caught me by surprise as Lana switched off my powers. Her elbow knocked me back. That same horrible rush of hot pins ran down my back, leaving a jagged, gaping emptiness, as if my abilities had been physically torn out from under my skin.

"You . . ." I choked out.

"She needs her medicine!" Lana growled at me. "I'm trying to help her!"

I lashed out a foot, knocking the syringe from her hand.

Something seemed to occur to her. A rare light entered her eyes.

"You don't even know," Lana taunted, her voice turning singsong. "You don't even know! Aw, did you think they were your friends? Did they tell you some sad story about how very awful their lives have been?"

"They told me enough," I said, as we circled each other. Lana licked her lips, obviously relishing this. "They told me about the Psion Ring."

Her face screwed up. "The Psion Ring? What are you talking about? We were raised by Gregory Mercer—you've heard of him, haven't you? I can see it in your face."

Mercer. Blue Star.

The connection snapped into place. I *did* know that name. He was on Interpol's wanted list for weapons trafficking. His had been one of the few crime syndicates to stay afloat and thrive after the United States' borders had been closed during the Psi epidemic.

Blue Star. His organization.

Blue Star. Like the tattoo on Priyanka's wrist. Like the tattoo Lana pushed up her sleeve to show me on her own wrist.

The cold shock of it left me standing in place, my feet frozen to the floor.

Liars. The word hissed through me, as bitter as it was ugly.

After everything, they'd still lied to me. The only difference was that this time, I'd been stupid enough to believe them.

Whatever happened to once bitten, twice shy? I asked myself savagely.

"Mr. Mercer made us. He *cared* for us," Lana said. "My brother and Priyanka let someone else fill their heads with lies. They hurt him when they left, so badly, and I—" Her face hardened with rage. "They'll need to answer for it. But the punishment won't be as harsh, now that they've decided to come back with me."

I straightened, unable to hide my surprise at the girl's conviction.

"They don't *want* to go back," I told her, my throat raw from the smoke. "They want to help you get away from . . . from Mercer."

"Do they?" Lana asked, her voice too sweet for the dark look on her face. "Why else would they be here, turning on the server and helping Mercer? That little worm wouldn't give us the actual server location. He would only give us remote access to it after we extracted him from the house."

"Who's *he*?" But I knew. I already knew.

Anger, as helpless as it was scalding, poured through me. It was impossible. Clancy's memory was locked down. How could he remember where he'd left a server in his past life enough to— The rest of her words caught up to me.

Extraction. Clancy had asked Blue Star to get him out of his house. Out of Charleston.

Somehow, he remembered.

Lana only smiled. "The boss's business is his own."

Behind her, a section of the wall collapsed. Neither of us so much as flinched.

"You don't believe me," she said. Reaching into her jacket's pocket she pulled out a familiar black device. The spare battery. "Tell me, why was Priya carrying the tracker from the drone? Why did she switch it on, if she didn't want me to come get them?"

I drew in a sharp breath, choking on it. The blood left my head so rapidly it felt as if the floor were tilting up underfoot.

If we keep chasing her, she'll run farther and faster, Priyanka had said. *We have to find a way to get her to come to us.*

Oh, Priyanka, I thought, glancing toward her shifting form on the ground. *Of all the stupid, desperate things . . .*

"She wasn't telling you she wanted a pickup," I told Lana. "She was luring you into a trap. And you fell right into it."

Lana's face transformed, hardening with rage. Her top lip peeled back, and it was my only warning before she charged.

The wind rushed out of me as she drove her head into my gut, knocking us both to the ground. I shoved back at her as she hissed and clawed, pinning me, her knees locked tight to my side. I tried kicking her off as her fist slammed into my cheek.

"It was you, wasn't it?" she screamed into my face. "You're the one who changed them! You're the one who took them away!"

Don't let them get you on your back. Vida's voice floated through my mind as dark spots clouded my vision. *You'll never be able to get up again.*

I wheezed. She leaned over me, her hands around my neck.

Get back up. . . .

My nails were broken or gone altogether, but they still left ragged marks across her nose and brow as I raked them across her face.

"I don't have to bring *you* back alive," she told me. "It'd be easier for him if you were gone. It *will* be easier."

Her pupils dilated until her irises were nearly gone, and the hate in her expression made my skin feel like it was being flayed off even before the boiling agony filled my skull. It blew apart my last thoughts. My feet drummed on the ground beneath us, my whole body writhing in pain as my vision feathered with black.

At the edge of awareness, I heard the explosive *crack* of a gunshot and the pressure and pain suddenly eased across my whole body. With the weight off my chest, smoky air rapidly filled my lungs. I gasped and coughed, fighting the phantom hands still squeezing my throat.

Lana stood, staggering back toward the small kitchen. Her palm pressed against her shoulder. But there was no blood; the bullet hadn't pierced through skin or muscle. There was only a rip in her jacket where the shot had grazed over the leather.

Roman had found the gun I'd lost and had lifted his torso off the ground just enough to get the shot off. I wasn't sure which one of them looked more stunned by what he'd done. "Lana—*wait!*"

She turned and vanished through the smoke, and, in an instant, I knew I hadn't taken out all the soldiers. Two figures, their pale faces burned to a painful, angry red, emerged out of the darkness of the kitchen, charging forward. Roman fired again, downing one of them, but the other already had him in his sights.

An enraged scream filled the house. Priyanka, illuminated by fire, was on her feet now. Every muscle in her body looked strung too tight as she gripped the server rack and hauled it, and all the attached devices, up off the ground as if it weighed nothing. She threw it at the soldier hard enough for it to crack the floor as it fell on top of him.

"Priya!" Roman shouted, his voice strangled. "Stop!"

She charged toward the man, crossing the room faster than I could blink. Shoving the server rack out of her way, she knelt on his chest, clasping her hands together high over her head and slamming them down on his face. Her movements were so erratic and sharp it felt like I was watching a film skip through frames.

She was too fast. Too strong. I could see her pulse beating through her skin, racing harder and harder as she drove her hands down.

Roman crawled forward, snatching up the syringe that Lana had filled. Priyanka was still turning the man's face into a bloody pulp when he stumbled up behind her and pressed the needle into her neck, jamming down the plunger.

"*No!*" she howled, swatting at it. "I'm not finished! This isn't enough!"

Her arm knocked Roman hard enough to send him sliding across the room. He collided with the bottle of pills and snatched it up, struggling to get the lid off.

Priyanka shot to her feet with almost inhuman ease, her eyes too glassy and too bright. There was a predator's focus to her expression. "Where is she? Where did she go?"

"I'll—I'll show you," I rasped out, standing on unsteady legs.

"Stop her!" Roman said, panic ringing in the words. "Don't let Priya leave!"

The servers still had a lick of power left in their warm bodies. As I passed the rack, I brushed my leg against one of them, catching that slight charge and carrying it forward that last foot of distance to Priyanka.

The snap of faint voltage jumped from my fingers to her skin. She straightened, her eyes wide as it momentarily stunned her. It was just enough time to wrap her up in my arms and pin hers to her side.

Roman pressed the pills into her mouth, holding his palm over it to keep her from spitting them out. Priyanka fought both of us. Her too-fast pulse pounded against my skin as her muscles and ligaments turned to steel.

"You have to swallow them, I'm sorry, I know," Roman was saying. "Please, take them, just *take them*—"

I could tell she hadn't meant to, but she did. Sweat streaked Roman's face as he pulled his hand back.

"Lana," she cried, still trying to get away. Her pulse was slowing, though, the strength sapping out of her. "*No*. . . . Let me help. . . . Please . . . I'm . . . not . . ."

"What did you give her?" I demanded.

"A sedative and . . ." Roman pressed his hand against his head. "And something to keep her from having a stroke."

Distant sirens underscored his words.

"Shit," he said, pulling Priyanka's arm around his neck. I retrieved the gun he'd used, then moved to her other side. Her legs had turned to sand beneath her, forcing me to absorb her weight.

"We have to get out of here," Roman said, blinking rapidly. Sweat dripped from my face. The smoke was making it hard to think, and if we stayed any longer, the roof would fall in on us.

But Roman seemed almost as unsteady as Priyanka. We made slow, staggering progress across the yard. The heat from the fire roared at our backs.

When we reached the car, Roman struggled to open the back door, his hand slipping off the handle like he couldn't get a grip on it.

"I'll do it! Just go start the car!" I ordered. It still felt like Lana's hands were on my neck, choking the words out of me by force.

Roman nodded, stumbling to the front of the car. The engine started just as I had gotten most of Priyanka's long body through the door. My muscles sang in relief as I laid her in the backseat.

I checked her pulse one more time, satisfied to find it slow and steady.

"Did you see where Lana went?" Roman asked, his voice thin.

Fury swelled in me again as I threw the front passenger door open and slammed it shut behind me. "She got away."

He brought both hands down on the steering wheel and swore again, this time in what I assumed was Russian.

"No," I told him. The emergency vehicle sirens were closer now, maybe only a few streets away. "*You* don't get to be angry about this. Just drive!"

Roman didn't move. He searched the street with a desperation that might have broken my heart in any other circumstance. So I did the only thing I could think of. I pulled the gun on him.

I gritted my teeth. *"Drive."*

He reached down for the stick shift, moving it out of park. The sedan lurched forward, banking up on the curve before slamming back down onto the road again. The engine revved as he tore onto the next street.

The static was back, pouring through my skull. The lights on the dashboard flickered.

"Tell me what's going on," I said, keeping the gun steady. I pressed my back up against the window, putting as much distance between us as I could. In the backseat, Priyanka moaned something insensible. "Tell me about Blue Star—what it has to do with any of this!"

Roman's eyes blinked rapidly, color draining off his face like ink bleeding from wet paper. One of his fists came up to mash against his temples, beating against it. His breath fluttered in and out of his bloodless lips, which pulled back in obvious agony.

"Stop it," I whispered. The gun shook in my hand. "Stop it! Stop hurting yourself—"

"Take . . ." he began. The car lurched right before he straightened it again. "Take . . . the . . . wheel. . . ."

It was the last thing Roman said before he slumped forward in a dead faint.

I shot across the seat, gripping the wheel. The speedometer climbed up and up and up past eighty, ninety, a hundred. The road came to a dead end at a school under construction just ahead; the headlights skimmed over a yellow banner proudly proclaiming OPENING FOR THE BRIGHTEST MINDS NEXT YEAR!

There wasn't time to pull him out of the seat. I climbed over him, sitting on his lap and kicking his foot off the gas. The car squealed as I slammed my foot on the brake and spun the wheel to the right until it finally locked.

The car skidded to a stop, but not before bumping the scaffolding surrounding the sign. The banner fluttered down onto the hood of the car.

Then, finally, everything was still.

"What . . ." I breathed out, "the . . . *fuck* . . . is going . . . on?"

TWENTY-SIX

I SAT ON THE EMPTY DIRT ROAD, BETWEEN THE BEAMS of the two headlights. The same dust we'd kicked up speeding down the deserted country lane still floated lazily in the air, as if unable to settle itself. With the light blurring out the dark landscape, I could almost imagine that this was what it would be like inside an electrical current. Everything was aglow. Everything was simplified. I watched the hypnotic dance of the dust particles as they drifted down again and ignored the tide of dark thoughts as long as I could.

All along, I'd felt like I was missing at least one piece of this mess. So many aspects of it hadn't made any sense, even after I found out about Lana. Some parts of it still didn't.

I told myself that was the reason I hadn't already left them on the side of the road. For a few minutes, I'd been angry enough to seriously consider it. The only thing more powerful than the suffocating feeling of betrayal, though, had been the need to know. To force the last few answers out of them, if I had to.

The air was fresh and dry here, and for a while, all I did was listen to my breath wheeze in and out as the smoke finally left my lungs. I'd hoped it would carry some of my humiliation out with it, but the momentary peace didn't last, and I couldn't hold back the torrent of thoughts. All my questions seemed to shift with the wind. *Why did they lie?* became *Why did you believe them?*

Their desire to help Lana had explained everything I needed to know, and their willingness to help save the Haven kids had told me everything else that mattered.

Was I really that desperate for friendship, for any real connection, that I'd stopped questioning and analyzing everything that was happening? Had it been worth it to trade control and survival for a few minutes of laughter and living?

This has only ever been about using you.

That was truth of my life, wasn't it? For a long time, I hadn't been able to accept it, never mind do something about it. I'd had friends once, but lately, people only pretended to care about me as long as I could do something for them. Even Mel had been assigned to me. It hadn't been a choice.

I couldn't separate the thought of Mel from that of her death, and I couldn't stop crying once I'd started. I leaned forward, bracing my arms against my knees, letting the tears drip off my face into the dirt.

"You're—" The words locked in my chest. *You're so stupid. How could you be so stupid?*

I wasn't stupid. I had *never* been stupid. I was just . . . alone.

Wiping my face with my shirt, I took in a deep breath. Somehow, in the last few minutes, I'd become smaller, folding down into myself. I straightened. My hands toyed with the loose gravel on the road.

"Stop feeling sorry for yourself," I said, repeating it until the words became stronger, a command. *"Stop feeling sorry for yourself."*

I didn't have time for this. The killers were still out there. My name was soaked in blood. The kids at Haven were counting on me to find Ruby and Liam.

"You didn't leave."

I hadn't even heard the door open, or his footsteps—but that was just Roman. For all his strength, for all his deadly training, he moved through life like a whisper. Standing outside the headlights, his outline was only a bit darker than the night sky behind him, a shade away from disappearing.

Despite everything, his voice still made my heart lurch. "Is that disappointment I detect in your tone?"

"Zu—Suzume," he corrected himself. I didn't understand why that formality, of all things, cut me.

"Where could I have gone?" I asked him seriously, looking back. "What could I have done that wouldn't have involved dumping your unconscious bodies on the side of some road?"

He moved unsteadily toward the hood of the car, sitting on it.

"You would have been within your rights," Roman said. "I wouldn't have blamed you."

"Is Priyanka awake?" I asked.

He shook his head.

"Are you worried about it at all?" I asked, unable to keep the bitterness from edging into those words. "Or is that something I don't get to know either?"

"I wanted to tell you—"

I pushed up onto my feet. "It doesn't matter what you *wanted* to do. It matters what you *did*. Which was lie to me."

Roman, at least, didn't try to dispute that. I came to stand in front of him, crossing my arms over my chest. His eyes found the bruises on my neck and stayed there, until what little color there had been in his face was gone.

"Are you all right?" he asked.

"Not really."

Roman didn't look away. His hands turned up in his lap in a pose of supplication.

"Will you hear my explanation?" he asked. "I understand if you want to leave. But I need you to hear this, because it affects you. Your safety."

"I'm willing to hear your explanation, but I can't promise I won't interrupt you with a hard punch," I said. "Right now, that's all I really want to do."

You made me like you.

His gaze had fallen onto the sedan's hood. At that, he looked up again. "You can. If it'll make you feel better. Priyanka tells me there are moments I am highly punchable."

I wanted you to like me, too.

I shook my head. "Just talk."

He released a long breath.

I leaned a hip against the hood of the car, letting the night seep into my skin. Waiting. Roman seemed to need a moment to gather his thoughts, or, at least, construct a story in his head. It should have been my first indication there were no easy explanations.

"Have you heard of an organization called Blue Star?" he asked.

"You mean the organization you actually worked for?" His eyes widened as I said, "I heard Priyanka saying the name in the house. Your sister charmingly filled in the details for me."

He blew out a hard breath. "Then you know that it's a crime syndicate. A family. Run by Gregory Mercer."

"I've heard of him," I said. "He's a smuggler. Mostly weapons."

Roman nodded. "Running guns is a lucrative part of his business. When he was first starting out, building his name, he would take on hired work—assassinations, art thefts, bribes, money laundering. But his business didn't expand until he started developing new drugs and flooding the market with them."

"Whadda guy," I said flatly.

"The drugs weren't originally meant for market. They were the byproducts of another one of his schemes—finding a way to re-create the chemical that induced the Psi mutation in children."

"Agent Ambrosia," I supplied.

"Right. Agent Ambrosia." Roman took one last deep breath. "Years ago . . . when I was only five, and Lana was three, our mother fell on very hard times. I told you about my father."

I nodded.

"She wouldn't take that money from him. She tried to keep us fed and safe and warm on her own. She *tried*." It seemed important to him that I understand that. "We were living in Tolyatti—in Russia—when we started to hear about the troubles in America. How they were cursed with illness and their children were dying. It frightened everyone when there were a handful of cases in our country. We were no longer sent to school. We were no longer allowed outside to play with the other kids in the nearby flats. But the worst came when the economy in America crashed. The illness did not spread like we expected, but the collapse of businesses did. The car manufacturer our mother worked for closed. She lost her job, and we nearly lost everything."

"I'm sorry," I said, and somehow, it didn't feel like enough. "But . . . how did you end up here in America?"

He tilted his head, letting it lean toward his right shoulder. "Our mother would work odd jobs at all hours of the day and night. We were left to ourselves most of the time. One day, when Lana and I were outside playing, a police officer approached us. He said that our mother had been in a horrible accident, and that we needed to come to the hospital with him."

I straightened. "Was that true?"

"No. We were loaded into a van with a few other kids and told to be quiet, or they'd kill us. We were going to a new home. They took us to an orphanage thousands of miles away, in Ukraine. They—these men"—Roman's hands tightened around the hood—"they tried to separate me and Lana, but she was so sick. She was sick all the time. They quickly realized I would take care of her and keep her alive. They didn't care how it was done, they just wanted their money. We were only at the orphanage for a year before Mercer bought us."

"*Bought* you?" I repeated.

"The United States had closed its borders. He couldn't legally bring us in. He couldn't legally adopt us. The man in charge of the orphanage was willing to secretly work with him. Times were bad, and he needed the money. . . ." Roman shook his head. "Mercer purchased me, Lana, and six others. They brought us to the country inside a shipping container. One of the boys who was traveling with us died—he froze to death, it was that cold. Occasionally, someone came to trade out the waste bucket or bring us food, but for weeks, we lived like that. When they put the three of us in that shipping container in Pennsylvania . . . *that* was Mercer. That is the level of detail in his cruelty."

The words locked in my throat. I could only stare at him, absorb the pain radiating from every inch of his body.

Roman's face fell. "You don't believe me. I understand why—I know. It sounds impossible."

"You're not that good of a liar," I said. "I believe you. I'm even horrified for you. But what I'm struggling to get over is the fact that you knew who was behind the kidnapping all along."

He shook his head. "I swear, I didn't. Priya and I wondered, but we didn't recognize any of the kidnappers. We didn't know for sure until we saw Lana. Mercer would never have let someone else use her, even for a job. She is his and his alone."

"Then you've known a few days," I pointed out. "You knew when we found Ruby's car. You knew when we went to see Gray. You knew when we went into that house. You saw how much I was struggling with not knowing who was behind the bombing and kidnapping, and you still didn't tell me?"

His face went tight with pain. "I wanted to. But until we had the information to prove it, to expose Mercer, it was too dangerous."

"*I* decide what's too dangerous for me," I said sharply. "That wasn't your call."

"It's more than that," he said. "We're not the only ones in danger."

"Well, we're the ones in immediate danger," I said. "Did you know Priyanka was the reason Lana and that team found us?"

He scrubbed at his face, making a sound of frustration. "Really?"

"She took the tracker from that drone," I said.

"Priya . . ." Roman's face was pained. "She doesn't want to wait until we find Ruby. She wants Lana out now, so she can

338

protect her. It's not that she won't listen to reason, it's just that her love is stronger."

"What happened to her in the house?" I asked. "Before you gave her that cocktail of drugs it was like she went superhero. Or took a hit of PCP."

Roman opened his mouth to speak, then shut it. "I have to back up again to explain it. Is that okay?"

I nodded.

"Okay . . ." he began. "Priyanka arrived about three years after we did."

"Mercer brought her into the country, too?"

"No, she was already in America. Priya's father was a rival of Mercer's, and Mercer kidnapped her as leverage. It didn't work. Mostly because if there is one man alive more ruthless than Mercer, it's Priyanka's father."

Oh God.

"Anyway, it doesn't feel right to tell the whole story for her." I nodded again, and he continued on. "For a while, nothing much happened. Mercer kept us all in a compound together, just outside New Orleans. We had survival training. Lessons on how to fight and shoot. Mercer acted like a benevolent father, always showering us with attention and praise when we did exactly as he asked. Then, one day, when Priya and I were twelve and Lana was ten, he brought in a man named Wendall—Jonathan Wendall. He worked for Leda Corp, in their research and development sector."

Leda Corp—the company responsible for both the creation of Agent Ambrosia and the years of testing that went into what caused IAAN. Even just the mention of their name sent anger shooting through me.

"That's when the experiments began," Roman said, rubbing at his forehead. "Every day, Dr. Wendall would take one of us into his lab. Do blood work. Scans. Inject us with something or other. Record the results. It made us violently ill, but nothing more. Two years of this. Then, finally, when the camps were closed and the United Nations swept in, things changed. Kids fell through the cracks in the system, and Mercer was able to get his hands on actual Psi. Unclaimed Psi."

Unclaimed. Those kids whose parents had abandoned them to the government all over again by not retrieving them after the camps fell.

"That's where the real money was. He hired all those skip tracer types to find kids, then he'd turn around and sell them again to other countries looking to study or use them. But some he kept for Dr. Wendall. He became obsessed with one Psi in particular, the one whose power he wanted more than anything else. Ruby Elizabeth Daly."

I stared at him in disbelief.

"She was in the newspapers. On the television. He tried to take her from a park once, but his men were repelled by the UN protection detail she had. One of them injured her father."

"I remember that," I whispered.

"Because of his background with Leda, Wendall knew, before the wider scientific community confirmed it, that the mutation couldn't be passed on naturally from parent to child. Using Agent Ambrosia on women he could hire to act as surrogates was too inefficient, and the results were too unpredictable. Mercer wanted Wendall to find a way to induce a specific Psi mutation in us, otherwise clean slates."

"What?" I managed to get out. "You didn't have the mutation to begin with? None of you?"

"None of us had Psi abilities at the start of this," he confirmed.

I took a step back, shaking my head. That was impossible. They were mutations that had developed while we were all in utero.

He made us. Lana had meant that literally.

"Just listen, please," Roman said. "Once the cause of IAAN was confirmed and Wendall had Psi to study, he became increasingly more effective. He came up with a chemical compound that was one part Agent Ambrosia, a thousand parts poison. To induce the mutation in our minds, he force-fed us the chemical and conducted operations. Most of the kids who'd been brought to the States with us died in different phases of the trials, until there were only four of us left. At one point, when she was only twelve, Lana went into cardiac arrest, too."

"What?"

"Her body never fully recovered from her illness as a child. Wendall managed to revive her, but . . . from that moment on, I just had this feeling, this sense that she'd somehow suffer worse for having survived. Priyanka's power manifested immediately, and mine soon after, but Lana went nearly two years without showing any ability. The truth was, she just didn't know how to access it. Up until that point, we had been able to find some sense of normalcy outside of the testing and experiments. That changed once Mercer understood what she could do."

"When did her personality start to change?" I asked. "Priyanka said it happened slowly."

"When Lana was sixteen, and the rest of us eighteen, we were sent out to do work on Mercer's behalf. But someone caught Priya and Lana slipping away together and exposed their relationship to Mercer. He made it clear relationships were not allowed. When they were caught a second time, he made good on his threat to separate them. He pulled Lana onto his personal security detail and began working with her. Shaping her. They traveled when we were at the compound, we traveled when they were. He had become paranoid that his rivals would use Psi to assassinate him. Lana was his guarantee they couldn't. She's a Limit."

"I don't fully understand how her ability works," I told him. "In some ways, it does remind me of Ruby's ability. Lana is obviously suppressing the part of our mind that controls and regulates our abilities, the way Ruby might suppress someone's memory."

"And she can do it with enough force for it to be painful," Roman finished. "None of us became Ruby. None of us were what he wanted, so he found uses for us and continued the experiments. Priyanka can use her mind to infiltrate complex machinery, like computers, and assume control of them. She calls herself a Hacker."

I closed my eyes and took in a deep breath. "The highway cameras and drones . . ."

"The phones did nothing," he said, confirming my suspicion. "She switched them on and off while we passed under them. Priya is the reason we've managed to stay undetected by Mercer for so long. He used to use her a lot for thefts. She can get through any security system and any electronic safe."

"And what about you?" I asked.

"Mercer's garbage, mostly," he said with a humorless laugh. "Priyanka calls me a Mirror. I can mimic another Psi's abilities for a short time through touch, but not without consequences. Mercer had to find other uses for me."

"Wait . . ." I began. "In the truck after we were taken . . . I didn't have enough power to kill the engine. You grabbed me, and there was a surge, like I'd tapped into another source of power. I thought it was because you were a Yellow."

"I wish," he said, smoothing his hands over his knees. "I just amplified what you were already doing."

"Is that what causes your migraines?" I asked. "Using your ability?"

"Yes. We all have side effects—well, everyone but Lana."

I blew out a sigh. "Of course. But what happened with Priya?"

"She explodes. Her adrenaline spikes along with her heart rate, and it's too much for her body to handle if it goes on too long. She loses all sense of fear. Her mind is telling her that she's invincible. The drugs are to counteract the adrenaline and to sedate her, so she doesn't go into cardiac arrest or experience a seizure."

"Holy shit," I said.

"Most of the time—for instance, when she was turning the cameras on and off—she's fine. It gets her going, and makes her anxious to move and get things done. But controlling those servers was too much this time."

"Why did she do it, then?"

"She doesn't . . ." He rubbed the back of his neck. "She wants to help, but that feeling, that surge, is like an intense high. For a while, she was addicted to getting to that point. Mercer loved it. He thought it made her extra effective, so long as we could bring her back down."

"How did you guys finally get away from him?" I asked.

"We were on a job we couldn't finish," he said simply. "It got to be too much, and we ran. I was so sure I'd be able to get to

Lana within a few days. Mercer was always traveling. We could extract her while he was busy with his meetings. But after Priya and I left, he kept her back at the compound. Haven was the first time I'd seen my sister in almost six months. And tonight . . ."

He clenched his right hand. Roman looked crushed, absolutely obliterated.

"You saved my life," I said softly.

"She wasn't going to stop," he croaked out. "I saw it in her eyes. She wasn't going to stop."

My hand reached for one of his, closing around the warm, calloused skin. "She'll understand when she's herself again."

"All I can do is hope," he said. "That's all I have left."

"That's not all," I assured him.

Roman looked up at me, his fingers squeezing mine. "The reason we didn't tell you about ourselves, about Mercer, is because he is still experimenting on kids." I opened my mouth but he pressed on. "And I know what you're thinking, but we can't report it to the government. Can you honestly tell me that they wouldn't do even more experimentation on them? That they wouldn't send them to live with foster families, or in one of those privatized training institutes that Moore keeps talking about? They would never be allowed to return to their families."

"You didn't trust me," I said, letting my hand slip out of his.

He shook his head. "No. I didn't want to put you in the position of feeling you had to withhold information from the government. And the truth is, you're exposed to a real risk now that Mercer knows you're with us. He keeps such a tight lid on his business dealings, he will do just about anything to keep you from talking to someone with enough power to stop him. You wouldn't even see him coming."

A little shudder worked through me. After a moment Roman added, "But I am sorry. I'm sorry about the lies and the partial truths. I can't say it enough."

I tilted my head back to look at the sky. The headlights didn't dim the blanket of stars. "Limit, Hacker, Mirror . . . I can't believe I thought you were part of the Psion Ring."

"That's another thing," he said. "The Psion Ring doesn't exist."

My gaze shot back over to him.

He shook his head. "There's no proof of them anywhere. Logic dictates two options: they are incredibly good at covering their trail, or they don't exist. Believe me, Mercer investigated. He sent me out on a thousand dead ends looking for them. He put real resources behind it, and each time, he came up with nothing."

"I saw reports, though," I said. "The Psi Council reviewed information about them at their monthly meetings."

"Who were those reports created and compiled by?" Roman asked.

"A lot of agencies," I said. "The UN, the FBI, intelligence services . . . they all have people who could have been monitoring them and feeding the information back to someone in Cruz's administration."

"Even if a ring managed to form in the months since Priya and I left Mercer, there's no way they could pull off a job like the airplane bombing. The planning alone would take months. The way they're using your name has me more convinced than ever that it's a cover for something else."

Something worse.

"How do I fit in? You were going to approach me at the speech, weren't you?"

"Yes. The plan was to separate you and force you to take us to Daly, where we'd plead our case."

"Kidnap me, you mean?" I clarified, almost amused.

He looked a little sheepish. "Kidnapping is a strong word for it. We were hoping you'd just agree to help us. All of my research made it seem like—"

"Like what?" I asked. I raised a brow.

"The reports I accessed, the newspaper stories, the documentaries, it all made you seem so . . . docile. Vulnerable. Compliant," he said. "Within moments after the explosion, I knew that wasn't who you are at all. They had crafted an image of you that erased all of your strength and capabilities."

My stomach churned.

"I couldn't appear dangerous," I said softly. "I couldn't be a threat to anyone. Mel used to say that people would use me as a token to represent all Psi kids. My actions, the way I conducted myself, would shape the public's opinion of us."

So I'd nodded, accepting the things they'd told me were important. I subdued the parts of me that focus groups felt were "too bubbly." Too "erratic." I molded myself to be calm and composed. Reasonable.

"I was stupid enough to underestimate you because of all that I'd read and seen. But, to be honest, I think the men who took us did as well. You were able to save our lives because of it."

"It was Priyanka who sent the message on the teleprompter, wasn't it?" I asked, slowly putting it together.

"To try to disturb your usual procedure," he said. "We studied your security protocols for a full month, and thought that an emergency would be the best time to try to get you alone."

"That would have been the best time to get yourselves killed,"

I corrected. "I don't know that I would have helped you find Haven, even if you'd been up front at the start. It's not just about protecting Ruby's location. After what she went through, I feel the need to protect her. She will always help others. But her ability hurts her more than she lets on. Not physically. She sees the trauma, the pain, the ugliness everyone keeps locked away."

Putting it that way, it reminded me of Roman. Someone who said yes, who never failed to help, and suffered all the inward consequences of it.

"Is that why you believed she willingly left Haven?" Roman asked.

"That's part of it," I said. "Everyone has a breaking point, and she's been storing up so much pain over the years, it wouldn't surprise me if she'd finally reached hers. But now I'm sure she didn't leave—that she didn't walk away from this of her own volition. Something happened."

"I agree," he said. "Blue Star set the explosion at Penn State. It might have been so that they could take in me and Priya, and they only framed you to take any suspicion off themselves. But you said one of the Defenders was going to fire on you, right?"

"Right," I said. "It had to be a setup from the jump. Blue Star causes the explosion . . . frames me to avoid suspicion . . . and someone else decides to pile on with the attack on Moore's campaign plane?"

Roman hesitated.

"Just say it."

"You're not going to like this theory, but it could be someone in the government who has a grudge against you, the Council, or Cruz—or all of you. If that Defender uniform was real, it points to some greater conspiracy."

"No." I shook my head. "Is it . . . is it possible that Mercer's the reason Ruby's vanished? That he has her?"

"I think it's more likely that she caught on to his interest and went into hiding," Roman said.

"She would have found a way to communicate with us," I told him. "We have a few different systems she could have used. I think someone has her. And it *has* to be Mercer."

"I really don't know," he said, running a hand back over his hair. "I hope like hell he doesn't."

I pressed my hands to my face, drawing in a deep breath. "Where is Ruby?" I whispered. "Where is she?"

There was a knock on the windshield. Priyanka stared back at us. When she spoke, her voice was muffled. "I think I know."

TWENTY-SEVEN

THE CAR ROCKED AS I CLIMBED BACK INTO THE DRIVER'S seat and shut the door. A moment later, Roman moved to the passenger side and did the same. The only sound that came from him was the hard click of his seat belt as he strapped himself in.

I glanced back at Priyanka as she stretched her long legs across the backseat, but she didn't, or couldn't, meet my gaze.

"You tell her?" Priyanka asked. Without the usual warmth in her voice, the lightness of her tone felt artificial. Put on for our benefit.

Roman nodded, not looking at her.

My hand hovered over the ignition, not sure if I should be driving, or if we needed a moment to find whatever little center we'd had before.

"Man, you missed out," Priyanka told me, in that same painfully airy tone. "I tell the tragic tale with a lot more flourish—or, at least, a lot more sound effects and shadow puppets."

"Priya . . ." I began, taking in the sight of her. Her whole body was covered in a sheen of sweat. It turned her thick head of hair into a tight cap on her skull, black curls sticking to her collarbone and shoulders like vines. She slipped her hands beneath her legs, but I could see the rest of her was trembling. "Maybe not right now."

She cleared her throat, sitting up a little straighter. "There was an address. On the server. It matched one of the address searches on Ruby's phone, but they—Blue Star—deleted the archive before I could get a good look at it."

"Do you actually see the files?" I asked, curious. "How does it work?"

"It's more like . . ." Priyanka began, "everything gets downloaded into my mind. Sometimes I can't access it right away and it'll pop up in my thoughts days later, randomly. My mind is like a net when I'm plugged in. Sometimes I can catch everything, sometimes pieces of it slip away. It just feels like . . . connection. A hot, bright flow of snapshots."

"Did you see anything else in the files?" I asked.

"It was a veritable potpourri of blackmail, and it stank to high heaven of corruption and secrets. Lots of good stuff on senators, and even a little on a sketchy real estate deal President Cruz made a while back."

I resisted the urge to press my forehead to the steering wheel. "Great. Anything particularly interesting?"

"There's one thing you should know," Priyanka said. "There were files on you and your friends. Actually, okay, two things—after destroying the archives, the very last thing their system did was to issue a GO command and money transfer."

"That's the deal done, then," I said. "Clancy's in the wind now." I filled them in on what Lana had revealed about Clancy's deal. Roman shook his head, disgusted.

Ruby, what did you need from him that was so important you were willing to risk unleashing him back into the world?

Priyanka dissolved into a fit of coughing, pounding against her chest.

"Are you all right?" I asked, handing her a bottle of water. Unable to speak, she nodded, gulping it down. She was sweating hard enough to turn her purple blouse into a second skin, but her color was already improving.

"Coming down from Super Priya Mode is never as enjoyable as the ride, which is why it can be tempting to stay on," Priyanka said, winking at me.

Roman slammed his hand against the dash. I jumped. "It's not funny. I don't understand what you were thinking jumping into the server and chasing whoever was on the other end."

"I was handling it," Priyanka said. "The high was useful, like I knew it would be—"

"You don't need it, Priya." If the harrowing expression on his face was enough to grip my heart, I could only imagine what it was doing to Priyanka's. "I don't understand how you can't see that you're *enough*."

"I wish that were actually the case," Priyanka said. "There was no other way past the firewall Blue Star put up. It was that, or let them get the material without us ever seeing any of it."

"We could have unplugged the servers and taken them with us to analyze later," Roman said, his voice ragged. "I could have—"

"Made yourself sick with a cracking migraine, like you did? Risk it being the one you might not wake up from again?" Priyanka shook her head. "That high is the only way I have of keeping up with you."

"I was always having to run to keep pace with *you*," Roman said. "It wasn't just about that."

"No," Priyanka said. "It was about reclaiming some power after what Mercer did to me. To all of his kids."

"We're not his kids!" Roman interrupted angrily.

Priyanka only shook her head. "You never understood. Lana and I wanted to use our abilities to help other vulnerable children—to burn out corruption, but you just wanted to run."

He jerked around in his seat. "I don't want to run from this, I just want us to be safe. You want to talk about useless? Powerless? Look at me. Look at me, Priya." She did. "The only thing Mercer ever saw me as good for was my loyalty and a steady hand. The only reason he didn't put me down like a dog is because I was willing to do whatever it took to protect you and Lana."

What does that mean?

I glanced between them, the raw anger and pain on their faces enough to make me wish I had stepped out. Priyanka looked genuinely shocked by his words. Roman faced forward again, pressing his fist against his mouth and staring out the window.

I needed something to do, so I turned on the engine and took us back the way we'd come down the access road. Dust whipped up in clouds behind us as the wheels ground into the dirt.

"Ro . . ." Priyanka began, softer this time. "You don't have to worry. It's not that I want to be in that high, it's just sometimes it feels like we need it. But I make it a point not to fall into traps I'm not completely sure I can climb out of, and this is one of them. And while we're talking about traps, I'm sorry I didn't tell either of you about the tracker. I just thought . . . one more try. . . ."

I glanced back at her in the rearview mirror. "I understand."

She shot me a look of gratitude that was still tinged with lingering guilt.

"I don't mean to lecture you," Roman said. "You don't need it, and it's your right to use your ability the way you want to. But I can't lose you, too, and I don't want your hatred of Mercer to play any role in destroying you. You deserve more."

"I won't let it destroy me," Priyanka said, sliding Ruby's phone out of the backseat. She pulled up an address in Baton Rouge and handed it to Roman to plug into the car's GPS. It was miles of silence later before she leaned her head against the backseat and let her eyes drift shut.

I barely heard her whisper over the sound of the wheels turning on the road. "Not until I destroy him first."

The thick, churning heat set in as soon as we crossed the state line into Louisiana. It rose in shimmering waves off the boiling asphalt and slowed my thoughts to a crawl. I'd surrendered the steering wheel to Roman hours before but hadn't let him coax me into sleep.

"I can't believe you didn't tell me about Priya's ability sooner. We'd still have all that money for food." I watched in the side mirror as Priyanka poured the gas she'd just acquired—simply by hacking the pump to make it believe it had read a ration card—into the tank. The walk down to the station hadn't been far, and she hadn't had to wait long in the ration line, but by the time she'd returned, she looked like she'd swum the distance. When she finished, she threw the empty red can into the trunk again. "Why were you always the one going to get the gas, not her?"

"She did get the gas those few times that you slept. We were able to stretch what cash we had by using her ability. She put in a used ration card and hacked the pump," Roman said. "But there's always a risk someone will take a closer look at what she's doing and report her. I'm trained to be as inconspicuous as possible. It's the least I can do."

"I'm trained, too," Priyanka insisted as she slid into the back-seat. "Well, in theory. But why be inconspicuous when your enemies can furiously shout your name at the sky instead?"

I looked at Roman. "Point taken."

"You didn't take more than the ration limit, did you?" he asked, glancing up at her in the rearview mirror.

"No, you can relax. Even if I had gotten brave and tried it, there was a cop standing right there, watching the meter. Ugh!" Priyanka fanned herself. "Can you turn the air up before I get a whiff of myself again? I think I somehow absorbed the burned-nacho-cheese smell that was radiating from that place."

I did as asked. The line of cars waiting for their turn at the station now stretched past us. The symphony of impatient honk-ing had begun. Roman had his hand on the door, and seemed to be talking himself out of it.

"Go," I told him. "We can wait. You deserve to wash up and change."

"Maybe the gas station attendant will take pity on your sad state and give you the week-old nachos," Priyanka said. "But if it's a choice between nachos and hot dogs, take the hot dogs."

"Yeah. That'll happen when the lobster whistles on the moun-tain." He saw our blank looks. "Really? That's not an English one, either?"

"More like 'when pigs fly,' but we're keeping yours because it's absolutely delightful," Priyanka said. "What is it with Russia and lobsters? What was that other one you used a while back—something about sleeping lobsters?"

"I'll show him where lobsters spend the winter," Roman said, a glum note in his voice. "It's a good threat."

"Very evocative," I agreed. "Even more menacing than *sleep with the fishes*, because you don't necessarily know where lobsters spend the winter."

"Deep, freezing water?" Priyanka guessed. "Ice? Someone's freezer?"

With an exasperated sound, Roman opened the door and stepped out. He stuffed his hands into the back pockets of his jeans and kept his head down as he made his way toward the gas station.

Priyanka came to sit in the front passenger seat, coughing as she buckled in. I gave her a worried glance.

"I'm all right," she said. "The only thing that ever came close to killing me was the sad look in Roman's eyes. That is some weapons-grade effectiveness."

We both turned to watch him fade into the distance.

"Thank you," she said after a while. "For not leaving when you found out the truth. I'm sorry about the lies. You didn't deserve that. But nothing makes me feel more protective than thinking about those kids trapped with Mercer."

"Once I had the whole picture, it made sense why you did it," I said. "But this time I mean it—we have to be honest with each other, or this isn't going to work."

"Well, in the interest of full disclosure, did Roman tell you about how I came to Mercer? My parents?" Priyanka asked.

"Not really. He told me Mercer kidnapped you as leverage because your father was one of Mercer's business rivals," I explained.

"Oh yeah, big-time rival in weapons smuggling. Like, nemesis-level rival." Priyanka pulled her legs up onto the seat and wrapped her arms around them. "Have you ever heard of Parth Acharya?"

"That rings a bell. . . ."

She picked up the burner phone and switched over to the browser. The *New York Times* article was already pulled up. The image of a handsome, gray-haired Indian man filled the screen below the headline ACHARYA ESCAPES INDICTMENT.

She gave a faint laugh. "I can't help myself sometimes. I search his name at least once a week. I tell myself it's because I want to know if he's still alive, but I think it's just a different kind of morbid curiosity. When I was a little younger, I used to pretend that he was trying to secretly communicate with me through photos in the newspaper and online, to send me signals. He was such a big figure in my mind—like an emperor—I assumed there had to be a reason why he was always getting busted and tried for this crime or that. Turns out, it was just Mercer constantly leaking information about him to the government. No one could ever pin anything serious on him, though. Seems like they still can't."

"And your father . . . he just . . . let Mercer keep you?"

"Not exactly." Priyanka let out a soft breath. "I wasn't born here. My mother—her name was Chandni. She and I lived in Delhi for the first seven years of my life. My father had gone to America to establish himself there—one day he was a driver, the next, some crime boss's driver, and the next, the new crime boss himself. It didn't happen quite that fast, but it was only a year before he sent a private plane back for us. It was a whole thing, because commercial flights to and from the States had been stopped owing to IAAN and how they thought it could spread.

"A few days before it was set to arrive," Priyanka continued, "my mom was killed by a car as she was crossing our street. So, I went alone. I lived in his massive, echoing marble mansion in Jersey and watched the constant stream of henchmen and overheard a thousand whispered conversations, and that became my new baseline for normal. If he was ever scared of me catching IAAN, my father never showed it. And then about a year after I arrived, a day before Christmas—because, yes, he's *that* asshole—Mercer sent someone to kidnap me. He offered a choice to my father: get out of the guns business, or he'd send me back to him in pieces."

"Jesus," I breathed out.

"Oh wait, it gets better." Priyanka shifted in her seat. "The deadline fell on the same day my father was due in court for racketeering charges. Instead of responding to the message, or trying to renegotiate those terms, Mercer and I both watched on the news as my father walked up the steps of the courthouse in lower Manhattan in head-to-toe white. When one of the reporters asked him why, he explained that his *beloved* daughter Priyanka had died from IAAN the night before and he was in mourning."

It actually took me a moment to remember how to speak. *"What?"*

"Oh yes. That's how strong his sense of pride is. He refused to admit that Mercer had kidnapped his daughter, that Mercer had won and put him in a position of weakness, so he chalked me up as a loss and moved on. I was a problem to him, which meant I no longer had value. For him, I wasn't enough."

"That is disgusting," I said.

"At the time, the bigger issue was what Mercer would do to me. I remember it so clearly—Mercer looked down at me and said, 'Well, how are you going to be useful to me now?' So I asked to join the other kids."

357

I gasped. "Priya . . ."

She shrugged, clearing her throat. "Mercer is a sick son of a bitch, but my father is a coldhearted bastard. That's the difference between them in the end. Lana isn't wrong. Mercer did take care of us, in a way. When he turned his attention on you, it was like warm honey. It wasn't until I was older that I saw how manipulative he is."

"God," I breathed out. "What about your mom's family? Could you go back to them?"

"I don't know," she said. "I keep up my Hindi so I'll be able to communicate with them to some degree one day, but it's not like I've really tried to get in touch with them, even after we left Blue Star. Every time I think about it, something stops me. I tell myself that it's because I don't want Mercer to go after them, to use them to hurt me, but it's more than that. I'm not even sure how to explain it. . . ."

"Just try," I said.

"One of the worst things about all of this is that I feel this strange disconnect with my wider family and culture. I still have my faith, my deep passion for malpua, and all these golden memories of living in Delhi with my mom, but . . . it feels like I got plucked out of my real life midstream. Does that make sense?"

"It does." She'd put into words a feeling I'd never been able to articulate myself. When we'd gone to the camps, it wasn't just our lives that had been interrupted, but our sense of self. It changed the trajectory of our worlds. For so long, our focus had to be on survival, and survival alone.

But that wasn't living.

"I think that about sums it up," Priyanka said. "I feel lucky in some ways, because Lana and Roman are more family to me than my father ever was. I never would have met them otherwise."

Still . . .

She turned her wrist up, pushing the sleeve of her blouse back until it revealed the blue star tattooed on it. "I don't know why I kept this. Roman burned his off a few nights after we escaped, but I couldn't bring myself to do it. Roman said he hated feeling like he'd been marked as someone's possession, but I never saw it that way—to me, it was always more of a unifying symbol. A sign that we were family. Now it's a reminder that nothing is all good or all bad."

My heart was exhausted. It just couldn't handle any more. I pressed my hand to my eyes.

"Don't start crying," Priyanka said. "Otherwise I'll start and won't be able to stop."

I cleared my throat. "I'm sorry. Sometimes it just feels like it's too much, you know? I always thought the world would feel easier as I got older, but I've only gotten more practice at pretending it is."

"It's hard for people like us," Priyanka said, leaning over the console to rest her head on my shoulder. I let mine fall against hers. "We feel everything."

Outside, Roman appeared along the road again, his dark hair damp and shining in the sun.

"I'm sorry about Lana," I told her. "It must be unbearable to see her like this."

"It'll only be unbearable when I give up hope of ever getting her back," she said. "And I won't. Not ever. My heart is a wheel. It breaks all the damn time, but, most days, it just rolls on."

TWENTY-EIGHT

I UNFOLDED THE MAP AND SMOOTHED IT ACROSS THE steering wheel again, looking between the X Roman had marked on it and the building across the street. We'd used the burner's limited GPS capabilities to search for the Baton Rouge address, but there must have been some glitch in the satellite feed, or he'd made a mistake in transferring the information over onto the paper. This couldn't be it.

"I think this *is* right," Roman said, shielding his eyes from the glare of sunlight to get a better look at the building. "Unfortunately."

"It's like I can hear the screams of ghost children from here," Priyanka said, shuddering. "Tell me Ruby loves roller-skating so much she'd drive across multiple state lines and risk capture by the government for a fun day out."

Riverside Rink was just outside of Baton Rouge proper, on a street yet to be touched by that magic reinvigoration we'd seen in other places. The flow of money and government-sponsored work had apparently stopped at the city's center.

We parked across the street, behind a shuttered McDonald's,

and ate our lunch of vending-machine food on a faded rainbow play set. Roman insisted on keeping watch to see if anyone was coming or going. So far, nothing. No one.

"I don't think she's here," I said, tossing the M&M's wrapper into the restaurant's overflowing trash can. A swarm of flies immediately descended on it. "I don't think anyone's been here in a good decade."

Half the letters on the rink's fluorescent sign were missing, plundered by neglect or thieves, I wasn't sure. Its parking lot was empty, all of its lines faded. The windows, like all the other buildings' in the neighborhood, were boarded up and spray-painted with warnings against trespassers.

"Well, we're here. At least we'll see what she found so intriguing about this place," Priyanka said. "You good?"

Roman checked that there was a bullet in the chamber of his gun, then nodded.

The roller rink was completely locked down, and the front door had been chained for good measure. It made finding the back door open that much stranger.

"Stating for the record that I don't like this," Priyanka said.

"There is no record," Roman whispered.

She gave him a look. He gave her one right back.

"Should I go first?" I suggested.

We kept our backs to the brick wall, facing the mountain of trash piled high in the nearby dumpsters. The smell was bad enough that I lifted the collar of my shirt over my nose and mouth.

Roman led us inside, sweeping his gun back and forth as he searched what once had been the rink's kitchen. There was still a grill, but all the other machines had been taken, leaving behind only a congealed bit of orange cheese on the tile floor as a relic. The light filtering in from outside faded the farther we moved into the building. I pulled the flashlight out of my back pocket and switched it on.

Roman had stepped into the main rink area, only to whirl toward us again, the back of his hand pressed hard to his mouth.

"Don't—" he started to say as I passed him.

Too late. I smelled it, too. The sickly sweet stench of rotting food had blended with the unmistakable reek of human waste and . . . something else. Something like death.

The flashlight's thin beam illuminated the skating rink in slices of horror. Cubbies of roller skates, left untouched. Garbage and buckets were scattered haphazardly across the rink.

A body.

The girl was curled on her side, facing away from us, hugging her knees to her chest. A long dark braid stretched out on the floor behind her, the end buried beneath a stray wrapper. Her plaid shirt was a deep red, shot through with black. She wasn't moving.

She wasn't breathing.

My feet slowed.

Stopped.

Ruby.

The flashlight slipped out of my fingers, cracking against the hard ground. Blood roared in my ears until I thought it would tear me apart.

Two hands landed on my shoulders. Priyanka turned me toward her, saying something I couldn't hear. I pulled back, watching as a grim-faced Roman circled the girl and crouched down in front of her.

Priyanka's hands dug into my skin painfully, but she couldn't look away from him either, not until he glanced up and shook his head.

I didn't believe him. I tore myself out of Priyanka's grip, my breath burning where it was caught inside my chest. I only needed a single look at what remained of her face.

Not her.

She was too young. Her hands and feet, bound by zip ties, were too small. From a distance, it had been an easy mistake to make, but up close . . .

I forced myself not to turn away. To look at the girl, alone in this dark place.

"God, she can't be more than twelve, thirteen," Priyanka said, her voice strained. "What was she doing here?"

Roman stood slowly, picking up the flashlight from where it had rolled to a stop beside the girl's legs. The light passed over the rink again, this time sweeping over sticky footprints in the grime and dust. I followed one trail of small footprints until it intersected with another one, and another, and another.

There weren't just a few tracks. There were dozens and dozens of them. Some smaller than the length of my hand.

"Whatever it was," Roman said, "she wasn't alone. And she didn't come here by choice."

"I want to leave," Priyanka said, all humor gone from her voice. The air was like someone's damp breath against my skin, but she rubbed her arms as if she needed to warm some feeling back into them. "Right now."

"No," I said. "We can't just leave her here."

Roman's eyes softened as he looked to me. "We're not going to. We'll use the pay phone across the street to call it in to the

Baton Rouge police. They need to see this—whatever this is."

"I don't . . ." *Trust them to take care of her.*

That single truth burned in me. I didn't trust them. I didn't trust the FBI, or Cruz, or anyone in her orbit. I only trusted us.

"I understand," he said. "I don't like it either. But she deserves to be identified and returned to her family for a real burial. That's not something we can give her."

My throat ached.

"Right?" he said softly.

I nodded.

You must remember this, I thought. That was my responsibility now. But it wasn't enough.

"I need the burner," I told Priyanka.

She handed it over with a questioning look. The camera wouldn't record this in excruciating high definition, but all that mattered was capturing this scene, this moment, and refusing to let anyone look away.

If I were going to put together a narrative from all these pieces—the drone footage, this rink, and whatever we found next—I needed to actually begin to document what was happening.

I flipped the camera view so that it was on me. My face glowed in the dark rink.

"It's . . ." I began, doing the math in my head. "August seventeenth. About four o'clock in the afternoon, at Riverside Rink, just outside of Baton Rouge." I flipped the camera view again, walking the length of the rink, sweeping it over the shadowed evidence of the people—the kids—who had been kept here. "We discovered this place while following a lead on the real culprits behind the bombing at Penn State. From what I can tell, it looks as if children, possibly Psi, were held here against their will, likely because they were being trafficked."

I moved back over to the girl. Roman and Priyanka stepped out of the frame.

"But they left someone behind." I knelt down beside her, bringing the camera closer to her face. "She's been here, forgotten, waiting for someone to care enough to find her."

I stopped recording, looking back at the others.

"I think it's obvious who's behind this," Roman said, his voice pitching deeper with anger. "Mercer must be back in the trafficking business. This has his fingerprints all over it—we're near a reopened shipping port, close enough to the compound in New Orleans. Even using an abandoned facility to hold them until transport could be arranged . . ."

"I really wish I could believe he's the only one trafficking kids," Priyanka said. "If anything, this feels messy. That's not his way. He would have sent someone to clean up."

"He doesn't let rivals in on his game," Roman said. "It's exactly what he did before. Keep the Psi kids he wants for experimenting, sell the rest to other countries or organizations he doesn't think will challenge him."

I clutched the phone tighter in my hand. "If Ruby really was here, then this is what she was chasing. Maybe Mercer does have her, after all. It would have brought her right into his path."

She'd been following the lines of a web that stretched between states, between one dark criminal element and the next. Unwinding clues and, hopefully, collecting evidence.

And now . . .

"Zu," Roman said, taking my hand. He repeated my name again, and again, until I finally looked at him. "If Mercer has her, we can start looking in his various real estate holdings. It's a place to start."

That didn't make me feel any better. And it didn't stop the swelling tide of pressure as it rose up in my chest. Overhead, the fluorescent light fixture hummed, buzzing like a trapped fly.

"And how long will that take? He could have her somewhere neither of you know about," I said. "He could be hurting her right now."

"There's only one way to pinpoint her location for sure," Priyanka said, looking to Roman. "You're going to have to call in your favor."

TWENTY-NINE

NO WAS THE ONLY WORD ROMAN WOULD SAY AS WE LEFT the rink and crossed the street back to the car. No, and no, and no.

"But—" Priyanka began, gripping the front passenger door.

"No." The word held no anger, just finality. Roman shook his head. "I'm calling this in to the police, then we can reassess the available options as we head out."

"You're being an idiot," Priyanka told him as he walked toward the pay phone at the edge of the McDonald's parking lot. "You know I'm right! We should have done it in the first place!"

Roman's body stiffened, but he didn't turn back to us. "Maybe. Or maybe we'd all be dead now."

"Argh," Priyanka said. She climbed into the backseat and slammed the door behind her. "He's being ridiculous. Of course it's a risk. What *isn't* a risk?"

"I'd love to sympathize, but I still have no idea what you're talking about," I told her as I buckled myself back into the driver's seat.

Priyanka let her head fall back against the seat, taking a deep breath. "Did Roman tell you that four of us survived Wendall's experiments?"

I nodded.

"I want us to go find the fourth member of our Sad Squad," she explained. "He's a Fisher. He can locate a person telepathically. It's like he casts out a mental line and hooks onto an image of that person, wherever they might be."

"You're kidding," I said. "How is that even possible?"

"You'd have to ask Wendall," Priyanka said. "He might have some insights, considering Max is his son."

My mouth fell open. "How does this story manage to get worse each time you add something to it?"

"I've learned to break up the bad bits because it's too soul-crushing to absorb all at once," Priyanka said. "But you can see how an ability like that would be very useful to Mercer, right? He could find almost anyone he wanted: spies in his organization, his enemies and competitors . . . Mercer took Lana into his security detail, but the three of us formed our own team. Max would locate the person, I would break through their security systems, and Roman . . ."

All at once, I knew exactly what Roman had meant when he'd said Mercer valued his steady hand.

"It got to be too much for Max—the guilt, I mean. He might not have been the one pulling the trigger, but he saw each death and kidnapping as being on him. It got to all of us in different ways, and everything came to a head on the last job Mercer sent us on. Mercer wanted Roman to kill a former business partner and make it look like a burglary gone wrong. But in a burglary setup, you don't just kill the mark. You have to kill any witnesses present, too. And the guy had young kids. Max saw them when he went fishing for the man's location."

I gripped the steering wheel. "What happened?"

"Max usually traveled with us, and we didn't always know the parameters of the gig until we were nearly there because his locating became sharper the closer he got to the mark. Well, the night before the job, he woke up and tried running. Roman caught him a few hours later, and Max finally explained that he'd seen the guy's kids, and that he was done, no matter what the consequences were. So Roman let him go. Escape. Knowing about the kids ultimately decided our fate, too, because it wasn't like Roman and I were going to go forward with the mission alone and kill a bunch of innocent children . . . but running meant leaving Lana behind."

"Did you think about trying to go back to Mercer alone?" I asked.

She nodded. "I almost did. I didn't want to leave Lana, but I couldn't go back and blame it all on Roman. Mercer would have sent team after team to kill him. And even though he'd never admit it, Roman needs someone to look out for his well-being."

At that exact moment, Roman rounded the corner of the playground again and made his way toward us.

He opened the back door, slamming it shut behind him. "They said they're sending someone over *just as soon as they can.*"

Before Priyanka could say anything, Roman added, "The only reason I don't like your idea is because of the risks involved with it. There's no way to get to Max without breaking him out, and from what I've seen, there's no way of breaking in undetected, either. He's in there for a reason, Priya. He doesn't want any part of this."

"Wait . . . breaking in where?" I asked.

I was really starting to fear the looks the two of them exchanged.

"Roman and I bailed from the mission about an hour after Max did, but that was enough time for him to disappear,"

Priyanka said. "We finally tracked him down a few days later, when I found police records saying he'd voluntarily turned himself in at a station in Texas, and they dropped him off at some kind of facility. The security was too tight to try to scope it out, and the fact that he did the thing he'd been threatening to do—turn himself in—made us decide to leave him alone."

"What part of Texas?" I asked.

"North, right near Oklahoma. What was the city we drove through?"

That last question had been aimed at Roman. "Wheeler."

That sounded familiar, but my thoughts were too scrambled to piece together why.

"Max could have been moved," Roman pointed out. "Or that place could have shut down. It's been almost six months."

"No, let's go," I said. "If he's still there, we can see if he's willing to help us. It's that, or storm any and all of Blue Star's facilities without all the facts."

"Again," Roman said, "the issue isn't just getting Max out, it's finding a way inside."

I shifted the car out of park and guided the wheels onto the road again. The sun was slipping down toward the horizon, bold and shining despite the oncoming darkness of night. I drove us into it.

It was a wild idea. The sheer recklessness of it made me feel like I was careening around inside my own body.

"We don't need to find a way to break in," I said. "We just have to let ourselves get caught."

Miles and hours passed, but I still couldn't shake the girl from my mind.

Priyanka was stretched out across the backseat, her head

resting against the door. She'd tilted it back just enough to look up at the highway cameras as we passed beneath them, counting each one under her breath. Roman fought the slow drag of sleep, drifting off, then startling awake a few seconds later.

I turned the radio on, and was pleasantly surprised to hear the zone announcer's voice jump out at us. *"Here is the current hourly summary of the news. . . . In Washington today, Interim President Cruz's campaign announced that they had met and surpassed the sudden surge in fundraising money collected by Joseph Moore's campaign. Cruz herself announced that a new budget agreement had been reached with the United Nations, extending the repayment deadline and securing additional funds to support the Department of Defense. . . . In local zone news, the mayor of Nashville . . ."*

On and on, each state giving an update about their progress, about the new UN-sponsored factories that were employing whole towns, new highway projects, new schools, reopened universities, the return of parades, road closures, rally stops by local and national campaigns. I held my breath as she reached Louisiana, waiting to hear about the body the police had to have discovered by now.

Instead, she skipped over the state and moved on to Florida's reopened public beaches.

I glanced down at the dashboard, then at Roman in disbelief, waiting for the newscaster to circle back to it. Mel had taught me that it was better to pad bad news with good, to soften it, but the announcer clearly hadn't been given the same advice.

"Finally, the press secretary announced today that the interim president has asked Congress to reallocate the funds set aside for the Psi reparations program to the defense budget to increase the number of Defenders who are tracking the whereabouts of the Psion Ring. The reparations program, which would have seen a small financial

stipend given to surviving Psi and debt forgiveness for their families, will be put on indefinite hold."

Having reached the end of her news summary, the station switched back to soft classic rock standards.

"Shit," I breathed out, banging my hands against the wheel. *"Shit!"*

"They can still change their minds," Roman said. *"You* can still change their minds. We have to stay focused on gathering evidence."

I shook my head. The reparations package had just barely survived being cut apart during the vote in Congress. Knowing they'd used me as the excuse to kill the project Chubs had fought so hard for made me sick; the betrayal of it was almost too much to take.

It wasn't just that, though. It was the fact that they didn't even mention the girl—that she clearly hadn't been deemed newsworthy—that made me want to roll down the window and scream at the world. *Wake up, wake up, wake up!*

They were covering up her death. Sweeping it ever so quietly under a rug. The zone news reports weren't meant to be in-depth, but Cruz's administration had always prided itself on its transparency after years of secrecy by Gray. From a publicity standpoint, though, it made perfect sense to trumpet the good news and not draw attention to the expected spots of trouble that came with resetting a whole nation.

Now . . . now I wondered if they had actually cut out the rot at all, or if they'd only applied a fresh coat of paint over it.

Something is happening in America, I thought. *And no one wants us to know.*

THIRTY

"I REALLY DON'T KNOW ABOUT THIS. . . ."

"I want you to do it," I said. "Just think of it as doing me a favor. I'm *asking* you to do it. I'll beg if it makes you feel any better."

The exterior bathroom on the gas station had been slowly baking in the sun all day. Despite the small vent for light and air, it felt like being inside a coffin. Even Roman was stoically fighting to keep his expression neutral as sweat poured down over his face, causing the eyeliner Priyanka had smeared around his eyes to run. I didn't have to look in the mirror to know that mine looked the same.

"While I do enjoy being begged for things," Priyanka began, "begging for me to punch you in the face is not going to make me feel better about said punching."

"The Psi Tracking System uses facial recognition to match to its database," I said, running a hand over my hair. Priyanka had helped me slick it back into little braids that ended in a short ponytail. We'd chalked the whole thing hot pink before applying

373

a liberal coating of gel to keep the color from running as long as possible. "We need to mess with that function."

"O, ye of little faith," Priyanka said, clasping a hand to her heart. Like the rest of us, she was wearing all black clothing that we'd salvaged from a donation bin. Unlike the rest of us, she was actually pulling off the look. Her hair was twisted into a high bun, and her black shorts, flowy black top, and over-the-knee black boots looked almost sophisticated. Roman and I looked like we enjoyed kicking little kids and stealing their Halloween candy.

"You think I can't handle hacking their device, duplicating your current profile, and then changing the name and any other necessary details in less than two seconds?" she asked.

I looked at Roman. "This isn't going to work, is it?"

He sighed. "What about us?"

"I created clean ID profiles for us in their system ages ago in case we ever did get scanned," Priyanka said. "We're fine. Two regular ole Greens."

"Then maybe we should go in alone," Roman said, casting a quick look at me. "If we can't get back out, at least we can find a way to get word to you about whatever Max finds. You could go on without us."

"No," I said, straightening my black skirt over the torn black tights. "This is an all-for-one-and-one-for-all situation. Given the secrecy surrounding the facility, I don't think we're going to be able to find a way out until we're on the inside."

I wasn't going to let them take this risk without me there to help them. If we really were trapped there, then I'd find a way to contact Vida with Ruby's location. There was always another way. But the thought of not finishing this—that, I wasn't sure I was ready for.

Someone banged on the door from outside.

"Can you hurry up?" a man called, sounding irate. "Other people need to use the restroom!"

"I'm puking in here!" Priyanka called back. "I'll be taking my sweet-ass time unless you're looking to get projectile vomit all over your face and the horrible slacks you're no doubt wearing!"

"Ew," I said.

"I'm getting the manager!"

"You do that," Priyanka called back. "Stomp away like a little baby and go cry to Mommy."

We all chose to ignore the venomous string of cursing that followed.

"Anyway, I still think you need to hit me," I said, trying to sound as reasonable as someone could while asking to be punched. "In the eye, and maybe in the mouth to bust my lip open again."

"Why?" Priyanka said. "Why do you want me to hit your adorable face? Why are you so cruel to me?"

"I've been on televisions and in newspapers and magazines for years now," I said. "You really don't think people are going to be able to make a visual ID of me?"

"Speaking from experience," Roman said, his hair wild and teased up, "don't underestimate the power of context. You've made it this long without being caught. They're not going to expect you to be this careless now."

"And *look* at you," Priyanka said, turning me back toward the cracked mirror. I could barely make out my reflection through the thick layer of graffiti, but what I could see was a study in extremes. Hard and soft, bright and dark. And, like always, the truth was somewhere in between.

"All right," I said. "But if something goes wrong, and they do make a visual ID of me—"

"Then we'll abort the mission and fall back on Plan B."

"Isn't Plan B the one where we drive to and fro aimlessly until we happen to find another clue about where Ruby might be?" I asked.

Outside, the sound of car engines had turned from a faint murmur to an unending roar.

Showtime.

"We'll be all right," Roman said, rising from his perch on the toilet seat lid. "But if they see you hesitate, they'll take a closer look. Whoever you're choosing to be, be that person boldly."

I gave him a small salute. "We doing this?"

Priyanka shook out her shoulders and arms, then reached for the tire iron resting against the door. "If I fall, avenge me."

I took up my own tire iron, which I'd grabbed from a nearby auto body shop. "No. No one's doing any kind of falling. If someone pulls a gun, and, this being Texas, they likely will, immediately put your hands up and get on the ground."

"How long have you been waiting to say that?" Roman asked Priya.

"Pretty much from the moment I forgot to say it while we were on the Turner job."

"That was three years ago."

"It calls for a very specific kind of situation, Roman. I have to *feel* the moment—"

"Focus," I said, passing Roman the baseball bat. "Ready?"

He inspected the chipped wood, running his hand over the broken end of it, then nodded. Priyanka took a deep breath, her look of confidence flickering. Then she shoved the door open with her shoulder, spilling the hot glare of bleach-white Texas sun over us.

An hour ago, when we'd arrived, there had been a few cars lined up for the weekly gas ration. Now they wrapped down the dusty, otherwise barren street. The businesses and homes nearby had recently been bulldozed and the debris was still piled high. It looked like a scene out of the apocalypse.

The man who'd yelled at Priyanka earlier was wearing slacks and a faded button-down, and looked old enough to be her grandfather. His sunburned skin flushed a deep shade of purple as Priyanka dragged the sharp edge of the tire iron down his front.

"All yours, big guy," she said, tapping him on the shoulder with the tire iron as she sauntered by.

The boots had added three inches to Priyanka's already towering height, and she worked them, swinging the tire iron as we passed by the convenience store and moved toward the cars already at the pumps. I kept my head down, watching for trouble out of the corner of my eye. Inside the store, the woman working the counter picked up the phone, her face visibly paling through the glass.

Roman veered away from us, coming up behind the police officer keeping watch. The man grunted as Roman snatched his gun out of its holster and tossed it away, letting it skid across the pavement. With startling efficiency, he got the policeman in a headlock, applying just enough pressure until the grizzled man collapsed in a dead faint.

Priyanka took a running leap onto the hood of a sedan at the pump, then stepped onto its roof. "Ladies and gentleman, you're just in time for today's freak show and, lucky you, you get to play a starring role! Turn over your gas ration cards and maybe we won't electrocute you or burn this place to the ground." She tapped her heel on the sunroof of the car she was standing on. "That means you, too, handsome."

The man all but fell out of the door, scrambling to run away.

The cars at the end of the line peeled off, racing down the street to avoid trouble. Phones lit up across my mind like fireworks, suddenly active as they placed emergency calls. A dozen. Two dozen.

I walked over to the nearest SUV, where a woman was cowering inside, and smashed the passenger window in. I shoved my arm through the broken glass, holding out my hand to her.

"It's—it's already in the machine," she stammered, pressing her back up against her window.

Oh. Right.

I tried deepening my voice, with mixed results. "Take it out, then."

Unsurprisingly, it was the obnoxious whirring of drones that came first, buzzing overhead. Priyanka waved an arm and they crashed to the ground, smashing into heaps of metal, glass, and fire.

The flurry of movement and shouts came to a dead stop.

"Did you think I was kidding?" she called to them. "Who's next? Who wants to bake inside their own car when I turn it into an oven?"

Roman brushed by behind me, muttering a faint "Jesus" before knocking a side mirror clear off a minivan.

"Stop where you are, you fucking freaks!"

All of us pivoted toward the far end of the line, where a man had braced a long rifle over the hood of his truck. Three others, two women and another man, had pistols and rushed toward us. One fired off a shot, likely by mistake—it slammed through the metal overhang above the pumps. Priyanka jumped down for cover.

"Careful!" someone shouted. "Christ, you'll light the whole place up!"

"All right, all right!" Priyanka said, holding her arms up.

"Get down!" one of the armed women growled. "Right now, before I plug one into your freak brain."

"Well, you don't have to be *rude* about it," Priyanka muttered.

A hard barrel pressed into my back at the same moment someone gripped my arm and wrenched me down onto the burning pavement. I saw Roman snarl, lunging for whoever was behind me, as the other armed woman appeared at his side, gun trained on him. The assessing look he gave her chilled my blood, even with the scorching air baking us through our dark clothing.

"No," I said sharply. He looked at me, at the place the man pressed my cheek to the ground. I struggled against his weight, the way his knee drove into the small of my back like he was trying to break my spine, twisting just enough to turn my face upward. The sound of the Amarillo police's sirens sang out in the distance.

And then I got what I'd asked for—the man's free fist sailed down toward my face, and I dissolved into heat and darkness.

THIRTY-ONE

THE STEADY ROCKING, THE LOW, EVEN DRUMBEAT, THE stifling, sleepy air, the scent of leather and warm, clean skin—it all made it that much harder to rouse myself from sleep. But the gentle pressure against my wrists was enough to remind my body of its many complaints. And my face . . .

I swallowed back a cry of pain. The taste of blood was in my mouth again, bitter and metallic, like a bullet casing. I tried to force my eyes open despite the gritty crust on them, but I couldn't get my left one open more than a crack. It pulsated with each small movement. Static-laced voices drifted by me.

"Code ten—"

"—suspect is on foot—"

The seat back I'd been leaning against suddenly moved. A zip tie dug into my wrists as I tried to bring my hands forward to shove whatever—whoever—it was away.

Roman.

He stared at me, his eyes hooded, as he made a soft hushing sound. Next to him, Priyanka kept her gaze on the window, on the landscape racing back. Their hands were also secured behind their backs, forcing them to awkwardly lean to the side to find a comfortable position. I cleared my throat, my skull ringing with a pain that radiated out from my cheekbone.

The grate separating us from the front of the police car rattled as one of the officers knocked against it with a familiar yellow device.

"What did I say about being quiet and still?" she asked. "You want me to use this on you again? I'm all for reminding folks the meaning of *cooperation*."

Priyanka opened her mouth, the corners of it tilting up into a smirk, but Roman knocked his shoulder into her.

The officer shook her head. "Sorry to say this, Sleeping Beauty, but you're going to wish you were still unconscious in about five minutes. See those distant lights?" We were on a dirt road surrounded by desert on all sides. The only thing *to* see was the smear of lights on the lone mountain ahead. "Enjoy the view while it lasts."

I sincerely worried that Priyanka was going to explode if she didn't snap something back at him. Instead, she took several steadying breaths, then slid her eyes over to me. She must have seen my question reflected there, because she swallowed hard, then nodded.

A cloud of dust appeared, heading toward us from the opposite direction. Another police car, leaving as we were coming. Both officers waved as we passed them.

"Looks like you won't be their only drop-off tonight," the driver said. "It's like y'all are coming out of the goddamn woodwork all of a sudden."

A tremor of rage worked through me, and I had to bite my lip to keep from saying anything. Everything I had done in the government had been with the goal of bringing us out of the shadows, letting us bloom in what sunlight society was willing to give us. I'd thought—I'd hoped—that we could slowly change their minds. But the truth was that they didn't want to think about us at all.

The road became rougher the closer we got to the structure; the faint nausea that had crept up on me over the last few minutes became more pronounced with each hard bump and jolt. I realized then we weren't looking at a mountain. We were looking at high concrete walls lined with floodlights and barbed wire.

I squeezed my eyes shut, but all I found there was another fence, more barbed wire. My skin was too hot one moment, too cold the next, trapped between summer heat and the distant memory of snow. Feeling drained from the tips of my fingers, from my feet inside my too-big black boots. Saliva flooded my mouth.

Stop, I told myself. *Stop it. You're not there. You're here.*

I was here now. I was here with the others. Roman's shoulder pressed against mine as he shifted, straining his arms so his fingers could find mine behind our backs. I hooked my thumb and index finger on his, and it was only then that some of the numbness eased up.

As we came upon the ornate sign, I understood why Wheeler, Texas, had sounded familiar.

PERSONALIZED INDEPENDENT TRAINING FACILITY
AUTHORIZED PERSONNEL ONLY BEYOND THIS POINT

Priyanka inhaled sharply, but I couldn't breathe at all.

No. . . .

Photos and video of the completed facility had indicated it

would be half the size of this structure, lavishly landscaped, and painted soft, welcoming colors. Like a *school*. What the hell had Joseph Moore's team sent footage of when he'd won the bid to build his training facility?

The building's cement walls had to be at least sixty feet high, and they sloped inward like cupped hands. Electricity radiated from the place like a molten star. Power lines connected to it from all four directions, thumping and moaning as they worked furiously.

He made another camp.

Congress . . . Cruz . . . they had to have no idea. They never would have approved this.

The road curved and came to an abrupt stop at one end of the massive structure, this one standing straight up into the sky, with too many floors and windows to count. It had been built for function and intimidation only—there had been no time wasted or dollars spent on design embellishments that might have lessened its bleak look.

I leaned forward, trying to see through the front windshield. There was a passage, almost like a tunnel, that ran through the building at the ground level.

The car sped toward a security booth; it sat a good hundred yards from the actual structure, and served as a point of connection between the building and the webbing of security fencing that came into sharp focus as we neared. Not just one chain-link fence, but layers and layers of them. Between each was a series of connecting chambers for a vehicle to pass through. A ripple of pure, undiluted dread slipped down my spine.

If one gate failed, there would always be another, and another, to stand in the prisoner's way.

I licked the sweat off my top lip, tasting salt and whatever chemical was in the hair gel. The police cruiser finally slowed as we approached a soldier. No—it wasn't a soldier, at least not US military or part of the UN's forces. He wasn't in any kind of uniform, beyond a camo shirt and a heavy black Kevlar vest.

The man stood in the middle of the road, waving until the officer slowed down. He came to the driver's side, his face like thunder.

"Oh, this should be good," the officer driving muttered. "Hi there. Good evening to you. We've got three Psi in the back. These idiots were picked up trying to rob—"

"You can't keep dumping kids here like they're your garbage," the man snapped, interrupting him. "The boss wants us to crack down. We've got a new system now. Did you even scan them before dragging them all the way out here?"

"You think the government gives us that kind of equipment?" the female officer asked, leaning over her partner to get a better look at the guard. "You know how this bureaucratic shit works. Look . . . I'll pass the word on to the department if you'll take these last three."

The man guarding the entrance let out a noise of disgust, pulling back into the security booth. Another one stepped out, shining a flashlight into the backseat. All three of us turned our faces away.

"Fine," the first one growled. "Next time call ahead and flag it in PTS."

"You've got it," the male police officer said. He rolled up his window, adding, "Asshole."

Up ahead, the first of the gates buzzed and dragged itself open. As we rolled forward through the first section, then the next, my fingers tightened around Roman's. At the third gate, the female officer turned to watch us through the grate. "Enjoy being someone else's problem."

The gates slammed shut behind us, the chain-link rattling with the force of it. Each layer of fence was electrified, singing out its cautions, its warnings.

We came to a stop at the base of the fortresslike building. As the last gate closed behind us, the lights posted on the low ceiling of the tunnel went off, flashing red in time with the alarm.

There were black metal doors on either side of the police car. Both opened, and six heavily armed men poured out. All of them were wearing different shirts, some long, others sleeveless, beneath the same black vests.

They're not an organized military force, I realized. Roman was fixated on them as well, clearly drawing his own conclusions. This group was a hired force, most likely mercenaries.

The officer behind the wheel unlocked the back doors. He quickly stepped away, and before I could even take in another breath, an armed man had reached in and clamped down on my shoulders and arms.

Don't make a sound, don't give them that—

The thought was knocked out of me as I fell to the ground, hitting my head against the door.

"Hey!" I heard Roman snarl, but I couldn't see him, not with the splotches of black floating in my vision. My muscles locked up as the armed men hauled me back onto my feet, shoving me through the door to my left and into a pitch-dark hallway.

THIRTY-TWO

Panic turned my thoughts to ash. There was no way to see past the soldiers congregating in the hall, but I tried, pulling hard against the grip one of them had on my arm. I couldn't see the others—I couldn't tell if they were still behind me, and the thought made me feel like my chest was collapsing into itself.

The soldier on my right reached up with his rifle and smashed the hilt down into the tender spot where my shoulder met my neck. I gasped more from shock than pain, staggering forward. The man let me fall onto my knees, then used his free hand to grip my hair and wrench me back up.

"Hit her again and I'll kick your ass so hard you'll be eating my foot!"

Priyanka.

I turned just in time to see a female soldier slam her elbow into her stomach. She gagged on the pain, but managed to stay vertical, even as her knees buckled.

Where is Roman?

The empty hall was bookended with shadow. Cold air blew

hard from the overhead vents, hissing and spitting moisture down at us like a crowd of spectators.

The tile, I thought, watching the gray stone pass underfoot. *It's the same.*

Memory swept over me like a dark wave.

"What the hell is the matter with her?" one of the men asked.

"She finally realizes they're in a deep pile of shit," the one hauling me forward said. "Did you radio into processing we have more coming?"

I felt the walkie-talkies. The charge from their batteries buzzed inside their plastic shells. I felt the White Noise machines hanging from their belts. I felt everything and nothing at all. The only voice in my head was the one telling me to seize that charge, to hurt them the way they'd hurt us.

I swallowed the knot in my throat, chanting the word inside my head: *Can't. Can't. Can't.*

We were here for a reason. I couldn't attack, couldn't give them a reason to hurt or *accidentally* kill us.

I remembered this. I remembered how this worked.

Another soldier opened the elevator door for us. As we stepped inside, I was finally able to get a look at Priyanka, the barely leashed rage on her face. There were fresh scratches on her cheek and swelling on the right side of her jaw. But she was here. She was with me.

And Roman wasn't.

The elevator car shook to life, knocking me back against the wall. We didn't go up into the building, like I'd expected. Down. Down and down, the machinery creaking, its power wrapping around me in sputtering ribbons of electricity.

You are not a little girl anymore.

I could protect myself and Priyanka. I knew that. Rationally, I *knew* that. But it was like I could feel myself disconnecting the farther we descended, leaving some part of me behind. Dizziness crashed over my head in waves.

You're fine. You have to be fine.

My vision was going in and out in bursts. A gloved hand gripped my chin, forcibly turning my head. The soldier was a blur of black. His face came into focus as he leaned down to peer into mine. His hazel eyes narrowed.

He sees it. He knows who I am.

With whatever last grip I had on self-control, I remembered what Roman had told me about seeing someone out of context. So I did the only thing I knew that government-trained Suzume would never do.

I spat in his face.

He shoved me away, into the female soldier holding Priyanka in place. Wiping his face against his arm, he reached for his baton again.

The elevator door opened with a cheerful *ding*. Three more armed figures stood there, waiting.

"Waterson," one woman said in a flat Midwestern accent, moving aside so the five of us could step out. She was older than all the other soldiers present, her hair turned silver with age. The wrinkles at her eyes and forehead were pronounced, made more so by her humorless smile. Her camo was darker than the others', and she wore it head-to-toe like someone in the service would.

I recoiled at the sight of her. My pulse stamped out a new panic, one that twisted through me too hot and fast to understand.

Why?

"Ma'am?" the man said.

"Are you having difficulty securing this inmate?" she asked.

Inmate. My stomach roiled. At least they were honest about what we were here. No pretenses now.

"No, ma'am," he said, straightening as he stepped back into the elevator. "Just assisting with the transfer to processing." The woman nodded curtly and took position on my right.

This hallway was exactly like the one we had left above-ground, only shorter—and not empty.

Two girls, caked with dust and what looked like soot, tugged at where they'd been handcuffed to the metal bench. One was visibly older than the other by a number of years, and by the matching shade of their dirty blond hair, and the set of their jaws, I guessed they were sisters. That suspicion was only heightened when the smaller girl cowered back at our approach and the other leaned forward as if to shield her.

What little control I'd wrangled in the last few seconds disappeared.

Where is Roman?

"You can't keep us here," the older girl snarled. "We didn't do anything wrong! It was an accident!" She lashed out a foot at the soldier who had knelt to remove the restraints at their ankles and wrists.

"Actions matter," the woman said. "And your actions have brought you here for your reeducation. Line up."

I glanced back at Priyanka. She'd lowered her head, glaring out from under the loose curls that had fallen from her bun. One eyebrow rose in question. I shook my head.

The smaller girl swallowed, a fat tear rolling down her cheek, silently taking her place in front of me. Doing as she was told. Listening, like school, her parents, and society had taught her to.

Like I had done nine years ago, when they'd lined us up outside the bus that had driven us to Caledonia, confused and scared, begging to know when we could go home again. I hadn't been any bigger than this twig of a kid, with scraped knees and a handful of baby teeth still left. Neither was the girl who had been standing in front of me in that line. Nor the girl standing behind me.

It's happening again.

Nothing had changed. In all the years we worked to reclaim our place in the world, we'd only scraped at the surface of the problem. The old system had slid back in, like a recurring nightmare.

Or it had never truly changed at all.

The older girl lunged at the soldier. Priyanka gasped as one of the other uniformed women reached for the Taser at her side and calmly fired at the girl. She fell to the tile, writhing in pain. The weapon's charge seared through the spiral of my thoughts, leaving only one word behind: *Stop.*

"No! She's sorry! She's sorry!" the little one cried.

I don't know who actually killed the Taser, me or Priyanka. Its power snapped and died, but, by then, it was already too late. The girl lay motionless, facedown on the gray tile.

"Turn her over so that I can scan her," the older woman said. One of the soldiers did as she asked, struggling with the moaning girl's dead weight. She blinked up at the woman, her eyes so white in the darkness of the hall, as a tablet-like device was unhooked from its perch on the wall and handed to the commanding officer.

She lined up the girl's face in the software and snapped a picture. "Ah, this is easier. Government's good for something after all."

Every inch of my spine straightened. That wasn't possible.

Cruz had refused to send supplies to Moore's training facility until he accepted inspectors on the property. Either someone had seen this place and checked all the appropriate boxes or . . . they'd just stopped caring.

Standing behind her, I could just see the screen—the flurry of faces the government Psi tracking program flipped through before finally bringing up an image of a scowling, clean-faced girl.

"Isabella Jenner," the woman read aloud, scrolling down through the data listed beneath it. "Of Black Rock camp. Blue. All you had to do was be good and you wouldn't find yourself back in a place like this." She clicked her tongue three times.

That small sound—one, two, three, with not even a breath between. That *sound*.

Now I remembered her.

This woman—this woman had been at Caledonia. She'd worked in the control tower, then did night rounds past each of the rooms, knocking against the doors at all hours of the night to startle us awake. Just because.

One, two, three clicks of the tongue. *Shut your stupid little mouths.* One, two, three clicks of the tongue. *What? Are you going to cry now?* One, two, three. *It doesn't matter who you tell, because you don't matter.*

What was her name? All I could think of was the nickname the kids had given her: Knocker.

Static growled in my ears, growing louder as she said, "And not cured, just like I suspected."

The Knocker clicked her tongue again, once, to get the attention of the woman holding on to me. "Take her to surgery. I'll send the little one after her."

The girl still had some fight left in her. As the younger girl screamed, one of the armed women seized Isabella by the collar and hauled her down the hallway, disappearing through a set of double doors.

I whipped my head around. Priyanka's gaze met mine, eyes as wide as I'd ever seen them as the realization struck her, too.

They didn't just imprison Psi here against their will. No, that only came after they were stripped of every bit of power they had. Which meant . . . we'd come all this way to ask for help from a Psi who no longer had his ability.

Priyanka's eyes shifted back over to the device, locking onto it. The soldier holding on to her used her free hand to touch the Taser at her side, giving me a meaningful look. The Knocker snapped a photo of the little girl's face.

"Ah . . . a Green. Excellent." Knocker smiled. "We're running short on them this month."

The other soldier returned for the young girl.

"This one's going to the hold," Knocker instructed. The soldier nodded, gripping the girl's arm.

"No! I want my sister! I want my sister!" She sank to the floor, screaming, curling into a protective ball. The bare walls echoed with her pain. She was still fighting when the soldier bent down and lifted the girl's slight form over her shoulder.

Priyanka's dark lashes fanned against her cheeks. Behind her eyelids, her eyes darted back and forth, her mind already linked and working.

Shit! If they had already scanned Roman before she'd amended our listings to include the lie that we'd undergone the cure procedure—if the adrenaline overcame Priyanka—

I didn't see Knocker move until the tablet was pointed at my face, the flash burning into my retinas. The silver thread reached out, touching the device's batteries, primed to fry them.

Can't.

It would be too suspicious, especially after the Taser failed. It would give me away.

"Anna Barlow," Knocker read, then looked at me again. She took a step closer, her brows lowered in thought. Her lips parted. She recognized me. If not from camp, then from the news. Something sparked in her eyes.

Context.

I didn't think. I just spoke, in my best impression of Liam's accent. "Do I have something on my face, darlin'?"

She blinked in surprise, but recovered quickly. Her top lip pulled back as she said, "Nothing but a smart-ass look I don't like."

Knocker turned her attention to Priyanka, nodding first to the soldier gripping her arm, then to me. The soldier nodded in response, a thin strand of red hair falling out of her neat chignon. Without any other warning, she released Priyanka and seized the collar of my shirt, drawing me forward down the hall.

I spun back, trying to catch Priyanka's gaze again, but we were moving too fast. It took all of my concentration just to keep my feet from tripping over each other. For one horrible second, I was positive the soldier—GILBERT, her tag read—would take me through the same double doors marked SURGERY she'd dragged the others into.

Instead, she marched me further down the hall, into the room labeled DECONTAMINATION.

I'm fine, I told myself. *I am fine.*

My nose burned with the smell of rubbing alcohol and fake

lemon. I had to squeeze my eyes shut against the intensity of the room's exposed fluorescent lights and white walls. Half the room was covered in sterile ivory tiles that stretched from ceiling to floor. Their simple pattern was only broken up by the shower-heads mounted on the wall. The other half of the room was lined with metal shelves. Racks of them, all at full capacity with stacks of clear storage tubs. As Gilbert led me by them, a trickle of dread turned into a roar.

Piles of clothing. Shoes. Personal effects that would be destroyed before they could ever be returned.

I remembered this.

"Stand right there. Don't move," Gilbert said, pointing to the nearest showerhead. I stepped over the slight lip of the tile.

I wanted to drag my broken nails along the walls of the room. I wanted to rip the faucets off the wall, tear at her Kevlar vest, burn out every light overhead until they exploded into a hail-storm of burning shards.

I had never hated myself more than when I stood there, my face turned down, my shoulders slumped, my hands still tied behind my back. A posture of submission. Surrender.

All the poise I'd worked so hard for over the years was gone. The clever words and carefully sweetened disposition abandoned me. We stood in a silence that suffocated me more with each passing second.

I'm supposed to be fine.

Caledonia was years ago. It was a *lifetime* ago. I knew that, but I remembered all of this. My body did, too. It shook, even as I fought it, clenching my hands behind my back to try to restore feeling to them. The door opened behind me, but the sliver of relief I felt at seeing Priyanka standing there disappeared with Gilbert's next words. "Strip down. Put your belongings in the bin—"

She pulled an empty one off the shelf behind her. It slammed onto the floor in front of us, loud enough to make me jump.

"*Now.*"

Priyanka took a step forward, taking advantage of the extra inches she had on the soldier. Her eyes had that feverish look of too much adrenaline, and it looked like she was trembling with the effort to keep still. "You expecting us to put on a show, or are you going to turn away?"

Gilbert bypassed her Taser and baton and went straight for the pistol. She unholstered it, aiming at our feet. "I expect you to shut the fuck up and do as you're told."

The soldier escorting Priyanka moved behind me, cutting the zip tie binding my wrists.

Don't fight, one of the girls at Caledonia had whispered to me as we waited our turn to enter. *It'll be worse. It'll be so much worse.*

There are moments in your life where your consciousness just . . . fades. You disappear into some dark place inside yourself that protects you, even as your body goes through the motions. It's pure survival, that quiet place. It had kept me from breaking at Caledonia, and it was the only thing keeping me from it now as I slowly unlaced my boots, as I stripped off my jeans, my shirt, every layer until I was nothing but shivering, bare skin.

I remembered this.

I crossed my arms over my chest as I moved beneath the faucet. Up close, I saw that Priyanka's pulse was jumping at the base of her throat, the muscles of her neck bulging with the effort to remain still. To not react.

I couldn't watch as the soldier cut Priyanka's zip tie and she repeated the process, never breaking her hard gaze at Gilbert, never losing that look of furious defiance.

How could I get back to that? I tried to drop my arms, to mirror her stance, but it felt impossible. All I could think of was the processing at the camp, how they had shoved ten of us girls under the same showerhead and laughed as we screamed at the icy temperature. Our feet had slapped against the cement, trying to dance away from it.

My body locked into place, and my heart was pounding so hard I thought it might actually burst. As I stood there, trapped in the silence of fear, that last fraying thread of denial I'd knotted around my heart snapped.

All that was left was a single truth:

I'm not fine.

The cold water hissed on overhead, soaking us in seconds. Priyanka grunted at the first icy blast, but I couldn't get a sound out. My body tightened, bracing itself against the stinging onslaught. The cold water felt like knives carving up my skin, but as the seconds passed, even that pain began to ease.

The pink chalk washed out of my hair slowly, painting bright streaks over my shoulders and arms. Instead of rinsing clean away, it flowed into the tile grout like blood through veins, staining them. It held on. It didn't fade. I couldn't tear my eyes away from it.

I am not fine. The words floated through me, crackling with power as they surged into something more. Something new. *I don't have to be fine.*

There was a vase at my parents' house, one that had been in my family for years. I could picture it sitting on the shelf in the living room, glowing in the warm afternoon sunlight. It didn't look like any of the other art pieces in the house. Years before, my grandmother's grandmother had knocked it to the ground, smashing it into pieces. Rather than sweeping them up and throwing them out, the vase had been sent away. It had come back months later, whole, the pieces rejoined by kintsugi, a method that uses liquid precious metal or lacquer with gold powder to seal cracks.

The scars of what had happened were still there, not glued together to try to minimize the appearance of them, but glowing with thin rivulets of gold—more beautiful for having once been broken.

I remembered thinking, when I was so little, that if our scars could be mended the same way, we would never try to hide them, or erase them. Back then, I hadn't understood that we didn't always wear our scars on our skin; some ran deep beneath it, unseen by the rest of the world, aching even as we wore happy masks, even as we assured others we were fine.

My family abandoned me.

I escaped the rehabilitation camp that tried to kill me.

Skip tracers, PSFs, soldiers, car crashes, raids, death—I had outrun them all.

I had survived, when so many other kids hadn't. And if I couldn't at least acknowledge what I had gone through, I was never going to truly be able to prevent another nightmare like it from crashing into the lives of more kids.

I was still on my feet. There was still breath in my lungs. I wasn't fine, but I was *strong*. And I was going to use every ounce of my power to get us the hell out of here.

The water shut off, drizzling to a stop. Priyanka shivered with the blast of cold air, but I wouldn't give Gilbert the pleasure of seeing me suffer, not again. The other soldier shoved two identical sets of tan scrubs at us, as well as slip-on sneakers. No towels. My scrubs were drenched by the time I had them on and was in the process of rolling up my sleeves and pant legs. Priyanka looked like she was wearing child-size clothing.

"These shoes don't fit," she complained.

"Doesn't matter," Gilbert said. "You'll be lucky if the ferals outside let you keep them."

Priyanka and I exchanged a look.

The woman only laughed.

Gilbert walked us to the double doors on the other side of the room, kicking one open and nodding her head toward it. She never re-holstered her gun. I felt the end of its barrel graze my damp shoulder as I passed her and stepped into another dim hallway. My mouth twisted at the vile smell that greeted me—manure and something rotten.

At the last second, she threw out an arm, blocking Priyanka's path. "We may have orders not to kill you, but it doesn't mean we have to stop your kind from trying to do the same. Remember that."

"Lady, you have your whole life to be an asshole," Priyanka said. "Don't be afraid to take a day off now and then."

I dragged her through the door before Gilbert could whip the gun across her face. Both of us startled when, instead of following us, the soldier slammed it shut and locked it.

The cameras on the ceiling sputtered with intermittent power. Priyanka must have sensed them, too, because she kept her face turned down and her mouth shut. I looked her over, checking for any fresh cuts or bruises, but aside from the burning anger still radiating off her, she looked unharmed.

"Okay?" I whispered.

"In control," she whispered back. "Still feel like I could punch a hole in the cement, though."

With the door shut behind us, there was only one way to go. We followed the corridor as it began to slant up. I searched for any kind of door or window—any place where Roman might appear.

The walkway ended abruptly at the start of what looked like a field of gummy black mud, a cage of chain-link fencing separating us from the hell beyond. With the walls stretching high above us, it gave the false impression that we were in a stadium of some kind. But there were no seats, and only two levels: the mud-ridden ground and a series of interconnected metal walkways a few hundred feet off it. Armed men and women patrolled the upper level. A few had taken up stationary watch positions, tracking the comings and goings of the imprisoned Psi through the sights of automatic rifles.

There was hardly anything to watch. There were no permanent structures, only filthy white tents—the kind the UN had distributed to homeless families before they transitioned back into "traditional" living situations. There were groupings of them here and there, including a sizable one that looked as if it had mutated and absorbed all the others nearby.

Psi stood on the other side of the cage, most still sporting a fresh buzz-cut and new surgical scars. Whoever had done these clearly didn't have the time or didn't care about making the small incisions most surgeons used to insert the cure device. These scars were long and jagged, following the curves of their skulls.

One of them began to rattle the fence. The others quickly joined in, until the metal sounded like the chattering of wolves excited for their next meal.

I ignored them, reaching out to grip Priyanka's arm. "Roman—"

"I know," she said.

"Did you change his record?" I breathed out.

"I did, but I don't know if I was fast enough. They took him in through the other door when we came in, so they must have a separate processing section for boys, but I don't know if they moved him through it faster, or if there was anyone else there to slow the process up. I just . . . I don't know."

"Inmates," a soldier shouted down through a bullhorn, "stand back from the gate!"

The kids at the gate were small, just on the cusp of being teenagers. Their thin uniforms had been ripped and reworked; the sleeves were torn off, or the pants had been cut into shorts. Others had woven strips of the faded uniform fabric through their hair, or used it to tie their hair back. The older kids stood a few dozen feet behind them, laughing up at the soldiers. For one wild second, I wondered if they were trying to intimidate us or just prevent the people controlling the fence from sending us in.

Where is Roman?

The teens and smaller kids at the gate bought us a minute, maybe two, to look for him before we were ushered inside. I turned quickly, mud sucking at the soles of my shoes as I surveyed the rest of the cage, then the back of the building we'd been brought in through. And there—rising out of its foundation, was another tunnellike opening, identical to ours.

"Look," I said, trying to subtly angle my head toward it.

Here was the lesson you learned quickly in places like this: if the people in charge saw that you wanted something, they would use all their power to make sure you never, ever got it. Even now,

I felt the weight of those eyes looking down at us as surely as if they had dropped something onto my shoulders.

No one stepped out of the tunnel. I strained my ears, trying to catch the sound of approaching footsteps, but it was impossible to hear anything over the hooting and screaming of the kids at the gate.

The rattling of the fence grew frenetic. The older Psi whistled and jeered up at the hired soldiers perched on the rafter-like walkway over the gate, and it only grew louder as they pointed their rifles down at the kids. A silver-haired soldier muttered something into the ear of the one with the bullhorn.

"Step away from the gate!" he bellowed again. There was a new confidence in his tone, but the other Psi didn't seem to recognize the danger in that.

I turned back toward the other opening, waiting. I forced air in through my nose, out through my mouth.

He wasn't coming.

The thought of him down there, being dragged into surgery like the girls had been—I squeezed my eyes shut, tasting bile and blood in my mouth.

Too late.

"Come on," Priyanka breathed out. "Come on . . . Jesus . . . I know I don't pray to you, but Roman does, and he's one of your good ones . . . and okay, yes, I shouldn't have made that joke about the sandals one of your reenactors was wearing, sorry about that. . . . Who knew Birkenstocks would come back into style? Well, you probably did . . . but I mean . . . why? Why did they have to?"

A sudden surge of electricity flared behind us, firing through the fence—through the hands of the kids still hanging on to it.

"Holy shit!" Priyanka said, whirling around. The kids screamed as they fell back, convulsing as the shock continued to move through their systems. The silver thread in my mind lashed out, spreading over them one at a time, redirecting the flow of electricity racing across their bones—away from them, away from the damp mud.

The other Psi scattered, bounding toward the tents like spooked rabbits.

"What's going on?" a deep voice asked from behind us.

"They electrified—" My brain caught on a second later.

Roman's brow was creased with worry, his arms crossed over his chest. A new swollen knot was forming at his right temple. The small cut was trickling blood down the high planes of his cheek and onto his uniform.

Priyanka looked like she wanted nothing more than to collapse into a puddle of relief. "I thought I was too late."

"You probably were," he said. "I heard one of the guards mention the procedure testing on the way down and head-butted the tablet out of his hands. We had to wait for them to find another one."

"I'm so proud of you and all your baffling first instincts," Priyanka said.

"Are you all right?" I asked him, reaching up to dab at his cut. I caught myself at the last moment, dropping my arm back to my side.

"Inmates!" the same soldier called down, this time to us. "Stand at the gate and wait to be admitted. Any show of resistance will be met with force."

"I'll live," he said as we made our way over to the entrance and lined up in front of it. The lights posted at its two corners flashed red. Just as the gate began to drag itself open, Roman turned toward Priyanka. "But if we make it out of here, I am going to *kill* you."

THIRTY-THREE

ALMOST AS SOON AS WE STEPPED THROUGH THE GATE, the same horde of older kids drifted back toward it. A dozen kids. Two dozen. They came in waves, encircling us.

"Personalized Independent Training, eh?" Priyanka said, glancing at me.

"He's not going to get away with this," I muttered.

I let out a hard breath through my nose, studying the kids as they studied us. Most had been reduced to rail-thin states; a bite of hunger moved through me just looking at them. But it was the expressions on their faces that told their story. Suspicion. Curiosity. Resentment. The heat and dire conditions had baked those raw feelings into them. Here and there, I saw a nervous or worried shift of eyes. Those must have been the newer arrivals.

The others had obviously been here for a long time. Long before Moore's company had supposedly broken ground and started building. Long before the supposed community's model had sat on the table beside me as I spoke to reporters about the government's tentative investment in the project.

It didn't matter that I hadn't been given the truth—I should have known to ask. To *push*. Instead, I'd bought into the lie out of hope, and I'd actively helped them spread it.

I needed to question everything. Even myself.

Maybe I wasn't as guilty as the people who had conceptualized this place and now ran it, but I was still complicit—and that made me responsible for setting things right. I'd been so focused on finding Ruby and Liam, never mind clearing my name and getting justice for the people who'd been killed in the Penn State attack, but what about these kids? Why was it more important to prove my innocence than it was to get justice for victims of the same system I'd been trying to preserve my place in?

The system wasn't broken. It was working at full steam—against us. I understood everything so clearly then. We were never going to be given reparations for what they did to us, unless we reached out and took them for ourselves. And we'd never have that opportunity if we hid in the woods, or tried in vain to work with the people who were slowly, steadily, quietly trying to erase us.

I didn't know where that left us, but I was sure as hell going to figure it out. And when I did, someone was going to answer for all of this.

One of the older kids stepped forward, pacing in front of the others. She gave us the once-over, smirking. Roman tried to step out in front of both Priyanka and me, but I eased him back with my arm.

"You can try it," I warned them. "But you'll regret it."

Places like this were ruled by a pack hierarchy. The strong rose to the top through will and viciousness, and those who recognized their own weakness surrendered control of their lives to

405

the big dogs. Even with Caledonia's rigidly controlled schedule and monitoring system, it had still taken root in smaller ways.

"That so?" the girl out front drawled. Under the splatter of black mud, her skin seemed naturally tan. She'd tied her long hair back into a mess of a bun. By her height and stature, I would have put her at sixteen, maybe seventeen.

A long strip of wood slid down into her hand from inside the sleeve of her uniform shirt. A tent stake, judging by the sharpened end. But my attention was on her hand, which was missing its ring and middle fingers. The knot-like scars over the bottom knuckles were evidence enough that she'd been born with them.

Once I'd recognized her old hurt, it was impossible to miss it in the other kids. They were covered in their own scars—nicks of skin missing from an earlobe, knocked-out teeth, an empty eyelid barely covered by a strip of cloth.

Priyanka did not look impressed.

"Would you prefer I ran this through your throat or spleen?" the girl asked, tapping on her stake.

Roman looked even less impressed.

"What do you think, Doc?" the first one asked, looking to another girl, her hair buzzed and her surgical scar still a vivid red. Doc stepped up beside her and tilted her head to the side, studying us.

"Break the little one first." Her voice was sleepy, almost bored. "The others like her and protect her. They will do whatever you ask them to do if you threaten her, but she will only listen to you if you hurt her."

"Um," Priyanka began, "I don't know what school of evil you graduated from, but everyone knows you wait to give the overly long explanation of your genius *after* your plan is in play."

The first girl snorted, but when she opened her mouth, the words were drowned out by the clanging of bells.

The Psi circling around us broke ranks, sprinting in the direction of the tents behind them. Other kids swarmed out, joining the flow of bodies as they rushed toward something we couldn't see.

"Come on, Cubby," the sleepy-voiced girl said, hanging back. "Deal with them later. You know how the others get when they don't see you there. Let the rooks live with the fear for now."

"No one's going to be afraid if you give them advance notice!" Priyanka said.

The girl—Cubby—resisted for a beat longer, then slid the stake back up her sleeve. As the fabric shifted, I saw how she had tied strips of cloth up her forearm to keep the weapon in place.

"Better listen to your babysitter," I said.

The bell shut off as abruptly as it had started. Just before Cubby turned to follow Doc, she pointed at me, as if in warning.

I pointed at myself. "What? You want me to be your babysitter now?"

"You two are distressingly good at making enemies," Roman said as we watched the two of them follow the same path through the tents.

"We've got to keep you entertained somehow," Priyanka said. "So what are we missing here?"

The question was tossed to me, as the resident—and only— expert on the workings of Psi camps.

"No clue. The only time we had alarms at camp, it was to wake up and—"

Oh.

"What?" Roman prompted.

"Meals."

At Caledonia, blocks of rooms rotated through the commissary. We'd walk in a straight, silent line up to the kitchen window and receive a Styrofoam plate of mushy food. Even if we finished early, we'd remain seated until the bell rang to dismiss us, then we'd walk our plates and plastic cups to the trash cans positioned at the exit. The rooms on clean-up duty for that week would stay behind to mop and disinfect the table under the watchful eyes of PSFs. It was as neat and orderly as a military operation.

Mealtime in this hellhole was . . . not like that.

"What is happening?" Priyanka managed to get out. "Am I hallucinating this? Is this a rage dream?"

Near the center of the main cluster of tents, there were four large trapdoors in the ground. We arrived just in time to see those doors bang open, sending a spray of mud into the faces of the kids eagerly gathered alongside them. Elevator platforms cranked up, bringing crates of what looked like the UN's prepackaged rations. The same ones they had distributed in cities right after they took control of the country.

Cubby pushed forward to the front of the crowd. Before she could reach the closest crate, a small girl darted forward and snatched a ration, bolting through the legs of the Psi clustered nearby. A few more tried it, but all were blocked by the same kids we'd seen at the entrance.

All those assumptions that they were somehow trying to help us flew away.

"Now, who do I hate least today?" Cubby said, climbing up onto one of the crates. She bent to pick up a ration kit. They reminded me of the old-school lunch sets you could buy in the grocery store: mystery meat that didn't need to stay refrigerated, stale bread, freeze-dried fruit, and packets of instant soup and oatmeal I doubted were very popular.

She tossed one ration to her nearest friend, who laughed, shoving back a boy who looked thin enough to be carried off by a strong breeze. One by one, Cubby's friends received their share—multiple shares, in some cases.

The others seemed to be wilting in front of our eyes. It was their blank faces that worried me—the apathy that had somehow overpowered any humiliation and anger at being placed in this situation. They looked like they barely had enough strength to keep their bodies upright, never mind the energy it would take to fight back.

The camps and places like this relied on that resignation. That final surrender of your dignity in exchange for routine. Survival in these places often meant accepting the path of least resistance to food, water, safety.

Meanwhile, the hired guns up on the rafters watched, doing nothing to stop it. If anything, they were entertained. Laughing, pointing out the smaller kids who stood at the edges of the crowd.

"This is disgusting," Priyanka said. "Everything about it. It's appropriate that they're feeding them like caged animals, because they're watching them like this is a goddamn zoo."

I swallowed hard. The dryness in my throat reminded me of how long it had been since I'd had any sort of water. There seemed to be faucets of some kind along the right wall. Three girls had taken the opportunity to quickly wash themselves while everyone else was occupied. With their uniforms clinging to them, I could count their ribs.

Next to them was a line of bathroom stalls that looked and smelled like they were little more than holes in the ground. While there was some measure of privacy from the ground, there was no ceiling over them. The patrolling soldiers could easily watch everything happening inside. In fact, there were a number of men up there now, leering down into the stalls.

That silver thread uncoiled in my mind, searching for something to connect to, some way to transform my anger into the explosion it demanded.

I wanted out of here. I wanted everyone out of here.

"Should we split up to try to find him?" I asked. "There's got to be a hundred Psi here, maybe fewer. It shouldn't take too long."

Roman shook his head. "I don't think that's going to be necessary. . . ."

He pointed to a black teenager weaving through the crowd of kids on the other side of the crates. Blood vessels had burst in the whites of his eyes and mud splatter partially disguised the worst of the bruises on his jaw. There were open sores on his arms, a patch of rough skin on one of his cheeks, and he seemed to be limping.

"Oh boy . . ." Priyanka said. "He looks like hell."

Almost as soon as I'd spotted him, Max Wendall had approached the second of the four crates and reached down into it.

The anxious chatter fell eerily silent. So silent, I could hear the crinkle of the plastic wrap on the containers in his hand from a good hundred feet away.

Max's face was serene as he piled one rectangular box of food on top of the other. He ignored the looks of disbelief, the warning hiss of Cubby's crew. He even managed to ignore Cubby herself, until she stepped over onto the crate and pinned his arm with her foot. "You got a death wish, Monk?"

Max calmly tried to remove his arm. Cubby leaned forward, putting her full weight onto it. She gave him a mocking smile, resting her arm against her leg as she watched Max struggle. The only sign of pain on Max's face was the tightening of his lips as they pressed into a hard line.

Roman took a step forward, but Priyanka caught his wrist and held him in place.

Somehow, it played out exactly as I imagined it would.

Max refused to give the rations back. He turned his face away, just as Cubby released his arm, leaned down, and punched him in the side of the head.

It was like the gun at the start of a race. Her crew took off, jumping Max. He disappeared from view behind the crate, and for several horrifying seconds all I could see were the raised arms and fists of Cubby's crew as they whaled on him. I jumped with each hit he took and had to force myself not to look away.

"Max, what are you doing?" Priyanka whispered. "Fight back. *Fight.* You know how. . . ."

The soldiers, high up in their perch, hooted. Whistled. Clapped. Egging them on with every kick, every slap.

I saw my own cold fury reflected on Roman's face.

Finally, Cubby waved them off Max. The rations he'd taken were redistributed to the kids who had helped take him down. The food supply dwindled quickly. The crowds of kids dispersed, some stone-faced and empty-handed. And, still, we didn't move.

Neither did Max. We didn't actually see him again until the

elevators lowered back into the ground and the doors slammed shut. Then he was impossible to miss as he lay stretched out, facedown in the mud. Cubby leaned over, whispering something to him with a smirk on her face. When she and the last of the kids finally drifted back to the largest tent, Max pushed himself up onto his elbows.

Gingerly, he probed the skin of his temple and left ear. Blood ran down the side of his neck, where someone had come close to tearing off his earlobe.

His eyes landed first on Priyanka, then on Roman, before sliding shut again. Max sighed, and let his face fall back into the mud.

"I don't know how he got you in here, but you need to get out of here. *Now*."

"First of all, Maximo, it is lovely to see you again. I'm glad you took my drama lessons to heart," Priyanka said. "I also like your, uh, hovel. Real nice."

He hadn't invited us to follow him, but we did anyway. His tent, if it could even be called that, had whole sections that were shredded, dangling into the cramped space. By the way other areas were knotted, I wondered if he hadn't taken ruined scraps of other tents to try to repair it. He'd dug down into the earth, likely trying to cool off in the warmer months, and had carefully molded mud and other pieces of cloth into something resembling a bed. There was a single blanket and a few empty water bottles. Other than that, it was just the four of us crammed into a space the size of the backseat of a car.

The fabric of the tent flap brushed by my hair. I turned, only to be met with three smaller faces. Two girls, one smaller boy. It was impossible to tell where their freckles ended and the dusting of mud began.

Max's face fell as he saw them. He shook his head.

"That's okay," the little girl said. "Don't be sad, Max. You tried."

"I still have these," he said, reaching under the folded blanket for a slim package of prewrapped crackers. "Try mashing them with some water to see if she can get them down. Is her fever gone?"

I looked back at the kids in growing horror. The boy took the crackers with a look of such acute guilt that I felt it drive through me like a knife.

The taller of the two girls shook her head, revealing a long scar where her hair hadn't grown back. "But she was talking to us and asking for water."

"That's good," he told them. "I'll come check on Elise in a minute, all right?"

The older girl narrowed her eyes at us. "These are the rooks Cubby said not to help. She's going to hate you more than she already does."

"She only hates me because I don't entertain her by fighting back," Max explained. "Go on, guys."

The kids dropped the tent flaps back into place, dimming the stark glow from the floodlights.

"Why is that?" Roman asked, finally. "You were trained to fight like the rest of us."

"Because that's not my life anymore," Max said. "I don't fight. I don't kill. I made a promise to myself and the world I wasn't going to add any more pain into it. I don't get it—why would Mercer send you in to get me instead of coming himself? When did he figure out I was here?"

Priyanka made a sound of frustration, throwing up her hands. "How are we supposed to know? When you got out, we had to follow. We couldn't go back to Mercer without you."

Max looked momentarily stunned, as if he'd never considered that.

"Is that why you surrendered?" Roman asked, gently guiding him back into the conversation. "You felt like you deserved to be punished?"

Max looked up from where he'd been smoothing the fabric of his uniform over his legs. "Don't I? Don't we all?"

"I don't understand you," Priyanka said. "What were you thinking, letting them take you here?"

"I was thinking about the lives we destroyed!" Max said, finally breaking. "I was thinking about all the men and women and children that we'd be asked to kill just to satisfy a man who is *never* satisfied. I'm not like you—I can't just forget it and move on!"

In the silence that followed, I heard the sound of the kids in the nearby tents, talking quietly amongst themselves. Someone's labored breathing as they fought their way through the thick mud.

"I've never forgotten it," Roman said quietly. "How could I? I was the one pulling the trigger."

"I . . . I know that," Max said. The shame in the words tore at me. "It's not my life anymore. I won't go back to it, and I won't let Mercer take me next time he comes."

I was the first one to process this. "What did you just say?"

"Mercer comes *here*?" Roman said.

Now Max looked confused. "You're not here on his behalf, and you're not here to confront him . , . ?"

"We're here for *you*," Priyanka said.

"Max," Roman said sharply, drawing the other boy's attention back to him. "Are you sure you've seen Mercer here?"

"You think I can't spot that monster from a mile away?" Max rubbed at his face. "It's a whole system. They set aside the Prodigies that come in for him, and, once a month, he comes with an armed guard and selects the ones he wants. I saw him myself. Twice. He was here two days ago."

Roman swore, his hands curling against his knees. Priyanka's mouth opened and closed wordlessly.

"Lana wasn't with him," Max said. "At least, I didn't see her."

"No," Roman said. "She was tracking us."

"Mercer must want you back bad," Max said. He let out a humorless laugh. "You know the sickest part? The kids here think he's some hero. They call him the Angel of the Pit."

P.I.T. Fitting.

"Holy shit," Priyanka said. "Moore has to know about this, right?"

"Mercer could have a direct arrangement with the security company Moore hired to oversee this place," Roman said. "It would be easier to bribe an underling than a rich man like Moore."

"No . . ." I said, my thoughts rapidly coming together. "No, this actually makes sense. Think about the types of companies that Moore buys out and collects. One of his biggest acquisitions in the last few years was a shipping company with both domestic ground service and overseas freight."

Trucks. Cargo ships. Almost exclusive permission to cross through zone boundaries and enter seaports without much government oversight.

Roman's lips parted, making the connection. I tried not to imagine him, or any of the other children who'd been stolen from their families and locked inside shipping containers. Here, in America, they'd only needed to find the kids who ran into trouble, or the ones who'd fallen through the cracks of our systems. The unclaimed. The unwanted.

"Mercer gets kids, but what would Moore get out of it?" I asked.

"That's a good question," Max said. "You're welcome to get out of here and go figure it out somewhere else."

Priyanka ignored him, drumming her fingers against her knees. "Moore does want an army, doesn't he? He can tell the world he wants to reeducate Psi and make them 'useful,' but the original plan was some kind of fighting force, no?"

"What are you getting at?" Roman asked.

"Isn't it easier to *make* yourself an army, instead of trying to force all the Psi back with their families into service?" Priyanka said. "Moore gives Mercer the kids, but Moore's going to buy them back one day. Trained, and with heightened abilities."

"Why take Greens if he had been working with kids without the mutation?" I asked.

"My father discovered that it's easier to mutate a preexisting mutation," Max said. "And the Prodigies have less power to fight back."

"Well, Maximo, time for you to make amends on your father's behalf," Priyanka said.

"I don't want to hurt anyone else," Max said, shaking his head.

"I think you mean that you don't want anyone else to hurt *you*," Priyanka said. "We were a team, and you broke us. You ruined any hope we had of destroying Mercer from the inside, so now he goes on hurting kids, trafficking them, training them, testing on them, killing them. I would think you'd feel a little more responsibility, considering *your father* is his main instrument."

"Did you seriously break into a black-site prison just to yell at me?" Max asked. "You shouldn't have bothered. There's nothing you can say to me that will make me feel worse than what I've been telling myself. I see them every single night, Priya. Every person we hurt. Every person he had me search for. So, yeah, I surrendered. I *wanted* the cure. I didn't want to be used like that ever again. If that's what you're here for, you've wasted your time. I never took either of you for being fools, and yet, here you are."

He took a deep breath, closing his eyes again. When he spoke, it was so quietly I wasn't even sure I was hearing him right. One palm lightly slapped against his forehead, as if he could embed the words deeper into his mind. *"I cannot change the world, I can only change myself. . . . I cannot change the world, I can only change myself. . . ."*

The scar on his scalp wasn't as prominent as some of the others that I'd seen, likely because it had had more time to heal. But it was there, and he was right. It had been foolish to come here, especially without trying to learn more about what we'd find. Foolish. Reckless. Desperate.

With good reason.

"We did come here to ask for your help," I said. "But I think you need our help more."

"And who are you, exactly?" he asked, looking up.

"My name is Zu," I said. "And I'm going to get you, and everyone else, out of here."

THIRTY-FOUR

THE IDEA HAD COME TOGETHER AS I'D SAID THE WORDS. Both Roman and Priyanka turned to me in surprise, but I kept my gaze on Max.

"We think a friend of mine was tracking down kids who went missing and might have been caught by Blue Star," I explained. "She's vanished, too."

"I'm sorry about your friend, but—"

"The friend is Ruby Daly," Roman said.

The change in Max's expression was immediate. His eyes widened, his nostrils flared. It all clicked for him. "*Zu* as in Suzume Kimura."

I nodded.

"Daly's been missing for years. . . ."

"No, she's been in *hiding* for years," I said. "There's a difference. If we can find her, we can use the information she might have gathered as evidence to expose Mercer and Blue Star." I thought of the girl in the skating rink, adding, "And any partners they're using to move these kids and sell them."

"Even if I wanted to help . . . it's too late," he said, rubbing a hand along the scar on his head. "You're too late."

"You think I can't take care of that?" Priyanka asked him. "I would have thought by now you'd know not to underestimate me."

"Wait—you can hack a cure implant?" I said. The device, as developed by Lillian Gray and others at Leda Corp, effectively worked like a pacemaker. It regulated the abnormal flow of electricity through a Psi's brain caused by the mutation, preventing them from accessing their power.

She shrugged. "Sure. I would just switch it off."

"And that wouldn't hurt him?" I asked, glancing over at Max. "I'd offer to try shutting off the implant's power myself, but they put a special casing around its battery to protect it from interferences and tampering, both technological and Psi."

"Well, I haven't tried this, either, so I can't promise it won't hurt, or that there won't be side effects," Priyanka told him. "The implant will always be in there. But it's not keeping you alive. I don't see why turning it off would impair you in any way."

Max looked down at his lap, where his chapped hands had fallen open.

"You're not getting out of here. None of us are," Max said. "And what's the point? This is the Island of Misfit Toys. Thieves. Troublemakers. All-out criminals."

"Yeah, and what crimes are they guilty of? Stealing to survive? Accidentally hurting others because they've never been able to safely learn how to control their powers? Self-defense?" I asked. "We were set up to fail. These laws have been slowly knotting around us like a noose and now the knot's too tight for any of us to escape. The more we struggle, the tighter it gets, the faster we die."

Max tilted his head, confused. "Don't *you* work for the government?"

"Not anymore."

There would be no going back now. I had seen too much and was too deep into the shadows. But I just needed to see the way forward little by little, until we were through the darkness, and heading toward whatever light was waiting on the other side.

"Would I be reading you?" Max asked me. "I could do it now, then you could do whatever it is you think you're going to do to get out of here."

"No," Priyanka said. "She hasn't seen Ruby in years. The reading wouldn't be accurate. We need to bring you to someone who has."

Max shook his head. He ran his hands back through his hair, clutching at it. "I should be here. I deserve to be here."

"You really don't," I told him. "None of the Psi here do, either. No one deserves *this*."

"Please," Roman said. "I'm asking you to help us. Not because you feel that we're owed it, but because it's the right thing."

"I thought you of all people would understand," Max said, his voice breaking. "It's just not right. . . . I shouldn't get to be out there, not with everything that's happened. How am I supposed to make amends? I don't know how to make it right. Tell me how to make it right. . . ."

"Penance can mean prayers for forgiveness," Roman said. "But it can also be works that do enough good to earn it." He looked around the tent. "You've suffered enough. Don't let your pain become a prison."

"You've never known a day of peace in your whole life," Max said.

"No," Roman agreed. "And maybe I don't deserve to. But it doesn't mean I'm going to stop trying to find it for the people I care about. That includes you."

"We were the ones who survived, Maximo," Priyanka said. "It's our responsibility to stop Mercer."

"And my father," he added quietly.

I straightened. "Does that mean . . . ?"

"Yeah. I'll help you," he said. "For whatever good it'll do. But it still doesn't solve the problem of getting out of here. I won't leave the others behind."

"We need to burn this place down," I said. "They need to know we aren't going to just fade away."

"Is this a figurative or literal burning?" Priyanka asked. "Because I'm ready to start spitting fire."

I rubbed at my face, thinking. "How many implants could you deactivate before it became dangerous for you?"

"Depends on how difficult it is to hit the switch," Priyanka said. "I can't imagine I'll be in trouble, but someone should keep an eye on me after the fact. I might actually try to burn this place down."

"I will," Roman said. "I'll stay with you the whole time."

"I'm thinking more than just deactivating the implants," I said with an apologetic look.

"Have no fear, Sparky, I'll keep it together. You don't get to have fun without me," Priyanka said.

"Well, we won't have that much time to convince everyone," Max said. "There's got to be close to a hundred kids here now, and one of them might rat us out for better treatment."

"What are you thinking?" Roman asked me. "Run surveillance on the soldiers to get their watch schedule down and then head out with a team?"

This would be a risk, there was no avoiding that. The assault on Thurmond had taken weeks of planning and involved coordination on the inside and out. We'd be dependent on surprise and chaos, not careful timing and strategy.

"I'm thinking we leave no one behind," I said. "Anyway, I don't need to convince everyone. I just need to convince one person."

"Well, well, well. Looks like the ladies have come to pay their dues."

Unsurprisingly, Cubby was in the biggest tent, and even more unsurprisingly, she was surrounded by all of her best meathead types. Two of them rose as Priyanka and I stepped inside. I eyed what looked like tent stakes in their hands.

"Chill," Priyanka said. "Unless you're going out vampire hunting, those aren't going to be necessary. We come in peace, or whatever."

The tent was really four or five of them tied together, and it was immediately obvious that most of the camp's allocation of rough wool blankets was here. They were used as everything from padding to create more comfortable sleeping arrangements to curtains dividing off the area where Cubby and a few others were gathered, surrounded by empty ration boxes and water bottles.

I glanced up, checking again to make sure that we were hidden from the sight of the soldiers above us. I couldn't sense any microphones or cameras, either. Priyanka confirmed it, touching my arm and giving a quick shake of the head.

I almost laughed. At least the hired hands weren't pretending they cared if we lived or died. The camp controllers at Caledonia had spun the lie about the cameras and PSFs being there for our protection for far too long. In reality, they'd only ever been there to make sure we behaved, and to punish us when we didn't. The soldiers here didn't have to work nearly as hard to keep everyone in line, not with everyone's abilities smothered out like flames. They seemed perfectly content to sit back and watch as we killed each other.

These were the unwanteds, after all. The unclaimed and the misbehaving.

So . . . my kind of people.

"Where's the boyfriend?" she asked.

Max had taken Roman on a walkabout to familiarize him with the Pit's layout and try to plot the escape route. "Which of these kids do you not trust with your life?" I asked instead of answering.

Cubby's eyes narrowed. "What's your game?"

"I have an offer for you," I told her. "But I'll only deliver it with the assurance no one is going to go slip the information to one of the hired guns, looking for special favors."

"Anyone who rats to the grays gets spiked," she told me, picking up her own tent stake to demonstrate.

"What about you?" I asked.

The kids clustered around her began to whisper, exchanging looks that ranged from nervous to curious. Cubby's face flushed scarlet, all her bluster and bravado gone.

The sleepy-voiced girl, the one she'd called Doc, was sitting to Cubby's left. She leaned back on her hands, narrowing her gaze on me. "She's trying to test—"

Cubby jerked up her hand, silencing her. The flustered look

turned to one of fury as she pointed the tip of the stake at herself, thrusting it toward her to emphasize each word. "I got here same as everyone, I got treated same as everyone—you think I'm going to lower myself to working with the shits keeping us here? You think that helped any of us at Black Rock? No way in hell. The kids respect me, is all."

Black Rock? I took a step closer.

I'd assumed she wasn't more than sixteen, but to have been at Black Rock, a camp second in size and ruthlessness to Thurmond, she had to be my age at the youngest. Chances were, she was actually older and had survived a life full of want that had nearly starved her down to her bones.

I stared at her, and she stared back, unflinching. Priyanka pressed her arm against mine.

"You were in a camp, yeah?" Cubby said, lowering her stake. "I see it in your eyes. You've got that dark that just won't quit."

The others drifted back into silence. No wonder Cubby had handily taken this place over; she'd known how places like this worked. Which was why I knew exactly what to say to her—what to say to all of them. Because the government hadn't just relied on my voice, they'd taught me how to use it to persuade minds and move hearts. And now I was going to use that tool.

"I know you're wondering what I can do for you," I said, relaxing my posture. "We're new to the game here, and we don't understand how things really are. Not yet. But you're right, I do know something about being locked up, and I know what it feels like to believe the key is a thousand miles outside of your reach. It's not."

Priyanka's eyes shifted toward me, clearly wondering where this was going.

"Places like this exist to strip us of any dignity, to make us submit. They know the power we have, and all they want to do is smother it. When they're not telling us we're *too young to understand*, or we need to *wait* or *listen*, they're doing everything they can to contain our potential to do something incredible. These people," I said, gesturing overhead, "literally think they deserve to walk above us. They don't care if we just lie down and die. It's less work for them. If anything, it's probably what they're hoping for."

A murmur of agreement rippled through the kids. Cubby leaned forward, pressing her hands against her knees.

"The soldiers call you ferals. Not kids, not Psi, not even freaks. *Ferals*, like wild animals people hunt for sport. It makes me sick. It makes me want to *scream*, and I know you all feel the same. I let people like this hurt me in the past. They tried to break me and they came pretty damn close, but I won't let them keep hurting you. If it's the last thing—if it's the only thing—I ever really do in my life, it's going to be to help you get out of here. We deserve to be free. We deserve *more* than this. We've inherited the darkest legacy, but they don't know that we've learned how to thrive in shadows and create our own light."

Repetition, hyperbole, dialogismus, expeditio—all those little rhetorical devices Mel and the speechwriters had taught me, bullets for driving my point home. But nothing came close to actually speaking from the heart.

I met Cubby's gaze again. "Do you know what happened at Thurmond, on that last day?"

Her answer was a smile.

I returned it with one of my own.

THIRTY-FIVE

THE HARD PART, AS IT TURNED OUT, WASN'T GETTING everyone on board with the plan. It was coming up with a reason for us to all be gathered in one place without drawing suspicion—one that would also ensure we'd have the soldiers' full attention.

"I cannot change the world, I can only change myself. . . ."

I looked over to where Max stood a short distance away. The others were flowing by him like he was a rock in their stream, but he never opened his eyes to return their curious looks. He just kept repeating that phrase, over and over.

I didn't know how to tell him it wasn't actually true. One person, for better or worse, *could* have enough power to impact many lives. It just depended on their platform, on that rare chemistry of being the right person in the right moment. But I understood the sentiment, probably better than most. I could not control the world, so I controlled my voice. When things were overwhelming and moving forward felt impossible, small steps were easier to take than big strides.

"Are you sure you're up for this?" I asked Max.

All of us had held our breaths as Priyanka switched off his

implant. Nothing had happened beyond what registered as a hard snap of static passing through his system, but he hadn't stopped trembling since. Two members of Cubby's crew had gone from tent to tent, bringing them back to Cubby's in groups of five to ten, spreading it out over a good two hours. A few of the kids had elected to keep their device active, but the ones who underwent Priyanka's reverse treatment were roaming the Pit like they had fire in their veins.

The bulk of them were Blue and Yellow, with a few rejected Greens mixed in—Kin and Sparks and Prodigies. Priyanka's names had come in handy for identifying members of each group without any soldiers potentially overhearing. The kids took to them immediately; the names we gave ourselves would always have more meaning than the labels others forced on us.

Watching each of them have their ability restored reminded me of the way electricity flowed through a string of lights. Alone, each had their own glow, but together, their excitement was dazzling. It was like the parts of them they'd hardened into armor had fallen away, and they'd let themselves feel again.

At the first spark of power flooding their minds, half the group's instinct had been to immediately test them, only to be shut down by Cubby.

"Any of you pull a stunt before you get the signal," Cubby repeated to each group of kids, "I kill you myself. You hear me? You can wait an hour. You've gotta wait, otherwise you get us all gutted."

"Max?" I said, a little louder this time. The chatter in the tent was carefully restrained, with the whispered plans happening in corners under its cover. Max was watching Roman and Priyanka discuss the timing with a few of the older Kin.

It was Roman who had suggested keeping the smaller kids out of harm's way, until the first phase of the breakout was through. After Max finished here, he'd go join them in the crowded tent to wait out the worst of the fighting.

He startled at the sound of my voice, then passed a trembling hand back over his head. "Sorry, I was thinking . . . I thought they'd be more afraid."

"Me too," I admitted. In situations like these, a little fear was probably healthy—it kept you on your guard.

"She can switch it back on when we're done," I reminded him, "if that's what you want."

"No. It's not that," Max said. "I'd just . . . forgotten what it felt like. It's like a storm trapped in my skull. If I pass someone who's thinking of another person, or missing them, the power wants to seek out that connection. To find them."

"To go fishing," I said, using Priyanka's word.

He nodded. "Lana would sometimes use her ability on us while she was first learning to control it—testing her limits as a Limit, you know? Those moments of quiet felt like a relief to me. When I fish for someone, it's like a fever in my brain. There's no separating my reality from the other person's. Sometimes I connect and fish when I don't want to, and I see things I never should."

"That's not your fault," I said. "The same thing used to happen to Ruby, until she finally learned to control it."

"I wondered about that," he said. "I used to think about her a lot, make a game of trying to guess what it was really like. My father had all sorts of theories about how her ability worked. She was his obsession as much as she was Mercer's."

"Roman and Priya mentioned that," I told him. "I have to

428

tell you, I don't understand your father at all. It wasn't even that he experimented on other kids—he did the same to *you*, his own son."

"He didn't have much of a choice," Max said, hugging his arms to his chest. "Do you remember all of that mandated testing for the kids who hadn't turned yet? My dad worked for Leda Corp, at the old Philly lab they shut down, and he would bring me in to work to have all of that done—and change the results to make it look like I hadn't been affected. Back then, I was a Prodigy." He paused, letting out a startled laugh. "Wow. I never even admitted that to Priya or Roman."

"Why not?" I asked.

"I already felt like an outcast because of my father. I didn't want to give them another reason to potentially hate me." I opened my mouth to protest, but he shook his head. "Anyway, I was just good with numbers and memorization. It was easy enough to play off. My father is the smartest man I've ever known. It wasn't a stretch in most people's minds I might be like him or my mom, who was a math professor."

The dreaded *was*. "Is she . . . ?"

Max's grip on his arms tightened. "Mercer had her killed. Her and my sister both, though I think my sister was an accident. She should have been working that night. She always worked Thursday nights."

"Oh my God," I said. "I'm so sorry. Why would he do that?"

"When the four of us came through the transition, Mercer felt like my father had intentionally messed up to avoid giving him a Fader—giving him his own Ruby," Max said. "Kill one family member to show that there are consequences for disappointing him, keep the other alive with the threat hanging over them. It's classic Mercer. Neither he nor my dad would have ever told me, I don't think—it would have turned me against Mercer, and I was useful to him."

"How did you find out, then?" I asked.

"I saw it happen," Max croaked out. "When I was trying to work out how to use my power, I figured out that I was able to connect to my mom. To see her and Neve. Once that connection was there, I could always come back to it. And then, one night . . ."

"Max . . ." I began. Everything else just felt trite.

"Come on, we doing this?" Cubby said, stalking up behind us. "Night's not getting any younger."

"Could you be a little less eager about this, please?" Max asked, sounding pained. "I realize you hate me, but—"

"I don't *hate* you, Monk," she told him. "You just piss me off."

"That wasn't—" Max began. "Never mind. It doesn't matter."

"You ready for this?" I asked her. "If things go sideways—"

"Then I'm gonna die a legend before I let anyone stomp me out like a worm," Cubby finished. "We know what happened at Thurmond, and I'm going to make damn sure that people know what happened at the Pit, too."

I turned toward Max, but he was already pulling back the tent flap to begin the show. He paused before he exited. "I know I'm not supposed to want it, that there's peace in releasing all this hate . . . but some people are just monsters. Their only goal is to keep devouring us."

"Well, Mercer's about to choke," I said.

With a faint laugh, Max slipped out of the tent.

"You don't look like someone whose master plan is about to fall into place," Priyanka said, coming up behind me. Her pupils had returned to their normal size, and she was no longer bouncing from foot to foot, having worked off some of the rush with a jog along the perimeter of the Pit.

"I *am* nervous," I admitted, tracking Cubby as she made her way through the tent, punching and slapping her crew's shoulders, telling them something I couldn't quite hear. "I was a little surprised she said yes so easily. There was always a chance she'd take more convincing."

"She lives in a literal mud pit," Priyanka said. "Pretty sure it was a no-brainer."

I worried my bottom lip. "I got the impression we could trust her, but I can't say my intuition has been great, as of late. She could still betray us."

"I'm happy to betray her first on your behalf, if that makes it easier," Priyanka offered.

"Your incredibly selective conscience is one of my favorite things about you," I told her, "but I don't think that's going to be necessary."

I looked up at her, then over to where Cubby was surreptitiously streaking her face with mud. The caked-on mask was terrifying to look at, which I supposed was the point. Her crew began to do the same.

"Seriously, though," Priyanka said, "we don't have to like the girl. We just have to trust she likes living in the mud less than she likes us."

"They're getting into position," Roman said, striding toward us. "Where do you want us to be, Priya?"

"I'm about to go look. We'll be able to get into the wider system as long as they have a device on them that connects to a server in the main building," Priyanka said. Just before she went outside, she wrapped her arms around both of us, squeezing tightly. "Be excellent, my friends."

"It's okay if you can't do it all," I told her. "And if it's too dangerous to get upstairs . . ."

This was the part of the plan that hinged on chance, and I didn't like it. After we got the gate down, she and Roman would try to locate whatever functioned as the control center. We needed evidence that Moore had lied about his training program, and if there was security footage from the last few days, there was a chance they'd caught Mercer on it. Linking him to Moore was crucial. Without any concrete proof, our version of events would just sound like conspiracy theory to the general public.

Priyanka waved off the concern. "I don't need my powers to pull security footage onto a flash drive. I'll be all right." As she turned to go, she pointed at me. "Come together, leave together."

"Come together, leave together," I echoed.

Roman started after her but stopped suddenly. He turned to face me and started to lift his arms, as if to place them on my shoulders, but quickly let them fall back to his sides. His face looked progressively more agonized as he glanced from my face, to his shoes, to something very interesting I couldn't see in the mud.

In the end, he stuck out a hand, and it took me longer than it should have to realize I was supposed to shake it.

We both jumped as I accidentally shocked him, but he didn't release his grip.

I didn't want to insult him by checking again that he would be able to mirror Priyanka; he'd said yes once, and that was enough for me. But he seemed to read my thoughts anyway.

"If I pass out . . ." Roman began, still grasping my hand.

"We're not going to leave you behind," I told him. "So don't bother suggesting that."

"Right . . . right. If I'm dead, though, you shouldn't bother with that, either," he said, visibly flustered.

For someone with such steady aim, I could feel his hand shaking.

I took an unconscious step toward him, giving in to the sudden warm tug in my stomach. My heart kicked against my ribs as I moved between nerves, excitement, and fear.

And then he dropped my hand and all but ran out of the tent.

"You tell him he smelled like shit or something?" Cubby asked.

Stunned, I shook my head.

"Well. Save whatever the hell that was about for later. Ready?" Cubby rolled her shoulders back, shaking out her arms.

"Don't hurt him," I muttered, following her out of the tent. "It's pretend, remember?"

She glanced back over her shoulder, the dried mud on her face cracking with her humorless smile. "I'm tired of always pretending, aren't you?"

"Cubby!" Max roared from outside the tent. *"Come out, you coward!"*

"That's my cue," she told me. "Don't fuck this up for us."

It was Max who threw the first punch.

It landed strong against Cubby's jaw, the force of it nearly spinning her back. The mud latched onto her feet, keeping her upright long enough to lash out a leg. Max hunched forward as the air blew out of his lungs. Back and forth, they hit, kicked, slapped at each other, their feet stamping a circle into the mud.

The occupants of the Pit descended on the fight, hooting and cheering as they circled around them.

I glanced up at the soldiers clustered above them, who were watching with amusement as two of their prisoners seemed poised to tear each other apart. More and more of them moved toward the fight, leaving the outer walkways they were meant to be patrolling.

"You think you're better than the rest of us?" Cubby shouted. "That you aren't scum?"

"I think you're the problem here," Max replied.

Priyanka and Roman stood beneath the walkway's faint shadow. His hand was on her shoulder as they looked up. A moment later, Priyanka's eyes found mine, and she nodded.

They're in.

I pushed my way toward the front of the ring, nodding to Cubby as she wound her way past me. She gave a small nod of acknowledgment, then rushed Max again.

Priyanka thought they'd need at least five minutes to get through their security system and get it offline. Five minutes. Three hundred seconds.

Two hundred ninety-nine . . .

Max charged at Cubby with a roar. Some of the soldiers started laughing. To them, this was only part two of the fight they had witnessed earlier. Nothing suspicious from the little monsters below.

Two hundred ninety-eight . . .

The seconds wound down. I tried to look back at Priyanka and Roman, but couldn't see them over the heads of the excited kids between us. I winced as Cubby's foot struck Max's throat, making his eyes bulge.

He stumbled back, bumping into the crowd of kids who were all too happy to shove him back toward Cubby. She wasted no time in laying him out flat on his back, just in front of me. Mud splattered against my shoes.

Max stared up at me from the ground, all vestiges of his serenity gone.

Sorry, I mouthed as Cubby hauled him back up onto his feet.

"Come on, don't give out on me," she said. "I'm just starting to have fun!"

Max swayed, trying to shake off the latest hit. He feinted right, and Cubby actually fell for it. There was a genuine look of surprise on her face as his left foot hooked behind her knee, and he pulled the leg out from under her.

The boy beside me let out an excited cry, punching his fist into the air.

I watched it happen in agonizing slowness, the seconds dragging until I thought they would stop entirely. The burst of power rippled up from his fist, lifting the laces on the soldier's boots before gripping his body completely. One moment he was standing there, smirking, the next, his body had arced, his mouth open in a silent, shocked scream. And then he was falling.

Landing in the mud with the rest of us.

THIRTY-SIX

THE SOLDIER SLAMMED INTO THE GROUND, SENDING UP a wave of tarry mud. Max jumped away, but Cubby was forced to roll out of the soldier's path to avoid being crushed. Every single one of us looked as stunned as the soldier did. The Blue boy clutched his arm to his chest, as if he had physically struck the man.

There was a second of stillness. Quiet. Then the moment splintered into chaos.

Startled gasps and the clattering of guns being drawn above us.

Cubby reaching for the downed soldier's gun.

Roman shouting, *"One!"*

I didn't think. Didn't speak. Just reacted. I reached for that silver thread inside my mind, tightening my grip on it until I was strangling the power that thrummed inside the two floodlights directly overhead. The glass covers and bulbs shattered as they blew out, sending soldiers and Psi alike scattering.

Panic swirled through the voices above us.

"Code White!" someone shouted. "We have a Code White—get on the radio—"

"—radio's dead—"

"—trying to hail them but the signal—there's something wrong with the signal!"

The other kids ran out through the Pit, their arms raised toward the rest of the lights, surging the electric current through each of them. One of the soldiers screamed as the bulbs exploded, raining down shards of glass and sparks.

The pitch-black darkness was momentarily disorienting. I stumbled, then caught my balance as I swung back toward the others. They were a shade darker than the night; I couldn't make out any of their features, but as my eyes adjusted, I could see them. Most of the kids had done as instructed and taken cover beneath the walkways where it would be harder for the soldiers to aim.

Like they were trying to do now.

"Two!" I shouted.

The girls next to me were Kin. Their arms brushed me as they lifted the soldiers into the air, following the lead of the others like them. The screams from the soldiers as they were knocked to the ground should have been unsettling. Instead, it was like I could feel their fear moving through me, gathering into a roaring current. It amplified the words growling like static in my mind.

We have the power.

We outnumber them.

We are in control.

And if we couldn't fix a broken system, we'd shatter it and remake it ourselves.

Distant shouts—the few soldiers working inside the main building flooded out from a door on its second story that connected to the walkways. Before they could even pass over the cage, they were flying, too, and landing hard.

Some of the hired guns were trying to climb out of the Pit by going over the cage's chain-link fence, only to be ripped off it by a small pack of Kin who descended on them with screams and fists. A dark shape up on the building's roof got one shot off before being dragged forward. His rifle fell to the ground a second before the rest of him did.

Gunfire screamed in the air, only to be silenced as the kids overwhelmed the soldiers, prying their weapons away from them, making a game of shoving the soldiers to the other side of the Pit, just as they got up onto their feet.

"Come in! Anyone! Code White!"

I reached down for the gun half-buried in the mud at my feet. My pulse surged as I cracked the butt of it against the soldier's head, sending him sprawling back down. There was a metallic *click* as someone removed the safety of their gun behind me. I whirled back toward the sound.

"Down!" Cubby said, then, with an unexpected calmness, fired at a soldier I hadn't seen rushing up behind me.

He fell, howling, clutching his busted knee. Just beyond him, I finally made out the smaller shapes of the younger kids as they ran along the wall toward the main building. Max limped along behind them, clutching a gun.

"Three?" Cubby asked.

I nodded. "Three."

"Three!" she shouted.

Her crew rushed to her side, clutching the weapons they'd

stolen. Most of the soldiers were on the ground, their hands behind their heads, their faces down in the mud, but a few were still up and firing. I heard the solid *click* of someone reloading and spun. A group of teen boys ran past me, their legs churning at full speed as they ran after Cubby toward the fence that separated the Pit from the main building.

Bullets sprayed out from somewhere behind me. I threw myself down, covering my head, gasping in a choked breath. The boys seemed to leap up as the bullets tore into their backs. Blood streaked the air the instant before they fell.

Every last bit of feeling seemed to leave my body. The mud clutched at me, as if trying to drag me down, to smother me. I couldn't get my hands beneath me. The Pit began to spin and blur.

Get up.

Cubby and several of the others charged back toward us, screaming as they fired at the soldier who had taken down the boys. They knelt beside the fallen kids, feeling for pulses, trying to shake them awake, and never once noticing the other soldier who took aim at them. I opened my mouth to scream out a warning, but it was too late. Another explosion of gunfire followed, and when it finally abated, Cubby staggered up from the ground alone.

Stand up.

The mud turned to snow beneath me.

Get up.

I tried to lift my head, but there didn't seem to be an ounce of strength left in me. Those boys . . . why did I think this would work? Why did I believe we'd all get out of here alive?

Stand up.

A figure ran toward me, firing at someone or something I couldn't see. For one wild second, I thought it was Liam. I waited for the gentle hands to lift me, carry me away from here. Instead, the figure stopped beside me and took a bracing stance, returning fire at someone. His gunshots were rolling thunder, keeping time with the frantic pounding of feet against the ground, heading toward the fence.

You can get up.

You have to get back up.

I could get back up. I could do it myself. Again, and again, and again. As long as there was breath in my body, I could get back up.

I slid my palms out from where they'd been trapped under me until they were in line with my shoulders. I spread my fingers, steadying myself as I pushed up off the ground. The figure beside me ran a hand down my back and along my shoulders—Roman.

His mask had slipped in the darkness, and there was only terror there.

"Are you hurt?" he shouted.

I shook my head, still unable to speak. I pressed my right hand to my left shoulder. *I'm okay.* Roman nodded, returning the gesture. *It's okay.*

I could stand up. I could do it on my own.

A sheen of sweat had broken out over Roman's face, and the telltale tremors were already starting to work through his body. We'd only have minutes before the pain overtook him.

I grabbed his free hand, relishing the hard clasp of his fingers around mine. Needing to make sure he didn't somehow fall behind. *Still here, still standing.*

Priyanka was waiting for us at the gate, her body thrumming with power, her expression wild. Seeing that we were okay, she turned and started after the others, running for the building. I pushed Roman toward her.

"Go!" I said. "I'll make sure the others are all right."

"Five minutes," he said, pressing his hand to his shoulder again. I returned the gesture, feeling lighter. *We are okay.*

He navigated through the crowd of kids, disappearing into the building. One of Cubby's crew was at the fence, rifle in hand, waving everyone in. At the sight of me, she stopped. I turned, trying to catch a glimpse of whoever was behind me.

Only soldiers. Mud-splattered and charging, yelling out their rage. Even without their guns, they still had Tasers. Batons.

"Was that really everyone?" I asked.

"You're the last one," the girl said, dragging the gate shut and throwing its lock in place. "Do it."

I nodded. Priyanka hadn't completely shut down the electricity in the Pit, she'd only temporarily turned it off. It took only three heartbeats to coax the electricity back into the fence. We turned to go just as the soldiers reached it and began screaming.

Someone, likely a Kin, had ripped off the decontamination room's door, easing our path back into the building. The storage tubs had been ransacked, but I didn't bother to stop long enough to see if my clothes were still there. We'd left our actual belongings in the car we'd parked a good fifty miles north of here, at the border between Texas and Oklahoma.

There was no sign of Priyanka and Roman as the remainder of us followed the trail of destruction down a set of stairs I hadn't seen before, when we'd first come in.

Give them time, I thought, trying to ignore the sharp twist of worry in my gut.

"Where are we going?" the same girl called up to one of the others, just as we turned the last corner of the stairwell and saw for ourselves.

It was a massive garage.

The size of it must have encompassed the whole length of the Pit. There weren't just the soldiers' personal vehicles, but military-style trucks and vans they almost certainly used to haul kids in here.

Along the back wall were a series of lockers and a bulletin board filled with keys on hooks. The lockers had already been pried open and their contents—purses, backpacks, clothing—ransacked. Cubby was there, tossing set after set out to the kids waiting in a surprisingly orderly line for them.

"Don't keep the cars for longer than a few hours," I shouted over the roar of engines revving and the excited, terrified chatter of the kids. "And don't stop for anything!"

A few shouted back, acknowledging the instructions. I spotted Max helping another teenage girl load some of the smaller kids into an SUV. He waved to them as the girl climbed into the front seat, and a boy climbed up into the passenger side.

Most of them were traveling together, it seemed. Good. But seeing them pair off and cluster in groups made me stop and look back toward the entrance, waiting.

Come on, I thought. *Where are you guys?*

Cubby made quick work with the rest of the keys, leaving two smaller sets for us. She tossed both at me as she passed by, grinning. "See ya in the next shit hole, Rook."

The keys weren't for an actual car, but two of the motorcycles parked in their own section along the far eastern wall. Max ran to my side, dodging out of the way of a green Jeep as it roared by.

"Do you see them?" he shouted.

Seconds passed. Minutes. More.

"Maybe I should go look for them—?"

"No, there they are!" Max took off like a shot, weaving through the remaining vehicles. I saw them a second later, Priyanka all but carrying Roman on her back. The veins and tendons in her arms stuck out, and she vibrated like a kettle on the stove.

"I got it," she said, seeing my face. "I got it, I got it, I got it!"

"Great—"

"Are we riding these? I *love* these, oh my God, I love it—"

I clapped my hands in her face. Priyanka turned to me, her pupils dilated and her face bright with eagerness. She had Roman's full weight across her shoulders and hadn't so much as broken a sweat.

"Are we going? Are we doing this?" she asked. "Why are you looking at me like that?"

I felt Roman's neck for a pulse. His eyes opened to slits, and, as Priyanka set him back down, he pressed his right hand to his shoulder. In it was a syringe.

"Raided their med bay, it's all good," Priyanka said. "I'll take it once we get the hell out of here, I'll come down, I promise, I'm in control, I'm fine, just let me fly—let me fly."

"If you can handle it," I told her, squeezing her wrist, "then that's the plan."

Roman took one look at the bikes and managed to get out, "Can't." His brow wrinkled in obvious agony.

"Can." Max held up one of the soldier's belts. "You remember how to ride?"

That last question had been directed at Priyanka.

"I remember beating you in every, every, every single race," she said, taking the belt from him. "Load him up behind me, and let's blow this joint."

Priyanka sat down on the first bike, leaving Max and me to maneuver Roman's unconscious form behind her. I looped the belt over their chests, securing it with a little prayer.

She kicked off and headed toward the door before Max and I had even climbed onto ours.

"This is . . ." he began.

"Don't think," I told him. "Just go."

The words were drowned out by the roar of the garage's door as the others finally got it all the way open. The kids honked as they drove out, smashing through the chain-link gates that had seemed so formidable when we first drove in. The fencing splintered and snapped, tossed out into the dirt as the first trucks and SUVs mowed through it. A cry went up from the cars behind them as they flew forward. The sound rippled back through the mass of us, feeding an electric sense of hope.

After the last car was out, Max hit the gas, bringing the motorcycle alongside Priyanka's. We sped up, and the world suddenly opened for us. With the exterior lights out, all I could see was an infinite sky, studded with stars.

If they wouldn't see us as human, I thought, we'd make sure they understood we were something more.

The car was waiting for us right where we'd left it behind a run-down, deserted strip mall at the edge of Oklahoma. I'd lost track of how many we'd had to steal at this point; it had taken two just to put this plan into play. We'd stashed a car here and then taken a second one back into Texas to leave at the gas station where we'd been taken into custody.

We took turns changing out of the uniforms, leaving them and the bikes for someone else to deal with. At some point, Max had wandered away from us, walking toward the cheerful sign that had greeted us as we crossed state lines.

"Are you accepting Oklahoma's invitation to 'Discover the Excellence'?" I asked him, watching as he paced back and forth, his head tilted back. In the distance, I could have sworn I heard helicopters. "We should get going."

Or maybe that was just the sound of the wind turbines. We'd passed by hundreds of them, all sticking out of the ground like petal-stripped flowers. They'd felt appropriately skeletal, for a part of the country that seemed as dusty as old, disintegrating bones.

"Everything . . . all right?"

Roman had woken up just before we'd reached the car, but he still didn't look well to me. His skin had a chalky quality to it, and he swayed slightly as he came toward me. Instinctively, I reached out to steady him. He shot me a slightly rueful look, but accepted the help.

Now that I'd burned through the heat of anger and fear, what I'd found inside me again was quiet. The kind of quiet that didn't keep you at its mercy, but clarified everything. The comfortable kind of quiet you'd find walking next to someone who no longer needed words to know your heart.

"I think we should lie low somewhere safe for a little while and regroup," Priyanka said, coming up behind us. The sedative was starting to take effect, and her feet were dragging through the dust. "It'll give Max time to prepare for fishing. If anyone has any suggestions on where that mythical place might be, I'm all ears."

Oklahoma . . . As far as I knew, there wasn't anyone in the old Children's League network that lived out here. But—I couldn't believe I hadn't thought of it sooner. Ruby's friends Sam and Lucas had moved out to Kansas after Ruby had disappeared, falsified identity documents in hand. They'd left an address with us to memorize, in case we ran into any Reds who needed their help.

I just wasn't sure I could bring myself to interrupt what little peace they had.

Desperate times, I thought. When were they not, though?

"I know a place," I said.

After the hell the last few days had brought, the next few hours unfolded with surprising ease. Once I was done driving my leg of the trip, I passed the wheel—and Sam and Lucas's address—to Roman. In our exhaustion, we just kept heading north, until the sun was up and we were in Kansas.

"Wake up, Dorothy," Priyanka said, giving me a slight shake. I sat up from where I'd been sleeping against her arm in the backseat. "We're over the rainbow and in Kansas."

For one disorienting moment, I heard a different voice.

I'm Gabe. This is Dorothy.

"Don't call me that," I said, rubbing my face.

"Aw, but Dorothy suits you, now that I think—"

Dorothy— Guess we . . . shouldn't have left Oz. . . .

"Priya," I said, letting an edge of that old pain into the word. "Don't ever call me that."

"All right," she said softly.

"That has to be it, right?" Max said, pointing through the windshield. A small farmhouse with some kind of detached shed or barn took shape in the distance. As we turned up its long driveway, I saw a few cows grazing, a handful of overexcited goats, and a separate sty for the two pigs.

"Looks all quiet on the home front," Priyanka said as Roman parked the car.

I stepped out first, trying to see through the house's windows. Thick white curtains completely blocked out the interior. The others waited by the car as I stepped up onto the porch and knocked.

No answer. I pressed my ear against the wood, trying to listen for any movement inside. Clearly someone was home. There were fresh footprints leading from the house to the pigs' trough, as well as to the chicken coop on the other side of the barn. A lone rooster strutted by us, heading toward the small, noisy structure. His path overlapped with another set of tracks, this one heading for the barn door.

"Zu . . ." Roman began, reaching for his gun. I waved him back, motioning for them to stay where they were. Sam and Lucas probably didn't get many visitors. We could have scared them into hiding, uninvited and unannounced.

I reached for the barn door, angling myself back as I walked it open. When no one jumped out, I stepped inside, slowly searching the darkness.

Only to be met with the hard jab of a gun's barrel against my back.

"Keep your hands up," a familiar voice said. "Back up nice and slow—"

Recognition lit through me, surging until I thought my heart might explode. Somehow, I managed to turn my head to look back at him.

"Christ!" Beneath his beard, his face paled. He lowered the shotgun. "I could have killed you! You about scared the life out of me—"

I launched myself forward, and threw my arms around Liam's neck.

Three Years Ago

WE BEAT THE SUNRISE TO BLACKSTONE, A SLEEPY LITTLE town that had yet to wake up from the country's financial slump. Nature seemed to have overtaken a number of the neighborhoods we'd driven through, looking for the mural that was mentioned in Liam and Ruby's coded message.

"All right," Chubs muttered. "This is getting ridiculous. . . ."

Back in the Betty days, we used to relish mornings like these, where our chances of being seen and reported dwindled enough for us to find a place to park and rest for a few hours. But it seemed to be having the opposite effect on Chubs. He shook his head at each abandoned house, sighed at the potholes we hit. It was clear that what I saw as a blessing, he saw as unfinished work.

There's so much left to do. The more I thought about it, the heavier the realization sat in me. It seemed insurmountable; how many roads, how many neighborhoods, were exactly like this one? How were we ever going to get to them all in our lifetime?

"There—" I said, pointing. There was a small road sign barely hanging on to its post. It was twisted and bowed backward, but still readable. "We have to go right to find 'Historic Main Street.' That sounds promising."

For all those hours we'd spent driving in circles, once we were on the right road, we found the mural immediately. A saintly hooded figure held out both of his hands, welcoming us. Compared to the dirty brick exteriors, the paints were bright and fresh. The image seemed to glow with the sheen of the drizzle on this overcast day.

A few cars were parked in front of the shops along the street. They had their choice of a grocery store, a pharmacy, and . . .

"There's the coffee shop." Chubs pointed to it. "All right, they said what again?"

"We're supposed to write a name on the wall and leave a rock?" I said, reading from the sheet again. "And then they want us to go in and buy tea."

He looked at me. "Why tea?"

"That's the part you find strange?" I asked. "Do you have anything to write with?"

We searched the car, eventually turning up an old pen in the center console. After looking up and down the street to make sure no one was watching, we got out and walked over to the mural. Cold air bit at me as I stared up at the towering image.

"This is ridiculous," Chubs muttered, trying to scratch his name onto one of the painted bricks. It was so faint, I didn't even bother trying to write my own when he handed the pen to me.

I told him before that this wasn't a scavenger hunt, and I still believed that. Clearly, the address wasn't going to suddenly flash across the wall because we'd completed the mysterious steps. If anything, the steps probably didn't matter as much as being seen attempting them did. Someone nearby must have been keeping an eye on this spot. If they didn't have the address, then maybe they were notifying Liam and Ruby we were here, and were ready to be picked up?

"He should have just given us a stupid address," Chubs said. "I feel insane doing this. Come on, let's go back to the car—"

"Wait," I said, searching the ground nearby. "The rock—"

I picked up a broken chunk of brick, turning back toward the mural. But that had been the end of our instructions. With no other place to really put it, I set it down against the wall, just under the painted figure's feet.

"This is ridiculous," Chubs said again, stuffing his hands into his pockets.

"You need to go buy tea," I said. "Remember?"

I wanted to go in with him, but I also didn't want the questions or looks I'd get from the others, especially if there was a chance that it would spook Liam and Ruby.

Chubs sighed, but started to trudge across the slushy street anyway.

"Hang on," I told him. He let me pull his hat down a little more and adjust his scarf so that it covered his identification pin. I took his glasses off too, just for good measure. I didn't think he'd even been photographed without a pair.

Chubs gave me a slightly unfocused, but definitely irritated, look.

"Just this once," I said.

Waiting for him in the car was pure torture. When Chubs finally appeared again, two steaming cups in his hands, he looked even unhappier than before.

"Nothing?" I asked.

He passed me my usual hot chocolate. "After making incredibly creepy eye contact with everyone in that café, I can only assume that they're either going to show up, or the local police will beat them to it—ah, shoot—"

Hot water from the tea spilled down his front. Chubs started to blot the stains with a napkin. The cup tilted dangerously again.

"Give me that," I said.

As he passed it over, the protective sleeve slipped down.

I set my own drink aside, sliding the sleeve off completely. I turned the cup so he could see the address scribbled there.

Chubs leaned back against his seat, letting the napkin fall to the floor.

"All right," he said. "Let me see the map again."

In the end, the address didn't even lead us to a house. It took us down a small back road and onto a cleared lot of land. I would have picked it out as the address even if I hadn't seen the numbers spray-painted onto the tree at the edge of the road, or the red truck parked just out of sight.

Chubs pulled up alongside the truck and killed the ignition. For a moment, we simply sat there, listening to the rustle of rain falling through the nearby leaves. It glazed the windshield, blotting out our view of the world.

"Should we get out and take a look around?" I suggested, my hand already on the door.

"Guess so," he said.

We wandered the lot, passing each other as we circled it. As I moved closer to the far edge of the field, the rain sounded different. Louder. I moved deeper into the foliage, pushing a shrub out of the way until I saw why.

"Zu?" Chubs called.

"Over here!" I waved my arms big and wide so he'd see me. *"Look!"*

Chubs looked all right. And he did not like what he saw. The only word to describe his expression was *grim*.

"What's the matter?" I asked.

Before he could answer, a dark shape appeared in the haze, moving in a quick, smooth path across the silver surface of the lake. Plaid shirt. Baseball cap. Whistling the Rolling Stones.

Liam.

He turned on the small rowboat's bench, finally noticing us. The drop from the trees to the water was steep—too steep to run down and greet him like I wanted to.

"Damn, I can't believe you guys beat me here!" he called up, turning his boat to bring it alongside the edge of the water. "There's a little beach-y area over this way, a few hundred feet. It's easier to grab you from there . . . unless you want to swan-dive into my arms, Chubsie? You know how much I love a dramatic reunion."

Chubs started in the direction Liam had pointed. From down in the boat, Liam shot me a questioning look. I shrugged. We both knew Chubs. Sometimes he needed a little time to warm up to a situation.

The curve of the hill was rockier than I'd expected. Chubs turned back to help me navigate it, steadying me as we climbed over a downed tree.

"Really, I'm fine," he whispered when he saw me studying him.

By the time we made it down to the flat, even ground, Liam had pulled the boat up onto the shore. I released my grip on

Chubs's hand, and Liam hopped out just in time to catch me as I took a running leap toward him. His laughter was slightly breathless as he swung me around until both of us were dizzy.

"Now that's a proper hello!" he said, tugging my askew hat back down over my ears.

As soon as my feet were back on solid ground, I punched him in the stomach. His laughter burst out of him as he doubled over.

"Don't you dare ever leave without telling us again!" I said, letting the last six months of worry and anger into the words. "It wasn't right—it's not right."

Liam straightened, the mirth slipping from his expression. "You're right. It wasn't. If there was a way to get you guys a message without risking someone else finding out . . . I should have tried harder. It was just so nuts at the end, especially with what happened to Ruby's dad. We had to get out before things got worse, no matter the consequences."

Those consequences being that they were now fugitives in the eyes of the government. Ruby had been more carefully monitored with curfews and check-ins than any other Psi, and when she and Liam had disappeared, she'd broken her word to the interim president and United Nations that she'd follow those strict arrangements. We weren't allowed to live outside the system the government had methodically set up for us anymore. At least not legally.

"It's not—" Chubs began to say, then cut himself off. His hands were still tucked into his jacket's pockets, but the fabric was thin enough for me to see that his hands had curled into fists.

Liam opened his arms wide. "I'm up for round two, buddy. Don't fight the twirl."

"Could we possibly get out of the rain first?" he said, taking off his glasses and wiping them clean on his undershirt.

The rain dripped off the brim of Liam's beat-up hat as he stared at Chubs. His arms fell back to his sides, and he glanced toward me again. I gave him a pained smile.

This wasn't acceptable. I knew there might be a little weirdness, and Liam pretending like nothing had happened wasn't exactly helping, but there was no reason for it to be *this* awkward.

I walked over to Chubs and planted my hands on his back, pushing him forward until, finally, he relaxed enough to fold Liam into a quick, hard hug.

"Sorry," he mumbled. "I'm just tired. We had an early start."

"I do recall how much you love your early rises. I also seem to recall having to carry you out of one motel room bridal-style to get you into Betty before sunrise."

Chubs took his glasses off to clean them again, even though they weren't wet at all.

The tense silence was back, winding through us.

"Is Vi still in the car?" Liam asked, glancing behind us.

"She had to work," Chubs said.

Liam's expression fell. "Oh. Maybe next time, then."

"Maybe," Chubs said. He nodded toward the rowboat. "Are we all going to fit in that? I'm guessing we have to go back across the lake to get to your hideout."

"You'd be correct in that assumption, my dear Chubston," Liam said, turning back toward the water with his hands on his hips. "It's not as big as Lake Lee is a ways up the road, but, then, all lakes should have something to aspire to. I feel lucky that we found this place."

"It does have that certain . . . comfort of familiarity," Chubs said slowly.

Another confused look dimmed Liam's smile, but he recovered quickly and moved to help me step into the boat. It actually was a tight squeeze. In the end, I had to nestle down into the foot well beneath them, using Chubs's sweater as a cushion. Liam pushed us back into the water and jumped in with the ease of someone who'd done it countless times. I passed the oars to him.

"Aaaand we're off." Liam pushed up his sleeves as the boat coasted. He didn't seem bothered by the chill or his soaked shirt. If anything, he was beaming. There was this . . . ease to him, one I hadn't seen before. The brightness was back in his eyes, and his face had filled out again. I remembered looking at him in those last tense weeks before the camps fell and not recognizing him at times. The strain of everything, his grief over losing his brother, the constant threats on Ruby's life, it all slowly broke him down and carved away at his health.

"Sorry about the cloak-and-dagger routine," he said. "We're working out the kinks for making contact. It all feels complicated now, but I don't think the old network will have any issues getting the instructions out in the next few weeks."

"Wait, who are you getting the message out to?" I asked.

Liam pulled the oars back through the water, smiling. "This isn't just our new home. Ruby and I decided that we're going to turn it into a safe place for other kids who need help. We've already gone to get three kids based on tips from some of our old Children's League friends."

"That's great," I said. And it was very *them*. I could easily see the two of them out navigating back roads, stepping in to help out the kids who needed it most. "Are they runaways?"

Liam glanced over at Chubs, who'd turned his back to us and was running his fingers through the water. "Actually, the three we have now had been returned to abusive households."

Chubs's hand stilled.

"Well," I said, too brightly. "That's . . . great. That is super great." The awkward silence was back. "How did you guys end up here?"

As Liam told the story, he relaxed back into his task. After he and Ruby had disappeared, they'd spent weeks simply camping out, until Harry, Liam's stepfather, was able to meet them. And when the apartment above her coffee shop came up for purchase by the bank, Mrs. White sold them her old house. It became too much for her to get back and forth to work, Liam explained, because the house was only accessible by crossing the lake on boat, or navigating through miles of the wild, tangled woods that surrounded the house. They spent most of the summer updating the house to comfortably fit more kids, and digging out an escape route through the basement.

The boat bumped up against the opposite shore and Liam jumped out again, dragging it up on land. While Chubs and I waited on the bank, he returned the boat to a small shelter, covering both with a tarp to help keep out the rain. It gave me the perfect opportunity to pull Chubs aside and level him with a look.

"A secret hideaway for kids in the middle of the woods, nestled beside a lake, under the protection of an Orange," Chubs whispered back at me. "No, this doesn't feel familiar *at all*."

I cringed. "Please don't repeat that to them."

"Believe me," Chubs said, looking over to where a dirt trail curved out from the cover of trees. "I'm not going to say anything."

That seemed incredibly unlikely.

"This way," Liam said. "It's just a quick walk, and Ruby's standing by with hot chocolate."

I almost resented Chubs for bringing East River back into my mind. This wasn't the same at all—with Ruby and Liam running the show, this was going to actually deliver on what East River had promised to be. Plus, instead of many little cabins, there was only one big friendly-looking house. It came into view quickly, as did something else.

"Is that a tree house?" I asked, pointing up at the platform that had been built into a nearby tree.

Liam chuckled. "Yeah. It doesn't look like much yet, but I thought it would be fun, you know? And if the kids want time alone, they can go there."

The screen door banged open as Ruby stepped out onto the covered porch. She had an exasperated expression on her face as she held up two umbrellas.

Liam gave her a sheepish look. "I was in a hurry."

"I set them right by the door," she said.

"Okay, I got excited and forgot, can you blame me?" Liam said. "We've got visitors, darlin'. Come down and say hello."

She rolled her eyes, opening one of the umbrellas as she came toward us. My heart felt like it was trying to jump free from my chest. The sight of her in her cozy white sweater and red rain boots, her face free of shadows—it was the best reward after all the frustration of waiting and searching. She pushed the other umbrella against Liam's chest, then wrapped me in her arms.

"You're frozen to the touch," she said, trying to fold me in closer. Her sweater was warm, and she smelled sweet, like cinnamon and cloves.

"I like your boots!" I told her.

She shook her head. "Liam's sense of humor is as good as ever. I'm impressed you resisted the urge to push him into the lake, Chubs."

He stared at her, looking almost dumbfounded. I understood it completely. It was like coming face-to-face with a different person. I'd never seen her so calm. So *peaceful*.

"Yes, well," he managed, finally. "I can't say the thought didn't cross my mind once or five dozen times."

When she moved to hug him, there was no resistance. Chubs held on to her tightly, his face half-hidden by her loose braid.

"For the record, the twirl thing *was* funny," Liam insisted.

"I'm sure it was," Chubs said, finally sounding more like himself, "when it existed only in your mind."

I let myself relax at the familiar rhythm of the conversation. Ruby kept a hand on Chubs's back as she led him up the porch and asked him about the drive.

Liam stared after them, his smile fading.

"It's okay," I told him quietly. "He was just worried. Give him a little time."

"That so?" Liam said. He playfully tugged my hat down over my eyes. "Stop reading my mind, will you? There's only room for one telepath in this house."

There was a small wooden sign with the word HAVEN hanging above the door. Within seconds of passing through the front entryway, the name became reality. The house was warm and bright, burning away the chill. A delicious buttery smell found its way to us from the kitchen, and I could hear a fire crackling somewhere down the hall.

Ruby pulled off her boots and left them beside three pairs of muddy sneakers. Liam kicked off his beside hers, which was our cue to do the same. As I took off my damp hat and hung it on one of the hooks to dry, voices trickled down from upstairs.

"I put together something that resembles lunch," Ruby said. "But would you like a quick tour of the house first?"

"Hi!" a voice called from down the hall. I looked up, unsurprised to find three faces watching us. The boy with the dark skin hushed the girl, but she waved, undaunted.

Ruby and Liam shared a warm, knowing look.

"This is Charles and Suzume," Ruby said. "And that's Lisa, Miguel, and Jacob."

All three of them looked about my age, fourteen, but the second, quiet boy, Miguel, was smaller than the other two, which made him seem younger. They joined us on our tour of the upstairs, the boys showing off their bunk beds and the quilts that Ruby's grandmother had made them. Lisa had her own room, which she didn't seem entirely happy about.

"It's only for a little while," Ruby told her, returning Lisa's grin with one of her own. She looked to us. "Sam sent us a message about a girl they're looking after who needs a more permanent situation."

I heard her, but her words didn't actually hit me until a second later. I saw the realization register on Chubs's face as well.

They'd been in contact with Sam and Lucas all this time?

"How are Sam and Lucas?" I asked, hating myself for needing the confirmation. "And Mia?"

"They're hanging in there," Liam said. "Mia wants to go back to school, but she can't without a guardian—well, I don't need to tell you guys. I think they're disappointed we had to put a hold on reaching out to the Reds, which is understandable."

It was the first time I'd seen Ruby's expression waver. The regret in her eyes was open and aching.

"I think we are *all* disappointed about that." It was the first time Chubs had spoken since we'd entered the house. "But at least with an official monitoring system in place, it's easier to ensure their safety."

The sound of rain on the roof filled the silence that followed. Liam rubbed the back of his neck, giving Ruby a look I didn't understand.

Do something, I thought. We needed something, anything but this horrible, stilted quiet.

"If the second floor is for the kids, where's your space?" I asked.

Liam's face lost some of its tension. "We put ourselves up in the attic like little mice. Here, I'll show you."

After an inspection of their small, cozy bedroom and its shelves of photos and books, the tour took us back downstairs to the living room. In one corner was an ancient-looking television set with some cartoon I didn't recognize paused mid-scene on it. Just beside it, a stone fireplace was working hard to warm the room and hall. Mrs. White's taste for shades of evergreen and ivory was on display, and it was clear that they'd inherited all the furniture, drapes, and rugs. While some of it had gone a bit threadbare, it gave the impression of a house that was well-loved. Liam couldn't have looked prouder of it.

The other kids joined us for lunch, interrupting Liam's stories with comments of their own. Ruby's stew was surprisingly delicious for someone who, like the rest of us, had subsisted mostly on prepackaged junk food for close to a year. Clearly, she'd had time to practice.

"Zu, do you want to see the backyard?" Lisa asked. "We just started a garden."

"Can we finish the movie first?" Jacob said. "We still have a whole hour left."

"You can see the garden from the living room window. Two birds, one stone," Miguel said.

"Yeah," Liam said, rising to put the dishes in the sink. "Why don't you go with them? Get to know each other a little better?"

I looked up from where I'd been rubbing the fabric of my place mat. Even though I knew it wasn't true, looking at the other three kids—how they elbowed and poked and glared and laughed at each other—made me feel so much older. The fact that Liam was trying to send me off with them left me feeling like a child dismissed from the table so the adults could talk.

"Maybe later?" I said to them.

Ruby shared another private look with Liam as she rose to pour hot chocolate into a set of mismatched mugs. The teens took theirs as they sped off for the nearby living room.

"Don't run with—" Ruby cut herself off, shaking her head. "I have never sounded more like my mother in my whole life."

"How is your family doing? Your dad?" I asked.

Back and forth, we traded updates. I told them about Cate and Vida and Nico and school and all the things that had become routine. I heard about Liam's family, Ruby's, and the Children's League kids who had scattered after the camps fell. The longer we spoke, the more obvious it became that Ruby and Liam had been in contact with seemingly everyone but us.

And the whole time, as promised, Chubs kept his comments to himself. A fact that did not go unnoticed by his best friend.

"All right, Chubs, come out with it," Liam said. "The last time you were this quiet, it was because you'd burned your tongue so badly on soup that you physically couldn't speak."

"Come out with what?" Chubs asked, sipping his cocoa.

"Maybe we should—" Ruby began.

"Whatever superior thought is crossing your mind right now," Liam said. "Whatever insult you've been holding back for the last two hours. You think I don't know?"

"I think you don't know me at all anymore," Chubs said simply.

"There it is," Liam said, splaying his hands out on the table. "Come on, get it out of your system."

Even I prickled at his tone. Chubs's jaw worked back and forth, as if he were grinding the words down.

"It's been six months," Liam said. "Look, I'm sorry about the way this all went down. There just wasn't time to explain. We had to cut and run before it got any worse for us or Ruby's family."

"I understand," Chubs said.

"Do you, though?" Liam said. "Because right now it's not understanding that's coming through, it's your very special form of hostility."

"It's not—" I tried.

"Forgive my *hostility*," Chubs began, his voice low. "I suppose I'm just wondering why, if the two of you are so happy and set-tled, you waited until now to finally get in touch to let us know you were still alive."

Ruby and Liam shared another look.

Chubs's hand slapped down on the table. "Stop that! Just say it."

"We wanted to make sure that . . ." Ruby's voice trailed off. "We needed time to set this place up, and to get a clear view of what was happening in Washington. Since they don't seem to have pulled back on the search for us—"

"They haven't pulled back at all," Chubs said sharply. "You want to know why Vida couldn't come? Because the only way she could avoid being detained for obstruction of justice was to agree to join the task force looking for you!"

I didn't know that. I just assumed she and Cate were working on a number of national security matters, like zone-crossing control.

"I'm sorry," Ruby said, rubbing at her forehead. "I should have realized something like that would happen."

"You don't have anything to be sorry for," Liam said vehemently. "Forgive us for thinking our friends might want to come live here with us and do some actual good."

Some actual good.

The words pierced my anxious swirl of thoughts. Chubs's whole body stiffened, absorbing that blow.

"You want us to . . . live here?" I asked, wondering why I couldn't feel my hands, why my whole body seemed to be going numb.

"Yes," Liam said. "It's safer for you. For *both* of you. Plus, you'll be with kids your own age. We can figure out a way to get Vida here, too."

He said it with such sincerity, with all that hope and goodness that was Liam, I couldn't bring myself to say the words that were locked in my throat.

This was the person who had lifted me out of the snow and carried me to safety.

This was the person who had held me after every nightmare.

This was a person I loved. Who I never wanted to disappoint, not ever.

But the only answer I had to his offer was *I'm not a kid.*

If I stayed here with them, it would always be this way.

I didn't want to live outside of the system, not anymore. I didn't want to live with the uncertainty of one day being discovered. I wanted to be hopeful. I wanted to help make things better for *everyone*, not just seek safety for myself. Liam and Ruby could help a dozen kids here, but I could help thousands.

I didn't want to feel powerless anymore.

"I didn't fight so hard to survive so that I could live out in the woods and commune with nature or whatever bullshit you're going to accomplish out here," Chubs said, rising out of his chair.

"Tell me how you really feel," Liam said, his voice colder than I'd ever heard it. Ruby closed her eyes, drawing in a deep breath. I wondered if, in that moment, she wanted to disappear. Or if she wanted the rest of us to.

"You're trying to protect kids? Great. Save them. Be the savior—that was always your favorite role, Liam, because it's uncomplicated. It doesn't make you doubt yourself. It doesn't make you feel bad about having to make hard choices. Meanwhile, the rest of us are back under every lens imaginable, under threat every single day, trying to make *actual lasting change* happen."

"Yeah?" Liam said, standing. "And what have you accomplished? Forcing everyone to wear those stupid badges so other people can scorn and belittle them? Making kids go back into the same homes that rejected them in the first place? How are those promised reparations going, by the way? Think we'll see any sort of apology, any sort of amends by the next century? Or are you going to roll over on that one, too?"

I couldn't breathe. I couldn't move. The world went out of focus. Chubs and Liam stared at each other from across the table, both trying to control their expressions. Finally, Liam turned, disappearing through the living room.

Chubs took one last look at Ruby. Then he was gone, sweeping out of the kitchen. The back door slammed shut. The front door followed a second later. I jumped both times.

Ruby leaned back in her chair, releasing a slow, heavy breath.

"I'm sorry." The words were strangled by the painful knot in my throat. "I didn't think it would be like this. . . ."

"This is pretty much exactly how I thought it'd be," Ruby said faintly. "I knew Chubs would be upset, but I think . . . I didn't realized he'd feel so betrayed."

"You left us," I whispered. Somehow, I got my feet under me even as it felt like my whole body was dissolving. It was embarrassing to cry, but I couldn't help myself. This didn't feel right.

"I did," Ruby said, her expression crumpling. "I know I did."

"I can't stay here," I told her. "This place is perfect. You will give these kids the love they need. But it's not for me."

"I understand," she said.

Did she? I felt like I needed to explain, like I had to pour my heart out to her so she'd know that I loved her, that I loved him, that I loved the us that used to exist. But I couldn't be powerless. I couldn't stay here.

"It's all right," Ruby said, coming around the table to hug me. "I promise that it'll be all right. Everything changes. It has to."

"Not us," I cried. "Never us."

She leaned down, whispering, "It's painful because we care. Don't ever stop caring. Don't let anyone make you cold. You are already the strongest person I know."

I shook my head as she eased me back, smoothing the stray hairs off my face. "You know where to find us now. You can come back anytime you'd like. No matter what happens, there will always be a place for you here."

"Will you . . . will you tell him I'm sorry?" I said, looking in the direction Liam had gone. "He's going to hate me."

"He would never," Ruby said. "*Never.* I know it seems like . . . like what we're doing is small, but this . . ." She took a deep breath. "I know what people expect from me, what they need from me, but *this* is what I can offer to the world right now. This is a piece of myself that doesn't need mending. It doesn't need to be healed. It's something new and fragile that I need to protect. I know that might not make sense to you now, but this is my place. Every kid we help puts the pieces of my heart back together."

I nodded.

"But you find what you're meant to do," Ruby said. "I will be there to help you, no matter what."

It felt like I was leaving my body as we walked toward the front door. Ruby hovered nearby as I slipped my shoes back on. I started to pull my hat off the hook, but stopped myself. "Maybe the new girl will need it?"

Ruby tried her best to smile, pushing back the flood of emotions. Hugging her arms to her chest, she said, "I'll see you later, okay?"

The possibility was a dream, and I think we both knew that. There could be no casual drop-ins. I wouldn't be calling them for weekly updates. We'd barely managed to get away this time, and I knew, after the stunt we'd just pulled, there'd be even more focus on our movements.

I looked back at her one last time, my hand on the door.

"Go on," she said softly. "Chubs needs you."

The rain had eased up by the time I stepped onto the porch. I waited there, just for a moment, to see if Liam might appear, but Chubs had already gone on ahead. I didn't want him to leave without me.

Tears blurred again in my eyes as I followed his fresh tracks back down the trail, the cold stinging my cheeks and hands. By the time I reached the lake, Chubs had already dragged the boat toward the water. As my shoes crunched on the pebbles, he spun around, nearly dropping the oars. The look of surprise on his face nearly broke my heart all over again.

Together we eased the boat back into the water and, together, we rowed back to the opposite shore. The fog swirled behind us, erasing the sight of Haven's trail.

"I hate this rain, you know?" Chubs said, turning his tear-slick face up to the overcast sky. "It just never stops."

THIRTY-SEVEN

"WHAT ARE YOU DOING HERE?" LIAM KEPT REPEATING the question, sounding as dazed as I felt. "What in the world are you doing *here*?"

I couldn't speak. I held on to him tighter, my face pressed into his flannel jacket, like he was a mirage that could fade at any minute.

Liam suddenly tensed, turning to face the entrance to the barn. Roman's gun was inches from his skull.

"Hey, Rambo," Liam said through gritted teeth. "You want to take it down a notch?"

I stepped back out of his arms, and, at my nod, Roman lowered the gun.

"Sorry," he murmured as he passed by us. "Old habits."

"Yeah, I've got some of those, too," Liam said, still eyeing him warily.

Roman stepped into the barn to scan its shadows and many hiding places.

"Hello . . . stranger Zu seems to like," Priyanka said, leaning into the barn to take a look. Her whole face lit up. "Ooh! A horse!"

Priyanka ran right past us, heading straight for the nearby stall. A white horse watched the scene unfold, casually chewing on its food.

"That's Snowflake," Liam said. He did a double take as Max trailed in after her. "Careful, she . . . uh, she bites when she's nervous."

Then he looked down at me with a clear who-are-these-people? expression.

"Something we have in common, precious Snowflake," Priyanka cooed, stroking the horse's nose. "Also, it's probably weird I know the horse's name before I know yours . . . ?"

"That's Liam Stewart," Roman said, circling back to us. "You *are* him, aren't you?"

I could see why they might be confused. The only word to describe Liam's current state was *rough*. His hair was overlong and shaggy, and he had a full beard. From what I could make out beneath the facial hair, his complexion looked almost ashen, which only served to deepen the dark grooves beneath his eyes. A whopper of a bruise covered his left temple, and the collar of his undershirt was torn.

"In the flesh. Most of it, anyway." Liam grimaced. "Could you introduce your friends to me, Zuzu?"

Oh, right. "Snowflake's new best friend is Priyanka, Roman is the only one who remembered to be careful about entering an unknown place, and Max is—" I looked around. "Where is Max?"

"Here," he called from the back of the barn. He stood directly beneath a sunbeam shining through a crack in the roof. "It's so beautiful. Like a golden ribbon."

Priyanka angled her head toward him. "Okay, I think you need some sleep, Maximo."

Liam let out a ghost of a laugh, shifting his weight. His movements were stiff, slow, almost like—

I grabbed his arm to keep him still. A small crimson stain was visible on his undershirt, just above his left hip. I pushed his jacket out of the way, revealing the splotch of dried blood and the jagged hole in the fabric. Panic jolted through me.

"Oh my God," I said. "You were *shot?*"

"I'm all right," he said, putting a hand over mine.

All this time we'd been looking for Ruby, he'd been hurt. He'd been shot.

"Zu," he said, tightening his hold until I looked up. "I'm all right now. Sam and Lucas have been taking care of my sorry self the last few weeks. But I need to know that *you* are okay. I saw everything on the news, and you know I adore you, but you look like fresh hell."

"I haven't been *shot,*" I told him, fighting the temptation to shake him. Instead, I wound my arms around him again and felt him sag against me. "I also don't smell like hay. Are they making you sleep out here? Where are Sam and Lucas anyway?"

Liam took in a deep, labored breath. "They're out looking for Ruby."

"Well, isn't that just a crazy coincidence," Priyanka said, all traces of humor gone. "So are we."

Liam took us to the front door, shooing the rooster off his perch on the porch. He leaned heavily on the railing. Waving a hand over the old lock, we all heard the definitive *click* as he moved the dead bolt.

"Old-school," Priyanka said approvingly. "I like it."

The house was small, enveloping you like a warm hug the moment you stepped inside. I'd only met Sam and Lucas twice—back then, we were all orbiting Ruby—but as little as I knew about the two of them, I saw shades of them in their home. Sam's boldness, reflected in the colors on the walls and the mismatched furniture that somehow worked together. Lucas's quiet, sweet demeanor in the many Polaroid photos framed in the house. In the corner of the living room, there was an easel with an unfinished canvas. All I needed to see were the jagged slashes of crimson and black paint to know who had painted it.

Liam's whole body tensed as we walked through the house. I was surprised he hadn't scratched up the walls by this point. He stopped in the tidy, old-fashioned kitchen, moved toward the counter beside the stove, and picked up a cell phone charging there.

"Water?" I asked.

"They pull from a well and have their own purifier," Liam said. "Give me a second and I'll grab you some glasses."

"Who are you messaging?" Roman asked from the other room.

Priyanka had sprawled out on an old leather armchair. Max was asleep at one end of the couch, his face mashed against his palm. But Roman sat at the other end, ramrod straight, eyeing both of us where we stood in the kitchen.

"Their friend Vida," Priyanka said around a yawn. "She wants to know if Zu had anything to do with the rumors she's hearing about 'an incident' at Moore's training facility. Apparently he's already trying to spin it on the news."

Liam almost dropped the phone. He shot me an uneasy look. "That is some guesswork."

"Not guesswork," I said. "My friends are different."

He raised a brow. "We're all different."

"Differently different," I clarified.

Liam started to type something in reply, watching Priyanka with narrowed eyes.

She looked over at him, bored. "Yes, I can read that."

He swore under his breath, deleting the text. "I'm going to need an explanation in a minute, but first I need to let Sam and Lucas know to come back."

"Is that their phone?" I asked.

"Sam's," Liam said. "I've been relaying messages between them and Vida as they've been searching. Seemed safer to have an intermediary, especially since Vi was only just able to shake the rest of the agents and head out alone."

"Are those lines secure?" Roman asked, taking a position by one of the windows. I watched him, wondering why he seemed unable to relax, even for a second.

Liam looked up from the screen again, this time in disbelief. "I was sending secure messages while you were still eating your own boogers."

I gave him a look as I filled the glasses. "He's my age, old man."

"Boys do develop slower than girls," Priyanka pointed out.

"Why are we talking about my mucus?" Roman said.

The phone buzzed again.

"What do you want me to tell her about the facility?" Liam said. "Moore's making it sound like you burned a sweet little red schoolhouse to the ground."

Priyanka rolled her eyes. "We would have burned it down, but there was too much concrete."

"Ask her if she or Chubs knew about it." I needed to know. I needed to understand why.

Liam's expression turned grim again as he quickly typed out the message. Finished, he reached out, running a gentle thumb over my black eye, examining the treasure map of cuts and bruises on my face.

I stepped away and took a long drink of water. "It's been a busy few days."

Liam's smile was strained. "Attagirl. Let me get you some ice for that shiner."

Gathering the rest of the glasses and jam up into my arms, I moved back into the living room. Liam trailed after me with the bread and a bag of frozen peas, which I took gratefully as I collapsed on the couch. When Roman glanced over from his position at the window, I motioned to the empty spot beside me.

Finally, he released some of that tension in his expression. I was aware of every place his leg touched mine as he sat down next to me.

"Vi says she'll be here in an hour," Liam said, looking between all of us. "She's been following your trail since you left Haven, apparently." He struggled to keep his face neutral. "Is it at all salvageable?"

That small bit of hope in his eyes almost did me in. I opened my mouth, but I couldn't force any of the words out. Instead, all I kept seeing was his face as he'd given Chubs and me the tour of the house. The pride and happiness that radiated off him.

Even Priyanka fell silent, leaving the job to Roman.

"The structure can be saved, but the location has been thoroughly compromised. You cannot ever go back there."

Liam gave him another long look. "Thanks for pulling that punch."

Finally, the pressure building inside my chest broke wide open. "It was my fault. I can't tell you . . . I can't begin to express how sorry I am. If I'd had any idea that we were being followed—"

"You did *exactly* what we wanted you to do, and don't you ever forget that," Liam said. "I'm just mad as hell I wasn't there to help protect the kids. Thank you for helping them get out." He looked to the others. "Thank you. The kids are safe with Mom and Harry for now, and that's all that really matters. It was always more of . . . Well, in any case, we'll all rebuild it together."

He wants to go back, I realized. He still didn't want any part of the wider problem.

"What happened to you?" I asked. "All Miguel, Lisa, and Jacob said was that you'd been in touch, but they hadn't been able to follow up with you about Ruby's last known location. How did *that*"—I gestured to the gunshot wound—"happen?"

Liam blew out another long, deep breath as he lowered himself into the worn leather armchair. "I got a tip through the usual network we use to find endangered Psi. There was nothing to make me suspect it wasn't a typical pickup, even when my phone started to flip out on me nearby—you know how unreliable the cell networks can be. Even the address for the abandoned apartment building in Kennett, just over in Missouri, wasn't anything alarming. Lots of kids will squat in places like that thinking it's safe."

"But it wasn't," I said.

"It wasn't. I walk in, and I'm met with no kid, just four guys armed to the teeth. I managed to fight my way out, but got this souvenir as a parting gift." He gestured to his wound. "I don't think they were there to kill me, though. In true Liam Stewart luck, I caught a ricochet. Actually, I don't even think they were there for me at all. I heard one of them say Ruby's name."

"God," I said. Each little detail was slowly weaving together.

"I drove like hell as far as I could, trying to message Ruby. She'd left a few days before me, and I hadn't heard anything—" He seemed to catch himself. His eyes darted toward me. "I was losing consciousness, but I knew I was at least heading toward Kansas. I sent Sam my location and pulled off into a ditch to destroy the phone, in case those guys had followed me. I feel rotten knowing everyone's been worried sick this whole time."

I didn't want to deepen his guilt by confirming it.

"Sam and Lucas somehow managed to find me, and brought me back here. They patched me up with the help of a sympathetic neighbor, then headed out to look for Ruby. I've been stuck on the farm ever since. Sam and Lucas took the only car. At one point, I even thought about riding Snowflake, but she really does bite when she's nervous, which seems to be with all people of the male persuasion."

"Don't blame her," Priyanka muttered.

"Then everything happened to you, and they started tearing you down like you had even a *shred* of ill will in you." The bitterness in Liam's tone was so unfamiliar to me. "Dammit—what the hell is going on? Do you know?"

I looked to Roman, wondering where to start. "I think we're finally putting this together. Do you know anything about Blue Star?"

"Son of a bitch," Liam said, running his hands back through his hair.

"You *do* know about Blue Star, then," Priyanka said. "Because that just about covers it."

Max finally jerked awake. I handed him a glass of water from the coffee table.

"Do you have any juice?" he asked, still sounding drunk with sleep.

Roman answered my questioning look. "He needs to get his blood sugar levels up to do a reading. Way up."

"A reading?" Liam asked.

"Differently different Max has a way of locating Ruby," Priyanka explained, standing and heading toward the kitchen. Liam's expression lit up, until she added, "But he needs a little more R-and-R, otherwise the reading won't be as accurate, or it might melt his brain."

Liam leaned back in his seat, frowning. I caught him stealing a few glances at Max, even as I brought us back to the topic at hand.

"I'm guessing you also know that Ruby was visiting with Clancy," I said.

Liam's lips tightened into a hard line. "Yes. His mother asked that she come by twice a year to make sure that his memory loss wasn't fading. I *knew* something was going on, that he was remembering his old life. There was no other reason why he started to wave all that information beneath her nose."

Priyanka, Roman, and I all sat forward.

"Go on," Priyanka said.

"You know how Lillian got their financial accounts unfrozen?" Liam asked. "Before he vanished, Gray got reacquainted with his paternal side and left some prime blackmail material with them. Seems like junior learned most of his tricks from his father. Even though Lillian kept it hidden, Clancy somehow managed to find it and started sharing pieces of it with Ruby. I could see what he was trying to do by dangling little bits of awful in front of her to see what she responded to."

"Damn," I said.

He nodded. "Even though he never gave her a reason to suspect it, I had a feeling he knew that she was the one who had repressed his memory. She started going back more frequently, trying to get information out of him. He told her about some server that was down and only needed to be switched back on. I fought her on it. She told me she agreed, that it was bait and she'd give Lillian a warning and stop going."

So *that* was what they had been fighting about.

"Now he's vanished," Liam said bitterly. "They're keeping it off the news, but Vida said he was 'abducted' as he was being driven to classes one morning. Clearly it was an inside job. I'm guessing by the looks on your faces that you might have already known that, though."

"Yeah," I said, letting out a breath. "A little."

"Do you . . . ?" He fought to keep his voice steady. "Can you tell me what you know? Because I've got this fear, and I'm not sure I can go another minute without knowing if I'm right."

"Of course," I began. But the words were drowned out by the crunch of wheels on dirt and loose rocks.

"That can't be Vida—it's too soon," Liam said, struggling to push himself up. I helped steady him, letting him use my shoulder as a crutch. Before either of us could make it to the door, Roman was already at the window again, nudging the curtain back.

Liam glanced down at me, mouthing, *Where did you find this kid?*

I bristled. We were lucky one of us was at least trying to stay on guard. I was not going to entertain mocking Roman for being ready to do the necessary thing—the thing that inwardly ate away at him.

Liam looked between us, and my face warmed under his close scrutiny.

"Don't," I warned, just as he raised a brow and said, *"Reaaally?"*

For a second, under all the strain and scruff, Liam actually looked like his old self.

"It's safe," Roman said, stepping back and holding the curtain aside for us to see for ourselves.

I only needed one look at the dark figure that stepped out of the car and cast an anxious look up at the front of the house. I slipped out from under Liam's arm and ran for the door, throwing it open hard enough to startle Chubs.

"Good God!" he said, clutching at his chest as I flew toward him. "As if I haven't spent the last few days in enough terror for you, you're the one who almost does me in—"

I all but tackled him. "Are you okay? Where have you been?"

"Where have *I* been?" he said, hugging me so hard that he lifted me off my feet.

"They said you disappeared on the news—I thought they took you in for questioning, or you were being punished because of me—"

"It didn't even come to that," he promised, finally setting me back down. His hands landed on my shoulders, giving them a reassuring squeeze. I reached up to straighten the glasses I'd knocked askew on his nose. "Cate smuggled me out of the city in her trunk before they announced the dissolution of the Psi Council. A good thing, too. After what happened last night, they would have put all of us in a hole and left us there."

Horror flooded through me. "You mean what happened at Moore's facility?"

"His facility—?" Chubs shook his head. "I hadn't even heard about *that*. No, someone tried to blow up Joseph Moore's motorcade through Chicago, and then someone else succeeded in killing a UN envoy that was headed there to investigate."

I released a heavy breath, closing my eyes. "Let me take a wild guess about who they pinned it on. . . ."

He gripped my hand.

"Someone at the FBI falsely leaked to the independent media that it was the Psion Ring," he said. "The other Council members are trying to regroup with a few former Children's League members to try to come up with a plan, but when I finally got a hold of Lucas, he said to just come straight here. Now I see why."

My heart gave an anxious thump as the front door creaked open.

"Well, I don't think I was the only reason," I said, stepping to the side.

Liam limped forward to the edge of the porch, gripping the railing. He struggled to guard his expression, even as his jaw worked back and forth. Chubs straightened, smoothing his hands down his neat sweater and slacks.

I took another step back, worried that I might have to knock both of their heads together.

But then Chubs turned his palms up at his sides and lifted his arms out in front of him.

"Come on," he said softly, "don't fight the twirl."

A small smile worked its way over Liam's lips. "Only if you promise not to drop me this time."

"Only if you promise we can stop talking in stupid euphemisms," Chubs said, "and you let me look at whatever horrific injury you managed to give yourself."

"All right, all right," Liam said. "Come on in. I'll let you fuss over me for a few minutes."

Chubs made his way up the porch steps, walking toward Liam's outstretched arm and slinging it over his shoulder under the guise of supporting him. "Honestly, if you'd just be a *little* more careful . . ."

"And," I whispered, trailing behind them, "they're back."

THIRTY-EIGHT

VIDA ROLLED UP TO THE HOUSE A HALF HOUR LATER. She blew in with the force of a gale, beating the actual thunderstorm that was flirting with the horizon. A piece of bread fell out of Max's mouth when she announced herself by saying, "That fucking drive through no-man's-land, Oklahoma, was the icing on a seven-layer shit cake."

I seemed to recover first, hurrying over to shut the door behind her and take the smaller of the two bags she carried.

"Thank God you're all right," she said when I hugged her. "I should kick your ass for making me chase you all over these damn zones. It was *really* hard to pretend I hated you."

"I'll try to remember that next time I get framed for a terrorist attack," I said dryly.

She slung an arm around my neck. "You look like a fucking street punk. I dig it."

"Hi to you, too," I said, then nodded at the bag she'd set down. "What's in there?"

"The last of my patience and a few assault rifles."

Chubs stood to kiss her, and it would never not surprise me that Vida let him. She took a step back, attempting to appear nonchalant as she inspected him. "Why do you look like you missed the bus to the science fair?"

He glanced down at himself. "You bought me this sweater."

"Not to wear with that awful shirt, I didn't." When Liam let out a strained chuckle, she fixed her dark eyes on him. "I don't want to hear a laugh out of you. *You* look like you've been living under a tunnel and subsisting solely on the flesh of rats."

"It's been three years since you called me ugly to my face," Liam said happily, pushing himself up out of his chair. Her put-on look of disdain wavered as she saw him struggle toward her.

Vida stared at the others over his shoulder as he came in for a hug of his own. "And I have no idea who the fuck you three are."

"That's Priyanka, Max, and Rambo," Liam explained. "They're our new little buddies."

Roman started to correct him, but Vida held up her hand. "No. I don't care what your real name is. You are now Rambo."

"It's Roman," I said, shaking my head.

"Thank you," he murmured. As long as we'd been talking, he'd kept that tense posture. His near-silence reminded me how overwhelming it could be to listen to this group's back-and-forth.

"Introductions over," Vida said. She and Chubs took seats on the floor, rounding off our circle. Max let out a burp, pounding his chest as he swallowed the last of the bottles of apple juice. It joined two other empty jugs on the coffee table.

Priyanka and I took turns explaining everything that had happened, pausing now and then to let Roman or Max elaborate. By the time we reached the body of the girl in Baton Rouge, all three of them, even Chubs and Liam, who had already heard the story, fell into a stricken silence. When I described the Pit, both Chubs and Vida looked inconsolable.

"You can say it," Chubs said, his voice strangled as he looked over to Liam. "You were right."

For his part, Liam only wiped a hand down over his face, pressing it against his eyes. He shook his head. "Not going to gloat about the suffering of kids. And I wasn't completely right, either. It's not like you guys didn't get good work done—I have no doubt that the world would be a hell of a lot uglier for us right now if not for you. Things were just weighted against us from the start, and we trusted them more than they were ever willing to trust us."

"The government equipment at the Pit is an indication they're expanding the program. I never thought Cruz would be that careless." Chubs looked to Max, who was staring into the empty fireplace. "I'm sorry about everything you went through. We're going to make this right."

"She's not being careless. She's desperate," I said. "We know better than to trust that others have our best interests at heart, but we did it anyway out of hope. That's the limitation of hope—everyone else's agenda."

"I understand what you're saying," Chubs said. "But if we stop trying to genuinely work with the government, what sympathy the country has left for us will wear thin very quickly. If we move against them, they'll start seeing us as a true threat, and then the Pit will be only the beginning."

"But you have to admit that you have your doubts about the system, too, otherwise you would have told me about Ruby being missing," I barreled on, letting the sting of betrayal back into those words. "You didn't trust that the government wasn't listening to everything we said over text, on the phone, in person. You didn't tell me because you *knew* what would happen to her if they somehow found her first."

"We couldn't let the FBI or the Defenders know that we were reaching out to the Children's League network, or that we were still in contact with her," Vida said. "And if the government had her at some black site, we didn't want them to move her before we could get to her."

"Jesus," Liam breathed out, paling.

I recognized that growing blend of horror, anger, and anguish on Chubs's face—I'd spent the last week lost in it. Only now, I could put a name to it.

Complicit.

He and the others on the Council had tried to protect us, but they had no way of truly blocking the government from enacting something like this. Their outward support of these policies to the public had inadvertently provided a shield that prevented closer inspection of their actions. We had all played a role in normalizing what was happening.

"I realize this is a shitty system, but it's *our* shitty system," Vida said. "Right *now* the choice is binary. If we can keep Cruz in office, then we have a shot at a better future where someone will at least pretend to care about us. If Moore gets elected, we're not just fucked, we're all conscripted into forced military service at best, and imprisoned for life at worst."

I don't know how I managed to swallow the scream of frustration building in me. We needed something *new*, and they couldn't see that. Not yet.

"How are you doing, Max?" Roman asked quietly. Liam's gaze shot to the end of the couch.

Max coughed, pounding his chest as he got to his feet. "Let me go wash my face and try to clear my head. I just need a few more minutes."

"While we wait, I want to hear more about the evidence you gathered," Chubs said. "Did you get something from the Pit?"

Priyanka pulled a flash drive out of her back pocket. "We got all the raw footage and material we could. Does anyone have a computer we could use?"

Chubs shot to his feet. "I do. Let me just get it out of the car."

Priyanka met him at the door, prying the laptop out of his hands and plopping down next to me on the couch. She went to work immediately.

"What exactly are we waiting on the other kid for?" Vida asked Liam.

"He's going to do some kind of reading," Liam said. "I don't know."

"Do you want me to tell it this time?" I asked Roman and Priyanka. They nodded, both looking a bit grateful.

By the end of my explanation, I could have tipped Chubs, Liam, and Vida over like a row of dominos.

"And Mercer has more kids he's testing on?" Liam pressed his hand to his face. "You're right—this has to be what Ruby was chasing. And Clancy was the one to put her on the trail initially, for the sake of his own endgame."

"What I don't understand is why Moore thinks other countries are just going to let him have a Psi army," Chubs said, sitting on the arm of Liam's chair. "If anything, it'll cause a war. Or the other countries will have to find a more terrifying way to counteract it. And why the fixation on Zu? If it's Blue Star framing her . . . *why*?"

"I don't think it is Blue Star," Vida said, a dark expression on her face. "I think it's Joseph Fucking Moore. He's the asshole that's been playing it up, floating mentions of the Psion Ring any chance he can get. He needs someone to prove his point. But Charlie and I were right there. Why Zu?"

"Too much security," Roman said. "Zu had a lighter detail. Moore could have asked for the frame job and had Blue Star kidnap Zu so that he could eventually claim the credit of being the one to 'capture' her."

"Damn," Vida said. "That's so evil, I'm almost impressed. He gets to be the hero—"

I took a deep, burning breath. "And win the election in a landslide."

"We need to find Ruby," Liam said, his eyes wild. He started to rise, only to be ushered back into his chair by Chubs.

Something came together inside me as I watched Liam fall apart. I wanted to lift him out of that dark, suffocating place, the way he had for me all those years ago. He had to be so strong for all of us back then, when we'd been at our most powerless. He could get up again and again after every hit. Even after his brother was killed, it hadn't occurred to me that Liam could be broken.

I had never once considered that he might have needed Haven as much as Ruby had.

"I know," Chubs said, locking him inside the circle of his arms. "Lee, we all know."

Finally, Liam went still, slumping forward to rest his forehead against Chubs's shoulder.

"I have to be selfish," Liam said raggedly. "I know kids are suffering. I know people have died. I want those bastards taken down, I want Zu to be cleared, I want some ounce of justice in all of this, but I'm *terrified* of what they might be doing to her. What they might have already done. I don't want to do this without her."

All along, I'd been so afraid of our circle of friendship falling apart forever. I'd wanted things to go back to the way that they had been before everything had become so painful and complicated. I'd believed that they could, if we only tried. Watching Liam now, I felt the last bit of that hope slip away.

I felt resolve slip into its place.

We would never get back to what we'd been, because we were no longer those same people. That private world we'd created and filled with love and protection had to expand, had to grow and flex into something stronger. There was nothing in the world that would ever be powerful enough to keep us from being there to carry each other forward in those moments when our strength gave out.

The floor creaked as Max stepped back into the room. He scratched at one of the sores on his arm. "I'm ready, if you are."

"What do you need to do this?" Vida asked. "Some kind of conductor? Silence?"

"I just need to borrow his mind," Max said. "Well, and a bucket."

"To knock me out with?" Liam asked weakly.

"Not . . . exactly," Max said.

"The ride's pretty gnarly," Priyanka explained. "A lot of people hurl."

"Great," Liam said. "Didn't like the lunch I ate anyway."

I switched places with Liam, giving him my spot beside Max on the couch. Roman dutifully retrieved the trash can from the small bathroom and set it down next to Liam.

"What do you need me to do?" Liam asked Max. "Do you want our audience to give us some space?"

"It's all right," Max said, taking one last gulp of his water. "Do you mind if I hold on to your arm?"

Liam rolled up his sleeve, offering it to him. I could see him trembling from where I sat on the arm of Priyanka's chair.

"Remember that you're not there," Max told him. "We're only riding a link between the electrical currents of your minds. No matter what you see, you have to let me pull you back."

Liam nodded.

"Think of the last time you saw her," Max instructed, his hand hovering over Liam's skin. "It'll help us locate her faster."

They both closed their eyes, shutting out the world and us with it. For a while, the only sound that filled the farmhouse was our breathing. To distract myself, I counted the electric currents moving through the walls and across, and under, the floor, taking stock of the digital clock on the bookshelf, the television, the refrigerator. . . .

Liam jerked hard, leaning back against the couch as if to get away from Max's grip. His feet kicked out, slamming against the floor.

"What's happening?" Chubs asked, bending to check his pulse.

"It's all right," Priyanka said. "He's connected."

The moan that escaped Liam's lips tore at me. "Are you sure he's okay?"

"He's all right," Roman promised. "Max, what do you see?"

I whipped back toward the couch. He'd gone so still, I'd just assumed that he was in some kind of trance state.

"Lights . . . sterile gowns . . . gurney . . ." Max said, the words sluggish. "Tired . . ."

"She's alive?" I pressed. "You're sure?"

Liam jerked again, his whole body tensing.

"Liam, it's all right," Chubs was saying. "You're not there, remember?"

Tears streamed through Liam's lashes. He shivered. The hair rose on his exposed arm, prickling with goose bumps.

Owen's words at Haven drifted back to me. *She's cold. She's so cold.*

"Door . . . label . . ." Max seemed to startle himself awake, a full-body tremor rippling through him as he released his grip. He blinked rapidly until his pupils were no longer dilated.

Liam gasped in a ragged, wet breath, folding forward at the waist. Vida dutifully passed him the trash can, but he waved it off, swallowing.

"You saw some kind of symbol?" Roman asked.

Max nodded. "It was on a set of sliding doors . . . some sort of bird?"

"It wasn't just a bird," Liam croaked out, his face bone-pale. "It was a swan. Blue Star doesn't have her. Leda Corp does."

THIRTY-NINE

THE STORM WAS DANCING.

Heavy clouds unfurled over me, but they brought no relief to the miles of dry land crying out for a drop of rain to drink. A wall of dust traveled through the fields each time the wind picked up. Now and then, I could taste it in my mouth, feel the grit of the earth between my teeth. And still, even knowing the power of the thunderstorm growling in the distance, I couldn't go back inside to those grim faces. Not yet.

Not until I'd figured out what I was going to do.

The lightning made me feel as if the clouds were living things; they streaked across the violet sky like pulsing silver veins. Each singed my nose with a sharp, almost chlorine-like smell. The longer I sat there, watching, the more static seemed to gather on my skin and crawl across my nerve endings.

I don't know why I did it, exactly, or why it even occurred to me to try. My world had tilted so sharply onto its side that I'd gone from questioning nothing to questioning everything, including what my own limits were.

The thread of power in my mind tentatively reached out,

stroking the charge in the air. I kept both of my hands planted on the stone fence post, drawing up my legs and crossing them beneath me so I was balanced on top of it. I closed my eyes, imagining the thread weaving through the blanket of power enveloping me, imagining that I could draw it near enough to paint my skin with light.

Warmth gathered at the center of my chest, building, feeding itself, burning brighter until it finally exploded, shooting across my nerves like the purest, hardest hit of adrenaline. I was floating and falling all at once, my body dissolved into particles that rolled with the deep thunder and flashed down to strike at the world with pure power. A laugh bubbled up in my throat and escaped, as surprised as it was thrilled. The dry summer air heated as the glow behind my eyelids intensified.

Behind me, someone gasped faintly. That small intake of breath was enough for me to drop the thread, to release the heat and light back into the air. I whirled toward the sound, my heart still pumping wildly in my chest.

Roman held up his hands, taking a step back. "Sorry. I walk now to clear—I *was* walking. Walking. Thinking in Russian. Speaking in English. Confused brain. I'm not sure why I'm still talking?"

"Do you usually think in Russian?" I asked, curious.

"Sometimes. Sometimes I dream in it, too." Roman still looked like he wasn't sure if he was supposed to stay or go. I slid down off the stone post, onto the wood fencing, hoping he'd at least read the invitation in that.

I would have felt embarrassed for wanting him to stay, maybe, if it hadn't been for the sparks still firing under my skin telling me *try*.

"I came out to look for you," he blurted out. "The storm . . . I thought it would be . . ."

"Dangerous?" I finished. My whole body felt like it was shining as he stared at me. The warmth was back, curling through my blood until I was sure I'd have to run miles to work off the raw energy. I wondered if this was even a fraction of what Priyanka felt after she used her power.

His expression was one of pure wonder. "You looked like a star."

Lightning streaked over us, and my heart gave that little kick again. He looked flustered, suddenly fixing his attention on his hands. "I don't even know what I'm saying. I'm sorry."

"You thought I looked like a star," I said softly. The words hung in the air between us, and not even the thunder was powerful enough to erase them.

He forced that careful mask back into place, the one that revealed almost nothing—but only to the people who didn't know him. His expressions were like a language; you only had to learn how to read Roman's face to decipher him. The line of his lips relaxed as he drew a breath and crossed the distance between us, sitting on the fence beside me.

I relished the easy silence between us. The way we let the wind and thunder carry on their own conversation, like we might listen in and learn a secret.

"Your friends are . . ." he began lightly, looking for the right word.

"A lot?" I suggested.

Roman looked a little relieved, nodding. "Vida made my ears wilt."

I smiled.

493

"No," he said, groaning. "What's the English phrase?"

"Your ears were burning," I said, then thought better of it. "Actually . . . you know what? I don't think there is an exact match."

He let his head fall back, clearly frustrated. "I've been here for so long. How do I still mess these things up?"

"You're not messing them up," I said. "You're expanding our idiom list with some fun new variations."

Roman gave me a dubious look.

"Really," I promised.

"When it happens, it makes me . . ." The sky flashed with the storm, capturing him for a heartbeat in perfect, gorgeous light. I could see the way his throat bobbed as he swallowed, how he angled his face away, as if to partly hide it. "It reminds me that I wasn't supposed to ever be here."

I watched him until he turned back to look at me. This time, neither of us looked away.

I finally had the courage to ask. "Priyanka seems to think that you'll want to return home once we help Lana."

Stay.

"I want so many things," he said. "And most of them are impossible. They contradict each other. They change and shift, and I hate them for being so far out of reach. Going home, telling our mother that we're alive and okay, is something I want to do, not something I have to do. Priya and Lana wanting to stay and ruin men like Mercer always made me feel selfish and foolish for dreaming about a place far away from here. Somewhere quiet and safe."

"That's not foolish or selfish," I told him.

Stay.

Longing for security was as much a human instinct as wanting more or wanting to retaliate after being hurt or wanting to protect the people we love. If I could call down the lightning and burn out every last trace of darkness for my friends, I would. I would do it in an instant, even if it left me in ashes.

After everything they'd seen, after everything Roman had been made to do just to keep from being separated from his sister, he deserved quiet anonymity. Away from Mercer and Blue Star. Away from a government who'd take an interest in breaking his mind down for analysis.

Away from me.

Stay, I thought again. *Please stay.*

"Helping Lana, returning home . . . I thought that was what I wanted more than anything," he said. "Now I'm not so sure."

Roman was still looking at me as he said it, his eyes the blue of a new morning sky. Earlier, he'd showered and shaved the last few days off him, leaving his skin soft and smooth. He looked younger, and there was an almost unbearable tenderness to his small smile. Hope and warmth lifted through me.

"It's okay to change your mind," I said quietly. I couldn't keep his gaze anymore, not with the painful, urgent squeeze of my heart. Instead, my eyes fixed on the small scar along his jaw. "About what you need. The things you want."

Roman's hand was only an inch from mine on the fence. I thought of the way he'd described the music he loved, those old songs. *Simple.* It would be so simple to just weave my fingers into the spaces between his.

"What do you want?" he asked.

His question brought me out of that small, sweet dream.

I turned. "If you had asked me that two weeks ago, I would

have told you the only thing I wanted was to be able to stand beside my friends as an equal, and protect them the way they had protected me. I couldn't accept that they'd left me. All of them, in their own way, had left me behind. My voice was never going to be loud enough to call them back. I was so sure the worst thing that could ever happen to us would be to lose one another. To break apart."

He didn't say anything, only watched.

"Of course, now I know breaking apart isn't the worst thing—it's failing each other," I said. "I can't stop thinking about Ruby, about what she's going through. The fact that she's alone. I know she was trying to protect us, but—did we disappoint her? Did she really not trust us to help her anymore? If she'd figured out that the government was somehow involved, or could be, and she'd lost faith in us . . . I don't know. I'm so scared for her."

"She didn't lose faith in you," Roman said. "I don't know her the way you do, but everything you and the others have said makes me think she wanted to shield you from any blowback."

It was the steadiness of his voice that I found reassuring, almost more than the reasoning itself.

"This whole time, she was with Leda . . . even before the explosion," I said. "*Weeks*. And I refused to believe it was possible."

It had been easier to swallow the idea of her choosing to leave Haven behind than it had been to consider the government might have her. But even if I'd known everything from the start, what could I have actually done to help her? I'd only ever had the illusion of power and influence.

Roman closed his eyes. The first drop of rain struck his cheek, curving down the exact path my fingers wanted to take. The cool water splattered against my hair, my bare arms, but it did nothing to dull the heat growing there.

"The irony is that these people destroyed my life, but in the process they freed me," I said. "They brought me to a place where I felt weaker and more afraid than I had in years, but it only forced me to recognize the strength I already possessed. They made me out to be a traitor and gave me the opportunity to discover all the right reasons to rebel. The way forward isn't to choose the best of two bad choices, it's finding a way to navigate between them. To create our own path. One that provides Chubs and the Council with the kind of material they need to expose the people working against us and make a case for stronger, more permanent protections for us. One that helps Psi in need find people like Liam and Ruby and give them a chance at living free. One that takes back our story from people like Moore, and shows the world who we really are."

The lightning tore up the sky, illuminating the admiration on his face. "I'm not powerful, and I might be more trouble than I'm worth most of the time," he said, "but . . . maybe I could help you with that?"

Stay.

"You *are* powerful," I told him. "In this whole world, there's no one like you."

"Thank God for that," he said wryly, letting his clean shirt darken with the rain.

"I mean you, as in *you*," I told him, gently elbowing him. My heart was beating hard in my chest, about to burst. "I'm no more or less powerful than you. We both channel power."

"You're wrong," he said. "You don't channel it, you *become* it.

Touching your power was like—I'm not sure I know the words to describe it."

"Generally speaking, it is pretty indescribable," I said. "I'm not sure I could even do a good job of it."

"It's connection," he said, looking back up at the storm clouds. "I know it was a lie, but . . . I liked that you thought I was the same as you at the beginning. I'm the only one like me, but you and the others, you're part of something bigger. Brighter. You're never alone."

"I liked it, too," I told him.

When I met Roman's eyes again, they were burning. A deep heat flowed through me again, burning away those last traces of uncertainty. My chest was so tight I could barely breathe. I saw what I was feeling reflected in the softest shade of blue.

"What did it feel like," he asked, "to hold a storm in your hands?"

I didn't even have to think about it. "Limitless."

"Will you let me feel that, just this once?" he whispered. "Just once."

My heart lurched inside of my chest, knowing what he was asking and how it would twist his mind into agony. "I don't want to hurt you."

"Some pain is good," he said. "It's necessary. I'd rather feel it than nothing at all."

You say that, I thought. *But then I'm the one who has to watch you suffer.*

This time, when I drew the crackling charge from the sky, I pictured myself covered in stardust—as something shining and luminous enough to push back against anything, even the night.

The feeling of power was exhilarating, and the confidence it gave me invincible. I never wanted to wake up from this feeling.

Simple, I thought. So simple.

Roman was glowing with my light. He lifted his hand from the fence railing, turning the palm up toward me. I didn't take it. Instead, I put both of my hands on his cheeks, and when he didn't pull away, when he leaned into the touch and shut his eyes, I kissed him.

The electricity streamed around us, wild and crackling. I was careful not to bleed too much from the air, or let it get close enough to burn, but static snapped at my fingers as they brushed his skin, and bit at my tongue. As his lips moved against mine, I couldn't separate the rush of sparkling power from the heady sensation of finding him there, feeling him.

Distantly, I recognized that the storm was dangerously close now, the lightning strikes near enough that they could be drawn to the power between us and kill us in an instant. I recognized that, but I still had to force myself to pull back.

Roman's face was stunned as we broke apart. The smell of the singed wooden fence and ozone filled my lungs, and my limbs were buzzing with the last traces of the charge between us, but I couldn't tear my eyes away from his face. Not as he laughed in pure, unbridled amazement, until tears came to his eyes. Roman's gaze found mine again, his throat working as if he wanted to explain.

I know, I thought. *I know.*

Neither of us spoke as we rose and raced back up to the house. Roman took my hand, ignoring the hard sting of the static that jumped between our palms. Cool rain struck the top of my head, then my face and shoulders, erasing the charge's warmth from my skin.

As we reached the porch, Roman glanced back over his shoulder, taking one last look at the towering clouds rolling across the farmland. But I couldn't bring myself to do the same; I didn't want to see those last traces of our light be devoured by the darkness of the storm.

The next morning, just as the sun had begun to paint the new sky pink, we gathered at the table to silently eat our breakfasts.

Silently, until Priyanka sat straight up from where she'd been lounging on the couch, the laptop perched on her chest. Her eyes were ringed with dark circles, and she looked slightly crazed from lack of sleep and excitement. "I got them."

Roman stood, shoving his chair back. "You found Mercer on camera?"

"I found *both*," she said. "Mercer *and* Moore. Together."

Liam set his spoon down in his untouched bowl of oatmeal, looking like he'd slept about as much as Priyanka had. "Tell me you're not joking."

"There was nothing in the security footage at all, but then I realized, duh, of course there wouldn't be. They'd delete it or turn the cameras off to give the boss full deniability. *But*"—she balanced the laptop on the back of the couch and turned it so that it faced us—"I went back and searched the time stamps for the day that Max said Mercer was last there and found something. I'm going to be honest, it's not the best shot. It's a reflection of the two of them in one of the building's interior windows. They clearly thought they were safe in whatever corner they were hiding."

"Genius, Pri," Max said, coming closer along with Chubs and Vida. "Good job. I would never have noticed it."

"Is there audio?" I asked.

Rather than answer, Priyanka twirled her hand and hit PLAY.

It was difficult to make the two of them out. But slowly, as they stopped walking and turned to face each other, it became easier to discern their faces.

Joseph Moore was a handsome man who looked ten years younger than his actual fifty. Forever tanned and impeccably groomed, it was actually a little shocking to see him look as disheveled as he did. One hand gripped his thick dark hair, tugging at it as he turned on the other man. His gray suit was rumpled, the lines of his face stark with obvious stress.

Beside him, Gregory Mercer was a study in opposites. His edges were grizzled, his face roughly hewn, and there was a long raised scar that ran over his left temple and cut down into his eyebrow. He was in a suit, too, only his was head-to-toe black. His blond hair had been tied back into a low ponytail, and he was as still as a snake in the grass. Eyes narrowed into slits. It was the only sign of his controlled fury until he said, *"This wasn't the deal."*

Both Max and Roman flinched at the sound of his voice.

"My job isn't to make you happy," Moore snapped back. *"My job is to make us both money, and I'm a little preoccupied with something else at the moment, if you haven't turned on the news lately."*

"I'm not here for your excuses," Mercer said. *"Don't fuck with me. I know more about you than anyone, even your show pony of a wife. You're too 'busy' to see to our terms? Then I'm too busy to make sure none of that slips out—nothing about your connections overseas, selling secrets. Nothing about your little bomb-making enterprise."*

501

Moore held up his hands. *"You think I wanted to do it? Turning her over to the feds myself would have singlehandedly won me this election. I took a loss there, too. Instead some sad-sack government employee will get the credit once they decide Cruz needs the PR boost."*

Roman looked over at me. I bit my lip.

But Moore wasn't talking about me.

"Don't lose sight of the bigger picture. The only way to avoid closer scrutiny was to give her to the feds, quietly trade her for their continued blind eye. I salvaged this project, and if you can't make this one sacrifice to keep it going, then—"

I jumped at the explosion of movement as Mercer violently shoved Moore up against the wall, his arm pinning him by the throat. *"Don't ever talk to me about sacrifice, you nepotistic, over-indulged sack of pig shit."*

Moore struggled against the hold, lashing out until finally the other man released him and turned to go. *"Where are you going? We're not finished here—I want an update on your progress!"*

Mercer didn't look back. As he moved farther from the camera, his words became almost inaudible. Almost. *"I'm going to get her myself."*

Liam leaned over, shutting the laptop screen. Without looking at any of us, he said, "Get ready. We're leaving now."

FORTY

WE MADE QUICK WORK OF FEEDING THE ANIMALS AND cleaning up the house. Once it was locked up, awaiting Sam and Lucas's return that night, we divided ourselves between two cars and siphoned the gas out of the third.

"I'd like to go with Zu," Liam told Chubs, then glanced over to where I was stowing our filthy, battered bags in the trunk of the SUV Chubs had driven. "If you don't mind?"

Liam had showered and shaved before coming down, and while his movements were still stiff, and he seemed to be vibrating with anxiety, he looked a little more like himself. Or, as Vida put it, he no longer looked like a cult leader who wanted to murder all of us.

"Of course not," I said. "But *I'm* driving."

A faint smile. "All right, then."

"I hope you're ready to snuggle up in the back," Priyanka told Max as they came down the porch steps. "I'm about to defend my repeat champion status in I Spy."

Max turned to Vida. "Can I *please* come with you guys? I could use some peace and quiet."

Vida opened the back door, sweeping her hand inside. "Be my fucking guest."

"Should one of us tell him that's not the 'peace and quiet' car?" Liam whispered, limping over to help me finish loading our supplies.

"Some things are more fun to discover on your own," I said.

"Are you *sure* you want to drive?" he asked, staring longingly over the backseats. Something in his expression changed.

Hopeless.

I reached into one of the backpacks, unzipping the front pouch. The photo I'd taken from Haven was still inside, burned and wrinkled, but still mostly in one piece.

I held it out to him until he looked down, his eyes widening.

"Everything's not lost," I told him. "It's going to be okay."

He took the photo in one hand, then reached over, resting his palm on the top of my head, the way he used to. "When you're the one saying it, I can actually believe it."

"Ready?" I asked him.

"It's a long drive," he said. "Maybe you'll need to take a break . . . ?"

I shot him a long look.

"There's my Zu," he said, pocketing the photo. Before I could move to the driver's side, he took my wrist.

"Liam, don't be ridiculous—"

"No, I just want to say—" He shook his head, a few strands of dark blond hair falling over his forehead. "I'm sorry I didn't even say good-bye."

"Which time?" I asked, fighting the need to hug him.

He winced. "Both. For leaving without warning, and for letting both of you go with angry words between us. I've never been perfect, but I've always wanted to be for you."

"I never needed perfect," I told him. "None of us did."

"After Cole died, after everything," he said, struggling with the words, "it was the only thing I could think to do."

"I *know*," I said. "Liam, I know. It's all right. Just . . . none of us are allowed to leave without saying good-bye, not anymore. Yeah?"

He nodded. "Yeah."

"All right," I said, giving him a nod of my own. "Then let's go."

Vida looked back at me before climbing into the driver's seat. "If you lose track of us, just keep going. We'll meet four blocks south of the lab."

I opened my own door. "What makes you think I'm going to be following you?"

Vida grinned.

As I slid inside, buckling my seat belt, Priyanka turned and looked out the back window. "Farewell, Snowflake, princess of my heart."

"Everything all right?" Roman asked.

"Much better," I said, breathing out and hitting the ignition button. A powerful thrust of electricity blazed through the body of the car. A faint pop song I didn't recognize came on the radio, but before I could change it, Liam opened the front passenger door.

Where Roman was already sitting.

Liam clucked his tongue, jerking his thumb toward the backseat.

After a long look at me, Roman unbuckled his seat belt and moved.

"What?" Liam asked when he saw my look. "I'm wounded. I need more room."

I shook my head, putting the car in drive. The car lurched

ungracefully as I got used to the looser steering. Liam pressed a hand to his chest.

"Settle down, old man," I told him, picking up speed as we turned off the long driveway and onto the dirt road. Vida was already leaving a blazing trail of dust behind her. The longer I drove, ten minutes, twenty minutes, the harder it became to ignore the way Liam was practically vibrating.

"You're starting to offend me," I warned him. "Not to mention annoy me."

"No—no, you're a great driver," he said quickly. "It's just . . . why would you listen to *this* when you could listen to literally anything else?"

I'd just tuned out the pop music, focused on keeping pace with Vida. "Change it, then."

He looked almost horrified at the suggestion. "Driver chooses, always."

"It is amazing no one has ever tried to push you out of a moving car," Priyanka noted.

He turned in his seat. "You were my favorite of Zu's new friends. Now it's him, because he at least respects his elders."

"Since when are you an elder?" I asked him.

"It's a fair statement," Roman said, staring out his window. "The brain supposedly hits peak performance at age twenty-five, and after that it's all downhill."

"Nice," Liam said, facing forward again. "This is the guy you're choosing to make out with on fences?"

"Whaaaaaaat?" Priyanka sang out, a false note of surprise in her tone.

"You were watching!" I said, reaching over to smack his shoulder. I glanced up at Priyanka in the rearview mirror, her eyes on the roof of the car. "You were *all* watching?"

Roman seemed completely unbothered by this revelation, and instead focused on drawing out alternate routes on the maps.

"Okay, yes," Priyanka said. "But it's not really our fault. Charlie went out to yell at you to come inside before you got hit by lightning, and he saw it, and then he ran back inside and got very flustered and embarrassed and told us it was nothing, which seemed deeply suspicious, all things considered, so of course we all had to go see, just to make sure you were all right and not a pile of charred remains."

I glared at her in the rearview mirror, then jabbed the scanner button to search for another station. Mercifully, it landed on the zone's official channel, not Truth Talk Radio's garbage of the day.

But, unfortunately, it wasn't good news.

"*—catch up those who are just tuning in. We interrupt our usual broadcast to bring you this breaking report from your local Zone Three station—*"

"Why did I just shudder at the words *breaking report*?" Priyanka asked.

Roman let the map drift down to rest on his legs. "Can you turn it up?"

"*Following last night's attempted attack on Interim President Cruz's motorcade as she returned to the White House, the Secretary-General of the United Nations has issued the following statement....*"

The blood seemed to swell inside my veins, the pressure driving my pulse up to the point of pain. Secretary-General Chung never issued public statements on behalf of America unless . . .

"*After a meeting with delegates from each nation of the coalition overseeing the restoration of the United States government, we have reached a unanimous decision to extend the United Nation's oversight for the next two years. These tensions, all of which have arisen over what would have been the first independent election since the removal of former president Gray's administration, have demonstrated a dangerous volatility that still exists in the country. For the sake of domestic and international stability, we will maintain the status quo as it exists today, and increase our support to both the Defender and peacekeeping forces. Thank you."*

"They actually did it," I said. "They actually called off the election like Moore predicted. He couldn't have wanted this. . . ."

He couldn't have wanted anything that kept him away from power.

"Residents of Chicago, Indianapolis, Detroit, and other major cities are advised to remain inside and keep roads clear for emergency services as they manage spontaneous demonstrations."

Spontaneous demonstrations. Classic PR-speak for what were likely raging protests.

"Did he overplay it?" Priyanka asked. "Isn't this what they've been fear-mongering all along? Churning out all that propaganda that the United Nations was too controlling, that they would never let this country go, even as they forced the UN into this position. This is exactly what he wants: open rebellion."

For weeks—for months—Moore and others like him had been launching dangerous sparks of dissension into the air. And now they were about to rain down over us. In the chaos, the public would turn to him for guidance, even the ones who hadn't necessarily believed him before. He'd manufactured the proof he'd needed that he was both a prophet and a savior.

"Well," Liam said, turning to gaze out his window. "Shit."

FORTY-ONE

By the time we reached Philadelphia, almost a full day of driving later, the city was on fire.

The smoke was visible for miles beyond the police blockades set up at every major access point to the city. I'd followed Vida as she navigated through the town of Lansdowne, pulling into the parking lot of a boarded-up grocery store. The words FAMILY OWNED PLEASE LEAVE US ALONE were spray-painted over the panels that covered the chained front doors. Garbage, glass, and tear-gas canisters littered the street, but there didn't seem to be a soul around us. The homes we had passed looked like they'd been abandoned and ransacked.

My back was killing me, even after trading off driving with the others. Standing outside the car, I tried to stretch out my cramped muscles and let adrenaline eat away at my lingering exhaustion. Vida stepped out of the car, her ear pressed against the cheap burner she'd picked up when we'd stopped for gas. "I will. Thanks. You'll be the first one I call, I promise."

"What's up?" Liam asked, stretching.

"Cate," she said. "She's been monitoring the situation in the city for us. Based on what she's heard on the FBI's channel, we might be able to get into the city by going on foot and cutting through something called Mount Moriah Cemetery. She overheard the coordinating agents talking about pulling security coverage of that area and relying on aerial patrols."

There was never any doubt that Vida was going to be the de facto leader of this rescue operation. Aside from Ruby, she was the only one of us who had real, proven experience. Still, taking the backseat now after days of leading my own charge left me feeling like I was crawling with static. The only thing that gave me some small sense of control was watching Vida, studying what she was doing to prepare us. As much as Vida preferred to go it alone on missions, she never backed down from stepping up in a group. There was something to learn from everything she did.

Roman went to retrieve the map from the glove compartment, then spread it over the hood of our SUV. "Here. It looks like we're about two miles away."

The location of Leda's lab in Philadelphia wasn't a secret. It was the same building that had been shuttered years ago in an attempt to hide the fact that Agent Ambrosia was responsible for the Psi mutation. It had been a shock when, rather than being scorched out of existence, the company had been given permission by Cruz to reopen it. The funding Leda had received from the United Nations—to continue their research into the mutation and the development of new, unrelated drugs—had been incredibly unpopular. Even I'd been able to recognize the unfairness of rewarding the people who had, however unintentionally, destroyed so many lives.

"And then how many more miles to Center City?" Liam asked,

his hands on his hips. "This is going to take *hours*. Isn't there any way to drive?"

"Not unless you're dying to remember what it feels like to be thrown into the back of an unmarked police van," Vida said. "If you've missed White Noise that much, I'm sure someone will be more than fucking happy to oblige."

He waved her off, glancing toward Chubs, who was leaning against their sedan, a pensive expression on his face.

"If the city is in this kind of condition," Chubs said, "would they have already moved her out?"

"I can do another reading," Max offered, coming toward us.

Vida shook her head. "Cate said they've locked down the office buildings in Center City, the lab included. The bigger thing is going to be circumventing the increased security, but we're going to have to assess the extent of it when we get there. They have a curfew in place, but they're still struggling to control the situation."

Frustration bled into Liam's expression, but he nodded. We all knew a little something about having to make the best out of a terrible situation.

"The lab building is about seven miles from here," Roman noted. "A little under two hours of walking at a good pace, but still a long way to walk for someone with a gunshot wound."

"Kid," Liam muttered. "Quit busting my chops. I'm fine."

Vida checked the cartridge of her gun before tucking it into the pocket of her leather jacket. I knew Roman had a weapon on him, but I was still surprised to see Priyanka take the extra pistol Vida offered.

"I don't need to tell you this, but don't let anyone catch you with it, especially not anyone in a uniform," Vida told her. "They might hesitate to shoot the white boy, especially if they don't think he's a Psi, but not the brown girl."

"I know," Priyanka said. "But they won't catch me to begin with."

"Good. I can't take another dead kid on my watch."

Priyanka saluted her sarcastically.

"I also don't need that attitude," Vida said sharply. "Are you capable of taking orders?"

"You have no idea what I'm capable of," Priyanka told her, her voice hard.

Vida's steely expression relaxed as her lips curled into one of her patented, unnerving smiles of approval.

We made our way through the town, carrying our water and the weapons. We didn't encounter the first helicopter until we were nearly to the cemetery's perimeter. Priyanka and I were the first to feel it, before the others even heard it. She grabbed Max and I grabbed Roman, dragging them under the cover of the nearby trees.

Up ahead, the others followed, diving for the heavy shade. Liam crouched a short distance away from me, resting his head against a tree trunk. He was red in the face, sweat streaking over his cheeks. A twinge of concern moved through me at his labored breathing. Then he clenched his jaw, and a fierce look of determination set in. He pushed himself up onto his feet the instant the noise of the chopper's propellers faded beneath the distant car alarms and the wailing of emergency services sirens.

"Cut across the cemetery two by two," Vida instructed as we climbed over the fence. "Except you, Stewart—you're coming with me and Charlie."

Each pair waited until the one ahead was through the maze of headstones and paths before running after them. By the time the helicopter came back to make another pass, the city had already ushered us into the cover of its smoky arms. We disappeared into its chaos.

At the edge of the city, buildings and shops were still glowing with flames, coaxed on by the wind. Looters smashed the windows of convenience stores and clothing shops. A white guy stumbled out through the smashed glass of a storefront, clutching a computer in his arms and running toward a group of friends wearing bandanas over the lower halves of their faces. A police car flew by us as we hurried along the sidewalk.

By the time we'd reached the river and found an unmonitored path over it, we'd wasted an hour just dodging the patrols and hiding behind dumpsters. I seethed with frustration; every minute we lost mattered. A life could be taken in seconds. Ruby might already be . . .

I saw Liam's face, steeled with grit, as he pulled himself up from behind the garbage containers and led the group forward. Roman and I brought up the rear, his gaze sharply assessing each individual threat as we passed it. While Priyanka had lengthened her strides to keep up with Vida and the others, Max had slowly drifted back to us, his face troubled.

"Are you all right?" I asked him. "You can turn back if this is getting to be too much."

I didn't mean it in a cold way; I was surprised that Max had decided to come with us at all. When Liam had called to update them, Sam and Lucas had invited him to stay with them until he felt ready to face the world. But Max insisted on coming, saying that he might need to do another reading after we got to the city.

"I'm managing," he said. "I didn't expect to find a path through violence again, though."

"You don't have to do any fighting," I told him. "I'm just glad you're here with us."

He nodded, turning his gaze back out to the street. I was beginning to see the pattern of the wreckage. Burning buildings gave way to still-smoldering ones as the fire department worked its way from the heart of the city out to its fringes. By the time we reached the blackened remains of a fleet of row houses, there were no actual flames in sight, just air that was thick with ash and clogging smoke. I lifted the collar of my shirt over my mouth and nose, trying to get a clean breath of air.

The only problem was, we were finding more and more people as we moved toward Center City. We stepped off the streets to let a roving crowd pass by. They were all different ages, all different ethnicities, but all of their eyes were rimmed with the same painful-looking red. As if they'd tried to scratch them out.

"Tear gas," Roman said, nodding toward them.

A middle-aged man supported another, younger man as they hobbled forward. The younger one had a gushing head wound that left his expression unfocused. They maneuvered through the burned-out shells of cars and fields of broken glass. As they passed by us, the older man looked at me, then looked again.

I cleared my throat, turning my face away.

"Don't go to Independence Mall," he said, his voice hoarse. "That's where they're rounding everyone up and checking IDs. You won't get to leave."

I risked a glance back. Even if the man didn't recognize me, he had to recognize how young we were. What that likely meant, even without buttons.

"The cemetery is the best way out," Roman told him, his hand closing gently on my elbow to guide us both forward. "Keep an eye out for helicopters, though."

"Thanks," the wounded man said, slurring. "Be careful. They don't have rubber bullets."

"Oh God," Max whispered as soon as they were out of earshot.

"Still okay?" I asked him. He swallowed, nodding.

We had to run to catch up with the others. Along the way, Roman fell back, bending to retrieve something that had been washed into the gutter by a sputtering fire hydrant. A Phillies baseball cap. Wordlessly, he offered it to me.

"Thanks," I whispered, pulling it down as low as I could over my face. The last thing we needed was to be recognized before we could even see the Leda building.

"Isn't Leda's building near Independence Mall?" I asked when we'd finally caught up to the others in the shadow of a boarded-up pizzeria.

"I think it's a good ten blocks away," Vida said. "Why?"

"It's closer than that," Liam said, the words strained. "About four."

"You're sure?" I asked.

"This is where my brother was in deep cover for the League," Liam said, his voice flat. "I waited to see if I could spot him from that park. I'm sure."

He was right. It was on the corner of Locust and Tenth Street, a nondescript white building with no logo or signage. The lab was an open secret for anyone who worked in the government and, likely, anyone who lived and worked in Philadelphia. The public had only been told that they'd closed this lab down and donated it to a nearby university, and that Leda's UN-commissioned research was being done under the watchful eye of the govern-ment in a building in Washington. If anyone didn't know what the low rectangular building was before the riots broke out, they had to know now by the heavy military presence that surrounded it. I couldn't even see the front doors past the armored vans they'd parked there.

We stayed a block back, slipping into the narrow alley space between what remained of a sushi restaurant and a dry cleaner. The combined smell mingling with the smoke made my eyes water.

"Don't make those pitiful-ass faces," Vida told us. "We were *never* going to be able to get in through the front doors."

"Won't all the entrances be monitored?" I asked. When we'd left Kansas we'd known to expect security in the building, but not assault rifles.

"Come on, we're not fucking idiots," Vida said. "Someone throw out a suggestion."

"I have an amazingly bad one," Priyanka said slowly.

"Now we're talking," Liam said. "Go for it."

"We're near a ton of rowdy protestors who are trapped in the park by people they're bound to outnumber, right?" Priyanka glanced to me. "It's a play on the Pit strategy. We get them to swarm Leda, floating the idea to them there's . . . I don't know, supplies? Remind them that Leda is the reason we're all here? If they surround the building, that'll draw the focus of the soldiers and security to the front while we find some shady back entrance to sneak into."

"That'll also probably get a number of people killed," Chubs said. "Even if we can use the chaos to slip inside, they might be prompted to evacuate the building because of it."

"U! N! No! More! U! N! No! More!" Until now the voices of the people who were packed onto the grounds of Independence Mall, the ones I'd seen with signs near Independence Hall and the Liberty Bell, had been a dull roar. But the chants were growing louder the longer we stood there, moving closer.

"We could steal peacekeeper or police uniforms," Roman suggested.

"That's the right line of thinking, but not exactly realistic," Liam said. "Even if we could come up with a brilliant reason for all of us to need to be in that building, we're never going to be able to find seven uniforms, let alone an eighth to get Ruby out. Our best bet is to hope things get a little bit rowdy outside to pull the security force's attention while we sneak in through a side entrance."

"I don't know about any side entrances, but there's the overflow parking garage."

We all pivoted toward Max.

"Your father used to work for Leda," I said, suddenly remembering what he'd told me in the Pit. "In *this* lab."

He nodded.

"So, that's the kind of information that would have been useful five fucking minutes ago," Vida said. "Anything else you want to add?"

"The main garage for staff is right under the lab, on the back side of the building. This one is a few blocks north, but there's an underground walkway that connects it," Max explained.

"You're sure about that?" Chubs asked. "One thousand percent sure?"

"The researchers used it when they didn't want anyone to know they were late or for corporate meetings when more employees were on hand," Max explained. "My dad used it with me when he brought me in for testing so I wouldn't have to face the stares in the lobby. There's still a security presence, cameras and at least one person in the booth, but getting in shouldn't be a problem. I've never known a lock to keep Priyanka out."

"Aw, Maximo," she said. "Now I *am* sorry I changed the password on your phone all those times to torment you."

His eyes narrowed. "I *knew* it!"

Liam clapped his hands together. "Focus. Where does this garage tunnel lead in the building? Up to the lobby?"

"It connects to the same elevator bank the main garage uses, just a level lower. It goes straight up and down the back of the building. You need a key card to tap in and out, but, again, Priyanka."

She flipped her long curly hair back over her shoulder.

"All right," Chubs said. "Seven floors, including the lobby. If we split up, a few of us can start searching from the top floor and the rest from the second story. We can meet in the middle."

"You are for sure coming with me," Vida told him. "No arguments. You haven't held a weapon in four years."

"I was *not* going to argue with that."

"I'll go with you, too," Liam said. "The kids can take the lower floors. We'll meet on the fourth floor, by the elevators. Is there any way to take out the security cameras?"

"When we get there, I can try," Priyanka said. "See if I can't get the whole system to loop."

Everyone was nodding. Everyone but Max, who looked a bit sick.

I don't want to hurt anyone else. . . .

We'd already made him break that promise to himself when he fought Cubby. I wasn't about to do it again.

Roman had taken notice, too. In his usual quiet way he said, "We're going to need transport out of the city. Can you take point on that? Find a quick escape route through the blockade?"

Max nodded eagerly. "Just leave one of the burners with me. I'll keep you updated."

Chubs gave him the one he'd been using, and Liam handed us Sam's old phone.

"Text only," Vida said. "And only on the encrypted app."

"U! N! No! More!" The chants were getting closer. "Let us vote for Joseph Moore!"

Vida went first, keeping her back to the wall as she moved to the edge of the alleyway. She motioned us forward, pulling Max closer to her by the collar of his shirt. "Are they moving in the direction of the garage?"

He nodded. "It's north of the building. If they stay on this street, it's a straight shot up Tenth Street."

That seemed like a good bet, given the police barriers that blocked access to either side of Locust Street where vehicles had been left abandoned and trashed.

"Our favorite lady's back," Priyanka whispered to us. "I've missed you, Lady Luck."

As the first wave of marchers passed us, heading the opposite direction as they carried their signs like flags and their flags like cloaks, Vida led us out into the fray. The protestors spilled over the sidewalks, packing themselves together to march forward, forward, forward, forcing us to push and weave through them to get past. A few soldiers gathered on the streets that connected to ours, both watching and keeping the crowd on their set path.

Liam ended up right beside me, stumbling as someone accidentally elbowed him in the chest. I reached out, looping my arm through his to steady him. Vida's dark hair was just visible through the waving signs. I kept track of her the best I could, trying to spot the others.

A familiar hot rush of pressure slid along the back of my mind, sending a shiver down my back. It was gone before I could process the feeling.

Liam shuddered, pressing a hand to his chest. "I feel like someone just walked over my grave."

I stood on my toes, searching the surrounding buildings. Nearby faces blurred as my anxiety grew. Up ahead, Priyanka turned, finding my gaze as she conducted her own search for the only possible source.

Lana.

FORTY-TWO

WE PEELED OFF FROM THE PROTESTORS ONE BY ONE, following Max as he led us down a sliver of a street, one that didn't even have a sign to identify it. If we hadn't been following Max, I probably would have walked by the entrance altogether. The garage door itself blended almost seamlessly into the graffiti on the brick wall it had been carved into. He pointed to the small black square that was posted over the top left corner of the entrance.

"That's the remote access," he said, glancing at Priyanka, but she only had eyes for the security camera posted above the other corner.

"Is she . . . working?" Liam whispered to me.

"I can hear you just fine," Priyanka said. "And yes, I am. Give me just one more minute. . . . This is a pretty firewall they've got. Lots of . . . layers . . ."

Roman shook his head. "We can't go through this door. There has to be some kind of vent. . . ."

He followed the edge of the building, somehow squeezing himself into the narrow space between the garage's wall and the office building adjacent to it. Finally, Roman reached an opening along the back of the building that looked about as big as a closet. My heart jumped as he disappeared, and then jumped again as he leaned back so I could see his face. "I've found it. Tell the others."

Liam raised his brows at me. "*Very* dreamy."

"Can you not?" I said, pushing him toward the opening. To make the fit work, he had to shed his belt and plaid shirt, leaving him in a gray undershirt. Chubs looked doubtful about his ability to slide between the buildings, but tried anyway. Priyanka went next, sucking in a hard breath and tearing the back of her shirt in the process.

Before I followed, Vida turned to Max. "We're going to need some kind of service vehicle, I think. Something with an excuse to be on the road that won't necessarily be stopped and searched. If you can't find that, see if you can figure out a road that isn't being monitored."

He nodded, his brow creasing. "I'll do my best."

"You have about twenty minutes to do better than your best," Vida told him.

The others had already pried off the metal vent, and Roman had crawled inside. We found him standing over an unconscious security officer in the booth by the massive door.

Roman led us down the length of the small, empty garage, until we reached a pathway shaved out of the concrete. It sloped down gradually before evening out. We were so far beneath the street that we couldn't even hear the sirens from the police or the chanting of the crowds. Overhead, the fluorescent lights flickered in time with my driving pulse.

Just breathe, I reminded myself. *Find Ruby. Get out.*

It was that simple. Don't set off alarms. Don't alert security. Find Ruby. Get out.

I rolled my shoulders back, feeling a static charge snap against my teeth.

The pathway fed into a small elevator bank, just as Max had promised.

"We're only going up three floors. We can take the stairs," Roman suggested to Vida. "It might draw less attention than multiple stops."

Vida gave a nod of approval. "Good idea."

Priyanka stepped forward, pressing her hand to the keypad. The elevator dinged with each floor it passed on the way down. We all cringed at the sound.

"Fourth floor in front of this same elevator bank," Vida said. "Twenty minutes. No matter what, that's the meet. We'll reassess if we have to."

I nodded as they stepped inside. "Good luck."

The doors shut, carrying them away. A sickening feeling of dread wormed through my stomach. Roman brought up a hand and rested it on the nape of my neck. At the touch, I turned toward him.

"Come together," he said softly, "leave together."

I nodded, setting my shoulders back. I pulled the burner out of my pocket again, and began recording. Priyanka had already bypassed the lock on the stairwell's door and was holding it open. With a deep breath, I followed them in.

The building's power was a low hum in my ears. The concrete of the stairwell had been painted and sealed, the edges of the steps covered in rubber to prevent slipping. A strip of glow-in-the-dark tape ran along the side of them, almost brighter than the small fixtures on the walls. Only every other one was lit, like they were on reserve power, not full.

"Maybe they did evacuate the building," I whispered.

"It seems more likely that no one's been able to get back into the city since the announcement," Roman whispered back.

Don't let your guard down, I thought, counting the floors we passed. Main garage, lobby, first floor . . .

Priyanka stepped up again, dealing with the keycard pad. There was a small window on the door that gave us a clear sight of the empty hallway. Roman pressed his finger to his lips and held his gun with his other hand as he slowly shouldered the door open.

My chest was burning, and my ragged breaths sounded louder in the complete and utter silence of the floor. A few scattered ceiling lights were on above the rows of gray cubicles. The lines of desks stretched from one end of the building to the other. I swept the phone's camera around, capturing them, then shook my head at the others. Next floor.

The second floor was just as shadowed as the first had been, but the setup was entirely different. The stairwell opened to two long hallways: one that stretched straight ahead to a dead end at a covered window and another that ran to its right, cutting off abruptly at two heavy doors labeled QUARANTINE.

My tennis shoes let out a horrible squeak as we took to the one ahead of us. I stopped dead, bracing myself for someone to jump out from behind one of the doors. Priyanka glided forward like she was stepping across clouds. Roman shook his head as she reached for the handle of the nearest door, but she ignored him, pushing it open. I kept the phone recording.

An office. A desk, a crammed bookshelf, piles of papers, and an extra pair of high heels under the desk. We didn't need to go any farther to know that the others would be exactly the same. All the electrical pulses I felt were identical. All of them were sparks compared to the roar of power that was coming from behind the heavy sliding doors at the end of the other hallway.

This time I led, and the others followed. The hallway seemed to darken at its edges as I moved toward the doors. My heart was beating so hard, so wild now, I couldn't have spoken even if I'd needed to. I reached out and pressed the button on the wall, letting the doors hiss open.

But the second I released the button to move ahead, the doors slid shut again.

"They probably only open from this side," Roman said.

"Only when I'm not here," Priyanka whispered back. "Open sesame."

Cold, sterile air swept past us, running its icy fingers along my cheeks and through my hair. I fought back a shudder as Roman went straight for the box of surgical masks posted on the wall, passing one to each of us. I held mine over my mouth, grateful to have something to ward off some of the chemical stench. Goose bumps trailed up over my arms and the back of my neck. This section was even darker than the others had been; only one light shone down from the ceiling as we passed the hospital-like rooms with their many machines. Priyanka slowed, peering in through one of the observation windows.

"What the hell is this place?" she whispered.

I had a horrible suspicion about what this place was originally used for years ago, back when IAAN first emerged and the world was convinced it was a contagious virus. This must have been where they kept the first few known cases.

Roman turned back toward the doors we'd come through, motioning for us to follow him. But just as I took a step forward, a faint strain of music reached my ears and I almost dropped the phone.

Not just music. The Rolling Stones. "Start Me Up."

It traveled over the tile floor, across the smooth surfaces of the walls. The other end of the hallway had been so completely blanketed in darkness, we hadn't even seen the way it intersected with another hall and turned right.

I went first, feeling like I was pulling one thread of myself loose with each step. Roman kept close beside me, his gun up and aiming.

The hallway ended at another pair of double doors, which were swinging slightly open and shut with the force of the air-conditioning blasting from above it. Blue scrubs. A surgical table. Large, wheezing machines.

Not here, I thought as I reached out and pushed one of the doors open. *Please not here.*

It was like something out of a nightmare.

A surgeon stood at the head of the operating table, waving the drill in his hand in time to the song's beat like a conductor's wand. A small figure stood on the other side, next to a tray of gleaming silver instruments. A third person sat behind a monitor, controlling the arm of some sort of scanner that was rotating overhead.

And on the table, her head shaved, her face like wax, was Ruby.

"Stop!" The word exploded out of me with a roar of power. The surgical light flared, shattering at the same moment the monitor did. The woman sitting there was thrown to the floor, knocking her head on the tile.

"I'm calling—"

Roman shot the man before he could finish. The drill in his hand fell to the floor a second before his body did.

The other woman screamed, running for the shelves of supplies along the far left wall. They pulled forward easily. Too easily.

Priyanka ran after her, all but tackling her. As the woman fought her, kicking and twisting, Priyanka leaned behind the shelves to see what was there. "We've got a door—where the hell does this go?"

"It's just—" the woman sputtered, sobbing in terror. "It's just an emergency exit out to one of the streets—please, we were just doing our jobs!"

I didn't see how Priyanka silenced her. I didn't care. I turned off the phone's camera and ran straight for the operating table.

Ruby's shoulders were too thin under my hands. Her face was gaunt, still shadowed by a bruise on one cheek. She looked . . .

Dead.

"Ruby?" I said. "Ruby, can you hear me?"

I searched for the IV drip, whatever drug they might have injected her with, but there was nothing. I grasped at her hand beneath the surgical blanket, my fingers feeling for her pulse. Faint. *There.*

I just wanted to save you. I just wanted to help.

"Do you—?"

Roman faded at the edge of my vision. The operating room took on a silky texture, brightening until it was completely blotted out with white. It felt like fainting, even though I could feel the ground steady beneath my feet. That same white light faded, and forms began to take shape from the darkness it left behind. A hallway, not unlike the other one on this floor, unfurled in front of me. I was moving down it, past the locked doors, past the small faces peering out at me through the observation windows, the small hands pressed against it.

Memory.

I released my hold on Ruby with a gasp, but the memory didn't fade. Not until I saw the number on the hallway's wall, the way she'd seen it. LEVEL 3.

"—okay? Say something!" When the image of the hallway cleared, Roman's worried face replaced it. All at once I felt the pressure of his fingers on my upper arms.

"What's going on?" Priyanka asked. "What just happened?"

"There are more kids here," I said. "They're on the floor above us. Ruby wants me to get them."

Priyanka looked between me and Ruby's terrifyingly still face.

"I don't have time to explain," I said, taking her arm. "You have to come with me to get their doors open."

"All right," she said, putting a hand over mine. "I'm coming. Ro, are you going to be okay?"

He nodded. "I've got everything handled."

I threw the phone to Roman, who caught it with his free hand. He looked like he wanted to protest, but there must have been something in my face that made him hold back. All I could feel was Ruby's fear; all I could see was her still, frail form. "Text the others that we found her. And tell Max we're going to need a bigger transport."

Priyanka opened the quarantine doors from the inside, leading the charge down the hall to the stairs. My head still had that cottony feeling, like something had been placed inside of it that didn't belong. Ruby hadn't woken up, but she was in there. Somehow, she knew it was me. She'd heard me or sensed me. . . .

We stopped outside the door leading into the third floor. Priyanka kept her back to it, trying to look through the small glass panel without being seen. Her whole posture stiffened. Without explaining, she stepped back so I could see for myself.

A security officer was sprawled across the hallway tile, a pool of blood beneath him.

I pulled back, looking to her with wide eyes. Maybe the others had already come through, or they'd crossed paths with him and he'd made it down this far. But there was no blood anywhere on the stairs. There was no blood beyond what was right there, soaking through his dark uniform. He'd fallen where he'd been hit.

Priyanka gave me a searching look, waiting for my cue. I peered through the window again. There was no one, and there was no time.

I opened the door slowly, one hand taking the gun from Priyanka as she offered it and the other turning the phone camera back on to record.

I covered her as she ran to the nearest door, then, when no one fired, followed her over. A child, one who looked to be about six, pressed his face against the glass, watching us both with wide eyes. My hand shook a little as I captured it on film, then turned to do the same with the others. The sight of the eight doors, and the kids behind them, sent a tremor through me.

The rooms had to be soundproof. Across the way, a girl—her hair shaved like the boy's—was yelling, her fists banging silently against the glass. Farther down, another boy was trying to get my attention, waving his hands toward the opposite side of the building, where another hallway intersected with ours.

Where Lana was watching us.

I raised the gun, but the rush of boiling needles was back, slamming through my skull with a new viciousness. I staggered, trying to stay vertical. None of the doors were open—Priyanka hadn't had enough time.

Lana's wavy hair had been pulled back into a neat ponytail. She was dressed in the same uniform as the security officer she'd shot and studied me now in a way she hadn't before, her expression unnervingly close to Roman's. The gun remained at her side, as if the one I was aiming at her was no threat. I shoved the phone into my pocket, freeing up both hands.

We don't have time for this. We had to get the kids out.

"There's a whole team here with me," Lana said. "You're not going to make it out. You might as well come with me now."

"Don't do this," Priyanka said softly, stepping in front of me. "Please, Lana. Please don't break my heart again."

"That's always been your problem, Pri," Lana said, her voice husky. One hand reached up, touching the charm on her necklace. "You use your heart and never your head."

"True." Priyanka's voice wavered. "I'm a romantic, as you might recall."

"I recall a lot of things," she said, her voice hardening.

"We didn't abandon Mercer, Lana," Priyanka said, taking another step toward her. "We *escaped* him. That man is a monster, and he's hurting kids, just like the people here are hurting the ones who are right in front of you. Please . . . *please* let Suzume get them to safety. You can take me back with you to Mercer."

Lana's face twisted in disgust. "As if you have a choice now. I didn't come here for you, but I won't turn down the opportunity to stop you."

Finally, she raised her gun. I kept my own on her, my heart banging in my ears. The jittery feeling of having my power repressed made it impossible to steady my hands.

I was right. This wasn't the talk of someone who'd been brainwashed—this was nothing like I'd seen in the Reds. This was someone deeply misguided and manipulated, who'd walked into the arms of someone who'd likely seemed powerful and strong enough to protect her.

"You think Mercer loves you? That he cares about you beyond what you can do for him?" Priyanka let out a hollow laugh. "That's not love—love isn't torturing innocent kids, it's not manipulating their bodies so that he can use them. *I* love you. *Roman* loves you."

"And I hate you," Lana said, the words seething. "I *hate* you."

Priyanka flinched. "That's what Mercer told you to believe."

Lana kept her gun trained on me. Her laugh made the hair rise on my arms. "I believe what I want to believe, and that's this: Mercer made me strong. He gave me the power to be the person I wanted to be. He didn't leave me behind, he built an army for me. For us."

"Leave you behind," Priyanka repeated, her voice ragged. "Do you have any idea how much that killed us?"

"Not enough to come back," Lana said. "Not enough."

Behind us, the door to the stairwell banged open. I turned in time to see Vida throw out her arms, sending Lana slamming into the far wall with her power. Priyanka gasped, and I had to catch her arm to keep her from lunging toward Lana's prone form.

The pressure of the girl's power lifted from my mind and electricity sang through me once again, filtering toward me from all sides—above, below, through the walls of the rooms.

"Where are the kids?" Vida barked. "We need to go!"

"I told you, you're not getting out of here."

Lana hauled herself back up to her feet. I started to dive for the gun that had been knocked out of her hands, but she made no move to reach for it.

She only lifted the plastic cover over the fire alarm and pulled it.

FORTY-THREE

THE ALARM SHREDDED THAT LAST BIT OF CONTROL I'D
had over my nerves. It blared out, piercing and relentless. Red
lights flashed on, sweeping over the bare walls and tile.

Vida pushed Priyanka's frozen form aside, firing after Lana as
the girl fled down the hall.

"She's going for Ruby!" I shouted over the alarm. "There's a
Blue Star team in the building!"

"The boys are already there," Vida said. "We just need the
kids— Priyanka—*Priyanka!*"

She reached out, gripping the girl's shoulder and giving it a
hard shake. Whatever prison of horror Priyanka had been locked
inside, she finally emerged.

"Can you turn the alarm off?" I shouted.

"It's too late!" Vida said. "They'll be here any second. Better to
have the sound to cover the gunfire. Watch the other entrance—
the elevators on the other side."

"Right," Priyanka said, moving toward the first room as if in
a trance. "I need . . . It's going to be . . ."

"It's fine," I told her, "just *hurry.*"

533

Before she took her position, Vida shouted to us, "If we get separated for any reason, we're going out through the quarantine."

Max must have had us covered, then. That small bit of relief was instantly stomped out by throbbing fear as I ran down the hall in the direction that Lana had gone. There was an elevator down that second corridor to my left. I planted myself at the corner, crouching down to use the edge of the wall as cover.

A shot rang out behind me as Vida took down the first security officer with ease.

"You've got seconds!" she shouted to Priyanka.

She didn't need them. The doors swung open together with a hard *clack* as the locks released. The kids stepped out, their skin stained scarlet by the lights from the alarms. They'd only been given gray scrubs and slippers to wear, but that wasn't the reason they were shivering.

"Follow me, all right?" Vida said. "We're going to get you to a safe place."

The kids stared at her with thousand-yard stares, as if shock had finally set in. They had no idea what was happening.

"We're like you," I shouted over to them. "And we are about to kick the asses of every single person in this building who hurt you. Got it?"

A little girl, ten at most, lifted her hand. It took Vida a moment to realize she was supposed to take it. Once she guided her forward, the others fell in line behind them, taking each other's hands and forming a chain. Priyanka brought up the rear, gently urging them toward the door as Vida pushed it open with her shoulder. She leaned into the stairwell, aiming up, then down at anyone who might be coming.

I waited a beat longer, just to make sure no one was coming

up the elevator, then ran after them. The gun was slick in my hands, but I didn't want to risk letting go of my grip to wipe them off against my jeans. I kept my gaze, and the barrel of the gun, on the stairs above us, mirroring Vida as she cleared the path below. A few of the kids screamed as the bodies, wounded and dead alike, rolled down the steps.

Bullets pinged off the railings, and the shouted orders from the uniformed security officers became roars of pain. Vida slammed her shoulder against the door to level three. I counted the kids' small heads as they trailed after her, the chain ending with Priyanka. One, two, three, four, five, six, seven.

But there had been eight doors. There were *eight* kids.

Breath slammed in and out of me as I turned and ran back up the stairs, bursting through the door again. My shoes slid through the pool of blood, tracking it across the floor. I shoved back against the panic that was rising in me like a wave, focusing on scanning each room for places where a child might be hiding. I concentrated on the memory Ruby had given me, trying to sort through the glossy-bright images to match their faces to the ones I'd seen. The last room on the left was identical to the others, with one major difference: the sleeping cot was bigger. My stomach bottomed out as I realized exactly how stupid panic had made me.

Ruby. Ruby was the eighth one on this floor. There wasn't another kid.

The elevator chimed, the doors dragging themselves open. Bootsteps thundered out, and it was all the incentive I needed to run back for the stairwell, legs and arms pumping harder than ever. I took the stairs too fast, barely catching myself from tumbling down onto the second level's landing.

Steady, I thought. *Calm down.*

I tried to look through the door's glass panel, but a bullet had left a web of cracks in it. After reaching out with my power to see if there were any electrical signatures nearby, and finding none, I pushed it open slowly, stepping out gun-first.

The alarm wailed through the corridor. Its red lights swept over the bodies scattered across the floor. I swallowed bile as I wove through them, running for the doors marked QUARANTINE.

It wasn't until I reached for the button that I remembered.

"Shit," I breathed out.

The doors slammed shut as soon as I lifted my hand from the button. I hit it again and darted forward, only for the heavy metal to snap shut in front of my nose. I pressed my face up to the small window on the right-side door, searching the darkness of the hallway there for any sign of the others. I pounded on it, holding my breath . . . and releasing it again when no one came.

Think. . . . There had to be something on that floor I could use to pry open the doors, or keep them from completely closing.

My breath was ragged as I rolled one of the chairs out of a nearby office, trying to cram it into place, but the doors shut with such force they splintered the chair's plastic frame and sent the wheels sliding through to the other side.

There were the downed security officers and soldiers on the floor, but . . . I shook my head to clear the gruesome images from it. Bones would break, but a Kevlar vest might be enough to withstand the force of the doors' impact. My whole body shook from the effort of stripping one off a soldier, feeling the hot blood that had soaked through the fabric.

I held the button to keep the doors open, then slid the bundled-up vest between them with my foot.

They didn't cut through the fabric, no. But the force of the impact flipped the vest out of position and into the other side of the hall. I slammed my fist against the button again, shouting, "*Hey! Priya! Vida!*"

But I could barely hear *myself* over the alarm.

Idiot, I thought savagely. I didn't have a phone. I didn't even know where the secret exit emptied so that I could meet them down on the street. My options dwindled, running through my mind like the last gasp of power from a battery.

Releasing the button, I stepped back, assessing the two slender windows on the doors. I was small . . . I could maybe contort my body enough to drag myself through. I took careful aim, my arms absorbing the kickback of the shot. Instead of shattering the glass, the bullet ricocheted off it. *Reinforced.* The cartridge clicked empty.

"Shit," I breathed out, wiping the sweat off my face. My thoughts spun out, dwindling with the last few possibilities. I could use my power to overload the doors' circuitry and fry the wiring. That might be enough to lock them in an open position. Or it might activate a fail-safe that would only lock them down further.

I blew out a shaky breath, trying to steady myself with reason. At this point, there was really nothing left to lose. No one was coming to get me, except for the soldiers and security officers currently combing the floors. If the doors opened, great. Easy. If they jammed, I'd take my last option: trying to get out of the building another way and rendezvousing with the others somewhere else.

I've wasted too much time already, I thought.

I reached out for the door control again, only to feel something hard jab against the base of my spine. The flush of hot, numbing needles in my mind left me screaming in frustration. The alarm droned on and on, forcing Lana to speak directly into my ear. "Be a good girl and put your hands on the doors."

Not like this.

The words burned through me, catching inside of my chest.

I just wanted to save Ruby. I just wanted to help.

Lana directed me forward with a push of her gun. I saw my shadowed reflection in the dull metal of the door. It was freezing to the touch as I rested my palms and forehead against it.

"If I can't bring him her, at least I can offer you up," Lana said, wrenching one of my arms behind my back. "This wasn't a wasted trip after all."

"You can definitely try," I told her, ignoring the cold dig of the barrel against my spine. I squeezed my eyes shut, narrowing my concentration on finding that silver thread, on digging that spark out from under the hold she had on my mind. These powers were *mine*—no one got to take them from me—*no one*—

The tightness that had clamped over my skull, the pressure, seemed to shiver.

"What are you doing?" Lana growled. "Stop it—"

It happened so quickly, I didn't realize I was falling until the doors disappeared from in front of me, and my body slammed into the freezing tile. My teeth clacked together, biting my tongue as pain rang through my knees and palms. I flipped myself over, lashing a foot out toward Lana, but the quarantine doors had already snapped shut again behind me. I gasped as the knot binding my mind snapped, and warm power surged through it again.

Mine.

For one insane second, I thought I had actually done it—but I was through the doors, and she was . . .

There was a muffled scream from the other side of the door, loud enough that I could hear it over the alarms. *What the hell just happened?* Red light washed over the hall as I pushed myself back up onto my feet.

Run, you idiot, I thought, even as I peered back through the window at Lana.

My blood stopped in my veins.

Someone had grabbed her from behind, gripping her across the torso and pinning her arms down at her sides. I saw the head of dark hair in the flashing emergency lights, and I knew. Even before he looked up, I knew.

"Roman!"

That's . . . That couldn't be right. I'd left him in the operating room. He'd gone down ahead, with Liam and Chubs and Ruby. Why wouldn't he have left with the rest of them?

Why was he on the wrong side of the doors?

I banged my fist against the glass, trying to get his attention. Lana was thrashing wildly, but he only tightened his grip, his face pained as he told her something I couldn't hear.

If I had my power, that meant—what *did* that mean? That he'd been able to surprise her and mirror her ability before she'd been able to turn it on him? That he'd nullified her power to nullify our powers?

"Roman!" I shouted, pounding harder. I raised my hands, ready to try frying the doors, but Roman finally noticed me. He swung the two of them around, his arm shaking as he shot out the control on the wall. There was a metallic clang inside the doors, and, just like I'd feared, the fail-safe kicked in. The power drained from it like a soul leaving a body.

"No! Roman!" I wedged my fingers into the crack between the doors, bracing my feet on the floor. I could melt the lock, I could do something—they were heavy, but—

He kept looking from me to his left shoulder, where his right hand, the fingers out straight and together, was pressed. He lifted the hand slightly, then pressed the palm to his shoulder again, repeating the motion. The signal.

I'm okay.

"No!" I shouted at him.

He did it again, struggling to keep Lana still.

This is okay.

I knew I was sobbing when it became impossible to take in any air, when my hands were too slick with sweat and my own tears to get any sort of purchase on the metal. I moved toward the window, trying to get his attention. The effects of mirroring Lana's power were already ravaging him. His face was locked into a grim mask of pain as he tried to maneuver them down onto the floor.

I screamed as the armed soldiers poured out of the stairs down the hall. Not the uniformed army officers, not building security, not even Defenders—these men and women were dressed in familiar gear and all black.

Blue Star.

The way Lana suddenly relaxed—that horrible, victorious smile that came over her face—turned my blood to ice and choked off my next breath.

"No!" I shouted. "Let her go!"

He couldn't go back—they'd kill him—Mercer would *kill him*, if not with a bullet, then through crushing emotional and mental torture.

But Roman wasn't going to let his sister go. Not again. Not even to get away and save himself.

He looked back at them, then turned his gaze toward me, his blue eyes as bright as the lightning had been in the stormy sky. His expression was terrifyingly calm. I read the word on his lips. *Run.*

A canister rolled toward them. Roman twisted, keeping his back to the soldiers to shield Lana. The soldiers formed a defensive line down the hall, several raising their guns to cover the ones who were approaching with handcuffs. It was the last sight I had before the flash of the stun grenade went off, and dissolved their images into light.

I pressed my hands against the glass, banging against it.

Run, I thought. *You have to run.*

I couldn't stay here. I couldn't leave.

But the others . . . Ruby and Priyanka and Liam and Chubs and Vida and those kids, they needed me. They needed me to *run.* I wasn't done yet.

I wasn't done.

I don't know how I got back to the operating room, or how I got down the narrow, crude stairs. I had enough sense left in me to drag the shelves back into place behind me, and to overload the keypad lock on the door until the metal hissed and melted into itself.

What I did know was that when I made it outside, the others were still there. The sight of them didn't make sense at first. I didn't recognize this strange little side street, tucked against the back of the building, where there was a loading dock with a brick overhang above the ramp, shielding it from any eyes above. Parked there was one of the white tankers that the UN and interim government regularly used to bring in clean water to population centers.

Max stood next to a middle-aged dark-skinned woman in army fatigues. She was gesturing toward the truck, her face tight with panic. Chubs was on the roof of the tank, lowering the small kids down through one of the hatches. Liam and Ruby must have already been inside.

The only others who hadn't climbed onto the truck were Vida and Priyanka, who were having a conversation of their own. Priyanka made a heated gesture back to the building. Vida pointed up, where helicopters were buzzing nearby.

It was Chubs who spotted me first. He called down to the girls, pointing to me as I made my way along the side of the loading bay toward them. I took a deep breath. The ringing in my ears sounded like screaming, and it tore at me a little more with each second. Each step forward.

For as long as I lived, I would never forget the expression on Priyanka's face when she saw me running toward them, alone. Her look of relief faded, twisting into anguish, and the wound became a lasting scar.

"No!" she said, jumping down off the ladder and running toward me. "*No!* Where are they?"

I grabbed her, and even with all of her height on me, with all of her wild panic, I still managed to drag her back toward the water tanker. "We have to go. They're going to be on us in a few minutes—"

Vida tried to help me wrangle Priyanka's lanky form, getting a fist to the jaw in thanks.

"Don't make me knock you out," Vida warned.

"They're still in there!" Priyanka said. "Roman went back to find her! Where are they?"

"Blue Star," was all I could say.

Vida looked at me. The pain in my throat radiated through my whole body. She reached out, stroking my hair back.

"You did the right thing," she told me fiercely. "You did the only thing."

"Please," the driver was begging Max, "we have to go. They're still patrolling the streets. I want to help you, I do, but I've got a family. If they catch me doing this, they're the ones who are going to pay."

"I'm not going to leave," Priyanka said.

"You clearly thought I was kidding about knocking you out," Vida said, pushing up one of her sleeves.

"We can't help them right now," I said, refusing to consider the likelihood they hadn't been taken alive. "He wanted us to go. Priya, he told me to go."

"They're together?" she asked. "The two of them . . . they're together?"

All I could manage was a nod.

She turned back toward the ladder, refusing to look at me as she climbed. My whole body felt like it was being crushed when she pulled out of my grip as I reached up to steady her.

I followed her over the top of the tanker, accepting Chubs's help down through the tight hatch. Water splashed onto my feet, surprising me. It stank of chlorine and the coppery chemical they added to all water to neutralize Agent Ambrosia.

I felt along the edges of the dark space until my eyes adjusted enough to see the kids huddled together along one wall, and Liam holding Ruby at the very back of the tank.

543

They'd wrapped her in layers of coarse blankets, covering her weak form from her neck to her feet. Liam supported her shoulders with his arm, pressing her head to his chest. The lower halves of their bodies were soaked in the water. I knelt down in front of them, reaching out to touch Ruby's face. She looked no better than the last time I'd seen her. The shadows deepened the hollows of her face.

"Come on, darlin'," Liam was murmuring. "Don't keep us waiting. You know how impatient I get."

Priyanka watched us from where she crouched against the wall opposite the kids. There was just enough light coming from the hatch to see the tears as they streamed down her face and dripped into the water beneath her.

Finally, Max and Vida climbed in, and Chubs dropped down, closing the hatch door over us. The kids gasped at the darkness, and I wanted to tell them to wait, that they would adjust to it like everything else. But, somehow, I didn't think they needed that lesson.

The tanker truck's engine roared, sending us flying forward, as the driver moved the vehicle up the dip in the loading dock and then swung us out onto the street.

"Where did you find her?" I heard Vida ask Max.

"She caught me trying to take the truck and told me she'd help us," Max said.

"You believed someone wearing a government-issue uniform?" Priyanka asked.

"She drove over to Leda, didn't she?" he asked.

"Fuck, kid," Vida said, letting her head fall back against the tank's wall.

The vehicle swayed as the driver took another corner.

"She's not going to turn us in," Max said. "We're going to make the meet you arranged. She promised."

"If I'm right, I'm going to carve those words into your fucking tombstone." Vida scoffed. "*'She promised.'*"

Chubs put a calming hand on her shoulder as he moved past her, coming back to check on Ruby.

"Any change?" he whispered.

Liam shook his head. "The kids say they aren't sure what happened, either. They just said she's been—" He swallowed, hard. "She's been like this for days."

"Did they give her the cure procedure?" I asked.

"I don't know," Liam said. "They told me that the Leda people were just running tests and taking samples from them, but who knows what they were doing to her."

The image of the surgeon, the drill in his hand, flashed through my mind. But as I reached out to run my hand back over Ruby's buzzed hair, the sight of her burned away with a glare of white light. That same strange sensation threaded through me, weaker than before. This time I knew not to pull back from it.

The memory assembled itself in my mind like drops of ink falling through water. Trees in full spring glory. A trail between them. A playground flanked by a graffitied, boarded-up building.

I recognized this place.

The broken swing set seemed to materialize out of dust and air. The former school's sign had been smashed in, but the edge of the logo was still there. *Blackstone Elementary.*

Why was she showing me this?

I walked—Ruby walked—past the swings toward the rusted jungle gym, dropping to her knees and crawling beneath a long plastic slide that had buckled.

Her hands dug into the wet sand, tossing mounds of it to the side. After a few minutes, she—I—reached into the pocket of her jacket. A small black box, the kind you'd use to gift jewelry, appeared in my hands. I opened it. Inside, there was a small flash drive. A slip of paper with only two words written on it: FINISH IT.

The cover snapped down over it, and the box was placed into the hole. My right hand ached strangely as I covered it with sand. Only, I hadn't felt anything the last time Ruby had planted a memory. This pain was real.

It was Priyanka. I latched onto the feeling of her hand crushing mine, using it like a tether to pull myself out of Ruby's fading memory. I looked to her one last time, but her face was just as impassive as before.

"Something's happening," Priyanka whispered. "There's a ton of tech nearby."

I felt it now, too.

Max should have been grateful for the darkness. It was the only thing sparing him from the look I was sure was on Vida's face.

"Here it comes," Vida said, her voice low. "Try to stay still."

The truck's brakes groaned. Water rippled around us, sloshing up the side of the tank. I pressed my ear against the damp wall, straining to listen.

"Why are we stopping?" Chubs whispered.

I could think of a few reasons: a blocked road, being pulled over by the police or any one of the military patrols, hitting one of the barricades leading out of the city.

"—told you, I made my delivery and now I need to move on before things get any worse," the driver was saying.

Barricade. I set my jaw and held Priyanka's hand tighter.

"We have orders to inspect every vehicle, even military transports," a man said.

"No—*don't* open it," the driver said quickly. "You'll contaminate the purified water with all this smoke, then it's useless and I have to fill out a thousand pages of paperwork."

"We have to inspect the contents of every vehicle," the man insisted. There was a thump at the back of the tank, where the ladder was. The kids pressed closer together, staring up toward the hatch.

"Here, then," the woman said. "Hold out your hand."

There was some sort of faucet beside my left shoulder. My body jolted at the metallic creak of a handle being turned on the outside of the truck.

The water line in the tank was too low to reach the depression in the wall. I scooped water into my hands, thinking I could pour it in. Before I could, one of the kids, clearly a Kin, raised his hand and guided a steady stream of water up through that faucet. He didn't stop until the handle creaked again. The excess water poured back over my shoulder, soaking my front.

Vida reached over, giving the boy's shoulder a tight squeeze of approval.

As the engine rumbled on again and the tanker began to vibrate, I could have sworn I heard Max say, "I knew she wouldn't."

But even as we drove on, only Liam dared to speak. Over and over again, asking the same terrifying question of the silence.

"She's not waking up—why isn't she waking up?"

FORTY-FOUR

THE DRIVER BROUGHT US BACK TO THE LOT WHERE WE had left the vehicles, and, to my surprise, there was already someone waiting there. Cate.

Her pale hair was covered with a baseball cap, and she was dressed casually in jeans and a loose shirt. I didn't recognize the van she had pulled up beside the dusty sedan and the SUV, but it hardly mattered.

The distance between the bottom of the tank and the opening was so great that Chubs had to use his power to lift each of us out, one at a time. By the time I was through, Cate and Vida were already talking over a map spread over the sedan's hood.

"I thought you said there were eight of you, plus the kids," I heard Cate say as I helped one of the kids down the slippery ladder.

"It was eight," was all Vida said in reply.

The driver had climbed out of the cab and was watching Chubs as he continued his work. Her face went slack with wonder, as if she were watching a magic trick. I started toward her, meaning to tell her how grateful we all were, but she only held up a hand.

"I don't have to know the details about what was happening in the lab," she told me. "I brought my boy there every week for testing until IAAN took him. You just take care of yourselves now, understand?"

Liam levitated Chubs up through the hatch first, then somehow passed Ruby from his arms up to Chubs before Chubs used his own power to raise Liam out.

At first I thought it was just the water soaking the side of his shirt, but the stain was too dark. He must have torn his stitches at some point. Chubs saw it, too, but neither of us tried to stop him as he carried Ruby across the back of the tank, and gently lowered her into Vida's waiting arms.

Max had gathered up the kids and was trying to distract them with some story as he led them toward Cate's van.

"I have a medic I trust meeting us at the safe house," Cate said as she and the others passed by me, heading toward the SUV. "She'll give us an honest answer."

"I don't want honest," Liam said, sounding exhausted. "I just want *good*."

"I know," Cate said softly, opening the back door so he could climb in first. They lifted Ruby in after him.

I waved a hand at the driver, knowing she probably couldn't see me. It didn't matter.

Vida had already taken the driver's seat of the SUV with Chubs next to her in the passenger seat. That left me to slip into the space in the back, with Liam and Ruby. Priyanka and Max took two of the kids with them in the sedan, and Cate ushered the rest into the van.

It was quiet and quick, with all the efficiency of people who wanted to get as far away from a place as humanly possible.

We followed Cate out onto the street, and then out of town completely.

The radio remained on, buzzing quietly with the news so that Chubs could monitor it. I tuned it out, focusing instead on Liam's labored breathing as he held Ruby. He caught me watching him, his eyes going soft. If I kept looking at him, I was going to cry, and right now, crying was the least useful thing I could be doing.

"I'm sorry about Roman," he said.

I knew he was. I knew it was eating all of them up, the same way the pain in my chest felt like it had knotted my lungs together. I couldn't tell him it was okay, and I couldn't bring myself to explain what had happened, or what could happen with Roman and Lana back with Blue Star, so I said nothing at all. The longer we drove, the deeper the shock seemed to set into my system. I didn't fight it. My silence had become a place of recovery, not a trap. Right now, I needed it.

Liam reached over with his free arm, drawing me close to his side and to Ruby.

Right now, I needed that, too.

The safe house in Dover must have been a relic from the days of the Children's League, but I didn't ask and Cate didn't offer to explain. It sat at the end of an otherwise empty street, a weathered American flag still hanging from the front porch. Deeply ironic, all things considered. But it seemed secure enough, especially once we got the van into the garage and the kids into the house, so I didn't understand why Liam looked like he'd seen a ghost.

"It's the only one we kept open after the League dissolved," Cate was telling him as she came back out to open his door.

"Believe me, it wouldn't have been my choice to bring either of you back here."

A short dark-haired woman stepped out of the front door.

"Bring her inside," she said, glancing up and down the street.

With visible effort, Liam carried Ruby up the path and up the porch steps. Chubs kept close to them, a supporting hand under her prone form. Just in case.

"Thank you for doing this, Maria," Cate said as the boys lowered Ruby onto a bed upstairs. It was bare, save for a sheet over the mattress. The doctor stripped off her own oversize cardigan, rolling it up to give Ruby some kind of a pillow.

"What do you need?" Cate asked, hovering anxiously beside the bed.

There was an array of small handheld equipment over the nightstand, as well as an IV bag.

"Clean water and a washcloth, clothing for her," Maria said. "I looked just in case, but didn't see much of anything in the cabinets."

"We stripped the house of anything that could ID us as its owners," Cate said apologetically. "But I do have purification tablets in my bag. I'll bring a pitcher up for you."

"I'd also like the room to do my examination," Maria said, giving Chubs and Liam a meaningful look.

Liam tensed, but Chubs put a hand on his chest and shook his head. "Come on. I can patch you up, at least."

I lingered in the doorway, even after the others left. I wasn't sure what to do, other than wander out to the cars and assess what we had by the way of supplies and what food we could give to the kids.

551

Hauling the bags inside, I was careful not to wake the kids sleeping on the couch and the rug on the living room floor. They'd curled up together like kittens, and it reminded me, again, of how resilient kids were, and how much this world was testing the limits of that resilience.

There was nothing for me to do but disassemble the packs and sink into the mindless task of laying out the supplies on the kitchen counter. Max and Priyanka drifted in and out of the edge of my vision, but none of us seemed capable of talking just yet. I reached for the last bag. My fingers brushed a bundle of fabric.

The familiar gray shirt took the air out of my lungs. This was Roman's pack. It was empty, save for this spare set of clothes, a flashlight, and the remnants of the first-aid kit we'd taken from Haven.

"Zu?" Chubs called from upstairs. "She's ready."

The words shook me from the trance I'd fallen into. I made my way back up to the room, not realizing I was still holding Roman's shirt until Vida gave it a quick glance. Someone had found an extra set of clothes for Ruby; the gray sweatshirt was too big for her, but it disguised her skeletal form better than the blankets had.

"As far as I can tell, there's nothing wrong with her," Maria said slowly. "She's dehydrated and slightly malnourished, and I found various cuts and stitches from where they probably took tissue samples."

Liam shook his head. "That's not *nothing*."

"I meant," Maria said, raising her hands, "they didn't operate on her."

I slumped back against the wall in relief.

"Then why hasn't she woken up?" Chubs asked, his arms

crossed tight over his chest. "Is it a bad reaction to the sedatives? Even a strong dose should have worn off by now."

"I don't have the right kind of equipment here to confirm that she doesn't have a traumatic brain injury. She needs a real scan and an actual neurologist, but if the point was to study her specific ability, they wouldn't have wanted to harm the normal processes of her brain," Maria said. "My guess is that it could be a medically induced coma to combat brain swelling incurred during their testing. I find it equally likely that they wanted her completely subdued, knowing how powerful she is."

Could some part of a person still be aware, even if they were trapped in unconsciousness?

Liam shook his head, pressing his face into his hands. "Dammit . . . She had to have been awake at some point, otherwise Max wouldn't have been able to do his reading. We wouldn't have seen what she was seeing well enough to find her."

Cate's brows rose at that.

"Has she shown any kind of reaction?" Maria asked. "To your voices, to being moved . . . ?"

I haven't told them. "Yes."

"Zu . . . ?" Liam said. "You saw something?"

"She showed me where to find the kids upstairs," I told them. "When we found her, I touched her to check her pulse and she . . . it was like I wasn't in the room anymore. I was upstairs, being walked down the hall. I know it sounds impossible, but it was a memory, and it wasn't mine."

Liam's face transformed, his expression blossoming with hope as he turned back toward Maria.

"I haven't the slightest idea of what's possible," she told him. "She could wake up in a few minutes, or she could wake up years from now, or she might not be able to wake up at all. Like I said, you need a specialist. What I *do* recommend, in the event that she's unable to wake herself up by this evening, is keeping her on an IV drip and using a feeding tube. I can do that much, at least. Let me get what I need from my car."

"Thank you, Maria," Cate said. "I owe you."

The woman stopped in the doorway, glancing at Ruby. "You don't owe me anything. I have to tell you, though, I got a call from Beth. Your absence has definitely been noted in the office."

"I figured as much," Cate said. "The Bureau needs all hands on deck right now."

Maria nodded. We listened to her footsteps padding down the stairs before we gathered closer at the foot of the bed.

"Are you going to be all right?" I asked Cate.

She gave me a fond smile. "I did manage to have somewhat of an excuse. My boss is sympathetic to the Psi and gave me the day off to find somewhere outside the city for Nico and a few others to stay until things calm down. But I don't have to go back at all."

"You should," Chubs told her. "For the time being, you're the only one of us who can keep watch on what's really happening."

"For the time being?" she repeated. "Do you have a plan?"

"We have *something*," Vida said. "Clearing Zu's name and exposing Mercer's and Moore's roles in all this will hopefully go a long way in mending what Cruz just burned the fuck down."

"We just have to hope it won't start another, bigger fire," Chubs said.

"It won't," I said. "Not if we focus on the part that'll get people angry: the fact that they're selling Psi outside of the United States to potential enemies. They may hate us, but it's clear the government doesn't want anyone else to have us or our potential, either."

"That's awfully cynical," Cate said.

I shrugged.

"Ruby wouldn't have acted without proof," Liam said. "After everything we went through, she knows to always gather evidence."

Because very few people believed our word without it.

"She does," I said. "And I think I know exactly where it is."

Vida raised her brows. "Zu, Our Lady of Complete Fucking Surprises. Anything else you've forgotten to share?"

I shook my head.

Liam rubbed a hand over his face, looking back over at Ruby.

"What's the matter?" Chubs asked him.

"I was just thinking about my kids—the Haven kids," he said. "I trust Mom and Harry to take care of things, but I don't know what's happening with everyone—if they're even okay. I can't bring Ruby back to them like this, but she would kill me if I didn't go check on them."

"You can," Chubs told him. "Stay a few more days to make sure she's stable and to see if she wakes up. If she's still like this, then you can go for a day or two and I'll stay with her and keep everyone updated. My dad will be able to bring the supplies we need from his hospital and can probably find a neurologist we can trust for a consult. Let me do this, please. I can't go back to DC yet, I can't get myself in front of a camera and tell the world the truth, but I *can* help my friend. And I will."

"Maybe . . ." Liam said, his expression torn. "But if something happened while I was gone—"

"Nothing will happen," Chubs promised. "It'll give me time to start figuring out where the kids downstairs came from, and if they have homes they need to be returned to. Or it'll give me time to figure out a different safe place for them to go."

Maria came back in, her arms full. I stepped into the hall to give her room to pass, but once I was out, I couldn't bring myself to go back in. That sensation, like static crawling beneath my skin, was back. The room felt too small to contain me.

A hallway light winked as I passed by, heading into one of the empty rooms at the back of the house. This one had no bed or dresser, just a window and a chair-less desk. I leaned against the latter and closed my eyes, pressing Roman's shirt to my lips. I breathed in the smell of cedar, leather, and smoke.

Priyanka and Max still had no idea why I'd gotten out when Roman and Lana hadn't, and I was too much of a coward to go down and tell them. As it was, the longer I thought about those last few seconds, the less they made sense to me.

I could see it so clearly, how he'd lifted his scarred hand higher, pressing it repeatedly against the opposite shoulder until I'd noticed it. Until I'd gotten his message.

I'm okay. This is okay.

He had to have known they were Mercer's soldiers, and what the risks were. That was what I didn't understand: Why would he give himself and his sister back over to Blue Star? Why not come through the door with me or try to fight them off to escape another way?

Because, a small voice whispered in my mind. *You.*

He'd stalled the Blue Star soldiers so I could get away, along with Ruby and the others. Maybe some part of him had finally recognized what Priyanka and I had upstairs: Mercer had emotionally and mentally manipulated Lana, but she couldn't see it, and that made her a danger to all of us. But Roman couldn't leave her alone with Mercer. Not again.

I'm okay. This is okay.

Anger pulsed through me, sweeping away the ache and guilt. "Like *hell* it is."

I wasn't going to lose him or anyone else to this cycle of nightmares. I was done accepting what little we'd all been given—I wasn't going to be tricked into believing that the wheel of our story would continue to roll on without being pushed forward by sheer force. There was no time to sit here and just hope it would all get better. If we'd only wait.

The time for waiting was over. If they wanted a Psion Ring, then they'd have one.

On my terms.

Downstairs, Max and Priyanka were sitting across from each other at the kitchen table. Max had put his head down and shut his eyes, but Priyanka's finger was tracing the knots in the wood, her expression haunted. I found a sticky pad and pen by the landline phone and wrote a quick note of explanation, slapping it on the refrigerator. *No leaving without good-byes.* That would always be the rule. I'd decide on the rest as we went along.

At the sound, both of them sat up.

"Are either of you interested in going for a drive?" I asked.

"Why?" Priyanka asked. "What's going on?"

"Ruby left us a gift," I said. "And we're going to go get it."

Two Weeks Later

WE DIDN'T BOTHER WITH THE DOOR. WE BLEW THE whole damn wall out.

I looked back, watching the flames reflected in Priyanka's dark eyes. The black ski mask hid her face, but satisfaction radiated from her as the last of the dust and bricks settled. Muggy, smoke-stained air swirled against my skin. I took in a deep breath, touching the comm in my ear.

"Three minutes start now," I told the others. "Vi, you in position?"

The response I got was another small explosion, this one at the front entrance to Mercer's warehouse, where Vida and her team of seven Psi were positioned.

"We're in," Vida said in our ears. The gunfire was immediate in response. I waved the group behind me forward, into the smoldering remains of the room Mercer had set aside for his stooges to sleep in. Jacob stepped up and, with a thrust of his hand, sent two of Mercer's men slamming into the nearby wall.

"Stay here," I told him. "Make sure no one comes in or gets out until we're back."

He and Lisa had answered my call for help, as had a dozen other Psi I hadn't seen or spoken to in years. Once the network was alive again, the current of change that moved between us was as unstoppable as it was growing.

One voice could be drowned out, but not a dozen. Not a hundred. Not a thousand.

Our goal wasn't violence, and it wasn't subjugating others through terror—it was working outside the law to gather information, protect Psi, and speak directly to the public with the truth denied to them by the people in power.

"We're in, Max," I told him over the comm. "Get ready."

Outside, waiting for us back in the transport truck, Max said, *"Ready."* There was a flicker of static over the line as he added, his voice softer, "My dad . . ."

"I know," I said, leading the others out of the room. "Don't worry."

One of Mercer's men was waiting in the hallway, half-dressed, half-wild with adrenaline from having been woken from a dead sleep. He fired off a shot that went too wide. One of the Kin lifted him into the air, then slammed him back down onto the floor, stunning him.

Priyanka cast an anxious look my way.

"I know," I told her. "But if they're not here, then we'll search the next one, and the one after that."

"He's going to move them," she whispered. "Once we hit this headquarters, he'll know. If they're even still . . ."

She didn't finish her sentence. *Alive.*

We had slowly worked our way through Mercer's known

warehouses and facilities, searching for any sign of Roman and Lana. Mercer wasn't traveling with Lana now, which gave me hope that she and her brother were still together. In all the times Max had tried to go fishing for their exact location, he'd only seen darkness.

"They are," I told her. "They're alive, and we're going to find them. But we're also going to get these kids out of here, no matter what."

She straightened. There wasn't a flicker of doubt on her face, not one, as she said, "You're damn right we are, and that'll be enough."

We'll be enough.

The interior of the warehouse was exactly as Priyanka and Max had described it: a single hallway of rooms and Mercer's office, which was currently locked. We'd waited, sending Max fishing for Mercer, too, every day for the last week and a half, until it was clear he'd left Blue Star's primary headquarters here for a trip to meet up with Moore and his people.

Priyanka had wanted him here; she'd wanted to burn the building down and force him to watch, bound and gagged, in the back of a car heading for the nearest UN checkpoint. But I think we both knew that would never be enough; someone would rise to fill the void he'd left behind and assume control of his interests. If we wanted Mercer out of the game, we needed to raze the foundation of his business and uproot all the criminal dealings he kept so carefully hidden.

We were here to save the children he'd stolen, but we were also here to recover files and records of his business dealings and associates. And if what evidence we found wasn't enough for the law, we'd subject him to our own.

Priyanka gripped the lock on his office door. Before she stepped inside, she caught my arm. "Come together, leave together?"

"Come together, leave together," I promised. "Lisa, Jen—you're with Priya."

The two girls peeled off. I waved the rest of the group forward to search the other rooms for the kids. "Head back to Jacob when you finish!"

I got a round of acknowledgments from them as I ran on, rounding the corner of the hall. According to Priyanka, Mercer—the paranoid bastard—traveled with a massive security force at all times. I felt the lack of them now, as I easily took care of the one lone man who tried firing on me from behind the shelter of a nearby doorway. There was a phone on him, but not for long. His screams echoed down to me as I finally found the set of doors I'd been looking for.

The room stopped the breath in my lungs. There were hulking machines in every corner, vibrating with power, even as they idled. A small metal operating table stood directly in front of me, and, behind it, there was a hospital bed and a little black-haired girl resting on it, unmoving. Her skin was a waxy white, as if the blood had drained from her.

For a moment, I wasn't seeing the little girl there at all. I was seeing Priyanka. Roman.

I clenched my jaw as rage spilled up through me. The monitors and devices on either side of the bed displayed her steady vitals, but I ignored them, focusing instead on the dark-skinned man in the lab coat. His back was to me as he carefully adjusted the girl's IV drip.

At the sound of my boot squeaking against the tile, he froze.

"Step away from the girl," I told him, keeping my gun trained on him. "And put your hands up."

We found the kids, Vida said over the comm. Underscoring

her voice was the sound of clattering and a scuffle. *"But Roman and Lana aren't here."*

My side crimped with a sharp pain. I released a hard breath, trying to let that bit of hope go.

"I could use a little more help," Vida said. *"Some of the kids are not coming quietly."*

"I'll be right there," Priyanka told her. A few others chimed in, but the voices faded under the sound of the machines whirring.

"John Wendall?" I confirmed, an ugly pulse of hate moving through my heart.

He nodded. I saw Max in that face, under the heavy wrinkles and strain.

"You're so damn lucky I promised your son I wouldn't kill you," I told him, my voice shaking. That little girl . . . if he'd hurt her . . .

"Max?" he whispered. "My Max? He's here?"

"Outside," I told him. "You can come willingly, or I can drag you, but either way you're going to spend the rest of your life making up for what you did here."

His Adam's apple bobbed as he swallowed. "Willingly. The other children—"

"We already have them." I glanced toward the girl. "Can she be transported?"

Max's father nodded, moving to unhook the machines. The girl didn't stir, sighing deeply in her sleep as he began to reach for her.

"Don't touch her," I said.

"We're out, Zu," Vida said.

"I'm coming back your way, are you still—?"

The door swung open behind us.

Dr. Wendall's face changed again, almost brightening. "Priya."

The feeling was not mutual.

"That's right," she snarled. "Came back to personally drag you to hell."

Knowing she had a weapon on her, I holstered mine and picked up the young girl. Her cheek fell against my shoulder and, instinctively, she wrapped her arms around my neck.

"March, demon," Priyanka told him. "*Faster.* Or do you need a cloud of sulfur to ride out of here?"

"There's no need for hostility—" Dr. Wendall began.

She pushed him forward, keeping her gun against his back. "Oh, there is *every* need."

We went out the same way we'd come in. Jacob had hung back, waiting for us, but now he took the weight of the girl off my hands and hurried up to the small freight truck that screeched to a stop on the street in front of us.

Priyanka put a hand on my shoulder, unable to hide her disappointment.

"We'll go to the next one," I told her. "And the next one . . . and the next . . . however long it takes to find them."

She drew in a deep breath and nodded.

I had wanted Roman to be here so badly, but this was enough. Knowing these kids were safe and would never again fall into Mercer's or the government's hands, knowing that they would never see the inside of another lab . . . It was enough for me.

Vida jumped down from the cab, leaving Max up in the driver's seat. With the interior light on, I had a clear line of sight to Max's tense face as Priyanka walked his father past him, toward the cab of the truck. The gate rolled shut, cutting off the sound of the kids' nervous chatter.

Vida glanced at the small girl as she lifted her head off Jacob's shoulder.

"She's the last one," I told her.

"Did you . . . ?" the little girl began, her voice barely a murmur.

Jacob's feet slowed. "What was that? Do you need something?"

"The girl . . . with the flower," she breathed out, fighting to open her eyes.

Priyanka's gaze sharpened on her. "What girl, love?"

The long silence that followed was almost agonizing. My chest was too tight to take in more than a small breath.

"In the office," she whispered. "In the dark."

Priyanka and I turned to each other, and I saw my own hope reflected on her face.

"We checked the office," Vida said, pulling her mask up over her face.

"We went into the office, but we didn't search it," I said, the words tearing out of me. "You go ahead with the kids. We'll check it out and catch up with you later."

Vida raised a brow, but she didn't look surprised. "Don't forget to send Chubs the all-clear."

"I won't," I said. "Drive safe."

"I prefer to drive like a motherfucker," she said with a wink.

The kids would be safe at the new Haven they'd established until we sorted out if there might be families looking for them. I worried about doubling the number of kids there in one night, but at least with Harry and his mom still there, Liam's hands wouldn't be quite so full.

I followed after Priyanka as she ran back into the building, her feet sliding through the loose rubble on the ground. I followed a step behind her, desperate to keep up as we raced down the hallway, back to Mercer's office.

She kicked the door open, fumbling with the flashlight. The

remains of servers and his computer were scattered across the floor, and his shelves had been overturned in the search for hidden files or flash drives.

Priyanka felt along the walls frantically, searching for some kind of gap or hidden door. I stood still, feeling my heart hammer all through my body as I released that silver thread from my mind.

It found our comms, two blips of power compared to the electricity moving through the nearby buildings and streetlamps.

I forced myself to take a deep breath, hands curling into fists at my sides.

And there, like the soft brush of a finger against my cheek, was a ripple of power. Weak, but there. Hidden.

I surged forward toward the desk. "Help me!"

Priyanka's breath was labored as she helped me shove Mercer's imposing metal-and-wood desk toward the wall. Our hands ripped at the rug, tossing it back to reveal an armored door and electronic lock.

"Holy shit," Priyanka breathed out.

I gripped the lock, but she was faster, her mind hacking the combination. The numbers appeared on its small digital screen one by one, ticking my pulse up with each new one that appeared.

With a last electronic *beep*, the lock clicked, releasing. Together, we hauled up the door, letting it crash down against the floor.

Lana's pale face stared up at us. She shielded her eyes against the flashlight's beam. Priyanka sucked in a sharp breath, her expression moving through shock and relief and fear. By the way her throat was working and her eyes were glimmering, it didn't seem like she could speak.

"Where is he?" I asked, instead.

"Here," Lana croaked out. One of her hands was on the ladder built into the hidden room's wall; the other gestured to a part of it we couldn't see. "Hurt."

Priyanka flattened onto her stomach, casting the flashlight's beam into the room, and in the direction Lana had pointed. A figure was curled up on his side, his bruised and bloodied back to us.

Lana stepped out of the way as I jumped down, followed closely by Priyanka. "What happened?" I asked her as I knelt beside him. "Roman? Roman, can you hear me?"

"Hurt," Lana said, backing into the corner. She turned her face away from us, but even in the dim light I could see her hands shaking. Priyanka looked torn between going to her and staying where she was, kneeling by Roman's side.

I turned to truly take in what they'd been subjected to and immediately wished I hadn't. The half-rotten food and crude buckets explained the horrible smell that permeated the lightless space. It was boiling hot down here, and they had nothing in the way of bedding or water.

"Roman?" Priyanka said, giving him a hard shake. "Ro, can you hear me?"

We turned him onto his back, but with his face so bruised and swollen he was almost unrecognizable. My body was gripped with horror at the sight of it.

Alive, I reminded myself. *He's alive.*

"Didn't want to . . . I didn't want to leave him," Lana mumbled. "He hurt him. He said he wouldn't. He said . . . it was . . ."

"Are *you* all right?" I asked her.

Lana couldn't stand to look at us. She turned and faced the corner, and began to cry.

"Roman!" Priyanka was practically shouting now. She cast a

helpless look my way. "We're going to have to carry him out—"

I put a hand on her arm, stilling her. "Wait. Let me try something."

I only needed the smallest thread of power, just one shock to bring him back to consciousness. I pulled the comm out of my ear, clenching it in one hand and pressing my other palm against his chest.

"What are you doing—?"

The power pushed through him, rippling out through his body. One heartbeat he was still, and the next—

Roman gasped, his upper body rising off the ground as his eyes opened wide. His hand gripped mine as he took another unsteady, sharp breath, his gaze bewildered.

"Easy, easy," Priyanka told him, her voice breaking. "It's all right, it's just us. We're going to get you out of here."

Roman's eyes landed on me, and even battered and swollen, I could see the amazement there, the wondering disbelief as he tried to catch his breath. I leaned down, pressing my forehead to his.

"You're okay," I breathed out. "You're okay. But we have to go. We have to go *now*."

He shifted his hand, moving it to his right shoulder. His throat bobbed with the unspoken word. *Okay.*

Somehow, Priyanka and I managed to get him propped up enough to half drag, half carry him over to the ladder. Before he would take hold of the closest rung, he turned back to Lana, reaching out for her.

"Come on," he rasped out.

Lana shrank back—but this time, it wasn't in defiance. It was in shame.

"You can stay here," Priyanka told her, her voice steady. "Or you can come with us. It's your choice. It's—" She cut herself off with a shake of her head, then repeated, "It's your choice."

After the last few weeks spent trapped in a cycle of hope and fear, I knew what those words must have cost her. But Priyanka was right. Lana needed to choose. If they forced her to come with us now, it would only deepen the confusion and resentment Mercer had planted in her.

"Please," Roman whispered.

"The kids . . ." Lana began.

"They're safe," I told her. "They're already out."

This time she looked to Priyanka and held out her hand. As their fingers brushed, she began to tremble, but, finally, she nodded. Priyanka held on to her and didn't let go, not even as they climbed up the ladder after Roman and me.

After helping him to his feet, I looped his arm over my shoulder and absorbed as much of his weight as I could. Priyanka led Lana forward into the smoke still lingering in the hallway. Roman's grip on me tightened as the headquarters' collapsed wall came into view, revealing the dark street beyond it.

Every muscle in his body seemed to vibrate with the longing and need to escape this place. I helped him navigate through the remains of the bunk beds and cinder blocks and steadied him as we stepped out onto the street. My reward was feeling his chest expand with a long, deep breath.

We rounded the corner at a limping gait, but his steps seemed to be growing steadier, and quicker, the farther we moved away from that place and the memory of what had happened there.

I slowed us only long enough to reach into my jacket pocket for the burner phone, and hit SEND on the message I'd composed before we'd stormed the complex.

ALL CLEAR. RELEASE THE PACKAGE.

We'd bundled all the records and photos we'd found on Ruby's flash drive, along with all the other footage we'd collected. I'd sat in front of another camera and stared into its dark eye, explaining everything Mercer and Moore and all of their associates had done in killing innocents and selling children. Chubs and Vida still thought there was a way forward inside the system, but I knew, as soon as I said those first words, I was burning my only bridge back.

My name is Suzume Kimura, and I'm the leader of the Psion Ring. But everything else you've heard about me is a lie.

Chubs had a list of contacts in the government and media that could fill miles of open road, and all of them were about to receive the footage. The only question for me was who would care enough to try to do something about it.

But instead of confirming receipt, Chubs sent something else. A photo of a frail figure with a shaved head, wrapped in blankets and sitting up in bed. Her face was turned away from the phone's camera as she looked out the window, the smallest hint of a smile on her face. To anyone who had seen her photo in the papers or on the news, she would have been unrecognizable. But not to me.

Ruby.

"You ready for this?" Priyanka asked as we caught up to her and Lana.

I looked into the darkness ahead, sparks gathering in my heart. "Beyond."

Then we were running, shadows racing the night.

ACKNOWLEDGMENTS

WHEN I FINISHED *IN THE AFTERLIGHT*, I KNEW THERE was a chance I'd want to return to the world of the Darkest Minds one day—it was only a matter of finding the right story, and the right character to tell it. In the years between then and now, I've been lucky enough to travel and meet so many new people. Every now and then, I'd think of the cast of characters and wonder what *they* were up to, and what adventures they'd gone on in the meantime. When an idea finally clicked into place, and I sat down to write the opening chapters of what would become *The Darkest Legacy*, it felt like coming home and reuniting with friends.

First, I have to thank you, wonderful reader. Whether you're new to the series, or returning to it after years away, it's a joy and a privilege to tell you stories. To the readers who stuck with this series from the beginning, you helped to keep these characters alive in my heart and mind. I would never have been able to write this book without your incredible support, and I hope I've delivered a story that brought you both joy and plot twists aplenty. If there's one message I wanted to convey with this book, it's that there's power in our voices: never be afraid to use them to ask for what you deserve, and to fight for the rights of others and what you believe in.

The Darkest Legacy would still be an idea floating around my brain if not for my incredible publisher, Hyperion. It still amazes me that we've been publishing books together now for seven years! (Where has the time gone?!) Thanks, as always, go to Emily Meehan and Hannah Allaman, who not only helped me shape this book into something special, but also kept us on track during some truly crazy deadlines. You guys are magnificent captains of this ship! To Seale Ballenger—you are one of the best souls in this world, and the kindness you've shown me over the years has made such a difference in my life. And Marci Senders? You retain your title as Cover Queen! Thanks for designing a cover that truly lets Zu shine.

There are so many other incredible people working at Hyperion that I owe a huge debt of gratitude to: Mary Ann Naples, Augusta Harris, Dina Sherman, LaToya Maitland, Holly Nagel, Elke Villa, Andrew Sansone, Jennifer Chan, Guy Cunningham, Meredith Jones, Dan Kaufman, Sara Liebling, Cassie McGinty, Mary Ann Zissimos, and the entire sales team. You guys are the true heroes of this story!

I would be completely lost without the incredible guidance and support of my agent, Merrilee Heifetz. It doesn't matter if we're eating pasta in Italy, drinking margaritas on the beach, or on a conference call, I always have the best time with you. I'm so excited to see what the next few years bring. Many, many thanks also go to Rebecca Eskildsen for all of the support in coordinating the business side of things, and for being a white knight when I needed you most!

Alyssa Furukawa, I'm *so* grateful you were willing to read this story and provide feedback on it, even when it was in a rough state. One of your notes in particular has forever changed the way I approach describing characters. Thank you for your time, thoughts, and energy.

To Morgan Watchorn and Lisa Jordan, thank you both so much for your generous donations last year. Morgan, I hope you loved the early read! Lisa, I'm so excited to finally be able to reveal which character I named after you. I'm sorry I couldn't work your last name into those chapters, but I hope you won't mind a shout-out on the acknowledgments page to make up for it.

I have to send love to my friend Miya Cech, the sweetest of the sweet and the best on-screen Zu I could have dared to hope for. I've loved getting to know you and your family over the last year, and I can't wait to watch you shine in all of your future projects. Thank you so much for keeping the secret about this story! It makes me so, so happy that you were one of the first people to know Zu was getting her own book.

The past few years have certainly had their ups and downs, and I've been lucky enough to ride out the waves with my friend Susan Dennard. Thank you for keeping us warm in our brainstorming cabin and for having such an incredible editorial eye that you helped solve story problems in *The Darkest Legacy* that I had no idea were even there. You are such a compassionate, generous person, and your friendship pulled me through the toughest bouts of deadlines and stress.

To Erin Bowman, Leigh Bardugo, Victoria Aveyard, Amie Kaufman, and Elena Yip: you are absolute gems and, to run with that metaphor, I treasure you all. Thank you for being there for me (and, at times, putting up with me and my many worries) over this past year.

This book is dedicated to my friend Anna Jarzab who—no exaggeration—was the first person to love *The Darkest Minds* and its characters. Even now, Anna, you see things in the story that I've completely missed, and sometimes I'm convinced that you understand this fictional world better than I do! For all of the hours you've spent critiquing these books and helping me brainstorm . . . there's really no way to convey the full extent of my gratitude. Thank you for answering my questions about publishing all of those years ago. I can't wait for our next reunion.

Finally, I am very, very, very lucky to have such a supportive and loving family. Mom, Steph, Daniel, and Hayley: writing a book is always a team effort, but somehow *The Darkest Legacy* turned into a full-on team marathon. For nine months, you guys stepped up to the plate and helped me with everything from running errands to handling any plans to watching Tennyson when I needed to pull all-nighters to get this book in on time. I will never forget that, and I love you all.